Final Option

Clive Cussler is the author and co-author of a great number of international bestsellers, including the famous Dirk Pitt® adventures, such as *Celtic Empire*; the NUMA® Files adventures, most recently *The Rising Sea*; the *Oregon* Files, such as *Shadow Tyrants*; the Isaac Bell historical thrillers, which began with *The Chase*; and the recent Fargo Adventures, which lastly included *The Oracle*. He lives in Arizona.

Boyd Morrison is the co-author with Cussler of the *Oregon* Files novels *Piranha*, *The Emperor's Revenge*, *Typhoon Fury*, and *Shadow Tyrants*, and the author of four other books. He is also an actor and engineer, with a doctorate in engineering from Virginia Tech, who has worked on NASA's space station project at Johnson Space Center and developed several patents at Thomson/RCA. In 2003, he fulfilled a lifelong dream by becoming a *Jeopardy!* champion. He lives in Seattle.

Final Option

CLIVE CUSSLER
and BOYD MORRISON

MICHAEL JOSEPH
an imprint of
PENGUIN BOOKS

MICHAEL JOSEPH

UK | USA | Canada | Ireland | Australia
India | New Zealand | South Africa

Michael Joseph is part of the Penguin Random House group of companies
whose addresses can be found at global.penguinrandomhouse.com

First published in the United States of America by G. P. Putnam's Sons 2019
Published in Great Britain by Michael Joseph 2019
001

Printed and bound in Australia by Griffin Press

A CIP catalogue record for this book is available from the British Library

HARDBACK ISBN: 978–0–241–38685–9
OM PAPERBACK ISBN: 978–0–241–38686–6

www.greenpenguin.co.uk

Penguin Random House is committed to a
sustainable future for our business, our readers
and our planet. This book is made from Forest
Stewardship Council® certified paper.

CAST OF CHARACTERS

THE CORPORATION

JUAN CABRILLO—Chairman of the Corporation and captain of the *Oregon*.

MAX HANLEY—President of the Corporation, Juan's second-in-command, and chief engineer of the *Oregon*.

LINDA ROSS—Vice president of Operations for the Corporation and U.S. Navy veteran.

EDDIE SENG—Director of Shore Operations for the Corporation and former CIA agent.

ERIC STONE—Chief helmsman on the *Oregon* and U.S. Navy veteran.

MARK "MURPH" MURPHY—Chief weapons officer on the *Oregon* and former U.S. military weapons designer.

FRANKLIN "LINC" LINCOLN—Corporation operative and former U.S. Navy SEAL.

MARION MacDOUGAL "MacD" LAWLESS—Corporation operative and former U.S. Army Ranger.

RAVEN MALLOY—Corporation operative and former U.S. Army Military Police investigator.

GEORGE "GOMEZ" ADAMS—Helicopter pilot and drone operator on the *Oregon*.

HALI KASIM—Chief communications officer on the *Oregon*.

DR. JULIA HUXLEY—Chief medical officer on the *Oregon*.

KEVIN NIXON—Chief of the *Oregon*'s Magic Shop.

MAURICE—Chief steward on the *Oregon*.

CHUCK "TINY" GUNDERSON—Chief fixed-wing pilot for the Corporation.

CAPE HATTERAS 1921

HANS SCHULTZ—Captain of the U-boat *Bremen*.

ISTVAN HORVÁTH—Hungarian scientist.

CREW OF THE USS *KANSAS CITY*

MICHAEL BRADLEY—Navy SEAL.

JEREMY NOLAND—Corpsman.

CARLOS JIMÉNEZ—Navy SEAL.

RIO DE JANEIRO

RICARDO FERREIRA—Organized crime technology supplier.

LUIS MACHADO—CIA field officer.

DIEGO LÓPEZ—CIA field officer.

JESSICA BELASCO—CIA field officer.

BUENOS AIRES

COLONEL SÁNCHEZ—Argentinean military officer.

SÃO PAULO

MATHEUS AGUILAR—Harbormaster.

CREW OF THE *PORTLAND*

ZACHARIAH TATE—Commander.
PAVEL DURCHENKO—Executive officer.
ABDEL FAROUK—Chief engineer.
LI QUON—Ship specialist.

CENTRAL INTELLIGENCE AGENCY

LANGSTON OVERHOLT IV—The Corporation's CIA liaison.
CATHERINE BALLARD—Field officer.
JEFF CONNOLLY—Driver and bodyguard.
JACK PERRY—Field officer on the *Manticora*.

CREW OF THE *DEEPWATER*

RASHONDA JEFFERSON—Captain.
AMELIA VARGAS—Chilean navigational pilot.
MARY HARPER—Chief scientist.

SHIPS AND SUBMARINES

OREGON—The Corporation flagship.
PORTLAND—Replica of the *Oregon*.
CARROLL A. DEERING—Five-masted cargo schooner.
BREMEN—World War I U-boat.
MANTÍCORA—CIA cargo ship.
USS *KANSAS CITY*—Los Angeles–class nuclear attack submarine.

DRAGÃO—Brazilian luxury yacht.

AVIGNON—French cargo ship.

WUZONG—Chinese Type 039A diesel-electric attack submarine.

ABTAO—Chilean missile boat.

DEEPWATER—NUMA research ship.

BAROSSO—Brazilian warship.

PROLOGUE

———

**THIRTY MILES NORTHEAST OF CAPE HATTERAS, NORTH CAROLINA
JANUARY 30, 1921**

Through his periscope, Kapitän Hans Schultz watched the chaos aboard the schooner *Carroll A. Deering* and smiled. The white hull of the elegant five-masted sailing vessel was easy to see against the gray storm clouds gathering in the distance. The crew of the cargo ship rushed back and forth across the deck in hopeless panic.

Schultz narrated what he was seeing for the sailors in the control room of his U-boat, the *Bremen*.

"One man is standing there methodically tearing his hair out. Another seems to be screaming uncontrollably as he runs in circles. Two of the men are randomly tossing papers and objects overboard."

"What kind of objects?" asked scientist Istvan Horváth with a slight accent. Although born Hungarian, he spoke German fluently. He was always intrigued by the results of his brainchild, an ingenious device he had dubbed *Irre Waffe*.

Insanity weapon.

"Trunks. Clothing. Books. Navigational equipment."

"Fascinating."

Schultz's eyes were drawn to a couple of men by the lifeboats. They were sawing at the davit ropes with large knives.

"They're cutting a lifeboat loose," Schultz said.

"They're not getting in it?" Horváth asked.

"No. It looks like . . . Yes, it landed in the water upside down. Now they're getting ready to jettison the second one." He looked away from the periscope at Horváth, a small man with horn-rimmed glasses and a receding hairline who was jotting notes in a leather-bound book.

"Even though it took longer for the effects to manifest this time," Horváth said with both curiosity and pride, "the outcome seems to be the same. I suspect that the fact this ship has a wooden hull may account for the difference."

"Then we'll stick to steel-hulled ships from now on," Schultz said. "I don't like staying at periscope depth this long near a Coast Guard patrol area."

They had their pick of targets along the United States' East Coast, one of the busiest shipping lanes in the world, so they could afford to be choosy. The *Deering* was the fourth ship they'd attacked in the past three weeks. Designed as a merchant submarine to smuggle supplies past the British naval blockade during the Great War, the *Bremen* had been diverted from her original purpose on her maiden voyage. She was declared missing so she could be used as a secret test bed for an experimental technology, one that could have won the war for Germany had it been perfected in time.

But the *Irre Waffe* wasn't ready before the Central Powers surrendered. So Schultz and Horváth made a pact to steal the *Bremen* and disappear with her willing crew and the radical weapon to undertake a new goal to get rich. For three years, the plan had worked beyond their wildest dreams, and this expedition was the most lucrative yet. The *Bremen* had the capacity to carry seven hundred tons of cargo, but she'd been so successful on this mission that her holds would soon be full. They'd have to return to base to off-load the hijacked spoils.

Schultz turned back to the periscope. The *Deering*'s second lifeboat tumbled into the water unoccupied. Then one of the crew jumped overboard after it. With the ship at full sail, she quickly left him behind.

"There goes the first one," Schultz said.

"Life jacket?"

"No."

One by one, as though compelled by some unseen voice, the crew members leaped into the chilly winter waters. Schultz counted them off as they went. The last to go was a man in his sixties with white hair and a beard. He didn't hesitate as he flung himself over the railing.

"That must be the captain. Willis Wormell, according to our contact in Barbados."

"That's twelve crewmen total overboard," Horváth said. "Going by the manifest, the ship is empty."

"Excellent," Schultz said. He took one final three-hundred-sixty-degree rotation with the periscope. Several shark fins were circling the men thrashing in the water. He doubted there would be anything left of their corpses for searchers to find. No ships were on the horizon, perhaps because they were steering clear of the oncoming gale.

Satisfied that they were alone, he lowered the periscope.

"Surface the boat," he said to the executive officer. "You may shut down the *Irre Waffe*, Herr Horváth."

Horváth nodded and flipped switches until the lights on his board went dark.

Once the U-boat was on the surface, Schultz climbed to the top of the conning tower and opened the hatch. He inhaled the clean sea air, a welcome relief from the stench of diesel fuel and body odor that always built up inside during a long cruise.

He lifted his binoculars and scanned the deck of the *Deering* once more. After he was satisfied that no stragglers remained, he ordered the *Bremen* to pull up alongside the cargo ship. Despite the storm on the horizon, the seas were relatively calm, with only a slight breeze pushing the schooner along.

When they were beside the *Deering*, the *Bremen* matched speed. His crew attached lines between the ships in a practiced ritual and climbed aboard using rope ladders.

To save the time it would take to lower the sails, Schultz told his men to drop both anchors. When they did, the *Deering*'s stately pace abruptly came to a halt, and a gangway was placed between the two stationary vessels.

Accompanied by Horváth, Schultz climbed onto the abandoned ship. His first stop was the bridge. He found the ship's logbook and tucked it into his peacoat. It was his souvenir, just like the captain's log of every other ship he'd commandeered.

They went down past the mess, where they saw uneaten plates of dinner still on the table.

"The critical moment must have arrived during their meal," Horváth noted.

"I'll have some of the men raid the larder for fresh supplies," Schultz said. The *Bremen* had been at sea for over a month, and the canned beans and pickled beets were getting old. His mouth salivated at the thought of a ripe orange.

When they reached the hold, Schultz grinned as he took in the prize.

The *Deering* was smuggling five hundred barrels of illegal rum from Barbados destined for Norfolk, Virginia. The price for liquor had skyrocketed during Prohibition, which meant the schooner's cargo was worth a million dollars.

With ramps set in place over the entire route to the gangway, the crew began rolling the barrels over to the *Bremen*.

The process for moving the massive casks was tedious and back-breaking, but the crew had dollar signs dancing in their eyes. They worked without complaint. They were just rolling the last few barrels over when the first officer, who was stationed on the *Deering*'s bridge, called to Schultz.

"Herr Kapitän! A ship is on the horizon and closing on our position."

Schultz sprinted up to join him. The first officer passed the binoculars to him.

It looked like a Coast Guard cutter. It was on the opposite side of the *Deering* from the *Bremen*. They couldn't have seen the low-riding U-boat yet.

"Prepare to abandon the *Deering*," Schultz said. "Release the schooner's anchors before you return to the *Bremen*."

"*Jawohl*."

With the sails still set, the *Deering* would continue on, so the cutter would have no reason to investigate the unusual sight of a stationary ship in open water.

His men efficiently carried out their tasks, and Schultz was the last to disembark as the *Deering* began to move. He was met on the *Bremen*'s conning tower by Horváth.

"This might be an interesting opportunity to test the *Irre Waffe* on a warship," the Hungarian said hopefully.

"We've already pushed our luck, Herr Doktor," Schultz replied. "Let's return home and enjoy our rewards."

Horváth looked disappointed, but nodded.

When the *Bremen* was buttoned up and Schultz was back in the control room, he ordered the U-boat to dive. He raised the periscope and watched the cutter approach until she abruptly turned north.

Schultz turned to see the schooner receding into the distance, the words CARROLL A. DEERING, BATH etched in white on her black fantail. She would likely be ripped apart by the storm, but even if she weren't, there was no evidence that the U-boat had ever been in contact with her. The *Deering*'s missing crew would forever remain a mystery.

Schultz lowered the periscope and said, "Set a course due south. Back to base."

That drew a raucous cheer from the crew, but Schultz was contemplating where they'd go next after they sold off the current load of cargo. With the *Bremen*'s range of twenty thousand miles, it really could be anywhere.

The entire earth was their hunting ground.

1

Jack Perry stared in amazement at the approaching cargo ship. He wondered not only how it had made the voyage thousands of miles from South Africa, but also how it stayed afloat in the first place.

With the afternoon sun behind him, Perry had a good view of the decrepit vessel. The peeling hull was painted in so many different hideous shades of green that it looked like a collage of rotting avocados. Gaps in the deck railing were patched together by rusty chains, and the five cranes were so dilapidated that they seemed capable of collapsing at any moment. The bridge windows on the dingy white superstructure set two-thirds of the way toward the stern were so caked with dust that Perry couldn't see the crew inside.

He shook his head in disgust at the ancient steamer called the *Portland*. Why his employers back in Virginia would trust such an important operation to this rickety ship was far above his pay grade. When he had the freight safely transferred over to his own container carrier, he'd breathe much easier.

The *Manticora* wasn't a fancy ship by any means, but she had to be fifty years newer than the *Portland*. The bridge where Perry was standing was set near the bow, and she was smaller. Designed as a containership for smaller ports, the *Manticora* had two recently over-hauled cranes.

Perry turned to the captain and said in Spanish, "Make sure we lift the containers aboard using our cranes, not theirs."

"*Sí, señor,*" the captain replied as he eyed the *Portland* with contempt. "I wouldn't trust those cranes to carry a feather pillow."

"How long will the transfer take?"

The captain looked at the bridge clock, which read 14:17. "Once you complete the transaction with the *Portland*'s captain, it shouldn't take more than an hour to haul four containers over and secure them."

"And when will we arrive in Nicaragua?"

"There's no significant weather expected along the route to slow us down, so less than a week."

"Good. Then let's get this over with."

Perry left the bridge and climbed a rope ladder down to the lifeboat that had been lowered into the water. The *Portland* was now stationary two hundred yards off the starboard bow of the *Manticora*. Perry couldn't be sure, but he thought the creaky ship was listing slightly. He didn't relish getting on her, but he had to check the cargo to make sure they were getting what they'd ordered.

When the lifeboat reached the *Portland*, he climbed aboard and was greeted by a man in his fifties with thinning gray hair tied back in a ponytail and a gut that threatened to pop the buttons on his Hawaiian shirt. His khaki pants were stained with grease, oil coated his boots, and he hadn't shaved in days.

The man stuck out a hand and smiled. "Chester Knight is my name. I'm the master of this fine ship." His New England accent made him sound like he was straight off a Gloucester swordfish boat.

Perry nearly recoiled, not wanting to get his clean clothes anywhere near the man, but he shook it anyway. The man's grip was surprisingly strong.

"Jack Perry. Can I see the cargo?"

"You don't waste time on chitchat, do you?" Knight asked with a laugh. "Come on, then."

He led Perry to four shipping containers lined up on the *Portland*'s deck. Knight nodded to a crewman, who opened the first container. It was full of crates marked STELLENBOSCH PRECISION FLANGES.

"It's all here just like you ordered," Knight said, and handed Perry a crowbar. "See for yourself."

"I will," Perry replied. He climbed up and pried the top off one of the crates.

Inside, carefully packed in Styrofoam, were a dozen South African–made Vektor R5 assault rifles. He checked another crate and confirmed that it also held rifles.

He climbed down and had them open the next container. This one held Denel Y3 AGLs, Automatic Grenade Launchers.

The last two containers contained the other weapons that were promised.

"You got enough in there to start your own little war," Knight said.

In fact, they were destined for Nicaraguan rebels who were going to use them in fighting the corrupt socialist government that was allowing the drug cartels to run wild.

"What they'll be used for doesn't concern you," Perry said.

"Not at all. Not as long as we get paid what we're owed."

"Do you have somewhere we can complete the purchase?"

"My office should do nicely," Knight said. He waved for Perry to follow him into the superstructure.

The interior was even worse than the exterior. Cracked linoleum covered the floor, the walls were covered in grime, and the flickering fluorescent lights gave the corridor a sickly glow.

Knight limped slightly while he walked, and he coughed from exertion as they climbed a flight of stairs. Perry wondered who would be the first to go under, Knight or the *Portland*.

They walked into the captain's office, and Perry was assaulted by a putrid stench that nearly knocked him over.

Knight noticed his expression and closed the door to the bathroom. "Gotta get that toilet fixed." He gestured to the teetering metal chair in front of his desk. "Have a seat."

Perry perched on the edge of the chair. He'd have to toss his clothes overboard after he returned to the *Manticora*.

Knight plopped himself into his seat and heaved his right leg up on the desk. He pulled the pant leg up to reveal a scuffed prosthetic limb grasping his leg just below the knee. He scratched at the edge of it and said with a grin, "I'll find that white whale one of these days."

"Captain Knight, can we conclude this transaction?" Perry asked. "We have a schedule to keep."

"Of course. I'm only too happy to get paid."

Perry took out his phone. "Please tell me the account number and I'll have the money transferred."

"We don't have WiFi on board the *Portland*."

"I'm connected to the *Manticora*'s router."

"Someday we got to get one of those." Knight picked up a scrap of paper and read off a string of numbers.

For a moment, Perry wondered if he could get away with simply faking the transfer of ten million dollars, but he thought better of it and keyed in the instructions. When the transfer was complete, he told Knight. The grizzled captain picked up the battered phone sitting on his desk and called the radio room to confirm.

After a lengthy delay, he smiled and nodded before hanging up the phone.

"Looks like we've got ourselves a sale," Knight said. Perry was relieved that he didn't offer to shake hands again.

"Then I'll let the captain of the *Manticora* know that we can start moving the containers."

"That sounds fine. Why don't you watch from the bridge with me?"

"All right."

They walked up to the bridge, where they were met by three crewmen. The bridge was just as revolting as the rest of the ship. Discarded cans and cigarette butts littered the floor. The glass dials on several of the instruments were cracked. One of the windows had been blown out, was now covered with plywood and duct tape.

One of the crew said, "The captain of the *Manticora* has asked for permission to pull alongside so they can start lifting the containers."

"Permission denied," Knight said, his accent suddenly gone.

Perry whipped his head around. "What are you talking about?"

"We got what we came for."

"You're backing out on the deal?" Perry asked in shock.

"Why not? The money is sitting safely in our account now. We've got better things to do with those weapons than let them be used in some private war of yours in Nicaragua."

Perry's mouth hung open. "How did you . . . ?"

"We have people everywhere."

"You've made a big mistake. There is a squad of commandos on board our ship, ready to take over the *Portland* just in case you doublecrossed us. You can't possibly think you'll get away from us in this atrocity of a ship."

Knight nodded at the *Manticora*. "You think you can catch us in that thing?"

"Easily," Perry scoffed.

"In that case," he said, speaking up as if he were talking into a microphone, "Weapons Officer, destroy their bridge."

To Perry's utter disbelief, plates in the hull and deck slid aside, revealing a six-barreled Gatling gun like those found on Navy warships for shooting down missiles. It spun up and unleashed a torrent of shells at the defenseless *Manticora*. Perry put his hands over his ears as they were assaulted by the deafening buzz saw noise.

The explosive rounds ripped into the cargo ship's superstructure, chewing through glass, metal, and flesh. The bridge was instantly transformed into a slaughterhouse. No one inside could have survived.

The *Manticora* began to drift, and the crew members in the lifeboat that had transported Perry to the *Portland* dashed to safety on the other side of the stricken cargo ship.

Commandos burst onto the *Manticora*'s deck with weapons at the ready. They knelt and raised their assault rifles. One had an RPG.

"Now, we can't have that," Knight said. "Take care of them."

The Gatling gun swung around and raked the deck. The commandos didn't stand a chance. The rounds were so powerful that there was little left of the men besides slicks of blood.

Perry felt like he was going to be sick. He stared at Knight in shock. "We had an agreement. Do you realize who you're dealing with?"

Knight shrugged, as unconcerned as if he'd swatted a fly. "Tell your bosses we don't need them any longer. We have more profitable clients now."

With incredible power for a man missing one leg, Knight took Perry by the shoulders and shoved him onto the bridge's wing. When they reached the railing, Knight threw him over the side with no more effort than if he were a doll. Perry fell five stories to the water below.

When he surfaced, gasping for air, Perry saw the *Portland*'s Gatling gun disappear behind the hull plates. Her engines hummed to life, and the ship pivoted neatly until her prow was facing the *Manticora*. Another hull plate in her bow slid aside, revealing a cannon the size of the main gun on a destroyer. The cannon took aim at the cargo ship and fired five shots in quick succession. The armor-piercing rounds blew massive holes in the hull at the waterline.

The *Manticora* began to tilt sideways as water poured into the holds. The remaining crew on board emerged on deck with life jackets and jumped overboard.

Knight stood on the bridge wing of the *Portland* enjoying the spectacle. He looked down at Perry and gave him a jaunty wave before going inside.

The plate covering the cannon slid closed again. The *Portland* turned and shot away as if launched by a catapult. Her speed was as impossible as her hidden guns, but Perry couldn't deny what he was seeing.

Seconds later, the *Manticora* turned turtle, water cascading off her keel. It was only a matter of time before she went to the bottom. The lifeboat was busy picking up the waterlogged survivors.

As he treaded water waiting to be picked up, Perry wondered how he was going to spin this disaster to his supervisor at the CIA.

2

Michael Bradley sat on a bench seat in the *Kansas City*'s mess hall while the boat's corpsman, Jeremy Noland, looked at his ears. The smell of bacon from the crew's breakfast still hung in the air. Like many Los Angeles–class submarines, the *KC* had no onboard physician nor a dedicated infirmary, but Noland could handle anything short of major surgery. Bradley drummed his fingers on the table's blue padding as he waited for a diagnosis.

The Navy SEAL had endured pain and loss of hearing in both his ears for a few days, but had avoided seeing Noland because he knew that might take him out of the upcoming naval maneuvers with Brazil. But when he'd woken up this morning, he couldn't understand anything his CO was saying, and he was sent to get checked out despite his protests.

"What's the bad news?" Bradley asked. His own voice sounded like he was speaking into a pillow.

Noland, a thin guy with wispy blond hair, stepped back and frowned. His mouth moved, but all Bradley heard were muffled vowels, like those spoken by the unintelligible teacher on TV's *Peanuts*.

"I didn't get any of that."

Noland took a pad and pen from his pocket and jotted something down. When he was finished, he held it toward Bradley.

I think you have acute bilateral otitis media. Massive infection. Filling the middle ear with fluid. Should have come to me earlier.

"Yeah, yeah," Bradley said, annoyed with himself even more than with Noland. "What do we do about it now?"

More writing.

Antibiotic shot, then oral antibiotics. Lots of fluids. Bunk rest.

Bradley's heart sank.

"How long?"

Three days. Depends on how long it takes for your hearing to normalize.

"Three days! Maneuvers start tomorrow. I've got to prep for an op."

Sorry, bud. Your eardrums are under massive pressure and could rupture. Then you might be out for weeks.

Bradley slammed his fist on the table. He was supposed to be piloting the SEAL Delivery Vehicle for the first time. He was even going to get to fire one of its two torpedoes. The SDV was stowed in the dry deck shelter mounted on top of the *Kansas City*'s hull.

He was there the day that the bus-sized shelter had been delivered by a C-17 cargo plane to be installed on top of the *KC*. The middle section was attached to a hatch aft of the conning tower. That hatch gave access to the shelter's air lock, also called a transfer trunk. On its bow side was a decompression chamber for treating Special Forces operators returning from missions in deep water. On the stern side of the lock was a protective water-filled hangar holding the sixteen-foot-long SDV—really, a miniature submarine that wasn't pressurized. The Mark 9 was the newest version, and Bradley had been training for a month how to use it in an operational setting. Now his mission was down the drain because of an illness for a six-year-old.

"Fine," he growled. "Give me the antibiotics."

Noland handed him a second pad and pen.

You'll need guys to write on that if you want to understand any-thing. Then Noland pointed to the door and mimed like he was thumbing the plunger of a syringe.

Bradley nodded, and Noland left him to stew about having to tell his CO he'd be out of commission for the op.

A minute later, Bradley saw two men race by in the corridor out-side the mess. He couldn't tell if they were just goofing off or if there was an emergency. If the crew had been sent to action stations, he would at least have heard an alarm even if he couldn't understand what was being said over the loudspeaker.

He decided it was nothing to worry about until a third man dashed past. For the instant that Bradley could see him, it looked like the sailor had blood on his clothes.

Bradley was about to go out to see what was happening when Noland came back into the mess.

"What's going on with the boat?" Bradley asked. "I just saw three guys run by. I'd swear one of them was bleeding."

Noland just stood there with glazed eyes. He seemed to look right through Bradley. A hypodermic was dangling loosely from his hand.

"Noland? What's the matter with you?"

Noland's eyes came into focus as if he'd realized someone was speaking to him. His lips trembled, and he looked terrified. He started yelling something, but Bradley couldn't understand a word of it.

"Hold on! I can't understand you, remember? Just cool it."

Bradley put up his hands in what he thought was a calming gesture, but that only startled Noland.

He raised the syringe like a dagger and tried to stab Bradley. Brad-ley was six two and built like a linebacker, so he didn't have any trou-ble brushing the skinny Noland aside.

The corpsman flew over a table, but he jumped back to his feet still brandishing the syringe like a weapon.

Bradley was mystified by Noland's sudden transformation from mild-mannered medical officer to crazed psycho.

"What's wrong with you, man?"

Noland shouted something again, waving his arms wildly like he was trying to make some kind of point. Bradley shook his head.

"Calm down, Noland! Jeez! I—"

Noland didn't wait for Bradley to finish and lunged forward again, slashing at him with the needle as if he were desperately trying to ward off a rabid dog.

Bradley grabbed Noland's wrist and twisted him around until he had his arm around the corpsman's neck. He clenched the wrist of the hand holding the syringe, but Noland wouldn't let go. Bradley would have to snap the wrist to get him to drop it.

Instead, he squeezed Noland's neck until the sailor went limp. Bradley gently laid him on the floor and went to find someone to help him get Noland under control before he woke up.

When he got out into the corridor, rather than finding assistance, he found a madhouse.

A few of the sailors in both directions were going at one another in free-for-alls that wouldn't be out of place in the Ultimate Fighting Championship.

But many of them simply looked scared out of their wits. Two were curled up on the floor openly weeping. One was wandering the hall in a daze. And another sailor was bashing his own head against a hatch so forcefully that he tore a gash in his brow.

Even with all of his intensive training, Bradley froze, unsure of what to do. He'd never simulated anything close to this. He wondered if some kind of nerve gas or radiation leak had caused the deranged behavior, but then he dismissed that possibility because he was unaffected. Surely he wasn't the only one immune to whatever was causing this pandemonium.

He had to get to the control room and find the captain. Maybe the condition was limited to the lower part of the boat.

Bradley ran down the corridor, warding off attacks by his crazed crewmates. He climbed the stairs and finally made it to the control room. Some of the command crew had fled, leaving many of the controls unmanned. Two men were lying on the deck with severe injuries. One of them was the XO, executive officer, who had a mortal wound on the back of his head.

The captain was sitting in his chair with his face cradled in his hands.

Bradley rushed over and shook him by the shoulders.

"Captain! We need to surface! Something is infecting the crew!"

Bradley had never seen the normally stoic captain get flustered, but now tears were streaming down the man's cheeks. He bore the same expression Noland had, staring into infinity.

Bradley slapped him across the face, but it didn't snap the captain out of his trance. Instead, he collapsed to the floor and started screaming.

The entire control room was bedlam. One man seemed intent on his task. It was the sailor at one of the two yokes steering the sub. He had a demented look on his face and was pushing the wheel all the way forward.

Bradley looked at the depth gauge. It was at twelve hundred feet and dropping fast. Soon they'd be at crush depth and the sub's hull would implode.

Bradley yanked the sailor from his seat and slammed his head against the instruments panel to knock him out. He took a seat in the chair and pulled back on both yokes. He'd never driven a Los Angeles–class sub before, but the principle had to be the same as for the SEAL Delivery Vehicle he'd been training on.

The sub leveled off at fourteen hundred feet and started rising again. Bradley would have blown the ballast if he knew how, but choosing the wrong switch could just as easily flood the entire boat as surface it. They were at maximum speed. He'd have to worry later about how to slow them down.

He breathed easier when they were back above nine hundred fifty feet, the *Kansas City*'s normal maximum operating depth. They were cruising off the coast of Brazil near the Amazon River Delta, but they must have been out past the edge of the shallower continental shelf because they hadn't slammed into the bottom of the ocean yet.

Bradley planned to radio for help from the Brazilian Navy as soon as he could. The SEAL mission for this war game had been to penetrate Brazil's defenses and infiltrate a base located at the mouth of the Amazon.

When they were at five hundred feet, a sailor wearing headphones came into the control room ranting hysterically. He grabbed Bradley by the arm and tried to drag him out of the seat. Bradley resisted, shoving the sailor away. His highest priority was putting the *KC* on the surface.

The sailor was now sobbing. He staggered over to a panel and pulled a switch.

Bradley jumped out of the chair and lunged toward him, thinking he might be doing something to endanger the boat, like attempting to launch a torpedo while its tube door was closed.

But he realized what the sailor was doing when he heard the faint noise of a siren rising and falling. The switch was the collision alarm. Now Bradley understood why the sailor had headphones on. He was a sonar operator.

Bradley couldn't hear what the sailor was yelling now, but it didn't matter. He could read the man's lips.

Brace for impact!

The man continued shrieking and stumbled out of the control room toward the bow while Bradley raced into the sonar room. The first monitor showed what was coming.

There was a huge cliff in their path. They were heading right for the edge of the continental shelf.

He ran back to the diving control and yanked the wheel around. The submarine began to turn, but too slowly.

The *Kansas City* jerked violently to port as they slammed into the edge of the shelf. Bradley hit his right arm as he was flung against the bulkhead. Searing pain shot up to his shoulder. He didn't have to hear the snap to know it was broken.

Warning lights flashed throughout the control room. Bradley could feel the sub grinding to a halt as it scraped across the cliff. He couldn't tell if the engine room was flooding, but it felt like the propeller was no longer turning.

Bradley pushed himself to his feet with his good left arm. By the time he was standing, the *Kansas City* was at a full stop. The depth gauge, which was at two hundred feet, started to fall. The sub listed to port as it scraped down the side of the cliff.

Bradley readied himself for the end, assuming the hull would implode from the rising pressure, but there was a sudden jolt, and the sub stopped, its bow tilted forward. The depth read three hundred twenty-five feet. They must have come to rest on a ledge.

Bradley made his way to the communications station. If he could activate the extremely long frequency radio, he'd be able to communicate the *Kansas City*'s situation and position to the Navy and request a rescue.

Then he smelled something that chilled him. It was the salty tang of seawater.

He placed his hand on the instrument panel and felt a rumble pulsating through the hull. They were taking on water. Fast.

Bradley turned toward the bow and saw the sea churning in, carrying men and debris with it. It would only be a minute before the entire sub was flooded.

His crewmates were as good as dead. There was nothing he could do for them anymore. His only chance for survival now was the SEAL Delivery Vehicle. If he could get to the dry deck shelter, he could use the mini-sub to propel himself to the surface and avoid drowning.

He raced aft to the midship hatch where the shelter was attached. Before he could reach it, he was blindsided by one of his SEAL team-mates, Carlos Jiménez. Jiménez pushed Bradley into the bulkhead and tried to stab him in the eye with a Ka-Bar knife. Bradley moved his head aside at the last second, and the knife hit metal instead of pierc-ing his brain.

As much as he hated to do it, Bradley didn't hold back and pounded his forehead into Jiménez's face, breaking the ex-Marine's nose.

Jiménez teetered backward and slipped in the rising water.

Bradley kept running until he reached the hatch connecting the *Kansas City* to the dry deck shelter. It was a struggle to hoist himself up with only one arm, but the terrifying thought of being trapped in the doomed sub kept him going.

He spun the hatch open and pushed it up. The transfer trunk, which served as the air lock between the sub and the compartment where the SEAL Delivery Vehicle was stowed, was lit because it was attached to the sub's electrical system.

Bradley climbed up and closed the transfer trunk's hatch behind him. He used a strap to lock it closed in case Jiménez tried to follow him. He felt like he was murdering his friend, but he had no choice.

Before he could cycle the air lock to fill it with water and equalize its pressure with the pressure in the storage bay holding the SDV, Brad-ley had to get one of the air tanks out in the decompression chamber. It would then take a few minutes to move the SDV out of the shelter. At this depth, he wouldn't be able to hold his breath long enough to do it, especially with one bad arm.

Despite the closed hatch, water began flooding into the transfer trunk. But it wasn't a leak. Someone in the sub, maybe Jiménez, had remotely activated the dry deck shelter's air lock to flood it.

In a panic, Bradley rushed into the decompression chamber and pulled the hatch shut behind him. He quickly started to connect the tank, hose, and regulator, then stopped when he realized what a grave mistake he'd made.

He looked through the window in the door and saw that the water level was almost to the top of the air lock.

There was no way to reopen the hatch. The water was pushing against the door with thousands of pounds of pressure.

He was trapped.

Bradley dropped the scuba gear to the floor and slumped onto the bench. He didn't know how much air he had. Even with all the oxygen tanks, he doubted it would last until someone arrived to save him.

He sat there totally defeated until he remembered the notepad and pen Noland had stuffed in his pocket. Bradley took them out and used his left hand to begin awkwardly writing. Before he suffocated, it was his duty to record what happened to the crew on the final cruise of the *Kansas City*.

3

VITÓRIA, BRAZIL

Juan Cabrillo enjoyed the solitude of swimming laps. It was an opportunity to turn his mind off for a while, the rhythmic motion and focus on his breath serving as his form of meditation. He didn't have to make any decisions other than what stroke to use. Right now, he was powering through the butterfly, using his broad shoulders and wide arm span to launch his body out of the water and pull himself forward. As he flipped and kicked against the wall as he turned, he counted his nineteenth Olympic-length lap, nearly two thousand meters.

Juan wore goggles to protect his eyes from the saltwater. The two-lane pool doubled as the ballast tank of his ship, the *Oregon*, so the sea was used to fill it. A combination of fluorescent and incandescent lighting simulated a sunny day, and the walls and floor of the tank were tiled in white marble that tended to become smeared with algae after being filled to the top.

This afternoon, he had the pool to himself. Most of the ship's crew were on R & R in Vitória, a small but vibrant city located three hundred miles northeast of Rio. Although it had a wealth of fine beaches, Juan didn't mind staying aboard to relax, exercise, and get some work done. He was looking forward to a generous cut of Brazil's best prime rib and a bottle of well-aged cabernet sauvignon at a cigar bar and jazz club later that evening.

He and the crew had earned the rest and relaxation after their most recent mission, a two-week cruise tracking down a squad of ISIS terrorists bound for the United States. Juan and his team nabbed them on a cargo ship en route to Latin America, where they intended to cross the U.S. border from Mexico and initiate attacks across the country. Vitória had been the closest city where the *Oregon* could deliver the six Syrians into the custody of the CIA.

Juan had once been a CIA officer himself. After distinguishing himself in clandestine services, he got fed up with the bureaucracy and left midway through his career to form the Corporation, a covert organization designed to undertake operations in a way that gave the U.S. government plausible deniability. To undertake those missions, they operated from the *Oregon*, which was specially built for the task. Rescuing kidnapped VIPs, infiltrating terrorist networks, retrieving critical intelligence from belligerent nations, and investigating threats against the United States made up a large portion of their work.

Although they could be considered mercenaries, Juan's number one rule was that they only acted in America's interests. Hiring themselves out to hostile foreign powers was unthinkable. It was dangerous work, and they'd lost several crew members over the years. But it was also lucrative. Every member of the crew was a financial partner in the Corporation and could expect to retire in well-earned luxury.

When he came up for his next breath, Juan heard his name echoing off the tile. The voice was calling from the other end of the pool, so he flipped around and switched to a faster freestyle stroke and accelerated his pace. He knew if someone was interrupting his swim, it had to be urgent.

When he reached the edge of the pool, Juan easily vaulted from the water to find Max Hanley holding out a towel for him.

"You know, swimming would be easier if you didn't wear those," Max said, pointing at the weighted bands on Juan's wrists and the drag suit he was wearing for additional resistance.

Juan removed the weights and took the towel. "At my age, I have to earn our steak dinner tonight," he said as he dried himself.

Max, who was more than thirty years older than Juan, scoffed as he eyed Juan's lean physique. "If I had abs like that when I was your age, maybe my second wife wouldn't have left me."

"It didn't stop you from getting a third wife."

Max shrugged and patted his ample belly. "That ex likes her men built for comfort, not speed. Believe me, I've seen a picture of her new husband."

While Juan was tall, blond, and tanned from a lifetime in the sun and water—the epitome of a California surfer—Max, a Vietnam veteran, retained the ashen pallor of his Irish ancestors. The bright lighting reflected off a bald spot ringed by reddish gray hair, and his ruddy cheeks were framed with wrinkles etched by time, weather, and laughter.

The one thing that Juan envied about Max was that he still had both his legs. Juan ran the towel down his right leg and over the titanium prosthesis that began just below the knee. The rest of it had been blown off by the cannon of a now sunken Chinese destroyer. Juan was now so accustomed to the prosthetic limb that it rarely limited him in any way, but the residual ache in his stump never let him forget the day he lost his leg.

"So what brings you here?" Juan asked as he put on a T-shirt and sweatpants. "I know it's not to go for a swim."

Max smiled and shook his head. "I earned my steak with the walk down the stairs." Then the smile vanished. "Unfortunately, I don't think either of us is going to eat one tonight. We got an urgent message from CIA headquarters. You and I need to go make a call."

"That sounds ominous."

"It sounds like a job."

Juan served as chairman of the Corporation and captain of the *Oregon*. Max was the president and Juan's second-in-command. Together, they had formed the organization, and Max was the engineer responsible for designing the *Oregon*. He also served as a valuable sounding board for Juan, and the two of them were best friends even though their respective ages should have made the relationship more like father and son.

When they were out of the ballast tank, Juan closed and latched the watertight door behind him. "We'll make the call from my cabin." They arrived there a minute later.

Since all of the crew members lived on the ship, each of them was allotted a cabin with a generous allowance for furnishing it. Juan chose a classic 1940s style based on Rick's Café Américain from the movie *Casablanca*. The anteroom where he held small meetings had a four-person dining table, sofa, and chair, while his bedroom was outfitted with an antique oak desk and a large vintage safe. Inside it were the *Oregon*'s valuables, including Juan's personal weapons, working cash, and gold bullion and cut diamonds for untraceable purchases.

All of the décor was authentic, down to the old-fashioned black telephones. An original Picasso hanging on the wall of his anteroom was one of the pieces of artwork that the Corporation had acquired over the years for investment purposes. A few paintings were kept on board to dress up the ship's interior, but most were stored in a bank vault for safekeeping.

Juan and Max took a seat at the table, and Juan picked up a computer tablet to dial up his CIA contact. What looked like a window that took up one entire wall of the anteroom was actually a high-definition video screen. It changed from a view of Vitória's skyline to a close-up of Langston Overholt IV, Juan's former boss at the CIA and the man who had suggested he create the Corporation in the first place.

Overholt was sitting at his office desk with the blinds on the window behind him drawn. Although the CIA administrator was well into his seventies, he still carried himself with the patrician air of a banker and wore three-piece suits to match. He came from old money tracing back to the first traders who'd settled New England, and he'd been with the Agency for so long that he knew where all the bodies were buried, both figuratively and literally. His revered status and reputation made it impossible for political appointees to get rid of him, so he was allowed to stay on in an advisory role far past the normal retirement age. Overholt, as usual, looked alert and fit, his vigor maintained by regular jogs and games on the racquetball court.

But he also looked troubled.

"I'm sorry to intrude on your well-deserved rest," Overholt said in his gravelly baritone. "I'm aware that it's been only two days since you completed your last mission for us, but I knew you were in the region, and there aren't many people I can trust right now."

Juan exchanged a worried glance with Max. Normally, Overholt would have made a clever comment about Juan's damp hair and casual clothes. It wasn't like him to be so anxious.

"Did something happen with the terrorists we captured?" Juan asked.

Overholt shook his head. "It's much worse. It looks like we have a mole in the Directorate of Operations."

"Why do you think that?" Max asked.

"Three days ago, a cargo ship called the *Manticora* was lost in the Atlantic not far from where you were operating. Survivors in a lifeboat were spotted this morning by airplane, and a ship is on the way to pick them up. We don't know yet how it sank, but the *Manticora* never reported making its appointed rendezvous. A large shipment of weapons is now unaccounted for."

Juan leaned forward. "And you think it's because of a leak in Langley?"

"We'll question the survivors when they're recovered, but it can't be a coincidence that we've had another maritime disaster in that vicinity in the last two days."

"Another?" Max asked.

"It hasn't been publicly announced yet, but the Los Angeles–class nuclear submarine *Kansas City* seems to have gone down with all hands. It was operating along the coast of Brazil, and a Navy SEAL team on board was scheduled to conduct a CIA mission under the guise of a training op. We're still looking for signs of wreckage. The emergency beacon was never activated."

"It could just be a communication glitch," Juan suggested.

Overholt shook his head. "We doubt it. The covert op was supposed to take place twenty-four hours ago. Needless to say, it didn't. Attempts to establish contact with the *KC* have gone unanswered."

"I'm not sure we can help much," Max said. "The Navy and NUMA are far better equipped to handle a seafloor search than we are."

Overholt sighed. "Sad to say, I'm calling you because we've had a third critical situation arise today. It's the reason I'm convinced the other two incidents are the result of a leak."

Juan and Max remained silent while Overholt gathered his thoughts.

"We discovered that an electronic file has been stolen from our mainframe. It contains the names of three operatives on deep-cover assignment to infiltrate some very nasty groups in South and Latin America. From what we've been able to ascertain, the encrypted file wasn't read by the thief, but it was copied onto a thumb drive and sent by regular mail. We believe the recipient will be a man named Ricardo Ferreira, a Brazilian who supplies technology to organizations throughout South America. Many of them are legitimate, but he also deals with anyone who has the cash to buy his illicit products, no matter how dirty they are, including drug cartels, rebel groups, and corrupt governments. One of the compromised agents, Luis Machado, is embedded in Ferreira's company."

"You want us to intercept the package?" Max asked.

"Not possible," Overholt answered. "Although we think it will arrive at its destination in forty-eight hours, we don't know where. Once the package has been received, it won't take them long to decrypt it and identify the agents. Machado and the others will be tortured mercilessly."

"I assume you can't warn them to leave," Juan said.

"Any attempt to contact them from our end could tip off the mole to their true identities."

"Where are they?"

"We caught a break and know exactly where each of them will be in two days based on their last updates. We're lucky all three agents will be in Rio for the Copa América, South America's international soccer championship that is held every four years. That's why I'm calling you. I want you to get them out. You're the only ones who can do it."

Juan took a deep breath, then said to Max, "Looks like we're going to have to cut the R & R short and call everyone back to the *Oregon* for a mission planning session." He turned back to Overholt. "Where will the agents be?"

"This is where it gets tricky," Overholt said. "Luis Machado will be on Ferreira's yacht in Guanabara Bay. Diego López will be at a soccer game at Maracanã Stadium. And Jessica Belasco will be expecting a dead drop at the visitor center on top of Sugarloaf Mountain. I'll send you a file with the information and photos."

Max whistled in amazement. "Let me get this straight. We need three different extraction teams operating simultaneously in three different areas of one of the biggest cities in the world?"

Overholt solemnly nodded. "Or all three agents are going to die."

4

Forty-eight hours later, Juan lounged on the rear seat of a speedboat as if he were completely at ease. His arms were spread, and he had a pleasant grin on his face. His relaxed posture didn't betray the usual mission-induced adrenaline surging through his veins. His eyes flicked over the two guards stoically watching him from the front of the boat, pistols bulging underneath suit jackets. They were no threat. Not yet. As he went over the operational details in his mind, he gave every appearance that he was taking in Rio's spectacular sights.

They were cruising on Guanabara Bay, the one-hundred-sixty-square-mile harbor serving Brazil's second-largest city. To his right in the distance was the giant statue of Christ the Redeemer spreading its arms atop Corvocado Mountain. Closer was Sugarloaf, a monolithic granite peak towering thirteen hundred feet above the entrance to the bay and the tiny Ilha da Laje, an abandoned island fort dating from the seventeenth century. Juan was also able to see three different naval stations and the Rio–Niterói Bridge stretching eight miles across the harbor. Their destination was a giant luxury yacht called the *Dragão* anchored between them and the bridge.

"Looks like the party is well under way, *mi amigo*," Juan said in a thick Spanish accent to Eddie Seng, the Chinese-American sitting next to him. He pointed at the crowd of bikini- and Speedo-clad guests dancing on the two-hundred-foot-long yacht's sprawling aft deck.

Eddie nodded and replied, "Too bad we can't join the fun." Although he spoke in English, any listener would believe Mandarin was his native language based on his pronunciation. In reality, Eddie was born and raised in Manhattan's Chinatown.

Both of them were in disguise. With brown contacts, darkened hair, and a fake bulbous nose, Juan was unrecognizable. Shorter and more wiry than Juan, Eddie was also a former CIA officer, with years spent undercover in China. He sported a temporary scar slashed across one eyebrow and a trim goatee.

"I forgot to bring my swim trunks," Juan said. Like Eddie, he was dressed in a sharp tailored suit instead of beachwear. Even with the breeze, he was sweltering as the blazing midafternoon sun made the day hot and muggy.

"I was thinking of a cool, alcoholic beverage," Eddie said. "I could use a *caipirinha* right about now."

"I'll buy you one later."

Brazil's national drink wasn't in the cards for either of them at the moment. Not when they were about to meet one of the most powerful arms dealers in South America.

He and Eddie hadn't been allowed any bodyguards or assistants on this visit. It was just the two of them at the orders of the *Dragão*'s owner, Ricardo Ferreira.

The speedboat pulled up next to the aft platform. Juan and Eddie stepped onto the yacht, where they were greeted by a Brazilian dressed in khakis, sandals, and an unbuttoned silk shirt that showed off a flat stomach and hairless chest. The man looked at the guards, who nodded, confirming that the two guests had been thoroughly searched not only for weapons but for any listening devices. Their phones had been confiscated at the dock.

Ricardo Ferreira smiled at Juan and Eddie. "Gentlemen," he said in excellent English, "I wasn't expecting you for another half hour. But we had a break in our appointments, so I'm happy to fit you in."

They took turns shaking hands, and Juan said, "Mr. Ferreira, it's a pleasure to finally meet you. My friends in Colombia are intrigued by your invitation." Juan was playing the part of Jorge González, a representative of the Bocas Cartel that was one of the biggest cocaine suppliers in the world.

"As are my friends in Shanghai," Eddie added. "The amount of product we need to ship is increasing exponentially. I hope you can help us solve our transportation problems." He was acting as Chen Lu, the envoy for one of the biggest heroin smugglers in Asia.

"I think I have just the thing for both of you," Ferreira said, beaming. "I will tell you now that the price for what I'm offering won't be cheap, but when you see it, I'm sure you'll agree that it will be worth every dollar. Follow me."

Ferreira watched Juan as they climbed the stairs. "You walk remarkably well for someone with a prosthetic leg. I don't see any limp. Which leg is it?"

Juan stopped and lifted his right pant leg to show the plastic calf. The guards who discovered it during the dockside frisking must have told Ferreira about it.

"Goes up to the knee," he said. "Your men made me take it off to confirm it was real."

"A necessary precaution," Ferreira said apologetically. "How did you lose it?"

"Motorcycle accident," Juan lied.

Ferreira nodded. "A dangerous hobby. The risks I enjoy are more business-oriented."

Juan was relieved that the intel he'd been given was correct. Ferreira might have seen a photo of Jorge González, but the two of them had never met. Otherwise, he'd know that the real González still had both legs intact. González was scheduled to arrive at the *Dragão* in thirty minutes with the actual Chen Lu, so Juan and Eddie had only until then to complete their mission.

The two of them were Alpha team, responsible for getting the first agent out. After they had successfully taken Luis Machado, Juan would signal the *Oregon*'s Beta team at Maracanã Stadium and the Gamma team on Sugarloaf that they were clear to extract the other two agents, López and Belasco.

Ferreira led Juan and Eddie through the crowd of partiers on the afterdeck, stopping every few feet to hug friends and exchange a few laughing words. When they went inside, he took them downstairs.

As they walked, Ferreira said, "I understand the two of you have a mutually beneficial arrangement."

Juan nodded. "We're both interested in investing in lucrative new markets. The price for our product has dropped in the U.S., while the price for Mr. Chen's product has skyrocketed because of the opioid crisis."

"And with the wealth in my country exploding," Eddie said, "the demand for cocaine by the upper classes has increased exponentially. At the same time, there is not much of a market for heroin, so we are looking for new opportunities. Our main problem is shipment. Both the U.S. and China have instituted major crackdowns on drug smuggling."

"We're losing tens of millions every month in confiscated shipments," Juan said.

"Then you've come to the right place," Ferreira replied with a huge smile. "Your worries are over."

One of the guards opened a door on the lowest deck. They entered a large space where ten other men were gathered. Some of them were additional guards, while four of them, dressed in technicians' overalls, were huddled around what looked like a torpedo. A man dressed in a thousand-dollar suit was overseeing the operations.

Ferreira waved the man over to him. "Mr. González, Mr. Chen, this is Roberto Espinoza. He's been a key player in the Slipstream Project."

When they shook hands, Juan looked at him coolly. The man's five-o'clock shadow was expertly detailed, and his slicked-back hair made him look like an extra from *Scarface*. Juan would be convinced he was a drug dealer if he didn't know that Espinoza was actually Luis Machado, the compromised CIA agent.

"Nice to meet you, Mr. Espinoza," Juan said for the benefit of the rest of his extraction team, who were listening to everything being said via a molar mic lodged at the back of Juan's teeth. The responses from the other end were sent to his ears via bone conduction, which made it sound like the voices were coming from inside his head.

"Now, can we see the equipment?" Eddie asked. "We have other plans after this."

"I hope you aren't planning to go anywhere near Maracanã Stadium," Ferreira said. "The traffic will be a nightmare when the Peru–Mexico match is over."

With tourists streaming in from all over the continent for the Copa América, it was the perfect time for the various trafficking organizations to get together and make deals without drawing undue attention.

Juan shook his head. "Our next meeting is by Ipanema Beach. But we are looking forward to seeing Colombia take on Brazil tomorrow."

Ferreira grinned. "I hope you won't hold it against me if your team loses."

"Not if you can solve our shipping problems."

"*That* I can do. The Slipstream can evade any detection equipment the U.S. or Chinese Coast Guards have in place. I guarantee you won't lose another shipment." He gestured to the technicians. "Step aside so they can see it."

The technicians complied and stood back from the object Juan and Eddie had come to see.

It wasn't a torpedo, though it was shaped like one and was approximately twenty feet long. Its top was split down the middle by two doors that swung up and out, revealing a watertight storage area.

Juan did a quick mental calculation. Based on the volume and the current street value of pure cocaine, it could hold over a hundred million dollars' worth of product.

Ferreira walked over to it proudly. "The Slipstream is the Holy Grail of drug smuggling, my friends. A totally reusable, undetectable submersible drone."

5
___

Linda Ross watched the *Dragão* from only two hundred yards away. The submersible she was piloting hovered covertly six feet below the surface of Guanabara Bay. The Gator was operating on battery power, so the snorkel that supplied air to its diesel engines didn't need to protrude above the water, which might have attracted unwanted attention.

When she heard Juan mention Luis Machado's alias, Linda set course to inch them closer to the yacht in preparation for the extraction. Even though she was a Navy veteran, Linda had never piloted a sub until she joined the Corporation. Her postings had always been on surface ships. Now she was the most proficient sub driver on the *Oregon* besides the Chairman, and the Gator was her baby.

The submersible was a versatile craft intended for stealth operations. It could maneuver for extended periods on batteries alone for undetectable incursions into ports and naval bases and carry up to ten fully outfitted operatives. The forty-foot-long deck was flat and sleek, and only the cockpit's cupola of slim windows poked into the air when it was on the surface, making the Gator virtually invisible during night raids. If a fast escape was called for, Linda could fire up the thousand-horsepower diesels, rise out of the water, its profile looking like a cigarette boat, and rocket away at fifty knots.

She was prepared for any of those eventualities. As the Corporation's vice president, Linda was closely involved in prepping missions, and this one was especially complex with lots of moving parts. She thought they'd come up with a solid plan, but she was well aware of Juan's tendency for going off script when unexpected difficulties developed. His famous "Plan C's," as they'd come to be called, arose because his Plan B's usually weren't enough for the crazy spots he had to extricate himself from. It had taken her a long time to get used to the improvisations required for this job because the Navy had such a rigid structure, one of the main reasons she'd left.

"Machado is with them," she said over her shoulder, her high-pitched voice deadened in the confined space. She couldn't imagine how someone as tall as the Chairman endured the cramped quarters of the cockpit when he was piloting the Gator, but she was quite comfortable. Her petite size had been a liability in the Navy, where her authority as an officer seemed to be constantly tested. But once she joined the Corporation, size didn't matter anymore. Here, her tiny frame fit perfectly.

"We're just about ready back here," Mark Murphy replied as he tapped on a laptop keyboard with one hand while he shotgunned a can of Red Bull with the other.

"Easy on those things," Linda said. "Remember, we don't have a bathroom on board. After the last mission, I had to throw away two full water bottles I found. And it wasn't lemonade they were holding."

"Couldn't have been me," Murph said. "I have a bladder like a camel. I once played Call of Duty for six straight hours without once getting up to hit the can. But, man, once I got in there, it was like Niagara Falls."

Linda shook her head, grinning. "Both not surprising. And more than I needed to know."

She felt a kinship with Murph, even though he was one of the few *Oregon* crew members who was not a veteran. He'd been a civilian weapons designer for the military before being recruited by the Chairman, and he was so brilliant, with multiple Ph.D.s earned before most kids were out of college, that he got away with a style that would never pass muster on any other ship but the *Oregon*.

An avid skateboarder, Murph looked the part. The unkempt shock of unruly brown hair and wispy mustache and beard complemented the all-black clothing he preferred. Today it was jeans, Converse All Stars, and a baggy T-shirt that had the name of one of his favorite heavy metal bands, Nuclear Lobotomy, who, according to the bloody lettering on the shirt, toured with another band called Hate Gorgon.

Linda could understand his desire to rebel against arbitrary dress codes. For him, it was clothes. For her, it was hair. Freed from the restrictions in the Navy, she now changed her hairstyle and color on a regular basis. Currently, she had wavy electric blue curls that cascaded to her shoulders.

"Don't blame me, either," said Gomez Adams, the Gator's only other passenger. "I've flown missions longer than that without a break."

George "Gomez" Adams was the *Oregon*'s helicopter and drone pilot. Before joining the Corporation, he'd served in the 160th Special Operations Aviation Regiment, an elite unit known as the Nightstalkers, which carried Army Rangers and Delta Force teams into combat. Linda knew he got the call sign Gomez because of a dalliance with a woman who looked just like Morticia from *The Addams Family*. She supposed he looked somewhat like the character from the musical she'd seen on Broadway, but he was much more handsome, with a handlebar mustache, alert green eyes, and an ace pilot's cocky swagger.

Not that Linda had ever considered dating Gomez. Friendships and working connections in the tight living conditions on board the

Oregon could go badly if the romance fizzled, so keeping relationships platonic was one of the Corporation's unspoken rules. Besides, mustaches didn't do it for her. Too scratchy.

"How are we with the drones?" she asked him.

Gomez gave her the thumbs-up. "The *Oregon* tells me they're set to launch. We'll go whenever the Chairman's set."

"Weapons ready?"

"If we need them," Murph answered.

The Gator was equipped with a wide array of hardware, from submachine guns and assault rifles to flashbang grenades and RPGs. If everything went to plan, they wouldn't need them. Once the Chairman and Eddie were in position with Machado, Gomez would direct a swarm of drones to buzz the *Dragão* and provide distraction for Juan, Eddie, and Machado during their getaway.

The small quadcopter drones would fly low across the water from the direction of the yacht's bow, where they were less likely to be seen approaching by the partygoers aft. When the drones reached the *Dragão*, they would land and set off tiny explosives and smoke bombs. Nothing that would cause damage or injury, but enough distraction and confusion for the three of them to jump overboard unseen in the haze of smoke covering the yacht. The Gator would surface just long enough to bring them aboard and then quickly dive again. Murph and Gomez were prepared to provide covering fire if needed.

Gomez controlled the drones using an antenna that floated on the surface instead of jutting into the air. To anyone passing by, it would look like a piece of seaweed or garbage. The transmitter allowed Linda to see the Gator's position on the cockpit monitor without using a periscope. A winged drone flying a thousand feet above them was disguised to look like one of the many seagulls circling over the bay. Its high-definition feed gave her, Murph, and Gomez a panoramic view of the scene, with the Gator's location marked by a red dot.

"Alpha team, this is Omega," she said over the radio to Juan and

Eddie. "Now approaching you starboard amidships. We're ready to go. Beta and Gamma teams are getting into position."

The Chairman acknowledged by tapping on his molar mic twice with his tongue.

Now all Juan had to do to get the operation under way was speak the signal words.

Dead quiet.

6

"Keep us going in a lazy circle," Abdel Farouk said to the driver of the small powerboat as he huddled over his control panel and listened through his headphones. "Make it look like we're out here sightseeing."

Li Quon, the newest member of the Imito organization, muttered, "No problem." He inched the wheel clockwise, and they began making a circuit of Guanabara Bay a quarter mile south of the *Dragão*.

Farouk glanced at him with annoyance. "Is this boring you?"

Li, in his early forties with an upturned nose and caterpillar-sized eyebrows, rolled his eyes behind his frameless glasses. "I thought I was going to get to do something more exciting than this. Do you know what I used to do?"

"Of course," Farouk said. He wiped his receding hairline and brow with a handkerchief. Fifteen years older than Li and out of shape, Farouk didn't do well with the sweltering humidity. "You owned your own shipping company in Singapore."

"I worked my way up from nothing. I started with one fishing boat and built my company up into one of the biggest shippers in Southeast Asia. Now I'm driving a dinky little boat around Rio de Janeiro and I don't even know why."

"You lost your company because you were selling American secrets to the Chinese. You're lucky you escaped to Brazil before you were sent to prison for life."

Li smirked at him. "I mean, I don't know why you and I are out here."

"There's a lot you don't know," Farouk said.

"Care to enlighten me?"

Farouk sat back and pushed the headphones down to his neck. His equipment was ready. He supposed he could take a few minutes to bring Li up to speed.

Li had agreed to the organization's terms. If he ever talked to anyone outside Imito about the organization or betrayed them in any way, he wouldn't just be killed. He'd suffer horrors that he couldn't imagine. Graphic postmortem photos of previous violators convinced Li of the potential consequences.

Once you became a member of Imito, it was for life. There was no going back.

"Do you know why the commander recruited you to join us?" Farouk asked.

Li shrugged. "You needed someone with few scruples and knew I fit the bill?"

"And you're an excellent seaman. But neither of those is the primary reason."

"What is?"

"You share something in common with everyone else in the organization. Do you know what I used to do?"

Li shook his head.

"I received a degree in acoustical engineering from the University of Southampton in England. Then I went on to become the chief sonar engineer for the Egyptian Navy. While I was there, I worked on a plan to sink a U.S. aircraft carrier in the middle of the Suez Canal."

Li raised an eyebrow. "I think I would have heard if that had happened."

"It obviously didn't," Farouk said with an exasperated sigh. "When the scheme failed, I just barely got away. Like you, I can never return to my homeland. Our plan was foiled by the crew of a ship called the *Oregon*."

That got Li's attention. He sat bolt upright. "The *Oregon*? You mean the stealth ship? I thought she was a myth."

"She's very real," Farouk said. "In fact, you can see her right now from where you're sitting."

Li gaped in surprise before swiveling his head around. There were at least two dozen ships docked at the port, anchored in the bay, or in transit.

"Which one is it?"

"Guess."

Li thought for a moment, then pointed at a containership being loaded by three cranes at the port. "That one?"

"No, but you're on the right track."

"I know it can't be any of the Brazilian Navy ships." He turned and looked at a modern tanker passing under the bridge.

"I bet it's that one."

"You'd lose that bet," Farouk said. "Too bright and clean and noticeable. Your eyes have passed over it multiple times without giving it a second glance. Exactly as they want you to."

Li's gaze settled on the one ship he'd never suspect. It was an ancient cargo vessel anchored in the middle of the bay. Its paint was peeling, and patches of rust dotted the hull. The crumbling superstructure matched the piles of junk that served as cranes.

"That thing?" Li asked in amazement. "I thought they were waiting for a tug to haul it to the scrapyard."

Farouk smiled. He'd thought the same thing the first time he'd seen it.

"What if I told you that ship is faster than virtually every other ship or boat in Guanabara Bay?"

Li scoffed and pointed at a speedboat zipping away from the yacht. "Faster than that?"

"Much."

"Come on!" He turned back to the *Oregon* and waved his hand at it dismissively. "That scow has to be more than five hundred feet long. I'd be shocked if she could move under her own power."

"The *Oregon* doesn't have normal diesels. She's propelled by magnetohydrodynamic engines."

Li furrowed his brows. "What are those?"

"Tubes running the length of the ship take seawater in through the front, strip the free electrons for power, and then pump the water out using supercooled electromagnets so that it shoots out through vector nozzles in the stern like air from a jet engine. Not only does it make the ship exceptionally fast but she's also highly maneuverable."

Li looked at the ship with new appreciation. "Her capabilities are hidden well."

"That's not all that's hidden. She's also a sophisticated warship. Offensive armaments include torpedoes, anti-ship missiles, and a 120mm cannon like the one found on an Abrams tank. Defensively, she features anti-aircraft missiles, three 20mm Gatling guns with explosive, armor-piercing rounds potent enough to sink a ship, and a hundred-barreled Metal Storm gun that has an effective firing rate of a million rounds a minute."

"A million rounds a minute? You're joking."

"Effective rate," Farouk said. "It only holds a thousand rounds at a time. But it can fire them all within a few milliseconds using electronic primer caps."

"I wouldn't want to go up against her."

"Many ships have tried, even naval destroyers. It didn't end well for them."

"How do you know all this?"

Farouk turned back to his control panel. "That is something the commander has not cleared me to share. But I thought you would want to know what we're up against."

"That still doesn't explain why we're out here."

"Don't raise your head. Do you understand?"

"Okay."

"Using only your eyes, look at the bird circling high above us. Do you see it?"

Li's eyes tilted up. "I see it. So what?"

"That's not a bird. It's a drone sent up by the *Oregon*. It's communicating with a sub closing in on that yacht. I can't listen in on the signal because it's encrypted, but I can tell where the transmission controlling it is coming from."

Farouk nodded at the screen in front of him, and Li leaned over. The screen showed a white dot nearing the *Dragão*.

"Let me guess," Li said. "That sub came from the *Oregon*."

"You catch on quickly," Farouk said, impressed. "The *Oregon* has a central space called the moon pool big enough to hold several submersibles. Huge doors in her keel open to launch them unseen."

"So the sub is our target?"

"Exactly."

"Why?"

"Because it's part of a mission that we are going to interfere with. The sonic disruptor will introduce a challenge they're not counting on."

"I've never seen it in operation," Li said.

"You won't see the effects on the sub's crew. You won't even see the equipment." The sonic disruptor was mounted on an underwater drone connected to Farouk's control system by a hair-thin fiber wire.

Ironically, the drone was based on the same technology as the design sold to Ricardo Ferreira.

"Then what *will* I see?"

"The results."

"Who's on the sub?"

"It's who is on the yacht that I think you'd be more interested in." Farouk activated the controls for the sonic disruptor. The target was locked in.

Li threw up his hands in frustration. "You're infuriating. Who is it?"

"Our common nemesis. The man responsible for you losing your company and me being exiled from Egypt. The same man who is the reason why you and I were recruited by the commander into the Imito organization. Juan Cabrillo." Farouk grinned wickedly. "We're about to make sure that he has a very bad day."

7

———

Juan was disgusted at the pride Ferreira took in his technology. The Brazilian gently patted the Slipstream drone as if it were a beloved dog instead of a device that would benefit the most vicious drug cartels on earth.

"The entire skin is composed of carbon fiber," Ferreira said, "with microchannels built in to deflect sonar waves and reduce its sound signature when cruising through the water. The battery can power it for up to twenty-four hours after it's cut loose from the ship or sub that's carrying it."

"And if the batteries are drained?" Juan asked, putting on the guise of a wary buyer. "We could lose hundreds of millions if this thing sinks to the bottom of the ocean."

"Slipstream will go into dormant mode," Luis Machado said, "with enough power remaining to surface, once the authorities have given up searching your vessel in vain, and for you to activate the recovery signal."

"Very clever," Eddie said, playing the more eager of the two of them. "How many do you have for purchase?"

Ferreira smiled. "This is the prototype, which is undergoing testing, but my factory is currently in production and we will have a dozen within a month. Of course, we've had an extreme amount of interest from other parties, but with the right price, we can certainly move you to the front of the line."

"I need to see it in operation," Juan said. "How do I know Slipstream isn't an elephant-sized boondoggle? I want to know it works before I spend my money on it."

When Juan said "elephant-sized boondoggle," Machado looked at him with wide eyes. That was his CIA code phrase indicating his cover had been blown.

"Do you mean, are we trying to pass off something that doesn't work?" Machado asked.

"I mean exactly what I say," Juan said, looking directly at Machado so he would know the phrasing was deliberate. "Is this an elephant-sized boondoggle?"

"Gentlemen," Ferreira said, "I assure you Slipstream will work as promised. I wouldn't be where I am now if I sold shoddy products. We can arrange a demonstration if you'd like."

Machado abruptly turned to Ferreira. "Boss, I'd like to show Mr. González our aerial drones."

"Absolutely. We can deliver your product in a variety of ways. Our drones can even provide offensive and defensive capabilities by carrying remotely activated explosives."

Juan glanced at Eddie to indicate that he wanted a few moments alone with Machado to explain the situation.

Eddie nodded slightly and said, "We have aerial drones. I want to talk pricing for the Slipstream with Mr. Ferreira."

Ferreira's grin got even bigger, dollar signs dancing in front of his eyes.

"You go ahead, Roberto," he said. "We'll join you in a few minutes."

Machado led the way out of the room and up one level. When they were alone in the corridor, he whirled on Juan with a furious look on his face.

"Who are you?"

"Juan Cabrillo," he said in his normal American accent. "We were sent by Langston Overholt to get you out."

"Why?"

"Your cover has been compromised. It's only a matter of time before Ferreira knows who you really are."

"I can't leave now!" He looked around to make sure nobody heard his outburst and lowered his voice. "I've spent two long years infiltrating Ferreira's organization. By the end of the day, I'll have the account information for every major drug cartel in the Americas. We'll be able to freeze billions of dollars in assets."

"If you don't leave, before they kill you you'll be tortured for information about the CIA's efforts to infiltrate the cartels, and that'll make a bloody mess for the U.S. government. Our progress will be set back years, and we still won't have the info you're trying to get."

Machado paced the hall in frustration. And Juan sympathized with the guy. He'd had his own fair share of missions blown up by bureaucratic idiots back at headquarters.

"I'm sorry," he said. "Believe me, if there was another way, I'd help you get the job done."

Machado stopped pacing and leaned against the wall in defeat.

"You realize Ferreira won't just let me walk away," Machado said. "It'll be too suspicious if I leave the *Dragão* now."

"We have an exit strategy. We've arranged a distraction. In the confusion, you, me, and Eddie—that's the man pretending to be Chen—will go into the water."

"And swim to shore?"

"We have a submersible to pick us up. We'll get in and dive before they even know it's there."

"This is nuts."

"Yes, it is," Juan agreed. "But we need to go. Now."

Machado sighed. "Fine. Tell me what to do."

"You need to come up on deck with us. When we get there, I'll have my team initiate the distraction."

"Okay, I'll be back in a minute. Meet me at the Slipstream."

"Where are you going?" Juan asked.

"I have to get something from my cabin," Machado said as he backed down the corridor. "You can't be seen there." Then he disappeared around the corner.

As Juan walked back to the room where the drone was on display, he said, "Omega, this is Alpha. Be ready to go in two minutes." Once he and Eddie were up on deck with Machado, he'd work "dead quiet" into the conversation to signal Gomez to set off the quadcopters carrying the mini-bombs and smoke.

He waited. No answer. That wasn't like Linda.

"Omega, this is Alpha. Acknowledge."

Still nothing.

He tried twice more, but all he heard was silence. Possibly a technical malfunction with the comm equipment. They had a backup signal for just such an event. When they were outside, Juan would stretch his arms, and that would be the signal for Gomez to begin the quadcopter attack.

When he reached the drone room, Ferreira wheeled around.

"So what do you think of our other toys?"

"Very impressive," Juan said. He glanced at Eddie, who gave him a barely perceptible shrug. He hadn't heard from Linda, either.

Ferreira smiled. "Then why don't we talk deal? Mr. Chen and I have come to an agreement very favorable to both of us. I will be happy to offer you the same terms."

Before he could answer, he heard Linda's voice inside his head. She sounded terrified.

"Juan!" she screamed, using his real name in violation of protocol. "Chairman! They're coming for us!"

Juan couldn't answer her, not with Ferreira and his seven men listening. He tapped three times with his tongue to tell her not to do anything.

Her voice sounded desperate. "We need to go now!" It was completely out of Linda's nature to panic.

"We can't," Juan said to Ferreira, but he meant the message for her.

She was sobbing now. "There's no time!"

Then, through the hull, Juan was shocked to hear the sound of one of the mini-bombs detonating.

8

Linda felt like her brain was shrieking at her. She ripped off her headset, but it didn't help. Something deep inside her told her that extreme danger was coming. The image of tentacles, slimy and covered with hungry suckers, filled her mind. She had to escape no matter the cost. Although she knew the Chairman was counting on her, the urge to flee was even stronger.

Gomez babbled behind her, flailing at his controls, trying to attack some unseen enemy.

"I'll get them!" he yelled. "I'll get them all!"

Quadcopters around the yacht erupted in flames and smoke in haphazard fashion. She didn't know who Gomez was targeting, but it wasn't the right enemy. A giant squid was coming for them. The drones couldn't do anything to stop it.

Murph clawed at the hatch, trying to open it, as he blubbered about the gremlins coming out of the sub's batteries.

"We have to get out of here!" he cried as he yanked at the hatch's wheel.

Gomez tackled him, shouting, "Don't be a fool! You'll let them in!"

Linda had to do something or the squid would catch the Gator and crush it. Then it would pry the sub's skin apart like an aluminum can and eat them all.

She knew she shouldn't, but she had to surface the boat. Only the power of the Gator's diesels gave them a chance to outrun it.

"Surfacing the boat!"

She pulled back on the yoke, and the sub breached the surface. Linda blew the ballast, and the Gator rose up on its hull.

Then, through the cupola windows, she saw her best chance of escaping those ravenous tentacles. It was a small boat cruising south of the *Dragão*. If she could get past it, the boat would become the squid's meal instead of the Gator.

She fired up the diesels and gunned the throttle.

Gomez and Murph tumbled to the floor as she accelerated, but Linda didn't care. She had to get away.

Murph pushed Gomez off him and hopped to his feet as if he'd taken a fall off his skateboard. He didn't know where Linda was going, but he knew that fleeing wasn't the answer. The enemy was on board.

He plucked a grenade from one of the containers and pulled the pin. In his haze, he couldn't tell what kind it was. But it didn't matter.

Just as he was about to throw the grenade toward the back of the sub, Gomez smashed into him and it flew from his hand.

It rolled into the cockpit, right behind Linda's seat.

The grenade exploded, and Murph fell to his knees in blind agony.

Farouk was fascinated to see the submersible rise out of the water and turn toward the speedboat holding him and Li.

"They're coming right at us!" Li yelled. "Was that part of the plan?"

Farouk wasn't worried, but Li threw the throttle forward and took off at high speed to avoid a collision.

"Not exactly," Farouk replied calmly. "The results of the sonic disruptor can be unpredictable."

"Thanks for the warning."

"I think it's time we ended the operation. We've accomplished what we intended."

Farouk switched off the disruptor and input the recall coordinates, which would cause the drone carrying it to return to their ship on the far side of Guanabara Bay.

He made a call on his phone.

"Yes?" came the answer at the other end.

"We're on our way back," Farouk said. "The mission was a success."

"I know," the commander said. "I've been watching." Then he let out an uproarious laugh. "I haven't had this much fun in a long time."

Linda opened her eyes to find herself slouched over the Gator's yoke. She'd passed out from a concussion, but she didn't know how it had happened.

Even though she was extremely groggy, the gruesome image of tentacles that had tormented her was gone.

She leaned back and would have fallen out of her seat if she hadn't been belted in. Her head throbbed in pain like it was being hit with a sledgehammer.

Before she could get her bearings, she felt hands unbuckling the belt and pulling her from her seat. Her vision was still fuzzy, but she could see Gomez and Murph talking to each other as they carried her to the rear of the sub. They laid her gently on the floor, and Murph put a blanket over her. He had tears in his eyes.

He was talking to her, yet she couldn't hear him. She couldn't hear anything. It was only now that Linda realized she was completely deaf except for the persistent ringing in her ears.

Gomez said something, and the two of them had a brief conversation until Murph nodded. He then knelt beside her and wiped his eyes while Gomez went toward the cockpit.

Moments later, Linda could feel the Gator turning.

Then she remembered with horrifying clarity.

She'd left them. Linda had left Juan and Eddie to die.

F erreira had a pistol in his hand and it was pointed at Juan's head.

"What's going on?" he demanded.

Juan stood next to Eddie with his hands up. Ferreira's three guards also had their weapons drawn, and the drone technicians had been ordered to leave. Not a good sign, getting rid of potential witnesses.

"You tell me what's happening," Juan said. "I have no idea."

A phone was in Ferreira's other hand. He'd been getting updates from the bridge.

"The captain says there are quadcopter drones exploding in the air fifty yards off the bow. One of you is trying to steal my technology." He moved the gun over so it was pointing at Eddie. "Maybe the both of you. Maybe you're working together."

"I want to buy your product," Eddie said, "not steal it. We have a deal."

"It's not a coincidence that you two happen to be here right when we're attacked."

He's right about that, Juan thought. The guy's not stupid.

"How would we steal it?" Juan asked, pointing at the Slipstream drone. "You think we'd carry this out with us?"

"I don't know," Ferreira said. "Right now, I have to get everyone off this yacht and regain control of the situation. But I'll find out when I get back."

"You'll never do business with our cartels again if anything happens to us," Juan said.

"Remember, I'm a risk taker. There are plenty of other buyers for my products. I'm sure your competitors won't mind being exclusive customers. In any case, I'm going to learn the truth about this assault."

Before Ferreira left, he said to one of the guards, "If they move, shoot them in the leg. I want them alive for questioning." Then he was gone.

The three guards adjusted their aim so that the pistols pointed at Juan and Eddie's legs.

Juan didn't have any doubt that questioning would turn to torture once Ferreira discovered they were impostors. He and Eddie had to figure out a way to escape ASAP.

The odds of them making it out of this room alive and unharmed weren't good. The guards were cautious, keeping a good twenty feet away, so Juan and Eddie would be shot long before they could attempt any kind of attack.

In Juan's prosthetic leg, there was a special compartment hiding a .45 caliber ACP Colt Defender pistol, a ceramic knife, a packet of C-4 plastic explosive smaller than a deck of cards, and a single-shot .44 caliber slug that could be fired from the heel. If he could open the compartment and draw the pistol, he might be able to take down all three of them before they could shoot.

The problem was, he believed the guards would follow their command faithfully.

"I'm going to bend down," Juan said. "I need to tighten my prosthesis. It came loose when I was walking."

The lead guard stepped forward, but only six inches. "You try that and I'll make sure you need another fake leg."

"It'll only take a second."

"Do I look like I'm bluffing?" the guard growled.

Juan shook his head. "No, you look really serious."

Eddie turned to him and gave him a look that said *It was worth a try*.

At that moment, Gomez's voice came through the comm system.

"Alpha, are you still there?"

Juan tapped twice on the molar mic.

"We've had an incident on Omega," Gomez said. "The distraction got activated prematurely."

No kidding.

Juan tapped again to acknowledge.

"Too bad we're stuck in the bottom of the *Dragão*," he said.

The guard stared at him like he was crazy. "Shut up."

"Ferreira said we couldn't move. He didn't say we couldn't talk."

"That's true," Eddie added.

"I don't care," the guard said. "Be quiet or I'll shoot you and tell Mr. Ferreira that you moved anyway."

"Are you free to move?" Gomez asked.

Juan tapped *No*.

"You're captured?"

Yes.

"That doesn't sound good. We'll figure a way to get you all out of there," Gomez said. His tone wasn't very reassuring.

The door opened, but it wasn't Ferreira returning. It was Luis Machado.

"What's going on?" he asked the guard.

"Mr. Ferreira thinks one of them had something to do with the attempted attack. We're holding them for questioning when he gets back."

Machado looked at Juan and grimaced. Juan could tell he was making a decision.

"I see," Machado said. "I'll go find him."

He turned, putting his hand into his jacket. Without a word, he whirled around, firing a round into each guard.

They didn't have time to even be surprised. All three of them slumped to the floor.

"Thanks," Juan said.

"Some rescue plan you guys came up with," Machado said. "I didn't think I'd have to save you within the first two minutes."

Juan and Eddie both picked up pistols from the dead guards.

"Something went wrong," Eddie said.

Machado smirked at him. "You don't say. Somebody must have heard those shots. Let's get out of here."

"Omega, are you still ready for evac?" Juan asked Gomez.

"Who's he talking to?" Machado asked Eddie.

"Our ride," Eddie said.

"It's gotten a lot more complicated," Gomez said. "We surfaced, so they've seen us. I've dived the boat again, but I'm used to flying, not piloting a sub. It's taking some time to get the hang of the controls."

"Why are you driving the boat?"

"We've had an injury."

Meaning Linda was hurt. Juan couldn't take time to ask how badly or how it happened.

"Are there any quadcopters left?"

"One. Smoke bomb."

"Good. We're going to come out near the bow. Be ready to cover us."

Juan hoped that the other guards would be herding the other guests onto the aft deck.

"Understood," Gomez said.

"Take us to the bow," Juan said to Machado.

"This way."

He led them down a series of corridors. They didn't encounter anyone until two guards spotted them climbing the stairs at the front of the yacht.

Juan fired three shots. He got one of the guards, but the other one escaped. Juan could hear him calling for backup over the radio.

"Omega, they're onto us," Juan said. "We're coming out hot. Set off the smoke bomb now."

"Roger that," Gomez replied. "The breeze has gotten stronger, so it won't last long. We're ten yards off the starboard bow. Surfacing."

Juan took the lead and eased the deck access hatch open. He saw the quadcopter land and deposit the smoke bomb. The bomb went off, releasing orange smoke that engulfed the deck.

He popped the hatch and climbed out. While Eddie came out, Juan had his gun trained aft.

By the time Machado emerged, the smoke was dissipating.

"Hurry," Juan said, hauling Machado out.

A sudden gust blew most of the smoke away, leaving them exposed.

Ferreira spotted them from the bridge. In a rage, he grabbed an assault rifle from a guard next to him and shot out the window.

"I trusted you, Roberto!" he yelled.

Machado raised his pistol to fire, but Juan could see more guards coming from both sides of the *Dragão*, so he grabbed Machado and shouted, "Come on!"

The three of them sprinted to the side of the yacht as bullets chewed into the deck where they'd been standing.

The rifle rounds chased them all the way to the railing, where they jumped over and dove into the water.

10

As they were plummeting from the *Dragão*, Juan heard a brief scream of pain, but he couldn't tell if it was Eddie or Machado. After he plunged into the water, Juan swam back up as quickly as he could.

When he reached the surface, he looked around and saw the cupola of the Gator twenty feet away. Gomez was looking out at him with concern.

Juan swiveled around and saw Machado's head bobbing above the water, but he didn't see Eddie. With two powerful strokes, he was next to Machado.

"Have you seen Eddie?" Juan asked him.

Machado didn't answer. Juan tapped him on the shoulder.

"Machado?"

Eddie broke the surface on the other side of Machado. He blew out some water and said, "He was hit as we went over."

Juan grabbed Machado by the shoulders and turned him. There was a bullet hole in his chest. He was blinking in shock, his face drained of color.

Juan immediately looped his arm under Machado's shoulder and began hauling him backward toward the Gator.

"Stay with me, Luis," Juan said.

Two guards appeared at the railing of the yacht. As they took aim, they shuddered from the impact of automatic fire. Juan glanced behind him to see Murph shooting an assault rifle with a grim determination.

Without the weight of Machado to slow him down, Eddie reached the Gator first. He climbed aboard, then pulled Machado up when Juan was beside the sub. While Murph covered them, Juan bounded onto the Gator, and they lowered Machado's still form through the hatch.

Juan took the assault rifle from Murph and trained it on the *Dragão* while Eddie and Murph got in. He heard Ferreira shouting for his men to shoot at the sub, but no one appeared at the railing before Juan dove into the hatch and closed it behind him.

"Submerge now!" he yelled to Gomez.

"Submerging, aye," Gomez replied.

As they descended, Juan could hear bullets pinging against the hull, slowed just enough by the water covering the Gator so that none of them penetrated, although one of them cracked a cupola window.

Out of the corner of his eye, he noticed Linda lying on her back, but Machado was his first priority. Eddie had opened the medical kit and handed him some gauze compresses.

Juan ripped open Machado's shirt and checked his back. No exit wound. The bullet had missed his heart, but not by much. Blood poured from his chest. His breathing was shallow and gurgling from the damage to his lungs.

Juan pressed the gauze against Machado's chest to stanch the flow of blood, but he couldn't do anything about the internal bleeding. They had to get him to the *Oregon*'s medical bay as soon as possible.

"Gomez, set course for the *Oregon* at top speed."

"Heading that way, Chairman."

"And alert Doc Huxley to be ready for casualties."

"She's prepped and standing by."

Machado grabbed Juan's arm with a surprisingly strong grip.

"Password," he croaked. Blood trickled from his lips.

"Easy, Luis," Juan said. "We're going to get you some help."

Machado shook his head. "J . . . Two . . . Seven . . . Y . . ." He paused to catch his breath, then continued, "Five . . . Nine . . . Z . . . Eight . . ."

His hand dropped from Juan's arm and reached into his pants pocket. He took something out and pressed it into Juan's hands.

It was a sealed plastic baggie. Inside was a USB memory stick.

"Use it . . . to stop . . . Ferreira . . ."

That must have been what Machado went back to retrieve from his cabin.

"Don't worry," Juan said. "We'll get him."

Machado didn't answer. His hand fell to his side. His eyes closed. He let out a death rattle and went still.

Eddie, who had some training as a medic, immediately began CPR. Even though they'd have Machado to the *Oregon* in minutes, Juan didn't think it would do any good. The blood loss was too great.

Leaving Machado in Eddie's care, Juan stood and handed the memory stick to Murph.

"When we get back to the *Oregon*, see what's on there," Juan said. "You memorized the password?"

Murph simply nodded.

Juan bent down to Linda's side. She was awake but looked confused.

"How are you doing?" he asked.

"She can't hear you," Murph said with a hitch in his voice. "I threw a flashbang into the cockpit. It went off right behind her head. She's completely deaf."

"What? Why would you do that?"

"I don't know."

"It was both our faults, Chairman," Gomez called back from the cockpit. "I knocked the grenade out of his hand for some reason."

"We went crazy out of nowhere," Murph said. "All three of us. I can't explain it. It was sheer terror. I couldn't control myself."

"He's right," Gomez said. "Then suddenly it was gone, and we were back to our normal selves. Except for Linda, of course."

What they were saying made no sense to Juan. Their reported behavior was the exact opposite of the controlled professionalism he'd come to expect from them.

"We'll have Hux check all of you when the mission is over." He looked at Eddie futilely performing CPR on Machado and seethed about the failure. "I want to know how this happened."

"Two minutes out from the *Oregon*."

"I want a fast turnaround. Have Eric Stone meet us at the moon pool. He and I will go back out with Gomez to rendezvous with the other teams."

"What about the crack in the cupola window?" Gomez asked.

"We'll duct-tape it," Juan said. "The reason that Ferreira brought Machado into his organization is because the other two agents vouched for him. It's only a matter of time before Ferreira figures out they must be spies as well and rats them out. Alert Beta and Gamma teams to initiate extraction missions immediately."

11

The midfield seats were the best in Maracanã Stadium, but Franklin "Linc" Lincoln paid no attention to the tense soccer match between Peru and Mexico that was tied at one all. Instead, he was focused on the man two rows in front of him, Diego López. The CIA agent was cheering the players' every move, along with the men on either side of him, both killers from the Juárez Cartel of Mexico.

The plan was to get López away from his companions long enough to escort him out of the stadium alive. At one time Maracanã was the biggest on the planet, capable of holding almost two hundred thousand spectators. Since renovations for the Olympics and World Cup, its capacity was down to seventy-eight thousand, but that was more than enough crowd to cover their exit at the end of the game.

"Beta, this is Omega," Gomez said in Linc's ear. "You have to move now."

Linc glanced at the game clock. Three minutes to halftime. "The plan was to wait until the end of the game so we can lose ourselves in the crowd."

"You don't have time," Gomez replied. "Alpha team's mission went badly. You may be compromised soon. I'll be calling Gamma next to tell them the same thing. Rendezvous is still as planned."

"Understood." The connection clicked off.

"Why was Gomez on the line?" asked Raven Malloy, who had been listening to the communication on her own molar mic. "Do you think something happened to Linda?"

Like Linc, she was dressed in a Mexican national team jersey, except on her it was tied at the waist and showed off her trim, athletic figure. On him it strained to contain his huge shoulders.

Linc, an African-American, and Raven, a Native American, blended in easily with the multicultural audience. In addition, their clothes, similar to the gear worn by the thousands of other Mexican fans around them, ensured that they didn't stand out.

"I don't know," Linc answered. "But if Gomez had to take over for Linda, it can't be good."

Raven nodded at López and his two companions. "You still thinking the bathroom is the way to go?"

Linc nodded. "Those two have been swilling beers since they got here," Linc said. "They'll definitely make a pit stop at halftime."

"At least López has been smart enough to lay off. He's drunk half a bottle at most."

Raven used to be an Army Military Police investigator, and nothing escaped her observation. Since she'd joined the Corporation, she'd proven herself the equal of any Special Forces veteran on the *Oregon*. She was also the fastest runner on the ship, and a dead shot with every weapon they had in their arsenal.

Unfortunately, neither of them was armed, since they couldn't get guns past stadium security. On the other hand, Linc was sure the two men with López were packing heat. The baggy shirts they wore concealed the bulges of pistols tucked into waistbands. No doubt they bribed someone to bring them in undetected.

As a former Navy SEAL, Linc was an expert at assessing threats, evac routes, and possible hiccups in mission planning. This situation was rich with both problems and opportunities because of the massive crowd. Lots of witnesses, which could be either good or bad depending on how this went down. But also the ability to get lost in the scrum as people swarmed the food and drink vendors and the bathrooms at halftime.

Linc was sure there were more of the cartel's people in the stadium watching López. He was still proving himself to the cartel as a banker who could launder dirty billions. They weren't going to let him out of their sight.

Linc looked at the clock. Two minutes left in regular time. He estimated there were four minutes to be played in stoppage time. As soon as the men started to leave, he and Raven would follow them out. Raven would isolate one man and take him out on the concourse while Linc followed López and the other cartel guy into the bathroom, knock the cartel guy out, place him in one of the stalls, and whisk López away before anyone knew what had happened.

That plan sounded great until one of the men jerked his thumb over his shoulder and walked up the aisle.

"Guess he couldn't wait to go," Raven said.

"That might cause problems. Think you could get rid of him now?"

"You read my mind."

Raven waited for him to pass, then followed him to the concourse exit.

Time to let López know what was coming. Linc picked up the beer by his feet and stumbled down the aisle as if he were drunk.

He plopped into the seat vacated by the cartel henchman.

López, who had thin lips and a Roman nose, looked at him in surprise and spoke in Spanish. Linc didn't speak the language, so he slurred his words in English.

"Who are you guys? Where's my wife?" He took a big gulp of the beer, which by now was warm and flat.

"Get out of here, *hombre*," López said. "This isn't your seat."

"*Hombre?* Hey! You must be Mexican! Just like my wife!" He patted López on the shoulder.

The man next to López sneered at Linc. "Listen to him, *gringo*. Go away now or we'll make you go away."

Linc put up his hands in surrender. "Hey, man, I'm sorry. I thought this was my seat." He looked intently at the bottle in his hand. "What do they put in these beers anyway? Must be tangerine liqueur from Madagascar. I've only had eight of them and I'm already feeling a buzz."

López stared at him with barely concealed surprise. "Tangerine liqueur from Madagascar" was his blown cover code phrase. Linc briefly narrowed his eyes at López to make it clear he wasn't really drunk.

The cartel assassin didn't notice the look. "I said go," he repeated. "Now!"

Linc went back into his drunk mode and lurched to his feet. "I'm going, I'm going!" He hiccupped. "Maybe I should go to the bathroom before I hurl right here. *Adios, muchachos!*"

The disgusted cartel man had turned back to watch the game, so Linc gave López one last look. López nodded ever so slightly.

He understood Linc. He was in mortal danger. And the only way out was through the stadium restroom.

Linc staggered back up the aisle to get set for the coming fight.

12

Most people got to the top of Rio's Sugarloaf Mountain by riding its famous cable car. Thousands of tourists a day visited the observation deck at the summit for the spectacular view, as well as its snack bars and shops. From down in the city, the monolith towering thirteen hundred feet above the entrance to Guanabara Bay looked like a bomb standing on end, with sheer, rocky cliffs on all sides. But from the bay, boaters could see a sloping ridge covered with low trees and scrub brush extending from the sea all the way to the summit. Almost none of the visitors took the alternative route up along this ridge, a rough and difficult hiking trail marked by steep stone faces and several near-vertical rock climbs.

"Whose idiotic idea was this?" Hali Kasim asked, wiping sweat from his brow as he trudged up the worn dirt path near the peak. The slim Lebanese-American served as the *Oregon*'s communications officer and seldom ventured into the field. He certainly wasn't used to the rigors of the three-hour trek carrying a huge pack on his back. His T-shirt and cargo pants were covered in dust and soaked in perspiration.

Marion MacDougall "MacD" Lawless chuckled.

"Ah believe it was yours," the blond Army veteran said with a honey-thickened Louisiana drawl. He followed behind Hali to catch him in case he stumbled and fell backward down some of the steeper inclines. Although MacD carried the same kind of backpack, he didn't think the hike had been so bad. "This is nothing compared to Ranger School. Our packs weighed twice as much as this one, and we'd go twenty hours straight on two rations daily and four hours' sleep."

Hali waved his hand dismissively. "Yeah, but I'm used to sitting in a comfy chair with a refreshing beverage by my side, and the heaviest weight I typically lift in my workday is the headset hanging around my neck. You, on the other hand, look like you were designed in a laboratory experiment to bring marble statues to life for Army recruiting posters. If a movie were made about your life, Chris Hemsworth would be considered too ugly to play you."

"And too wimpy," MacD said, happily going along with the premise. "Ah do think Ah was a Spartan in a previous life."

MacD laughed as Hali threw a glance over his shoulder and rolled his eyes. "Ugh. I'm just thankful I don't have to see you in a loincloth. My humiliation would be complete."

"This might be a good time to remind you that it was your hobby that convinced the Chairman to let us try this."

"I didn't think he'd actually go for it," Hali said.

"Neither did Ah. But that video of you flying over Mexico was impressive. You've got a knack for it."

"So do you. It's infuriating that in only two days you mastered the hobby I've been pursuing for three years."

"Ah wouldn't say 'mastered.' But Ah've jumped out of my fair share of airplanes. It ain't that different."

"Is there anything you're not good at?" Hali asked.

"Ah don't know," MacD said with a smile. "Ah haven't tried everything yet."

They were within a hundred yards of the dirt trail's transformation into a paved path when they got a call on the comm system.

"Gamma, this is Omega," Gomez said. "We've had some issues down here. You need to push your timetable up as fast as you can."

The two of them stopped walking and exchanged glances. That didn't sound good, especially because it wasn't Linda Ross, as expected, talking to them.

"Everyone all right?" MacD asked.

"We've had some casualties. The CIA agent's identity may be compromised sooner than we thought it would."

"Is our extraction rendezvous still a go?"

There was a pause before another voice came through their molar mics. This time, it was the Chairman on the other end.

"Rendezvous will be as planned," Juan said. "We'll meet you at the designated coordinates whenever you get there. Let us know when you're on the way."

"Acknowledged. Gamma out."

Hali's face was a study of concern. "Sounds bad."

MacD shook his head in confusion at what he'd heard. "Ah don't get it. Should have been a simple op on their end. But we can't do anything about it right now. We need to focus on our job."

As if they needed any more distractions, three monkeys hopped through the bushes beside them, begging for food, but MacD and Hali ignored them. The monkeys chattered in disappointment but hovered nearby just in case.

MacD looked at both sides of the trail and saw that there was a relatively level spot to the right that sloped down to a cliff twenty-five yards away. The tiny island of Ilha da Laje, with its deserted concrete fortress, was far below them at the entrance to Guanabara Bay, and, beyond it, was the eight-mile-long Rio–Niterói Bridge stretching from one side of the bay to the other. Farther in the distance he could make out the shape of the *Oregon*, which was probably in the process of recovering the Gator so they could treat the casualties. Since the ship was turning, that meant it'd raised anchor.

MacD and Hali were low enough on the hill that tourists on the observation deck above couldn't see them, and a mass of trees obscured the view of the path higher up. MacD walked over to an area that was covered only by tall grasses and shrugged off his backpack.

"This is as good a place as any to launch," he said. "Can you get them both set up while I'm gone?"

Hali studied the terrain and put his hand up to feel the direction of the light breeze wafting up the side of the mountain. Then he nodded.

"Shouldn't be a problem as long as the monkeys stay out of my way."

"Let me know if you run into any snags," MacD said. "Ah'll give you a shout when Ah've got her."

"I hope she's not afraid of heights."

"She had to take the cable car to get up here."

"Not the same thing," Hali said, unzipping his pack.

MacD peered over the ledge to the water a thousand feet down. "You're right."

While Hali unpacked the equipment, MacD went back to the trail and walked up the remaining section until he could hear the sound of voices coming from the crowd gathered on the observation platform.

The huge deck spread in a semicircle around the building housing the cable car loading area and winch. There were several buildings housing the snack bars and the stores selling knickknacks and souvenirs. Hundreds of visitors leaned against the railings to take in the view, took selfies, or sat at tables, gazing at the incredible scenery.

MacD was looking for a CIA agent named Jessica Belasco. According to the photo and bio he'd studied for the operation, she stood an athletic five-six, held a black belt in tae kwon do, and she had long black hair, full lips, and a white three-inch scar down the side of her neck. He'd also noticed she was very cute, so he had no doubt she'd be easy to spot.

Belasco had infiltrated a Bolivian cocaine cartel and was tasked with discovering links between it and a series of government assassinations throughout South America. She was in Rio to connect with their Brazilian counterparts.

According to her weekly report, Belasco and some of the cartel's big bosses had cable car tickets that would have put them at the top fifteen minutes earlier. This was the only place where she'd be in public during the Rio visit, so the extraction had to occur there.

MacD wandered through the stores and around the deck, just another tourist among many who was taking in the sights. But unlike the rest of the people, he wasn't looking at the statue of Christ the Redeemer or at Copacabana Beach. He was systematically scanning the crowd for his target.

He finally spotted her sitting at a table with two men and a woman. They were eating cups of gelato while speaking animatedly in Spanish and laughing. Belasco looked like she was having fun. MacD was about to spoil it.

He walked up to the table and used the French he'd learned growing up near New Orleans.

"*Pardonnez-moi,*" he said. "*En aurez-vous bientôt fini avec cette table?*"

Pardon me. Will you be done with this table soon?

As he'd expected, the three people with Belasco looked at him blankly. But MacD knew the CIA agent spoke French. She responded, "There are plenty of free tables around us, monsieur."

She switched back from French to Spanish and explained what he was asking. They all looked at him like he was a moron.

"I know," he continued in French, "but this is my favorite table. It reminds me of a place where I grew up, a small country village outside of Chamonix."

"A small country village outside of Chamonix" was her blown cover code. She swallowed her ice cream and looked up at him, her smile faltering only slightly.

"It does?"

He nodded with a serious expression to let her know that she'd heard correctly. "While I wait for the table, I'll browse the gift shop on the other side of the deck. I want something that reminds me of this place when I leave. *À bientôt.*"

See you soon.

He smiled at the group, then turned and walked away, certain that she understood the message.

Two minutes later, as he scanned the postcards, she sidled up beside him, but facing the other direction.

"I only have a few minutes," Belasco said. "I told them I wanted to do some shopping before I went back down."

"You can't," MacD said. "Your cover is blown. They'll get a text at any moment that you're really a CIA agent. They might not even wait to get into the cable car before they kill you."

"And you are?"

"MacD Lawless. Rescuer and all-around nice guy. To my friends, at least."

"How do you know my cover is blown?"

"There was a leak at CIA headquarters. You and two other agents were compromised. That's all Ah know. But they wouldn't have sent me if they didn't think it was serious."

She threw up her hands in frustration. "All my work down the drain. I don't believe this."

"Believe it. Would Langston Overholt have given me your blown code if he didn't think you were in danger?"

The mention of Overholt's name seemed to convince her that she had no choice but to abandon her operation.

"Even if we take care of the three people with me," she said, "there are half a dozen more killers waiting for us at the bottom of the mountain."

"Ah know. You wouldn't get twenty feet from the cable car station before they'd stuff you in a van and make you disappear."

"So, what now?" she asked with a sigh. "You're going to escort me down on the cable car all by yourself?"

"Not exactly. Have you ever been skydiving?"

"Twice. Both tandem jumps." She turned to him and cocked her head in suspicion. "Why?"

MacD grinned. "Because we've got a flight to catch."

13

Raven Malloy lingered near a trash can as she nursed the last of her water. The concourse of Maracanã Stadium was still fairly empty, but in a few minutes it would be full of people heading for the restrooms or food stands. Right now, other than the few who couldn't wait for the break at halftime, the only people nearby were the ever-present police officers patrolling the grounds in teams of two.

She kept an eye on the closest men's room door. The Mexican assassin had gone in two minutes before, and she was going to intercept him on his way out.

Raven and Linc had planned on waiting until the end of the game to make their move. With seventy-eight thousand fans leaving the stadium all at once, it would have been easy to get lost in the crowd during the exodus. Now with an accelerated timetable, they had to hope the commotion at halftime would provide them with enough of a distraction.

She looked at one of the monitors displaying the game for those people who couldn't be at their seats. The clock was ticking down, with only three minutes left in stoppage time. López would be leading the other Mexican to the bathroom as soon as the first period ended.

If the first guy didn't exit the men's until then, the mission would get far more complicated.

Raven hoped her target wasn't having intestinal problems. Just thinking about the possibility made her gag.

She didn't have to imagine for long. Seconds later, the Mexican emerged. In her mind, she dubbed him Feo because he was snaggle-toothed and had a bushy unibrow. Although she was fluent in Arabic and Farsi, Raven only dabbled in Spanish, but she did know that *feo* meant "ugly."

She threw away her water bottle, adjusted her tied-back shirt to ensure that it revealed some of her flat belly, and made a beeline for Feo.

When she reached him, she put her hand on his shoulder and said in English, "I saw you a few minutes ago and thought I just had to meet you."

He stopped and looked at her in confusion because he didn't know any English, so she gave him a high-wattage smile. Smiling was not her thing, so it was killing her to put on the act.

He looked her up and down and smiled back at her with Tic Tac–sized teeth that went in all directions. The way his hungry eyes ogled her body made her skin crawl.

Despite her discomfort, she continued the performance, pointing back and forth from him to her before making the universal gesture for taking a picture. She took out her phone to emphasize the point.

The idea of a selfie with a pretty girl—better yet, one who was wearing a jersey of his native national team—was too good for Feo to pass up, just as she'd hoped. He nodded and grinned even wider.

She indicated a spot under one of the team banners hanging in the concourse. It also happened to be only twenty feet from where two policemen were standing and talking to each other.

Feo nodded again and put his hand on the small of her back to guide her over there. She swore if his hand drifted down to her butt, she'd break every one of his fingers no matter how it affected the mission.

However, it did give her an excuse to reciprocate and put her hand on his back. She brushed against the pistol tucked under the waistband. With a casual motion, she lifted Feo's shirt so it exposed the gun.

When they reached the spot for the selfie, she nestled in close to him, trying not to inhale the ungodly amount of nauseating cologne he was wearing. She held up her phone with one hand while she took a small ampoule of fast-acting superglue out of her pocket with the other.

She pretended to have some trouble taking the picture, but that was only to give her a little extra time. In the hand behind Feo's back, she flipped the top off the ampoule. She squeezed a few droplets of glue onto the hammer of the pistol before dropping the shirt back over it and throwing the ampoule away.

The glue would take a few seconds to harden, so she snapped several pictures with the phone in multiple angles and orientations. Feo was in no hurry to finish. He was eating it up.

By the count of ten, Raven knew the glue had hardened and she suddenly flinched as if he'd pinched her. She slapped him and started yelling in English.

"Hey! This guy just groped me!"

She turned and waved frantically to the police officers.

As she expected, Feo started cursing back at her and getting in her face. He wasn't going to take a hit from some disrespectful girl without fighting back.

She reared back again, but slowly enough so that he could grab her forearm.

Exactly as she wanted him to.

She rotated her body and clasped his wrist so that his arm bent at an awkward angle. Feo let out a yelp of pain. Raven used his body weight against him to flip him over and slam him to the ground facedown. The pistol was now fully exposed because his shirt was pulled over his head.

She backed away and screamed, *"Ele tem uma arma!"* She'd memorized the phrase.

He's got a gun!

The police officers saw the pistol and rushed over as they drew their weapons.

There had been a small chance that Feo would have opted for a shoot-out instead of risking a stay in a Brazilian prison. That's why she had glued the hammer down. Even if he had tried to fire it, nothing would have happened. He would have gone down in a hail of bullets, and neither of the police officers would have been injured.

But that would have been messy. This way was a lot tidier.

One of the policemen put his boot on Feo's back while the other removed the weapon, before handcuffing him. They lifted him to his feet while he spewed rapid-fire, angry Spanish. Raven couldn't understand it, but she bet it consisted of a few choice words about her.

She put on a scared look and tried to make some tears flow. She couldn't squeeze any out, but the officers got the picture. One of them even tried to console her. He said some kind words in Portuguese and then nodded for her to go.

As they led a still-fiery Feo away so the disturbance wouldn't attract onlookers during the halftime festivities, she turned and went back to her spot across from the men's room.

"First guy is out of the picture," she said over the comm system to Linc, who was just going inside the restroom.

"I saw," he replied. "Nice job. If it weren't for that sweet judo move, I would have thought you were the prototypical damsel in distress."

"It was easy. Men are suckers."

"Present company excepted?"

"I stand by my statement."

"I'll try not to let that hurt my feelings," Linc said with a laugh.

"Maybe I should teach a seminar on the *Oregon* someday about how not to be one," Raven said.

"I'll be in the first row."

That got a split-second grin from her, but it disappeared when people started streaming out of the stands. She checked the monitors, and they showed players heading toward the locker room for halftime.

A minute later, she saw López and his companion head into the men's room.

Raven said to Linc, "Your turn."

14

___

Linc pretended to use one of the urinals and kept his eye on the entrance. The modern bathroom, remodeled for the Olympics, was filling with drunk spectators rushing to make room for their next beer.

"López and his friend are coming in," Raven said over the molar mic. "López is in the lead."

"Got it," Linc replied.

He acted like he was zipping up and headed toward the sinks, which were across from the stalls. In his hand was a small spring-loaded syringe filled with a fast-acting barbiturate formulated to knock out the assassin in a few seconds.

Linc caught López's eye as the CIA agent rounded the corner. López nodded back, and Linc went back into sloshed mode.

"Hey! There's my friends again!" he cried out sloppily.

He stumbled forward, and López neatly sidestepped him so that Linc fell into the Mexican's arms.

"Aye!" the assassin yelled, but that's all he got out as Linc sunk the needle into his shoulder.

The man, distracted by the knee Linc sent into his groin, doubled over and went limp before he could recover.

López and Linc took him by either arm and carried him to one of the stalls.

"You're not feeling so good, huh?" Linc announced for the benefit of anyone who might be listening. "Throw up in here."

López took the cue and said something similar in Spanish.

They shoved him into the stall, and Linc put him head down on the toilet seat. By the time anyone checked on him and found him unconscious, Linc and López would be long gone.

Linc turned and saw López backing away to give him enough room to get out of the stall and close its door. What the CIA agent didn't see was another man lunging toward him with a knife.

Linc shouted, "Look out!" It probably saved López's life.

López spotted the attacker at the last moment and swiped at the man's wrist, which had been aiming at his heart. The fast reaction kept him from being murdered, but López wasn't quick enough to dodge the knife altogether.

The switchblade plunged into the side of his abdomen. By this time, Linc was able to extricate himself from the stall and grab the stranger by the neck. Linc towered over the man and outweighed him by a good forty pounds, so it took no effort to pick him up and slam his head into the granite countertop of the nearest sink.

The knife-wielding assailant instantly became a lifeless rag doll and fell to the floor, the blade dropping from his hand and bouncing under a stall door nearby.

Linc whipped around and saw López clutching his stomach. Blood was oozing from between his fingers.

"How bad is it?" Linc asked.

"Bad," López said through gritted teeth. "But not bad enough to wait for the cops to show up."

Not only would an investigation cause a diplomatic incident but they didn't know who in the Rio Police Department was on Ferreira's payroll. If they wound up in custody, they could easily be dead by morning.

A crowd of men was gathering to look at the prone man on the floor with the caved-in head.

"He slipped," Linc said to no one in particular. "Someone call an ambulance!"

He didn't know if anyone saw the fight or spoke English, but casting doubt on what happened might give them a few seconds.

"Let's get out of here," he said to López. "Raven, López got knifed in the side. He's on his feet but bleeding."

"On it," she replied curtly.

As they were leaving the men's room, Linc had his head on swivel looking for any more assassins in the crowd. Nobody caught his eye, but he did see Raven bartering with a female fan wearing a baseball cap and a scarf with the Mexican flag on it. Raven handed over a wad of bills and got the scarf and cap in return.

She joined them as they made their way through the spectators toward the exit. She put the cap on López's head as a simple disguise and wrapped the scarf around his midsection. He winced as she cinched it into a tight knot.

"What happened?" she asked.

"Someone was following López," Linc said. "They must have gotten word from Ferreira that he was a possible spy."

"And seeing you conk his friend out convinced them of that."

"Apparently."

"Where are we going?" López asked.

"We've got an extraction rendezvous five miles from here," Linc said. "Can you make it?"

"Car?"

"We've got three motorcycles waiting in the parking lot." They'd planned on that mode of transportation since they knew López was an experienced rider and getting through the dense after-match traffic would be much easier than with a car.

López shook his head as he hobbled along. "I don't think I could handle a bike."

"He can ride with me," Raven said. "You provide us cover."

That made sense to Linc. She was good on a cycle, but Linc was the most experienced biker on the *Oregon*. He even had his own, heavily customized Harley-Davidson that he occasionally brought out of the ship's hold for rides during R & R. He could fire a gun while driving through traffic if needed.

They were at the north exit of the stadium when two men spotted them from across the concourse.

Linc and Raven hustled López to the exit while their pursuers tried to get through the swarm of people between them.

Three BMW motorcycles were waiting in the parking lot where they'd left them. While Raven helped López on her bike, Linc opened the storage case on the back of his and withdrew a Glock pistol. He turned and saw the two men bolt from the exit with weapons in hand. One was talking on his phone as he ran.

Linc didn't wait for them to fire. He took each of them down with a single shot as they came toward him.

The sound of the gunshots would surely draw police attention. Linc took a backpack from the motorcycle case and put it on, then got on the bike and started it up. None of them took time to put helmets on, using sunglasses only. López leaned against the backrest of Raven's motorcycle, one hand around her waist and the other pressing on his wound to stem the blood loss.

As he flipped up the kickstand, Linc saw three vehicles screech around the corner. The phone call from the bad guy must have gotten through. Two men on red Ducati racing bikes were followed by a black Porsche SUV with men hanging out of the windows holding MP5 submachine guns.

"Go! Go! Go!" Linc shouted.

Raven's rear tire squealed as she took off, and Linc was close behind. They sped onto the relatively empty boulevard.

"We've got to lose them before we get to the bridge," Raven said, her voice in his head as clear as if she were right next to him despite the wind rushing past.

"Working on it," Linc replied.

Their destination was the midpoint of the Rio–Niterói Bridge. If they didn't put some distance between themselves and the pursuers, they'd never live long enough to make the rendezvous with Juan.

15

When MacD got back down the Sugarloaf Mountain trail with Jessica Belasco, the monkeys chattered to announce their presence to Hali. Belasco abruptly stopped at the sight of the equipment he had been prepping.

"You're kidding me," she said.

"Jessica Belasco," MacD said. "Meet Hali Kasim, our resident expert on paragliding."

A gold and white semicircular parachute wing was spread on the ground, its suspension lines converging on a harness tacked to the ground to keep the chute from taking flight early. The canopy, as the wing was called, constantly threatened to rise into the air as the breeze took hold of it.

MacD was beginning to enjoy paragliding almost as much as Hali, who had fallen in love with the sport during a stop in Jamaica when he went parasailing. In that case, the parachute had been dragged by a boat and winched out from the stern as it rose into the air. That's what usually was done with uninitiated tourists.

But Hali had become such an enthusiast that he learned how to paraglide by launching from a high cliff and soaring freely through the sky, eventually becoming an expert. His record for duration and distance riding thermals was two hours thirty-eight minutes and forty miles, still far short of the three-hundred-fifty-mile record. They'd even rigged a winch at the back of the *Oregon* so Hali could be towed by a launch behind the ship like an airborne water-skier.

"Nice to meet you." He was busy unrolling the second parachute, so he nodded to a helmet and said, "Brought that for you."

She walked over to it in a daze and picked it up. "I can't fly one of these things."

"You're not going to," Hali said. "I am. We've got a tandem harness."

She looked at MacD, who shrugged as he helped Hali finish prepping the second canopy, which was red and blue. "Fastest way down. Can't take the cable car, as you already pointed out. And hiking back down would take hours, during which time your friends would be able to intercept us."

"This is insane. How can you be sure my cover is blown?"

"Ah can't. Langston Overholt seems to be sure, though."

"But—"

"Listen. You can stay and hope they haven't found out about you or you can come with us. That simple."

Her griping was starting to get on MacD's nerves. He pointedly looked back up the trail. They were still alone, but that wouldn't last long.

Belasco followed his gaze, then grimaced and put on the helmet.

"Where are we going?" she asked.

MacD pointed at Ilha da Laje at the mouth of Guanabara Bay.

"See that little speck down there? We're landing on top of it. No way your friends can get to us there."

"And then what? A boat picks us up?"

"Sub."

She rolled her eyes. "This just keeps getting better. Who *are* you guys?"

"Private contractors. We're all partners in the firm. Ah can get you a brochure later so you can learn about our time-share opportunities."

"Great. I'm being rescued by Chuckles the Clown."

"Hey! You guessed my Ranger call sign!"

Belasco turned to Hali, who helped her into her harness. "You have to put up with this all the time?"

Hali smiled. "That's why I get paid the big bucks."

"How long will it take us to get down?"

"Ten minutes tops. Light breeze. Should be a smooth ride."

"And I should still be on my undercover mission," Belasco said. She wheeled on MacD. "If I find out you burned me for no reason, I'll make sure you regret it."

"Is it too early to regret it now?" MacD asked.

"Maybe I should let you two ride together," Hali said. "That way, you can continue this whole 'will they, won't they' tension."

"Oh, please." She jerked a thumb toward MacD. "My ex was a better-looking version of this guy."

MacD looked at Hali and shook his head. "It's good we're getting paid for this. Ah've never heard somebody complain so much about getting his life saved."

Hali just grinned and gave him a shrug. While Hali put on his own harness and connected it to the suspension lines and to Belasco, he told her how they were going to launch.

"We're going to face the canopy, and I'm going to pull it into the air," he said. "Once it catches the wind, we'll turn around and head down the hill toward the cliff until we take flight. Got it?"

Now she was starting to look nervous.

"You've done this before? The tandem thing?"

"Hundreds of hours," Hali said assuredly.

MacD knew that wasn't true. Hali had practiced it for the last two days with MacD to literally teach him the ropes. Before that, he'd done it maybe half a dozen times. Guess he wanted to calm Belasco. Panicky people did stupid things.

She nodded, and MacD and Hali checked the molar mics to make sure they were communicating. Then MacD clipped into his harness.

Just before Hali pulled the canopy up, the monkeys started going crazy.

"Someone's coming," MacD said.

The sounds of footsteps pounded down the trail, and Belasco's three companions emerged from behind the trees twenty-five yards away. They were momentarily dumbfounded by the vision of the colorful canopies spread on the ground.

But their surprise didn't last. Although they drew weapons, they had to dive for cover when MacD pulled out his SIG Sauer semiautomatic pistol and shot at them.

"Take off," he yelled to Hali. "Now!"

Hali jerked his canopy off the ground, and he and Belasco swiveled around. With a couple of running steps, they leaped into the air.

Despite several more shots from MacD, the three assailants fired back from behind some rocks.

MacD couldn't wait any longer. He shoved the pistol into his waistband and yanked the suspension lines up. The canopy caught the wind and billowed fully.

He noticed several holes had appeared in the nylon, but all he could do was hope they didn't become larger.

He turned and ran forward until his feet left the ground. As soon as he cleared the cliff, he bled lift from the canopy and sank out of sight of the people shooting at him.

He saw Hali and Belasco in front of him, but something looked wrong. Belasco was hanging much lower than she should have been.

"Hali, is she hit?"

"No," Hali replied, the strain evident in his voice. "But one of the rounds cut part of her harness. She's hanging by a thread."

"Can you make it?"

"I think so, even though it's throwing off my balance. But we've got a bigger problem."

"Bigger than nearly falling out of the harness?" MacD asked in amazement.

"I think we've got interceptors headed our way."

Hali pointed in the direction of the large yacht that Juan's Alpha team had infiltrated.

At first MacD didn't see anything, but then several dots resolved against the blue sky, and he knew Hali was right. They did have bigger problems.

Four large quadcopter drones were headed straight for them.

16

Raven and Linc had planned to race down the broad boulevards that led straight to the long highway bridge connecting Rio to the city of Niterói on the other side of Guanabara Bay. But with little traffic to provide a means of escaping their pursuers, they had to come up with an alternative route. The men on the Ducatis were gaining. The bikes were faster than the BMWs, and it didn't help that Raven had an additional rider with her.

"How are you doing back there, López?" she asked her passenger.

"I'll make it," he said, but his voice was weak, as was his grip around her waist. She didn't want to drive too wildly for fear that he would fall off.

"Name's Raven. Just save your strength and hold on."

"Okay."

Linc was behind Raven, occasionally firing shots in an attempt to ward off the pursuers. It didn't seem to be working. She glanced in the mirror and saw the two Ducatis, followed closely by the Porsche SUV.

She keyed the molar mic with her tongue. "Omega, this is Beta team. We have an injured man, and we've got a bunch of angry drug dealers on our tail. Need a little help with directions."

"I've got our resident guide on the line," Juan said on the other end, meaning Mark Murphy. "What can we do?"

"How about a traffic tie-up?"

"You're clear all the way to the bridge," Murph said.

"No, I want to *find* a traffic tie-up," Raven said. "We can at least lose the SUV that way."

"Gotcha," Murph said. "No jams near you on the main roads."

"Then get us onto a side road. A narrow one."

Raven knew Murph was monitoring their position using the GPS on their phones.

"I've got a new route," he said. "At the next street, turn right."

"Turning," she replied. As she leaned into the turn, a bullet ricocheted off the BMW's fender, barely missing the tire. Linc was right behind her and fired off three shots in return.

"Getting low on ammo," he said.

"At the end of this street," Murph said, "there is a canal perpendicular to you. You're going to cross it."

"How does that help?" Raven asked.

"It's a pedestrian bridge. Too small for the SUV. It's only ten feet wide and has steel barrier posts, according to the online street view. Do you have the backpack on?"

"Ready to deploy," Linc said.

"After you cross the pedestrian bridge, you can turn left and it's a straight shot to the Rio–Niterói."

"Got it," Raven said.

She could see the pedestrian bridge ahead. There were five steps up to it.

"Hold on," she yelled to López. He tried to tighten his grip, but his arm was weak.

She jerked the handlebars back, gunned the engine, and popped up on her rear wheel to climb the stairs.

Linc followed, and they raced across the thankfully empty bridge.

"Deploying," Linc said.

That meant he was releasing the drawstring on his backpack like a ripcord on a parachute. The pack was filled with four hundred caltrops. Shaped like jacks, the small steel weapons had four needle-sharp spikes, one of which poked straight up no matter how the caltrop landed. During the time of the Roman Empire, they'd been used to hobble horses and camels. Now they worked just as effectively on pneumatic tires.

When Linc pulled the ripcord, the caltrops spilled out and scattered across the pedestrian bridge behind him.

As Raven turned, she glanced to the side and saw the motorcyclists launch themselves up the steps. They ignored the tiny items falling onto the bridge surface and roared across.

The moment the tires hit the spikes, they blew out. One rider went tumbling across the remaining caltrops while the other flipped his bike into the canal.

The Porsche SUV skidded to a stop at the metal barriers, but it wasn't giving up. It backed up and began to follow them on the other side of the canal.

Raven gunned her engine. She and Linc accelerated much more quickly than the SUV could and left it trailing far behind.

Still, it had to be obvious to their pursuers where they were headed. The entrance to the Rio–Niterói Bridge was only a mile ahead.

They were doing over a hundred miles per hour by the time they got on the bridge, one of the longest causeways in the world. Because cargo and cruise ships crossed beneath it into the port, the bridge rose to two hundred thirty-six feet at its highest point over the water.

"How long will it take us to get to our rendezvous point?" López asked in Raven's ear. Every word sounded like it took supreme effort.

She gauged the distance on the eight-mile-long bridge that stretched out before her. "Ninety seconds."

"Ninety seconds?" He must have done the mental calculation because he coughed and said, "The middle of the bridge?"

"Right. We're going to jump off."

"At this height? We'll kill ourselves!" His yell produced another coughing fit.

"No we won't. We're going bungee jumping."

Raven slowed when she saw the orange paint they'd sprayed on the railing the night before. It was nearly at the highest section, carefully chosen for that reason and for the distance between pilings.

She screeched to a halt in the right lane beside the paint marker and got off the bike. She removed a flare from the side case, lit it, and threw it behind the motorcycle so they wouldn't get run over. Linc, who pulled to a stop next to her, did the same.

The guardrail was designed like a series of three-foot-high concrete benches abutted end to end.

"We're at the rendezvous," Linc said.

"We're prepared to catch you," Juan replied. "I've got a medical team standing by."

López pulled himself off the bike. He looked woozy and pale. His lower torso was soaked in blood.

"You people are nuts."

"It's a living," Raven said, pulling three harnesses from her other side case. Linc had the bungee cords they would attach to them. The orange marker told him where to connect the cords to the bridge, at intervals twenty feet apart, so they wouldn't slam into each other on the way down. The bungee lengths had been precisely measured to match the height of the bridge at this spot and according to their respective weights.

Raven eased López into his harness and was impressed that he didn't cry out in pain. Maybe he was in shock. She slipped on her own, and handed the last one to Linc, before attaching herself and López to the bungees.

"Ever done this?" she asked him as she kept an eye on the road behind them. She was expecting either the Porsche or the cops to show up at any moment.

"Been skydiving twice," López said. His teeth were starting to chatter.

"Same thing. Don't think about it. Just jump."

"Our friends are back," Linc said, pointing down the road. The black SUV was weaving through cars, trying to get to them faster. Blue lights flashed farther behind them. "If we can get over the side before they arrive, we'll be safe. No way they'll stop to tangle with the police."

They escorted López over to the railing and helped him climb up so that he was sitting with his feet dangling two hundred feet above the water.

"This is going to hurt," Raven said.

"I know," López said. "Push me."

Raven didn't have time to ask him if he was serious. She gave him a shove.

Then she went over to her own spot and jumped.

For a couple of seconds she floated weightlessly, enough time to wonder if the bungee was going to hold or if she would just plunge straight into the water at a speed that would render the surface as hard as cement.

But she started to feel a gentle tug as the cord began to stretch. She slowly came to a stop three feet above the water and then snapped back until she was halfway up to the bridge deck. She turned her head to see Linc and López rebounding just like her.

After several bounces, they all came to rest, dangling from the bridge like marionettes. Below her and to the side, she saw the Gator. The hatch slid open, and Juan pulled himself out.

Raven activated the quick release on her harness and dove into the water. She surfaced, and Juan pulled her aboard the Gator. Linc quickly followed.

López remained hanging where he was. He was unconscious.

Juan yelled down the hatch, "Move us over to get him."

The Gator maneuvered until it was directly under him. While Juan and Linc held López, Raven unlatched his bungee cord. The CIA agent fell into their arms.

They lowered him into the Gator, then followed him down.

Juan closed the hatch and ordered the Gator to move at top speed without submerging. Two med techs from the *Oregon* treated López while Raven and Linc slumped into seats, drained from the chase. Gomez Adams was prepping two drones as if he were getting ready to launch them.

"What are those for?" Linc asked.

The Chairman looked at López's inert form and shook his head in disgust and rage. Raven had never seen him so angry.

"MacD and Hali are in trouble," Juan said. "And we're not losing anybody else today."

17

Hali struggled to keep the paraglider in the air. Jessica Belasco's right harness strap had been severed by a bullet, so she had her hand looped through his harness to keep from falling all the way out. But in doing so, she was shifting more of her weight to the right, which made it difficult for him to maintain a straight flight path. If they went into a stall, he'd have to throw out their reserve chute or they'd plunge into the water from a thousand feet up.

Making an uncontrolled landing like that in the water in a tandem harness might drown them, so Hali told Belasco to remain calm and keep her grip steady.

All she could do was nod in terror. Hali was scared as well, but he had something to focus on. Still, his heart was hammering in his chest, and he had to remind himself to breathe slowly and smoothly, just like he had to handle the paraglider.

"I'm not going to be able to maneuver very well around those drones," he told MacD. "It'll be a challenge just getting to Ilha da Laje intact."

"They aren't from the *Oregon*, are they?" MacD asked.

"Not ours," Juan replied from the Gator. "They came from Ferreira's yacht. Belasco's friends must have called him back when she disappeared. The drones may be equipped with explosive devices, so try to stay away from them."

"Fantastic," Hali said.

"What is?" Belasco asked.

"We're on schedule to be picked up," he said. No need to scare her even further. "But, prepare to hold on if I need to roll quickly."

"Why? Wait a minute," she said, pointing with her free hand at the dots that were approaching. "What are those?"

"Drones."

"That can't be good."

"It's not."

MacD came up next to him only twenty-five yards away so that they were flying in formation. "Got a plan?"

They were still half a mile away from the island fortress, passing eight hundred feet in altitude.

"When the drones get close, we'll split and dive. You go right. I'll go left. We'll descend in a spiral pattern, which might be hard for them to follow if they're being flown manually."

Hali didn't have to add that they were toast if the drones had automated targeting systems. He knew Gomez had that kind of software in his drones, but he didn't know if Ferreira's were similarly outfitted.

When the drones were within a hundred yards, one of them split off while the others hung back.

"They must have a single operator controlling them," Hali said. "Otherwise, they'd attack all at once."

How Hali wished they had a shotgun. Pistols were useless against such small maneuverable targets.

"Tell me when to break," MacD said.

"Not yet."

Hali kept the paraglider descending straight and true as if they didn't understand the danger heading their way. When the drone was only fifty yards away and closing fast, he said to MacD, "Break right . . . now!"

Hali pulled down on the handle in his left hand, which yanked the canopy down on that side and sent him and Belasco into a tight turn and descent. She screamed from the stomach-churning drop.

The drone shot right between him and MacD and exploded in midair a hundred feet above them.

Hali felt the heat and concussion from the blast and looked up. The canopy was undamaged. The drones were so small that they could only carry a tiny payload. Unless the explosion happened right next to them, they might live through this.

Hali looked around and saw another drone break from the others. The operator wouldn't make the same mistake twice.

MacD apparently knew that as well. "Strike one for the bad guys. Now what, mister expert flyer?"

"Our best chance is to get down to the island as fast as possible."

"And the drone?"

"Dodge it," Hali said.

"Very helpful."

"I'm out of ideas."

"Think quick. Here it comes."

The drone was ignoring MacD and heading right at Hali and Belasco.

Hali pulled the paraglider first one way, then the other, in an attempt to shake it, but the drone was too quick. It would only be a matter of time before it closed within ten yards of them and blew them apart.

"I have an idea," Gomez said on the comm system.

At that moment, another drone came out of nowhere and slammed into the attacking drone in a kamikaze fashion. The propellers on both drones shattered, and they tumbled toward the water. The operator set off the explosive, but by then it was too far away to have the desired effect.

"Thank you, sir," Hali shouted. "Nice flying."

"I've only got one more on hand," Gomez said.

"Make it count."

Hali watched as Gomez flew his second quadcopter into another drone. Both were demolished in the collision.

That left a single attacking drone, and it raced toward them. Hali could see the Gator knifing through the water, but it was too far away for anyone aboard to have a clear shot at the drone. The *Oregon* was following in the distance, ready to recover them all. Assuming, of course, that they lived through this.

The fortress on Ilha da Laje was now just a few hundred yards away. From above it looked like a flying saucer had landed in the water. The tiny rock poking out of the bay was completely covered by the stronghold that had been built in the eighteenth century to guard the entrance to the harbor. The concrete roof added since then was several feet thick and could withstand almost any assault. A cantilevered steel jetty extended from one side for boats to dock, but the military installation hadn't been used in decades.

Since MacD had more maneuverability, he was ahead and nearing the island. He dropped quickly and landed in a roll on the fort's roof.

He quickly detached from the canopy and got to his feet. He drew his pistol and began firing at the drone, but it was useless.

It was up to Hali. He had a plan, but it was almost suicidal. Still, it was their best chance.

He found a thermal coming off the warm bay waters and used it to rise as he approached the island. He had to gain some altitude for this to work.

"Make sure you have a good hold on my harness," he said to Belasco.

"I'm not going to like this, am I?"

"Doubt it. Get ready to fall."

"What?"

But he didn't have time to explain. The drone came at them. When it was about to get within lethal range, Hali dumped all the air from the canopy and put them into a stall. They dropped like a boulder.

The drone exploded above them, shredding the canopy.

Just what Hali was expecting. He had his hand on the reserve chute and threw it away from his body.

As they plummeted, the parachute filled with air long enough to bleed off a good chunk of speed before they hit the ground.

Still, they landed with a bone-jarring impact, and Hali cried out as he felt his knee buckle at an unnatural angle while Belasco's helmet slammed into the hardened concrete.

MacD rushed over and knelt beside them. "Are you all right?"

"No," Hali said, his jaw clenched in pain. "I think I tore something in my leg."

MacD detached Belasco from him and turned her over, removing her helmet. Her eyes were closed.

"Knocked cold," he said.

He lightly tapped her cheek until her eyes fluttered open.

"What happened?"

"Hali saved your life, but you probably got a concussion in the bargain. Unfortunately, we need to get out of here in case more of those drones show up."

Belasco pushed herself up with his help. When she got to her feet, MacD helped Hali onto his good leg. With one person hanging on each side, MacD took them toward the jetty.

Getting down off the roof was a painful adventure for all three of them. By the time they were on the steel pier, the Gator had pulled up alongside it.

Juan hopped up onto the suspended jetty and with the help of Linc and Raven they were able to lower Hali and Belasco into the sub without incident. Juan immediately ordered them to dive and rendez-vous with the *Oregon*.

Hali took a seat on the bench while one of the med techs from the *Oregon* inspected his leg. He winced as she manipulated his knee.

"Looks like a torn ACL," she said. "We'll have to do a CT scan when we get back to the ship."

"Looks like I got off easy," Hali said to Juan, nodding at the inert man lying on the floor.

"Knife wound," Juan said. "Although he's lost a lot of blood, López is tough. They say he's going to live, but he'll require surgery."

"And Machado?" MacD asked.

The Chairman's eyes darkened. "Doc says he didn't make it."

"Anyone else hurt?" Hali asked.

"Linda. Looks like both of her eardrums were ruptured by a flash-bang grenade that went off next to her."

"How could such a colossal mess happen?" MacD wondered, in shock at the extensive list of casualties.

"I don't know," Juan said with a look of grim determination. "But I promise you, we're going to find out."

18

PORTO DE SANTOS, BRAZIL

Harbormaster Matheus Aguilar wished he hadn't eaten such a big lunch. The stench surrounding him in the captain's office on the *Salem* wrestled with his stomach, and the smell was winning. But he wasn't going to leave without his payoff, even if he had to throw up in the wastebasket to get it.

"I'm sure you understand that we have to be strict in our checks and precautions, Captain White," Aguilar said, trying to hold down the bile rising in his throat. He glanced at the filthy bathroom, where the toilet was gurgling nonstop. He worried it would belch up its contents at any moment.

The fat old seadog behind the desk leaned back in his squeaky chair, nodded, and stroked his silver beard. Then he massaged his right pant leg around his stump. The captain walked with a pronounced limp and had shown Aguilar the prosthesis after the harbormaster had tripped over it accidentally during their tour of the ramshackle bridge.

"I'm sure security is very important in these parts," White said. "You've got to make sure the port is safe."

"Which is why I need to inspect your cargo areas and engine room. Look at what occurred in Rio de Janeiro yesterday. I don't want a similar incident to happen here."

The explosions and gunfights all around Rio and Guanabara Bay had dominated the Brazilian news for the past twenty-four hours. The *Salem* was currently tied up at the loading dock of Porto de Santos, which served São Paolo. It was the biggest port in South America, so any significant disruption to its operations would affect the country's entire economy.

"So what are you looking for?"

"Excuse me?" Aguilar countered.

"The price," White said. "Name it."

"I'm not sure what you mean."

Aguilar had received many bribes during his stint as harbormaster, but no one had been so forward about it before.

White leaned forward, his shirt straining against the surprisingly ropy muscles underneath.

"I mean, I have a cargo to unload quickly and a few minor repairs to make in my turbines. Any bureaucratic hassles are going to slow me down. I've got to be out of here in three hours, and I don't want to be late. So what's your price?"

The way White's eyes drilled into Aguilar was unsettling. There was something wrong about the situation, but he couldn't tell why he was so on edge. Suddenly, the bribe didn't seem worth it, no matter how much he could get.

"Maybe I should bring some more people on board to conduct the inspection," Aguilar said, rising from his chair.

"Sit down," White said without moving.

Aguilar puffed up his chest and projected his haughtiest voice. This was his port and he was in charge. No one talked to him like that.

"I'm leaving. We'll go over this ship with a magnifying glass, down to every last rivet."

He turned to leave.

"I wouldn't do that," White said with a mocking tone. "Not unless you want the port authority to know how much you've been skimming off the docking fees."

Aguilar froze.

"It will set you up for a nice retirement one of these days," White continued. "Of course, you won't be able to spend it if you're in prison. Once the papers find out about your scam, your trial will be a mere formality."

Aguilar whirled around. "How do you know about that?"

"I have a computer guy who is a whiz at finding hidden documents. All I need to do is release them onto the Internet, and you'll never get the cork back in the bottle. Corrupt politicians don't like being cut out of the money flow by corrupt bureaucrats."

Aguilar's legs felt wobbly. He collapsed back into the chair.

"What do you want?"

"I expect to breeze through your inspection with a flawless rating. And if I come back through here again, I want the same kid-glove treatment the next time around. I'm a stick-and-carrot kind of guy, so here's a fee for your troubles."

White slid a thick wad of American dollars across the desk.

"There'll be more of this when I return. I don't want you to be unhappy with our arrangement."

White stood and glared down at Aguilar, whose stomach was nearing full boil.

"But if my ship gets so much as a demerit for a typo on the manifest, you'll be lucky to see the outside of a jail cell before you're seventy. *Entende?*"

Aguilar gulped and nodded. "I understand."

White beamed with a mirthless smile, which creeped out Aguilar even more. "Good. Now, I don't want to see you or anyone who works for you near my ship again during this visit."

Aguilar teetered to his feet and snatched the money off the desk. "You passed the inspection with flying colors, Captain White."

White nodded and waved good-bye. *"Adeus, amigo."*

Aguilar rushed out of the office. He made it all the way up to the outside deck before he vomited over the side.

As soon as Aguilar bolted from his office, Zachariah Tate laughed and started pulling off the false beard and nose, revealing his lean face, pinched nose, and cleft chin. The white wig came off next. Underneath was a shock of jet-black hair. Whether he was playing Charles White on the *Salem* or Chester Knight on the *Portland*, he always got a kick out of the acting gig.

"He's gone," Tate said to the hidden microphone. "Can we get rid of that hideous smell now?"

Fans sucked the artificial stink out of the office in seconds, replacing it with a pleasant sea breeze scent that Tate preferred.

Abdel Farouk walked into the office and smirked. "You didn't have to use the nuclear option right away, Commander."

"Oh yes, I did," Tate said, pulling the stuffing out of his shirt. "That weasel would have nickel-and-dimed me for an hour. I'm a busy man. I don't have that kind of time. Let's go get our cargo off-loaded and make some money."

The fake prosthetic leg was the last thing he removed. The plastic molding around Tate's intact right calf was the least favorite part of his disguise because it was so itchy.

He left everything on the desk and led Farouk down a dingy hall with flickering fluorescent lights to a broom closet. The cleaning supplies strewn on the floor and shelves were unused and moldy, and the slop sink was crusted with grime. Tate turned the handles in a preset pattern like a combination lock. A soft click announced the opening of a secret door at the back of the closet.

Tate pulled it open and walked into a hall illuminated by tasteful wall sconces and with a floor covered with plush carpeting. It was as if he'd entered the lobby of a five-star hotel.

Farouk closed the closet door behind them. "Our buyers are ready to transfer the four containers over to their ship once we've unloaded them."

"Have they agreed to our terms?"

Farouk nodded. "It was a fair offer. I wonder where the weapons will end up."

"Who cares?" Tate dismissed it with the wave of a hand. "What I like is getting paid twice for the same shipment." The *Manticora* operation had gone just as planned. The payment from the CIA front company had been moved through myriad dummy accounts. They'd never be able to track it.

Tate went through a doorway into the *Portland*'s op center. The control hub embedded in the heart of the ship actually served as the bridge. Up above, the dilapidated bridge in the superstructure was merely for show.

Every function of the ship could be handled in the op center, from propulsion and steering to communications and weapons activation. The room itself was designed to resemble a starship, with flat-panel displays, touchpad controls, and a massive screen on the front wall. High-definition cameras mounted all over the exterior of the ship provided surveillance.

Tate took his seat in the swiveling command chair at the center of the room. It was built with controls in the armrest so that the commander could operate the most critical functions of the ship from this one spot.

"Status?" he asked.

His first officer, a Russian naval veteran named Pavel Durchenko, said, "We're unloading the first container now, Commander."

He nodded to another officer, and an image of the dockside crane lifting the shipping unit appeared on the main view screen.

"As soon as the last container touches the dock," Tate said to Farouk, "I want that payment in our accounts."

"Yes, sir."

Two of the crew high-fived, and the rest murmured approvingly. They all shared in the spoils for every job pulled off by the *Portland*.

"Did we get the supplies we needed?"

"All food and ammunition stores will be replenished within the hour," Durchenko said.

"All right. Show me our target for this evening."

A different exterior view came on the screen, this one to the *Portland*'s stern. It showed a huge freighter being loaded with timber and coffee bound for France.

"That ship looks brand-new."

"It is," Farouk said. "That's why the owners are drowning in debt. They can't break the lease on it, and they're bleeding red ink. They say the only way they can cover their losses is for the ship to sink and Lloyd's of London to pay the claim."

Tate held up his fingers and played the world's smallest violin. "Cry me a river. They'll pay our normal cut?"

"Yes."

"Then let's make this a twofer."

"How do you mean?"

"Our old buddy Juan Cabrillo had a bad day yesterday. We want to continue his misery, don't we?"

Heads all over the op center nodded.

"Then we'll make sure to sink that freighter before sunset and get some good video of the *Portland* doing it. I got word that the crew of the *Manticora* was found in the middle of the Atlantic. The U.S. Navy is still searching for the missing *Kansas City*. Now it's time to up the pressure on the *Oregon* by framing her for another atrocity."

Once she was blamed as the culprit in these incidents, the *Oregon* would become a pariah to the United States, and so would her captain. Nobody in the CIA knew that she had a doppelgänger, an exact twin, down to her weapons systems and advanced magnetohydrodynamic engines.

Tate's extensive plans were finally paying off, plans he'd developed during years of torture and solitary confinement. Like everyone else aboard the *Portland*, he wanted his revenge on Juan Cabrillo, the person responsible for all their collective misery.

But Tate wasn't going to kill his former partner in the CIA. That would be too simple. What he wanted was far more punishing. First, Tate would ruin his reputation. Then he would kill Cabrillo's crew, sink his ship, and leave him to rot in a Third World prison for the rest of his life with the knowledge that he'd lost everything he held dear.

Tate savored the thought of such complete suffering and grinned.

He was going to utterly destroy Juan Cabrillo.

19

Juan entered the *Oregon*'s infirmary to find Julia Huxley making notes on a tablet computer. As the ship's surgeon, she had been extraordinarily busy in the two days since they'd beat a hasty retreat from Rio Harbor. He could see the toll that the extended hours had taken on her.

Instead of a white lab coat, green scrubs hung loosely over her short, curvy figure. She drooped as she leaned against a counter, and there were dark circles under brown eyes that normally looked much more alert. Her dark hair was tied back in her usual ponytail that swayed back and forth as she yawned.

"Not getting much sleep lately?" Juan asked.

"Or any," she said with a shake of her head. "It's been nonstop around here."

"I came to tell you that López and Belasco made it onto the CIA charter back to the U.S. along with Machado's body."

Juan had decided to return to Vitória because it had a major airport as well as a network of fine hospitals and doctors.

"How did López look?" Julia asked.

"A lot better, thanks to you."

"Luckily, the knife didn't penetrate any vital organs. It was a pretty straightforward procedure to stitch him up once we got the bleeding under control. He should be up and about in a few days."

Before joining the Corporation, Julia had been a skilled general surgeon and chief medical officer at the San Diego naval base. With the operating room and diagnostic facilities aboard the *Oregon*, she and her staff could handle any wounds that would normally require a big-city trauma center.

"What about the prognosis for Belasco?" Juan asked.

"She got a nasty concussion when she slammed her head into the concrete roof of that fort. She'd probably be brain-damaged or dead without the helmet. As it is, she'll need weeks or months to recover."

Juan crossed his arms and grimaced as he leaned against the counter next to Julia.

"I thought we had such a good plan for getting them out safely," he said.

"Don't beat yourself up," Julia said. "This is a dangerous business. We all understood that when we signed up."

"But this time, it wasn't bad luck. We screwed up. Did you find out what happened to Linda, Gomez, and Murph on the Gator?"

She looked puzzled and shook her head. "I did a full work-up on all of them and didn't find anything unusual. The tox screen came back negative for chemicals in their systems. Other than Linda's injuries, there weren't any residual effects."

"What could cause them to lose their minds like that?"

"You know I hate saying that I'm stumped, but I've never run across anything like this. I'll do a deeper search of the medical literature after I get a little sleep."

The sound of creaking crutches preceded Hali's tottering into the medical bay.

"I heard everything went well," Julia said to him.

She had found an orthopedic specialist in Vitória who was renowned for his expertise in laparoscopic ACL repair.

"Only took an hour," Hali said. "Did you know that doctor does the knee surgeries for all the famous soccer players here in Brazil?"

Julia nodded. "He studied at Harvard Med with me before coming back here. I had to pull some strings to get you in so fast."

Hali smiled. "So that's why he said I should be doing flying scissors kicks again in no time."

"Why don't you go into exam room one, and I'll take a look at the incision in a minute."

He gave her the thumbs-up and plodded away.

"He seems to be taking it well," she said.

"I told him we'd get him a brand-new paraglider for his efforts, above and beyond, to save Belasco," Juan said. "What's the news on our other casualty?"

"Linda?" Julia affirmed. "Two ruptured eardrums. Almost total hearing loss."

Juan swallowed hard. "Is it permanent?"

"I hope not. But it'll be a while until we know. The tympanic membranes in both ears were severely damaged, but I'm hoping they will repair themselves. In the meantime, she can only understand visual communication."

"I'll check in on her later." Juan sighed and stood up. "Right now, I have an uncomfortable call to make."

"Langston Overholt?"

He nodded. "Time to give him an update on this debacle."

"You saved two of them," she said, putting a gentle hand on his shoulder. "Without you and the teams from the *Oregon*, all three agents would be dead right now."

She was right about that, but it was small consolation to Juan.

He headed back to his cabin to contact Overholt. When he got there, he found Maurice, the ship's elderly steward, setting a coffeepot, mug, and fruit plate on the table. Maurice was the sole non-American on the *Oregon*. He'd served in the Royal Navy for decades before being lured to the Corporation. As always, he was dressed in an immaculate white jacket with a pristine linen napkin draped over his arm.

"I thought you'd like some refreshment for your call, Captain," Maurice said. He was the only person on board who didn't call Juan "Chairman." He insisted on adhering to naval tradition.

"Thanks, Maurice," Juan said, amazed at how the steward kept apprised about everything on the *Oregon*. Maurice was the epicenter of crew scuttlebutt, yet everyone also trusted him with their private thoughts. "How's the crew handling the fallout from our recent mission?"

"They seem to be in relatively good spirits," Maurice said as he poured the coffee. "We all know that the unfortunate results were due to difficulties you couldn't have anticipated . . . Will that be all, Captain?"

"Yes."

Without another word, Maurice glided out of the cabin.

Juan took a breath and made the call.

Upon answering, Overholt frowned. "You look a little haggard, Juan."

"That's why I'm due at the spa for a facial and manicure later," Juan joked halfheartedly before turning serious. "I'm sure you've read my report by now."

"I have, and I must say I'm perplexed. It's not like you to be caught off guard like that. Have you determined what caused your people to panic and jump the gun?"

"Not yet. I have Julia Huxley on it. If anyone can figure it out, she will."

"Well, I'm sorry to make things worse for you," Overholt said, "but I have some news that is disturbing."

Juan sat forward, expecting a reprimand from Overholt's superiors for botching the mission.

"The crew of the *Manticora* was rescued," Overholt continued. "As we feared, the ship was sunk, and they lost nine crew members in the tragedy."

Juan tilted his head in confusion. "I don't understand. What does that have to do with us?"

Overholt looked troubled. "One of the rescued men was a CIA agent named Jack Perry. Do you know him?"

Juan shrugged and shook his head. "Must have joined after I left."

"Perry was supposed to be covertly buying arms for a rebel action that we are supporting. The transfer of the containers was to be done at sea from a freighter called the *Portland*."

Juan didn't like where this was going.

"According to Perry," Overholt continued, "the *Portland* opened fire on the *Manticora* with Gatling guns and a tank cannon hidden behind hull plates and sent her to the bottom. They also stole the payment for the weapons."

Juan gaped at him. "What did the ship look like?"

"Perry's description fits the *Oregon* perfectly, down to the five cranes, peeling paint, and filthy captain's office."

"So he met the captain?"

Overholt nodded gravely. "The name the man used was Chester Knight, clearly an alias." He paused for effect. "And he had a prosthetic leg."

Juan was stunned. "Is Perry trustworthy?"

"His story was corroborated by the other survivors, except for the description of Captain Knight. Perry was the only one who saw him."

"We didn't sink the *Manticora*."

"Of course *I* know that," Overholt said. "But it doesn't help that the attacking ship had a name similar to your own, which makes it sound like you used *Portland* as a pseudonym."

Juan thought about how this would look. "And we were in the general vicinity four days ago."

"Exactly my problem explaining this to the CIA brass."

"They think we've gone rogue?"

"That's the conclusion I'm trying to steer them away from," Overholt said. "But now it's become exponentially more difficult to make my case defending you. Additional incriminating evidence has come to light."

Juan's stomach sank as he waited for the other shoe to drop.

The wall monitor switched from a view of Overholt's face to his laptop screen. A video started playing. It showed a large red cargo ship at sea, lit by the setting sun.

"That's the *Avignon*, a French freighter. She sailed from São Paolo's Porto de Santo yesterday."

"We were on our way to Vitória last night," Juan said.

"The problem is, we both know that at the *Oregon*'s top speed you could have been at sea near São Paolo and still made it to where you are now."

Overholt was right. Their alibi was worthless.

"Where did you get this video?" Juan asked.

"It was sent to us anonymously. There's no sound. We think it was taken from a cell phone on a fishing boat. You'll see in a moment why it has the CIA Director very concerned."

A missile streaked in from out of frame and slammed into the side of the *Avignon*, ripping a gaping hole in her side. A second later, the camera wobbled from the blast concussion.

Whoever was taking the video pivoted, and that's when Juan knew the Corporation was being framed. He was horror-struck as he watched a tramp cargo freighter fire a second anti-ship missile at the *Avignon* to finish her off.

The attacking ship looked just like the *Oregon*.

20

Langston Overholt didn't often have to leave CIA headquarters to meet with people. Because of his position and experience, they almost always came to him. But as liaison to the Corporation, it was his responsibility to deal with the seemingly rogue actions of the *Oregon*. The Director himself was expressing doubts about Juan Cabrillo, and it had taken all of Overholt's considerable charm and persuasion to convince him not to declare the Corporation a criminal enterprise and traitorous organization.

Overholt needed to buy Juan some time. He had to drive into D.C. to visit the State Department and keep the situation from becoming a full-blown diplomatic incident with both France and Brazil. Meanwhile, he'd instructed Juan to do whatever he could to find out who was pinning their crimes on the *Oregon*.

As he reached the main entrance, Overholt heard his name called. He turned to see Catherine Ballard hurrying toward him carrying a briefcase. With flaxen hair, a trim build, and a long stride, Ballard still carried herself like a field agent even though she'd been promoted to running her own operations at Langley three years earlier. Her tailored pantsuit and tortoiseshell glasses did little to hide the beauty she'd used to her advantage on more than one mission.

"It looks like you're off to the State Department now," she said. "We've just received some new information about the *Portland*, so I'm going down to NUMA headquarters to follow up on it. Can I talk to you about it when I get back?"

Ballard was running the Nicaragua rebel operation and had become friends with Jack Perry, the agent who met Juan Cabrillo's impostor.

"Since we're headed in the same direction, do you want to ride with me and give me the briefing on the way?" Overholt asked.

She looked surprised at the offer, but after thinking about it she agreed to join him. "I can get an Uber back here after the meeting."

Overholt's black Suburban SUV was waiting at the entrance. As they walked to it, he said, "How's Perry doing?"

"He was pretty dehydrated when they found the lifeboat, but he's recovering well. He should be back at work in a few days."

"Don't you think it's odd that their lives were spared?"

Ballard shrugged. "Remember, the man calling himself Chester Knight wanted him to convey a message to us, that Knight didn't want to work for us any longer."

Overholt nodded. "Still, I find it strange. It was Perry who hired the *Portland* to bring the weapons from South Africa, correct?"

"Yes. He found them through a referral from an emir in the Persian Gulf who had used them for security purposes."

That did fit Juan's MO. The Corporation didn't work exclusively for the CIA and had a web of contacts for finding other jobs, one of which was providing security at sea for friendly governments and companies.

When they arrived at the Suburban, Jeff Connolly, Overholt's driver and bodyguard, was holding the rear door open for them. Ballard smiled a thank-you to the burly Connolly and got in.

"What's the traffic look like this afternoon, Jeff?" Overholt asked, before he joined her.

"Surprisingly, the G.W. Parkway doesn't look bad today, sir," Connolly said with a Texas twang. "We should be there in half an hour."

"Ms. Ballard needs to go over to NUMA headquarters after you drop me off, if you don't mind taking her."

"Not a problem, sir."

As they pulled away, Overholt asked Ballard, "What's that new information about the *Portland* you wanted to tell me?"

She hesitated and pointedly looked at Connolly.

"It's all right," Overholt assured her. "Jeff is a former Navy SEAL, and his security clearance is almost as high as mine. He's just pulling this duty for a few months so he can be closer to his family."

"Kids?" she asked Connolly.

He shook his head. "My mother has been recovering from chemo. I've been helping out my dad."

She gave him a sad smile. "I'm sorry to hear that."

"Thanks."

Overholt saw them make a connection in the mirror. He suspected that Connolly's bare ring finger didn't go unnoticed by Ballard.

"Back to the *Portland*," he said to her, knowing she and Connolly would have plenty of time to banter on the way to NUMA. "Did you find anything that tells us who is operating it?"

"Nothing. I can't find any record of the *Portland*. According to my research, the ship that sailed from Cape Town with our cargo was called the *Norego*."

Overholt's stomach went cold. That was one of the aliases Juan used for the *Oregon*.

Ballard continued, "We also discovered that the *Norego* took on containers from Stellenbosch that weren't in our order. We now think they contained a load of twelve Exocet anti-ship missiles."

"The same kind used to sink the *Avignon*."

She nodded. It was looking worse and worse for the Corporation. Exocet missiles were part of the *Oregon*'s weapons complement.

"And you hope NUMA can help you track down the origin of the *Portland*?" Overholt asked. The National Underwater and Marine Agency had the most comprehensive database of ships in the world.

"I figured with an issue of this sensitivity, it was better to make the request in person."

"Smart thinking."

They'd been making good time along the parkway just as Connolly had predicted, but he suddenly hit the brakes as they approached the Chain Bridge Road exit. The highway narrowed temporarily to a single lane at the juncture, and a truck pulled out from the shoulder directly in front of them.

"What an idiot," Connolly muttered. He laid on the horn, and the truck accelerated until they were back at highway speeds. But now it took up both lanes.

"You believe this guy?" Connolly asked. "Wait . . . What the . . . ?"

Overholt leaned forward and saw the rear door of the trailer snap up. In the darkness of the interior, he saw the points of two huge harpoons aimed at them.

"Get us out of here!" Overholt shouted. It was too late.

The harpoons fired and rammed through the front grille, embedding themselves in the engine block. Steam from the destroyed radiator gushed into the air. At the same time, a ramp extended from the back of the trailer.

Cables attached to the harpoons went taut and started drawing them toward the truck.

Connolly stood on the brakes. The tires squealed and smoked, but the cables pulling them were too strong and dragged them forward while they were careening down the highway. He wrenched the wheel right and left, the Suburban swerving side to side, to not much effect. Jumping out wasn't a viable option, not at the current speed.

"Do you have a weapon?" Overholt asked Ballard. He could see her mind working overtime considering their options.

"No," she said.

Connolly gave up on wrestling with the steering wheel, bent down and gave her the revolver from his ankle holster, before drawing a Colt semiautomatic from his jacket.

In seconds, the Suburban hit the ramp and was methodically drawn into the darkened trailer until the door snapped down behind them.

"I can see four of them," Connolly said. "They've got ballistic shields. But if we—"

A single shot snuffed out Connolly's last words. But it didn't come from outside. Catherine Ballard had shot him in the back of the head with his own gun.

She turned it on Overholt, who looked at her in shock. She held up her hand for the men outside to wait. She seemed to want to savor the moment.

"So, you're the mole," Overholt said.

She nodded and grinned, apparently pleased with herself. "You would have eventually figured out that I was the one who compromised the identities of Machado, López, and Belasco. It was a risk, but I was confident we'd kidnap you before that happened."

"How could you know I would invite you to ride with me?"

"Oh, I didn't. That was pure luck. I was planning to follow you in my own car to signal the truck. But since I was in the car with you, tracking with the GPS on my phone made the job even easier."

Overholt was furious at himself for being duped. "So the *Oregon*'s whole extraction mission was a setup?"

Ballard nodded. "From the very beginning. And you played right into it."

"Of course, I wouldn't have any reason to suspect a decorated agent like yourself."

"Of course not. Why would you? I'm as pure as fresh snow."

"Then why throw it all away like this? What do you want from me?"

"You and Juan Cabrillo owe a debt to Zachariah Tate for what you two did to him," Ballard said, motioning for the men in the truck to come get Overholt. "For what you did to us. Now it's time for payback."

21

After leaving Vitória, the next forty-eight hours on the *Oregon* were spent reconfiguring her profile to make her look different from the ship that sank the *Avignon*. They spray-painted the hull a patchy dull gray, added a false block to the superstructure, and were now taking apart two of the disabled cranes. Juan hoped it would be enough of a change that they could search for the doppelgänger ship without being readily targeted by the Brazilian Navy.

Juan walked across the deck to join Max, who was overseeing the alterations. His Hawaiian shirt was drenched in sweat from the mid-day sun.

"How long until we can get going?" Juan asked him.

"Shouldn't be more than an hour to finish up here," Max said. He had developed a modular system for assembling and disassembling the nonfunctioning cranes quickly.

"It's time to give the ship another name."

"Great minds think alike. I was just going to suggest that we make up a new one. We have to assume all of the go-to names we've used are compromised."

Everyone in the crew called the ship the *Oregon* no matter what was listed on the stern, but they changed the visible name each time they arrived at a new port. The jackstaff often flew an Iranian flag to disguise her country of registry, and iron filings sprayed onto magnets embedded in the hull allowed them to change the name in seconds.

"Can we get away with *Queen Anne's Revenge*?" Max asked with a twinkle in his eye.

"Naming ourselves after Blackbeard's pirate ship might be a tad obvious. How about *Anacapa*? We've never used that before."

"In honor of the Q-ship? I like it."

The Q-ship had its heyday during the Second World War. Like the *Oregon*, they were merchant vessels armed with concealed weaponry. The aim was to look like helpless cargo transports in order to lure submarines to the surface, rendering the subs vulnerable. The Q-ships were also used to target enemy freighters by coming close before revealing their true nature and opening fire. The *Anacapa* was an American Q that had operated in the Pacific Theater.

The sound of footsteps pounded across the deck behind them. Juan turned to see Eric Stone sprinting in their direction. Eric was the *Oregon*'s helmsman and a Navy vet. Although he and Mark Murphy were the same age, both certified geniuses, and nearly inseparable in downtime, spent largely on video games and computer hacking, their appearances couldn't have been more different. While Murph favored the slacker look, Eric was always neatly dressed, usually in khakis and a blue button-down shirt. The two of them had worked together on a Department of Defense missile defense project before joining the Corporation. And they shared similar difficulties courting the opposite sex, despite MacD's extensive coaching efforts.

As Eric came skidding to a stop in front of Juan and Max, he adjusted his black-framed glasses.

"What's got you in such a hurry?" Max asked. "Did they announce a new Batman movie or something?"

"Unfortunately, no," Eric said. "We've received a call from Langston Overholt's private number."

"What do you mean 'from Langston Overholt's private number'?" Juan asked.

Eric shook his head. "It's not Mr. Overholt on the line. It's someone else. He won't say who it is. And, he'll only talk to you on video chat."

"He asked for me by name?"

Eric nodded. He looked just as puzzled and concerned as Juan felt.

Max left the dismantling work to be completed without him, and they all hurried to the op center. When they got there, Juan took a seat in the command chair, while Eric sat at the helm and Max took his spot at engineering. Hali was back at his communications post, with his leg in a brace and crutches perched next to him, and Murph was at the weapons station. He didn't seem his usual bright self, and Juan caught him glancing at Linda's empty seat. Murph still blamed himself for her absence. Juan made a mental note to talk to him later.

"Hali," Juan said, "focus the camera tight on me and put the guy on the main screen."

At first all Juan could see was a blurry room with several indistinct people moving around in it. One person was closer, in the center, but his face wasn't visible.

"Who am I speaking to?" Juan asked.

"Ah, Juan Cabrillo!" a man jovially replied. "I'd recognize that voice anywhere. I hope you remember mine."

The voice sounded familiar, as if echoing from his past, but Juan couldn't quite place it. "It would help if I could see your face."

"Of course. My bad."

The image resolved itself. Juan was bewildered by what he was seeing.

The room on the screen was an exact duplicate of the *Oregon*'s op center. There were four people in it, including the man at the center.

All of them had Juan's face.

It looked like it was actually Juan talking when the man said, "Here I am. Now, we have some important things to discuss."

Juan motioned for Hali to mute the feed.

"What's going on here?"

Murph swiveled in his chair. "They must be using an app like deepfake. It lets you paste a person's face onto someone else in a video and make it look like they're talking."

Eric nodded in agreement. "The most famous example is when some joker put Nicolas Cage's face on characters in a dozen different movies that he never appeared in, like *Lord of the Rings* and *The Terminator*. It can be done in real time. And the software special effects have gotten very realistic."

"Does it change their voice?" Juan asked.

"So far, that's been harder to do," Murph said. "It's probably his real voice."

"Are you still there?" the man asked, waving. "Hello?"

Juan looked at Hali. "Put me back on."

Hali nodded.

"We're all laughing hysterically here," Juan said in a monotone. "It was getting so loud I had to put us on mute."

"I thought you'd like this," the man said. "You've always had a high opinion of yourself."

"And what should I call you? Juan Squared?"

"I think you know what name to call me, although it has been a while. I think the last time we saw each other was at that little bar in Chechnya. What was it called? The Brown Bear?"

Juan felt the blood drain from his face as he suddenly realized who it was. The voice he heard now was more gravelly than he remembered, but it was definitely the same man.

Juan slowly stood up. "You were declared dead."

"So you do remember me!"

"Zachariah Tate."

"If that's what you want to call me." Tate lounged in his own command chair, rotating side to side like a hyperactive child. Now that Juan knew who the impostor was, it was even more revolting to see his face plastered on Tate's body.

"By the way," Tate went on, "I know you're recording this call. But if you were stupid enough to send a plainly faked video to the CIA to exonerate yourself, they'd never take you seriously again. You realize, of course, that there are no recordings of Tate's voice to compare the audio to. So, for all they'd know, you hired one of those guys from *Saturday Night Live* to do an impression."

"We got your message," Juan said. "We heard about the *Manticora* and the *Avignon*."

"Not very subtle, I know, but it got your attention, didn't it? Now I have an important task for you. Two tasks, actually."

"Why would I do anything for you?"

"You don't have to, but I think you will. The first item on your to-do list has to do with a Los Angeles–class nuclear sub called the *Kansas City*. I'm putting a bomb on its hull, and you have to disarm it before it goes off. It's in two hundred fifty feet of water, but that should be well within your abilities. Fun challenge, huh? But, then again, you guys specialize in that kind of fun."

"You could be sending us on a wild-goose chase," Juan said. "How do I know you had anything to do with its sinking?"

Tate motioned to the side, and someone handed him a three-foot-long tube. "Do you know what this is?"

Juan nodded. "It's a SEPIRB. It stands for 'Submarine Emergency Position Indicating Radio Beacon.' It's ejected from the hull when a sub goes down and floats to the surface to broadcast its location."

"Exactly." Tate held the SEPIRB closer to the camera. It had the name KANSAS CITY stenciled on the side. Although it could have been a fake, there was also a serial number printed on it. He would have

Murph and Eric check Navy databases to make sure it was authentic, but Juan had to assume it was the real thing.

"Are you going to tell me where the *KC* is?"

"Well, not its exact location," Tate said. "Not right now. That would be too easy. How about this? I'll tell you the precise coordinates an hour before the bomb goes off, which means that fancy ship of yours needs to be in a spot a hundred miles southeast of Montevideo ready to deactivate the explosives." He read off the latitude and longitude coordinates.

"What's the catch?" Juan asked.

"You *knew* there'd be one," Tate said, wagging a finger. "You always were smart. It's actually more like a dilemma. Is that the right word? Anyway, I expect you personally to be in Buenos Aires at the exact same time."

"Why would I do that?"

"To save this guy." Tate pointed to his right, and the camera slewed around.

It was Langston Overholt, gagged and strapped to a chair. His eyes smoldered with defiance.

Tate continued. "I'm going to sink him in a diving bell somewhere in Buenos Aires Harbor, and you'll have to get him out before he suffocates. At the appropriate time, I'll start sending you live video from the bell and all you have to do is just find it. Piece of cake."

It made Juan sick how much Tate was enjoying this. "How do I know this isn't a trap?"

Tate rolled his eyes. "Of course it's a trap! That's part of the challenge. I just don't see how you have much choice but to go along with it."

He was right. There was no choice.

"We'll be ready."

"I would expect nothing less. Oh, and I shouldn't have to say it, but if I see anyone but you and your people trying to save either this guy or the ship, the game is over. *Ciao* for now!"

Before the screen went blank, it flickered.

"Put up that last frame," Juan said.

In that last split second, the deepfake software turned off before the feed did. The image was a bit fuzzy from motion blur, but Juan recognized the older, more worn version of Zachariah Tate.

For a moment, there was only stunned silence in the op center.

Max walked over to Juan. "Who is Zachariah Tate?"

"He's a former CIA agent I worked with. He's also the most dangerous man I've ever met."

"But you thought he was dead?"

"According to the official reports, he was killed by another inmate in a Chechen prison."

Max stared at the picture on the screen. "Why is he after us?"

"He's after *me*," Juan said, scowling at Tate's image. "I was the one who put him there."

22

BUENOS AIRES

Overholt's cabin on the *Portland* was plushly furnished and comfortable, with his own bathroom and a soft bed, but it was a prison cell all the same. There were no windows or portholes, the door was guarded, and he had no doubt he was being watched at all times. Although he was quite healthy and strong for his age, breaking out by force or stealth wasn't even close as an option. His days as a field agent were long behind him. Words were his weapons now. And if he was going to get out of this situation, it would be with wits, not brawn.

He would have liked a change of clothes, but his jail was more pleasant than the ride that had gotten him to Argentina. After Catherine Ballard had killed his driver, Connolly, and taken Overholt captive, he assumed he would be driven to an undisclosed location for questioning, torture, or both. Instead, the truck was driven to a warehouse, where he was transferred to a smaller container with a cot and some food and water. The walls were insulated, so any attempt to yell for help was futile. He couldn't tell what was happening except when the container finally moved. It quickly became clear that he was being loaded onto an airplane. After that, he slept most of the way to the destination.

When they arrived and he was taken to the port, he was shocked to see former CIA officer Zachariah Tate welcoming him aboard a ship that looked like a carbon copy of the *Oregon*. He surmised it was the *Portland*, the ship that sank the *Manticora* and *Avignon*. The only stop before coming to the cabin was to participate in Tate's odd show for Juan in the op center.

That had been a day ago, and Overholt had no visitors other than the guard who brought him food. He spent the time developing a plan for how to approach Tate when and if he got the chance to speak to him.

Overholt heard a woman's voice speak to the guard outside. He stood and put on his jacket as the door opened.

Catherine Ballard smiled when she saw him. "Do you think we're going back to your office? Even your tie is still knotted."

"I presume we're going somewhere," Overholt said. "That's why you've come, isn't it?"

"You're sharp for an old-timer."

"Not as sharp as I was when I was younger. I should have spotted your deceptions."

"Don't beat yourself up," she said. "I'm very good. So is Zach."

"I know. I trained him myself long ago."

"Then you're going to be proud of what he's been able to accomplish."

"I sincerely doubt that."

"Come with me and find out."

She led him into the luxurious corridor, and the guard followed behind. The guard and Ballard both looked at ease. Overholt wasn't a physical threat. He was just a creaky old man. His mind raced for how to use that as an advantage.

"I understand why Tate would have a grudge against me," Overholt said as they walked, "but why have you thrown your life away to follow him?"

"'Thrown my life away'?" she parroted with a contemptuous laugh. "It's your reputation that will be in shambles. I left behind some very damaging information that will implicate you in a rogue operation involving Juan Cabrillo. I'm going to be regarded as an innocent bystander who was made to disappear by you for discovering your secret. It's what you deserve for letting Zach rot in that Chechen prison."

"He knew the risks when he took the job."

"The risks shouldn't have included being sold out by your own country."

"He was the traitor. He betrayed everything we were fighting for." He turned to Ballard and saw her seething hatred for him. Then it clicked. "You're in love with Tate."

"And we were able to keep it a secret for all those years. That shows our abilities in the trade."

"When?"

"We started dating when we were both fresh recruits. We knew it would damage our careers if we came clean about it, so we kept it hidden. It became a kind of game to see how long we could stay under the radar of the great Langston Overholt. And you never found out. Neither did Juan."

"So when Tate was imprisoned," Overholt said, "you couldn't very well reveal your relationship."

"And be branded a co-conspirator?" she asked with a chuckle. "Give me some credit."

"I do. You're quite devious. That's why I knew you'd make a good agent. I just didn't realize how deep that deception went."

"Thank you," she said sincerely, taking it as a compliment.

Overholt waved his arms at the surroundings as they got onto an elevator appointed in brass and mahogany. "This all must have cost a fortune, including smuggling me out of the U.S. Who is funding this operation? China? Russia? I know the Muslim extremist groups have access to oil money, but this isn't their style."

"We're a private organization with a group of highly motivated volunteers who believe in our mission. Just like Cabrillo's Corporation."

Overholt knew there was more to that story, but he didn't want her to put up roadblocks, so he played to her vanity.

"You must have helped Tate get out of prison. Only a talented insider could have done that."

"And helped him fake his death," Ballard said proudly. "It was all very clever and done right under your nose. Aren't I just the best?" She smirked at him. "Please, I know all your tricks."

The elevator opened, and the smell of saltwater washed over them. They emerged into a cavernous space percolating with activity. A gantry crane high above was lowering a yellow diving bell toward what looked like an Olympic-sized pool, and workers on the catwalks and the decking around the pool were shouting instructions that echoed through the space.

Zachariah Tate saw Overholt from across the pool and strode toward him, Ballard, and the guard.

"Isn't it impressive?" Tate asked, showing off, his hands out wide. "Welcome to the moon pool."

"I know what it is," Overholt said. "I saw it in the plans of the *Oregon*. How were you able to copy Juan's ship?"

"That is a long story involving some thievery from a Russian naval yard in Vladivostok a few years ago after I escaped from prison."

"Juan destroyed all of those records."

"He might have, after I got there, but we don't have time to go into that now. We have a tight schedule to keep." He turned to Ballard and gave her a kiss. "Have you told him any of the juicy details yet?"

"I would never rob you of that pleasure," she replied with a sickly sweetness.

"Thank you, my dear," Tate said with a clap of his hands. He pointed at the diving bell. "Do you know what that is?"

The sphere had one window and was surrounded by a protective cage of thick metal struts that extended below the bell to provide a base for when it rested on the ocean floor. The hatch was on the bottom, and the struts supported a dozen large air tanks and like number of batteries.

"It's a Personnel Transfer Capsule, to use its technical name," Overholt said. "It's for housing divers during deep saturation dives."

Tate wagged a finger at him and smiled. "Excellent! I see you're still as formidable as ever. This one dates from the seventies and was used for North Sea oil rig maintenance. I got it for a song."

"And you're going to put me in this old diving bell as a lure to get Juan to save me."

"Right again! We're going to plant you at the bottom of the harbor and then put some distance between us and that location. You'll have twenty-four hours before your air runs out. Carbon dioxide suffocation isn't a terrible way to go, I'm told."

"You'll kill me no matter what."

"That's up to Juan."

"Is it?" Overholt asked, nodding at a device mounted on the sphere. "That's an explosive device, if I'm not mistaken."

"You are not," Tate said, "but that's just there to keep Juan honest. I doubt he'll call the Argentine Coast Guard, but, if he does, I can't have them saving you."

"So you'll set it off once he's next to the diving bell?"

Tate shook his head as if Overholt just didn't get it. "Hardly. I don't want to kill Juan. I want him to suffer. He can't suffer when he's dead. When Juan fails to rescue you, I want him to live the rest of his miserable life knowing he had a chance to succeed and blew it. Pun intended."

"Are you so sure he'll come?"

"Juan's a Boy Scout with a competitive streak. You're his damsel in distress, so to speak. He wouldn't turn down this challenge for anything. Believe me, I know him well."

"And he knows you just as well."

"That's what makes this so much fun for both of us." Tate seemed giddy over the prospect of matching wits with his former partner. Ballard beamed at him, reveling in his enjoyment.

"So you're planning to capture Juan?" Overholt asked, hoping to goad Tate into revealing some useful information. "Good luck with that."

Tate smiled. "Nice try. I realize it sounds like I'm monologuing here, but you know only the barest part of my plans."

"I know that you sank the *Manticora* and *Avignon*. And you're responsible for the disappearance of the *Kansas City*."

"Not bad for a week's work, wouldn't you say?"

"I understand why you destroyed the ships, but a U.S. nuclear submarine? That's risky."

"It was a good chance to show off our capabilities to potential customers. Besides, that SEAL was too curious about his cousins' deaths."

Overholt saw Ballard's eyes narrow slightly, and he knew Tate had given away something important without realizing it.

"That SEAL may be your undoing once the *Oregon* finds him," Overholt said.

Tate shook his head. "Not likely. The sub was so damaged that the entire crew will be dead by now even if they weren't killed in the initial collision. Besides, all Juan knows is the actual depth of the sub. The *Oregon* will be two thousand miles away from the *Kansas City*'s real location." He gestured to the diving bell, which now hovered beside them with a ladder resting against its open hatch at the bottom. "Now, time to get in. You'll find a couple of protein bars and water bottles inside, as well as a camera to monitor you. I want you awake and alert when Juan sees your air run out."

"And if I refuse to play along?"

"Then we tie you up and shove you in. Your choice, but your last twenty-four hours will be a lot more unpleasant that way." The grin on Tate's face radiated with gleeful malevolence.

"I see your point," Overholt said.

He started climbing in.

23

As the *Oregon* headed southwest toward Buenos Aires at top speed, Juan sat in the infirmary while Julia Huxley injected the GPS tracker into his right thigh. All crew members were outfitted with trackers so that they could be found in the case of abduction.

She wiped away a drop of blood and said, "Done. You sure this new design will work?"

"Murph double-checked it." Juan inspected the injection site. "How long until you can't see that hole?"

"It should be invisible in a day. Let's hope you don't need that thing."

He stood and pulled up his pants. "You know me. I always like to have a backup plan."

"From what I've heard," Julia said, pointing at his leg, "this doesn't sound like a backup plan. It sounds like the plan's plan."

"It is," Max said from behind them. "And I don't like it."

Juan turned and said, "We're going to have to put a bell around your neck."

"I have a tracker, just like you."

"Then I'll be sure to set a phone alert when you get close to me."

"That would get annoying fast," Max said. "For both of us. Where are you headed now?"

"To the Magic Shop."

"I'll come with you."

Julia waved as they left.

"I got a call from Tiny," Max said as they walked. "He's on his way to Buenos Aires in the Gulfstream. Should be there in eight hours." Chuck "Tiny" Gunderson was the Corporation's dedicated airplane pilot. When they needed to get somewhere fast, Tiny flew them by private jet or on just about anything else with wings.

"Did he find the charter we need?" Juan asked.

Max nodded. "He's got an old buddy in the city who hooked him up. It's a single-engine Pilatus PC-6 Porter. Tiny says it's a cinch to fly."

"How's the weather in Buenos Aires tomorrow?"

"Clear. Zero chance of rain."

"Then it sounds like we're a go."

"Are you sure you don't want me to come with you?" Max asked.

"I need you in command of the *Oregon*. I know Tate has something up his sleeve about the *Kansas City*, and I want you here to handle it."

"Fine," Max grumbled. "For the record, I still think your plan is stupid."

"You don't think it'll work?"

"No, I think it will. That's the problem."

Without knowing exactly where Overholt would be or how the diving bell would be booby-trapped, the mission would require a good bit of improvisation. Since Linda was still out of commission with ruptured eardrums, Eric Stone would be driving the Nomad, their large submersible equipped with an air lock. The *Oregon* was going to approach twenty miles off Buenos Aires and launch the Nomad. It would take more than three hours to reach the harbor at its maximum cruising speed. Eddie and Linc would also be on board the sub. At the same time, Juan would launch the Rigid-Hulled Inflatable Boat, or RHIB, an extremely fast hydroplaning boat favored by Navy Special Forces around the world. Murph was in the process of adding some special modifications to it. Juan was going to take the RHIB alone into Buenos Aires Harbor to receive the further instructions from Tate.

Once the sub and RHIB were away, Max was going to take the *Oregon* to the supposed vicinity of the *Kansas City*'s sinking southeast of Montevideo, only a hundred fifty miles away across the Rio de la Plata estuary.

Getting Overholt out of the diving bell alive would be the tricky part. The depth of the harbor averaged thirty feet, so diving on the bell in regular scuba gear wouldn't be an issue, but Juan expected Tate to be monitoring it on video feed. And he'd be nearby, watching the location and set to capture Juan the moment he got any clue that a boat or sub was approaching the location. That's why Juan would be offering up an eye-catching distraction. A very risky distraction.

"We've gone over all the options," Juan said, "and all of the other plans have less chance of success. This is the only way to save Lang and stop Tate. I have to do this."

They were passing the ship's armory and firing range when Max stopped and frowned at him. Then he motioned for Juan to come with him into the reinforced single-lane, twenty-five-yard-long range where they tested weapons and maintained shooting proficiency. Max closed the door behind them.

"All you've told us is that Tate is a traitor to the CIA who deserved to go to a Chechen prison. Now he's after us. What happened between you two?"

Juan sighed. "I'm not proud of how I handled the situation."

"Why?"

"I worked with Zachariah Tate for more than a year. He was the smartest and most resourceful agent I ever met. I learned a lot from him about tradecraft, and he could get us out of the most difficult situations you could imagine. He's fluent in Russian like I am, so we were a natural fit. Or so I thought."

"What went wrong?"

"He did." Juan shrugged. "I don't know. Maybe he was born in the wrong country. Or maybe at the wrong time. Or both. He would have thrived in any number of ruthless regimes, from Genghis Khan's Mongol horde to Nazi Germany. I only recognized too late that he was a complete sociopath. No means was off-limits if it achieved the ends he wanted."

Juan stared off into the distance as he remembered the last time he saw Tate.

"You look like you've seen a ghost," Max said.

"Just nasty memories," Juan replied. "We were trying to acquire some information about an impending terrorist attack in Moscow that would have targeted the U.S. embassy. The plotters were Chechen separatists, and we'd tracked their origin to a tiny village in the Caucasus Mountains. According to our intel, the attack was only hours away, so we needed to find out who they were and where they were hiding in Moscow. Hundreds of lives were at stake."

Juan swallowed hard as he thought back to that day.

"We had one of the terrorists tied up in a farmhouse," Juan continued, "but he wasn't talking. His family—wife, sister, and three children, all under ten—were in the next room. I left to follow a lead on his partner somewhere else in the village. Looking back, it was obvious that I shouldn't have left Tate alone with them. He had a look in his eye, a complete lack of compassion. I thought he was simply pushing aside his emotions like I was. But the emotions simply weren't there, except for excitement about what he was planning."

Max had a stricken look. He knew what was coming.

"I had a gunfight with the second terrorist," Juan said. "He died, so I got no more information. When I returned to the farmhouse, I found Tate outside with the terrorist, who was on the ground crying. The house was going up in flames."

"Tate had set it on fire?"

Juan nodded. "He was smiling, actually grinning ear to ear. He said he got the terrorist to tell him the location of the hideout in Moscow, already bragging about the promotion he'd get for stopping the attack."

"He burned up the guy's family?"

"He locked them inside and threatened to torch the house to get the man to talk. The terrorist didn't believe him until he tossed in a gas can with a lit rag stuck in it."

Max shook his head in disgust. "He murdered five innocent people."

"No, one. I wanted to go in to save them, but Tate wouldn't give me the key. And it was a heavy oak door, so they would have burned alive before I could break it down. Tate said the terrorist was getting what he deserved. So I shot Tate in the leg and took the key from him. He called me a traitor, and every other name you could think of. I was able to get the three kids and the sister out, but I couldn't reach the mother."

"I never heard about an embassy bombing in Moscow. You obviously stopped the attack."

"We did, but not because of the information the terrorist gave Tate. Turns out the guy was lying. The info about the hideout was actually in a notebook he'd hidden in the pocket of the youngest child."

"Which you wouldn't have gotten with Tate's methods."

"I later found out that Tate had done similar things before in his career to get ahead." Juan took a breath. "When I got out of the house with the last child, Tate was gone. He took our SUV and fled with the terrorist, leaving me to hike for two days through the forest to my rendezvous. Tate got caught at a roadblock because one of the rebel soldiers noticed the blood on his pants from the gunshot wound. They threw him in prison, and the CIA had to disavow his status as an agent."

"I can see why he hates you," Max said, "but I'm glad to know we don't have someone like that on our side anymore. You did the right thing, as usual."

"Yes, but not soon enough. I thought that was all in my past. I received a report from Langley three years ago that Tate was killed in prison by another inmate."

"That must have been when he escaped," Max said.

Juan nodded. "It appears that he faked his death and that he's been planning his revenge ever since."

"Including building the doppelgänger *Oregon*."

"I guess he got to Vladivostok before we did and found the blueprints." The Russian shipyard was where the *Oregon* was constructed with the help of a corrupt Navy admiral. Juan and his team went back later when they realized a secret copy of the ship schematics were still in storage there and shredded them.

"Where do you think Tate had the *Portland* built?" Max asked.

"I'll ask him." Juan opened the door. "I better get to the Magic Shop. See you later."

He left Max mumbling sarcastically, "'I'll ask him,' he says . . ."

If a mission required any specialized gadgets, disguises, or false credentials, the Magic Shop was where they were created. It was run by Kevin Nixon, an award-winning Hollywood special effects and makeup artist who left show business behind to join the fight against terror after losing his sister in an attack. The CIA was his first choice until the Corporation came calling. Juan was glad he'd been able to snag Kevin because he was also the person who designed all of the clever versions of Juan's prosthetic legs.

When Juan got there, Kevin was rummaging through the extensive racks of clothing, which included military uniforms from around the world. If Kevin didn't have something in stock, his team had everything they needed to tailor it from scratch.

"Did you find a match?" Juan asked.

Kevin poked his head out of a wardrobe full of suits. He had a slim face and thick brown beard, and the stick end of a lollipop stuck out of his mouth. When he saw Juan, he pushed his way through, triumphantly holding up a gray Armani suit and red tie.

"This close enough, Chairman?" Kevin asked.

Juan squinted at the suit and nodded. It was nearly an exact duplicate of the outfit Overholt was wearing in the hostage video.

"By the time they're close enough to notice it's not really Lang's, it won't matter," Juan said. "Just don't get that lollipop stuck to it. It'll be a dead giveaway."

Kevin chuckled and said, "Oh, sorry," before tossing it in a wastebasket. "Sugar-free. Keeps me from snacking."

Years of craft services on movie sets had caused Kevin's weight to balloon far past obesity, but once he joined the Corporation, he went on a strict diet designed by Julia Huxley and controlled by the *Oregon*'s Michelin-rated chef. He'd kept the weight off for the most part, but it was a constant battle for him.

"I think the suit will look even better once I have it on Fred over there," Kevin said, pointing at one of the makeup chairs.

Juan smiled when he saw the articulated dummy sitting there. They often used it for testing the safety of new equipment. Today Fred was wearing a gray wig that looked remarkably like Langston Overholt's hairstyle. His facial features were altered to look like the CIA administrator.

"You even got the wrinkles right," Juan said in amazement.

"Don't worry," Kevin said. "All of that will stay in place even when Fred is wet."

Juan was impressed by the top-notch job, but not surprised. Like the rest of his crew, Kevin didn't settle for doing anything but his best work, especially when he knew his fellow crewmates' lives depended on it.

He understood that Fred would be a key player in the effort to rescue Overholt. The crash test dummy was going to be Juan's distraction.

24

BUENOS AIRES

Less than a day later, Juan stood alone next to the Obelisco de Buenos Aires, the monument commemorating the city's founding in 1536. It was one of the most famous landmarks in Argentina and sat in the middle of Avenida 9 de Julio, a twenty-lane boulevard known as the widest street in the world. He choose to take Tate's phone call here because it was recognizable and near his next destination.

Right on time, Juan's phone buzzed with a call from Overholt's number.

He answered in video mode, as instructed, and saw his own face on Tate's body again.

"Good to see you again, Juan," Tate said.

"I can't say the same."

"Take a spin to show me you're really in Buenos Aires."

Juan turned the phone around and showed the midday traffic on the easily recognizable street.

"Good enough?" Juan asked.

"You're on La Avenida, I see."

Juan started walking toward a side street. "I won't be here long enough for you to find me, in case you're thinking of capturing me before I get Lang out of that diving bell."

"And interrupt the game before it's started? I wouldn't dream of it."

"I know you're here as well. I saw the *Portland* in the harbor." Juan had spotted it during his morning reconnaissance. The name on the stern read SALEM, and the ship was configured differently than the *Oregon*, but its length was identical and the superstructure was in the same location.

"She's a beauty, isn't she?"

"Nice ship that you stole from us."

"I didn't steal it, I copied it," Tate said. "Didn't Picasso say, 'Good artists copy, great artists steal'?"

"You're no artist."

"Maybe you'd think differently if I stole the *Oregon* herself."

"You can try."

"Yes, I can."

"I'm tired of this," Juan said. "Where's Overholt?"

"As promised, he's under the water not far from you. I just texted you the coordinates and a link to a live feed."

Juan entered the coordinates into his phone's mapping app and saw that the diving bell was a mile away from the *Portland*. He had to assume the location was correct. He believed Tate couldn't bear the thought of having to cheat to beat his nemesis.

Then Juan clicked on the link. It brought up a video feed showing Overholt sitting in a tiny diving bell, sipping from a bottle of water. He seemed in good health. In the corner of the screen was an air pressure gauge. Given how much was left in the tanks, Juan estimated Overholt had less than thirty minutes before it ran out.

"This might be prerecorded," Juan said. "How do I know he's still alive?"

"Tell me something you'd like to see him do," Tate said.

Juan thought for a second and said, "Have him give the hand signal he uses when he finishes a race."

"I get it," Tate said. "You want him to know it's you asking."

There was a short pause before Juan saw Overholt look at the camera. Then he gave two thumbs-up, his traditional sign whenever he completed a 10K.

"Happy?" Tate asked.

"No," Juan answered. "But I believe he's alive."

"For now. Better get going. I'll see you soon."

As soon as Tate was off the line, Juan called Tiny Gunderson.

"I've got the location. Are you ready to go?"

"Engine is idling," came back Tiny's deep baritone. "Ready for takeoff."

"I'll be there in five minutes."

Juan got into his rental car and headed north of downtown toward Aeroparque Jorge Newbery just a couple of miles away. The airport abutted Buenos Aires Harbor, not far from where Overholt was being held captive. When Juan got there, he bypassed the exit for the airline terminal and drove to the general aviation tarmac on the other side of the runway.

He drove up to a white plane with its propeller spinning. It looked different from all of the other airplanes because it was sitting on two pontoons that had landing gear extending from them. This particular Pilatus Porter was an amphibious floatplane. Once the gear was raised, it could land on the water.

Tiny waved from the pilot's seat. His nickname was given to him ironically since the blond Swede was actually six foot five and built like a rugby player. He pulled the headset aside and leaned out the window.

"We've got clearance to take off anytime."

"Good. Let's get in the air."

Juan climbed the pontoon to get in and closed the door behind him. As soon as the plane was sealed, Tiny revved the engine, and the Porter began to taxi.

Tiny called over his shoulder. "What's our destination?"

Juan read off the coordinates.

Tiny shook his head. "That's pretty close to the airport's glide path. I might have to get a bit creative in my approach."

"Good," Juan replied. "Then it's less likely that Tate will expect our plan."

He called up Eric Stone, who was currently piloting the Nomad submersible through Buenos Aires Harbor.

"Did you get the coordinates I sent you?" Juan asked, testing out his molar mic. He'd texted the position of the diving bell to Eric on the way to the airport.

"Affirmative, Chairman," Eric answered. "We're motoring our way there now."

"Be careful. We don't know all the ways Tate is monitoring the capsule. And we don't want to tip him off to our intentions."

"All my running lights are off, and the water down here is pretty murky. Eddie and Linc are in their scuba gear and set for extraction."

"Acknowledged. As we expected, Tate has a video feed from the diving bell."

"Then the plan is a go?"

"Yes. I'll let you know when I'm on my way down."

"Copy that."

As the Porter took off, Juan went over the controls for the RHIB. Murph had modified the boat to be operated remotely. With a press of a button, the RHIB would start up and race at top speed to Juan's location in the harbor. It would give him the choice of escaping the diving bell's spot by boat or by floatplane.

Next, he checked Fred, the dummy. He was packed into a case designed to absorb a tremendous amount of shock. Juan shrugged into a sturdy harness and clipped the case to his waist.

Finally, Juan put on his parachute.

25

As the *Oregon* approached Tate's specified coordinates a hundred miles off the coast of Uruguay, Max entered the moon pool to see how the preparations were going. If the *Kansas City* really was in the vicinity and had a bomb planted on its hull, this would be an incredibly dangerous operation.

Murph and Hali were up in the op center, getting ready to search for the *KC* using the ship's sonar array, while MacD prepared the heliox dive gear. According to Tate, the nuclear sub was grounded near the edge of the continental shelf at two hundred fifty feet, well below the maximum depth for using normal scuba tanks. Heliox was a combination of helium and oxygen that eliminated the danger of nitrogen narcosis in deep dives. The Gator would be used to support MacD, and Linda Ross was doing what she could to help get the submersible ready for work, despite her hearing loss. She was communicating with the other technicians via a special set of glasses that Murph had rigged for her, in addition to hand signals and a whiteboard.

Julia Huxley was watching anxiously from the catwalk, and Max stepped up beside her.

"How's she doing?" he asked the doctor.

"As well as can be expected," Julia said, "but she's frustrated by her limitations. I told her she needed to rest, but she said she was going nuts staring at the walls in her cabin."

"I'd be the same way. Any better idea of what happened to her, Murph, and Gomez in the Gator during the Rio op?"

Julia shrugged. "Lots of theories, but nothing definitive."

"Like what?"

"There are a few things I think we can rule out. I did a full work-up on all three of them and didn't find any residual evidence of unexplained chemicals in their systems."

"So they weren't poisoned?"

"No. Or drugged. Besides, there was no vector for them all to be drugged simultaneously. They didn't consume any of the same food or drinks, and the only other possibility would be an aerosolized gas pumped into the Gator while they were submerged. Murph went over the sub with a fine-tooth comb and didn't find any hardware that didn't belong."

"What about an illness?"

"I didn't find any virus or bacteria in their cultures, but that was unlikely anyway. They all described the visions hitting them quickly and then turning off like a switch. An infection would take hours or even days to develop and then clear up."

"So what does that leave us with?"

Julia shook her head, puzzled. "There are a few prospects, but they're all pretty out there."

"Hit me."

"Microwaves could have the effect of causing neurological changes in the brain. Is it possible for such waves to penetrate the water as well as the hull of the Gator?"

"No way. The water around them would absorb the waves and boil first. What else have you got?"

She looked a little embarrassed when she said, "Hypnosis."

"Brainwashing? Really?"

"I told you these ideas were out there, but I'm otherwise stumped. Intelligence services have experimented with hypnosis combined with psychedelic drugs to improve the power of suggestion and subliminal direction, but the results have been mixed at best. Again, I didn't find any hint of drugs in the systems, so it's far-fetched, but I can't rule it out."

Max tried not to roll his eyes. "Anything else?"

Julia took a breath. "Auditory psychosis."

Max frowned at her. "What's that?"

"In my review of the literature, I found research that suggests high-volume auditory stimuli at certain frequencies can cause the vestibular system to convulse, producing a disturbing resonance in the neural pathways."

Max gave her a look that said *You're going to need to dumb that down for me.*

"We get our sense of balance and gravity from the inner ear," she continued. "Those sensory organs can be thrown out of whack by high-intensity sounds, even if they're ultrasonic or infrasonic—high and low frequencies that are out of the range of hearing for humans. Sonic warfare dates back to World War One. And the Nazis developed a parabolic dish to emit extremely loud noises as a battlefield weapon, but it was never put to use."

Max nodded. "I've heard of something similar called LRAD, a Long Range Acoustic Device. It emits ear-splitting sounds that are unbearable. Cargo and passenger ships are mounting them on deck to use as a nonlethal way to repel pirates."

"Right. And remember the incidents in the U.S. embassies in Cuba and China? Personnel were experiencing all kinds of ill effects that were later attributed to being bombarded by high-frequency noise."

"How would the crew in the Gator be affected by something like that?"

"They were wearing headsets. I asked Mark Murphy to inspect all of the software to see if something was installed to broadcast a signal directly into their ears. In the meantime, if you see anyone wearing a headset that's behaving strangely, remove it immediately."

Max nodded. "I'll send out an alert to the crew to be aware of that possibility."

Max's phone went off. It was Hali.

"I've got Tate on the line," he said.

"Patch it through." Max nodded at Julia and exited the moon pool on his way to the op center.

The phone clicked. "This is Max Hanley."

"Yes, I remember you. So Juan left you in charge? Interesting choice."

Max had no patience for Tate's games. "Where is the *Kansas City*?"

"You are correct. No time for chitchat. You've got sixty minutes until the bomb on the *KC*'s hull explodes, so you're going to have to move quickly."

"Where?"

"If you're where I told you to be, you're only eight miles away. I'm texting you the precise longitude and latitude now."

"How do I know the bomb won't go off just as we get to it and kill my people?"

"That wouldn't be very sporting, but, then, I'm not very trustworthy. It's just a risk you're going to have to take, isn't it? Good luck."

Tate hung up. Max put the phone in his pocket, grinding his teeth in fury. It didn't help that Tate used a phrase that wasn't uttered on the *Oregon*. It was considered bad luck to wish someone "Good luck" before a mission.

When he got to the op center, Max asked Murph to pull up the depth charts for the location Tate had texted to him.

"Two hundred fifty feet, just like he told us," Murph said.

Max ordered the *Oregon* to set course for that spot. "When we get there, I want to begin a full sonar search of the seafloor." He called down to the moon pool and told them to be ready for the dive in twenty minutes.

"Any radar contacts?" he asked Hali.

"One boat eight miles to the west. Forty-footer. Looks like a fishing vessel. Nothing else on the scope."

The boat could belong to Tate for observing them, but he didn't have time to go check it out. He'd keep an eye on it, even though a boat that small was no threat to the *Oregon*.

Normally, the *Oregon* would be too far over the horizon to observe from their chartered fishing boat, but Abdel Farouk was using a drone high above them to watch the *Oregon*. Doubling the owner's normal fee gave him and Li Quon the boat to themselves. He was pleased to see the spy ship rushing off at top speed to the northeast.

"Are they coming toward us?" Li asked uneasily.

"No," Farouk answered. "They're sailing for the coordinates the commander gave them."

"Showing them the SEPIRB from the *Kansas City* must have been convincing."

"The commander is no fool."

"How long do you think it'll take for them to realize the sub isn't there?"

"Long enough for us to hit them with the sonic disruptor." The drone holding the weapon was in place. As soon as the *Oregon* was in range, all Farouk would need was the commander's order to activate it.

"Do you think it'll have the same effect as in Rio?"

Farouk shook his head. "Better."

"Even on a ship that size?"

"I'm turning it up to full power, just like we did with the *KC*. The crew should begin to react within seconds."

"What do you think the chances are that they blow up or sink their own ship?"

Farouk shrugged. "Hard to say. Of course, that's not the commander's first choice."

"I'll bet you a hundred bucks they do it."

Farouk lowered the binoculars and grinned at Li. "Make it five."

"You're on," Li said. He had turned away and was walking into the bridge when the radio crackled. As Farouk thought about how he'd spend his winnings, he made some final adjustments to the sonic controls.

When Li returned, he said, "The helicopter is in position forty miles out. They're just waiting for your signal."

The Sikorsky hovering to the north was carrying a ten-man assault team. It would take the chopper fifteen minutes to make the trip to the *Oregon* once the acoustic weapon was transmitting. By that time, the crew should be incapacitated, overboard, or dead. When they landed on the deck, the assault team would encounter little to no resistance.

"They'll be in the position in five minutes," Farouk said, shaking his head in admiration for how Tate had foreseen everything. It had all lined up so perfectly.

The commander's plan wasn't to sink the *Oregon*. The plan was to steal it.

26

Juan put on his goggles, braced himself in the open door of the sea-plane, and stepped out onto the pontoon. He looked down and saw Buenos Aires Harbor five thousand feet below.

"Approaching drop point," Tiny said over the comm system.

"Roger," Juan answered. He pulled out the pack containing the dummy until it was balanced on the edge of the plane's floor. "Ready."

"Five . . . four . . . three . . . two . . . one . . . Jump!"

Juan pushed the pack over the side and followed it into the slipstream.

The sound of the plane receded quickly and was replaced by the sound of the wind buffeting him in free fall. The pack exerted less resistance to the wind than his body, so it dangled below him, dragging him toward the water. He imagined Tate watching him fall, scrambling to get whatever plans to capture or kill him in motion.

He wouldn't have much time once he hit the water, so he was going to open his chute as low to the surface as possible. A thousand feet was the target. The altimeter counted down every five hundred feet in his ear. It went awfully fast.

Juan took a moment to verify that the pack was still securely attached to his harness. During D-Day, U.S. paratroopers invading Normandy were given heavy equipment bags that strapped to their legs. Apparently, they'd never been tested in battle conditions before because most of the bags ripped loose when the chutes deployed. The packs then plummeted to the ground and were lost in the darkness.

If Fred the Dummy detached prematurely, Juan would plunge right to the bottom of the harbor, and his mission would fail almost as soon as it began. He'd never tested this scenario out in a real-world environment, either, but his buckles seemed latched and tight.

"Two thousand," the mechanical voice called out. "Fifteen hundred."

Juan anticipated the thousand announcement and pulled the ripcord when it came. The parachute yanked him upward, as the harness around his chest and waist cut into his wetsuit, but it held. The pack swung wildly beneath him. Tate was surely wondering what it was.

The water came up fast, and Juan took one last glance around him. No boats were anywhere close to him. He pressed the RECALL button on his wrist, which started the remote control on the RHIB. The speedy boat would now be heading his way. At the same time, Tiny would be descending to land as backup.

When he splashed down, Juan pulled the release on the chute and turned around until he saw the small buoy indicating the location of the diving bell. He swam to it, trailing the floating pack behind him.

When he reached the buoy, he removed a tiny tank called Spare Air that was clipped to his harness. It was for divers to use in the case of emergency and held enough air for fifteen breaths. That was all Juan would need.

He put in the mouthpiece and cracked the pack containing the dummy to release the air inside. It sank and pulled Juan down with it.

Juan snapped on his headlamp and saw the yellow diving bell resting on the muddy harbor floor.

As he got closer, he spotted the bomb stuck to the hull. As he expected, it was Tate's fail-safe. But Juan's old CIA partner wouldn't have gone to all this trouble just to kill him. At least that's what he was hoping.

When he got to the top of the diving bell, he took out a small electronic device and clamped it to the cable carrying the interior and exterior camera feeds from the bell to the buoy. The unit was designed to insert itself into the middle of the connection, buffering the video and then rebroadcasting it. The display indicated that it was successfully intercepting the signal.

Juan double-tapped twice on the molar mic with his tongue to indicate that the feed was in place.

"Acknowledged," Eric said from the Nomad's cockpit. "Two hundred meters out and approaching."

Juan double-tapped again and lowered himself to the window of the diving bell. He saw Overholt inside, alive but looking worn out. The interior wheel of the hatch had been removed. Juan caught Overholt's eye and held a whiteboard up to the window.

Stay perfectly still for one minute.

Overholt knew not to ask questions. He nodded slightly and remained in his seat, looking blankly at the wall.

Juan pressed the button on his remote, and the unit was now recording the video from the diving bell and any cameras on its exterior. In a minute, it would begin broadcasting that video as a loop. To Tate, it would look like nothing was going on in the capsule.

Juan opened the pack and extracted Fred's inert form. As promised by Kevin Nixon, the dummy's hair and facial prosthetics had stayed in place. From any distance farther than ten yards, it would look like a soaked version of Overholt.

He dropped the pack and looked at his watch. Based on his math, the RHIB should be approaching any moment, which was great because he only had one or two breaths of air left in his mini-tank. Then he heard the engine of the speedy boat as it raced toward him.

As he rose to the surface, he saw the headlights of the Nomad below him as it approached the diving bell.

Linc and Eddie were in scuba gear holding on to the railing around the Nomad's air lock hatch. The diving bell came into view as the submersible's lights focused on its resting place on the seabed. Silt rose behind them, mixed into the water by the Nomad's propellers.

Eric, who was driving the sub, brought it to a halt only a few yards away from the bell and expertly hovered there.

"I'll turn around while you go get him," Eric said.

"On our way," Eddie replied. He and Linc were wearing full-face masks so they could talk.

They let go of the Nomad and swam toward the capsule. Linc was carrying a snorkeling mask for Overholt, who would buddy breathe using one of their backup octopus regulators.

Eddie checked his watch. It had been more than a minute since Juan started the countdown on the camera feed interrupter. He held a whiteboard up to the window and knocked.

You can move now. We're getting you out of there.

Overholt looked at it and nodded.

Linc pointed at the bomb stuck to the capsule.

Eddie nodded. "Let's move."

They sank to the bottom of the diving bell and swam to the hatch.

Eddie yanked on the wheel to open it. The wheel spun, and Eddie felt the mechanism click, but when he pulled on it the hatch wouldn't budge.

"Tate wasn't going to make it that easy," Linc said and traced his finger along the edge of the hatch.

Eddie looked more closely and understood what he meant. Scalloped beads of hardened metal were evident around the entire circumference.

The hatch was welded shut.

27

Zachariah Tate watched the diving bell's video feed from the *Portland*'s submersible, the Deceiver. Like the *Oregon*'s Gator, it could operate underwater for lengthy periods of time on its batteries alone, but it could also surface quickly and engage its twin diesels to shoot across the water at high speed. They were keeping station only a hundred yards away from the diving bell.

Tate could see the marker buoy via a high-powered telescopic camera mounted on the *Portland*. It was clear that Juan Cabrillo hadn't lost his planning skills. The parachute jump to the bell was clever, but it wouldn't do Cabrillo any good if he couldn't get Overholt out. Of course, Tate's ex–CIA partner would have been expecting the hatch to be welded shut, so the case he descended with might have held a mini-blowtorch or some other device to break the seal.

On the well-hidden exterior cameras, he saw Cabrillo descending to the capsule. Cabrillo clipped something to the cable leading to the surface, which Tate assumed was some kind of signal interrupter for the camera feeds. Sure enough, a few moments later, when Juan had swum to the diving bell's window, the interior and exterior feeds went to loop mode. Soon after that, Tate could see Cabrillo on the monitor descending to the diving bell all over again. Overholt just sat there inside.

"Set course for the diving bell," Tate ordered the Deceiver's pilot. "He must have a sub ready to pick him up."

"Aye, Commander."

The Deceiver was armed with miniature torpedoes. Tate would destroy the sub before Cabrillo and Overholt could board, along with any chance for their rescue.

Before the Deceiver got halfway there, Tate was surprised by what he saw on the video feed from the *Portland*. Cabrillo had surfaced. And he was holding Overholt under the arms.

"We've got a Rigid-Hulled Inflatable Boat nearing the buoy," said Catherine Ballard over the radio from her position in the *Portland*'s op center. "But I don't see anyone on board."

"It must be remote controlled," Tate replied. "That's how he's planning to escape." He turned and yelled at the Deceiver's pilot, "Surface the boat and intercept them!"

The RHIB was closing fast, but it would take time for Cabrillo and Overholt to climb aboard once it stopped. The Deceiver would be there in moments, plenty of time to disable the RHIB and capture them.

The submersible popped out of the water, and the pilot started the diesels. They rocketed forward.

The RHIB raced toward the swimming men, but it wasn't slowing down. At that speed, it would overshoot the two of them by a considerable margin. A malfunction in the remote control? Tate wondered, before quickly dismissing the thought. Cabrillo didn't make mistakes like that.

Then he noticed a thin nylon rope trailing behind the RHIB. The boat was towing a boogie board.

"Faster!" Tate yelled.

They had closed just half the distance when the RHIB's motor cut out. The boogie swung by Cabrillo, who snagged the rope and pulled it to him. He clipped his parachute harness to the board and lay on his back with Overholt cradled in his arms. The RHIB went back to full power, yanking Cabrillo and Overholt through its wake.

It turned away from the Deceiver and flew across the harbor. In the distance, the floatplane that Cabrillo had jumped from was descending toward the water.

Tate leaped into the cockpit and shoved the throttles against their stops, and snarled at the sub's pilot, "If you let them get away, you're a dead man."

Eddie and Linc hovered below the diving bell's hatch as they pressed a ropy length of plastic explosives against the weld. They'd been anticipating the hatch to be locked, jammed, or welded and had different equipment to deal with each scenario.

While Linc finished applying the plastique, Eddie went back to the capsule's window and held up a different sign.

Sit far back from the hatch and cover your eyes.

Overholt nodded and put his hands up to shield his face.

Linc met him at the side of the diving bell holding the detonator, its leads twisting back to the shaped charge.

"Ready?" Eddie asked.

Linc nodded.

"Do it."

Linc pressed the button, and a loud thump rippled through the water, shaking the bell. Eddie looked through the window and saw a small puff of smoke curl up from the blown hatch, but water didn't flood in because the air pressure inside was equalized with the water pressure outside.

When they swam to the bottom of the capsule, they saw the hatch resting on the seabed. A jagged hole in the floor of the diving bell had taken its place.

Eddie took the snorkel mask from Linc and swam up through the opening. When he surfaced inside, he took his regulator out.

"Mr. Overholt, we don't have much time. As soon as Tate figures out that the Chairman is holding a dummy, he'll blow this thing."

"Just tell me what to do," Overholt replied, taking the mask and putting it on.

"I know you've dove before, so this should be easy for you. You'll use my spare regulator, and Linc and I will each hold an arm as we swim. We won't bother trying to enter the Nomad. We'll grab its hatch handle, and Eric will get us away from here as fast as possible."

"Understood." Overholt calmly removed his jacket and tie. Although he looked tired, he didn't seemed fazed by the sudden rescue.

The hatch opening was only large enough for one person, so as soon as Overholt had the regulator in his mouth, Eddie descended as far as the hose connected to his tank allowed. Overholt put his feet in the water and dropped in. His pants and shirt billowed around him.

When he was free of the diving bell, Eddie asked, "Are you okay?"

Since Overholt didn't have a full-face mask like Eddie, he could only nod and sign OK with his hand.

Eddie took his left arm, Linc took his right, and they furiously kicked toward the waiting the Nomad.

"Eric, we're on our way," Eddie said through his comm system.

"I'll crank it up to max speed the moment you're secured," Eric responded.

Eddie knew that this was the risky part of the mission. The Nomad wasn't a speed demon. They just had to hope the Chairman could delay Tate long enough for them to put some distance between them and the diving bell before it exploded.

The RHIB weaved back and forth as it tried to evade assault rifle shots from the men on the deck of the Deceiver.

"Don't shoot Cabrillo or Overholt!" Tate shouted at them.

Their bullets were missing the fast boat as it was approaching the floatplane that was coming in for a landing.

Tate had had enough. He didn't care that it was broad daylight in one of the busiest harbors in South America. He took an RPG from the weapons rack and climbed out onto the Deceiver's deck.

He took aim on the RHIB and fired. The Rocket-Propelled Grenade shot across the water and hit the RHIB dead amidships. It blew in half, and the boogie board it was towing plowed to a halt.

The floatplane's pilot must have seen the carnage because he abruptly pulled up and banked away from the Deceiver.

Cabrillo and Overholt bobbed in the water with nowhere to go.

Tate tossed the spent RPG launcher into the water, and the Deceiver pulled alongside the two men. His crew pulled them aboard.

Cabrillo got to his feet and blew water out of his mouth. "Can't say it's good to see you again, Tate."

"You should have known it would end this way," Tate said with a smile.

"I did," Cabrillo answered with his own grin.

Tate frowned at the odd response, then looked down at Overholt, who just lay there facedown.

"What's wrong with him?" Tate asked. "Did you kill him during your 'rescue'?"

"Not at all. He was never alive."

Tate looked closely and saw that something was wrong with the man's limbs. He yanked an arm to turn Overholt over and discovered it was merely a dummy with the same suit and hair as the CIA administrator.

"No!" He kicked the mannequin off the Deceiver and sneered at Cabrillo as he ordered his men, "Get him inside!"

Tate dropped through the hatch first and looked at the video coming from the diving bell. It was no longer showing the loop. He could see a wisp of smoke inside the capsule and the real Overholt lowering his hands to look down at a diver surfacing through the opening.

Cabrillo landed next to Tate with four different guns trained on him. He peered at the video screen and shook his head.

"There he is," Cabrillo said with mock annoyance. "I knew something was off with the other guy."

The hatch closed, and Tate said, "Dive the boat and get us back to the *Portland*."

He turned back to the monitor and saw Overholt donning a mask. Tate flipped the cover off the DETONATOR button for the explosives attached to the diving bell.

As he placed his finger over the button, he looked at Cabrillo. Tate wanted to see his expression when he pushed it.

"You just killed your friend."

Eddie and Linc had a tight hold on Overholt and the sub as the Nomad motored away from the diving bell at a stately eight knots. The video feed now being broadcast was on a one-minute delay, but Eddie didn't know how long the ruse would protect them.

He got his answer a second later.

A bow wave of pressure and noise pummeled them as the explosives ripped the diving bell apart. The Nomad bucked from the impact, tearing the handhold from their grips.

They also lost Overholt.

Eddie tumbled for a few seconds, and his mask was torn from his face. When the shock wave had passed, he steadied himself and reached around to find the hose connected to his mask. With a practiced hand, he put it back on, clearing the water, so he could breathe again.

The buddy hose dangled in front of him, the damaged regulator bubbling. Overholt was no longer attached to it.

Eddie retrieved the flashlight lashed to his wrist and rotated until he saw Linc putting on his own mask in the swirling mud. When he was breathing again, he gave the *OK*. Then he noticed that neither of them had Overholt.

They frantically searched the seafloor for him, but it wasn't until the Nomad swung around and focused its powerful lights through the gloom that they saw Overholt floating motionless nearby, his mask askew.

Eddie grabbed his arms and pulled him toward the Nomad's open air lock hatch. There was room for only two people, so Linc closed the hatch behind them and waited outside while Eddie held Overholt as he waited for the air lock to drain. Overholt was unconscious or dead, Eddie couldn't tell.

The moment the lock was empty, Eric pulled the interior door open, and Eddie lay Overholt on the floor.

"Oh, man," was all Eric said, before closing the door so he could refill it to let Linc in.

Eddie turned Overholt onto his back to clear the water from his throat and then felt for a pulse. Nothing. He began chest compressions, being careful not to press too hard and break the elderly man's ribs.

He counted to thirty and checked again. Still nothing.

Eddie tilted Overholt's head back to open the airway and administered two quick mouth-to-mouths. Then he started CPR again.

After five pumps to the chest, Overholt coughed. He convulsed, and water spewed from his mouth.

Eddie turned him over, and more water drained from Overholt's lungs. He shuddered as he struggled to draw in air, and he finally gasped in a ragged breath.

The air lock cycled again, and Linc emerged as Eddie helped Overholt sit up. Linc let out a sigh of relief and clapped Eric on the shoulder.

"You had us worried there, Mr. Overholt," Eddie said.

Overholt coughed again, then said, "I never doubted this would work . . . Where's Juan?"

Eddie looked at Eric, who said, "Tiny called in from the plane. He saw the Chairman get pulled aboard a sub that disappeared."

"Then Tate has him," Overholt said, shaking his head. "Juan traded himself for me."

"Just like he wanted to," Linc said.

Overholt looked at the three of them with a puzzled expression. "You mean, that was Juan's plan the whole time? He wanted to get captured?"

Eddie nodded. "To fool Tate, we had to make the rescue look well executed until you 'died.' Everything went exactly how the Chairman sketched it out. I just hope the rest of his plan works."

28

Juan climbed out of the submersible Tate called the Deceiver and into what looked like an exact duplicate of the *Oregon*'s moon pool. The only thing missing was the Nomad hanging from the gantry cradle. The catwalks above were packed with gawking crew members.

All work had stopped. All eyes were locked on Juan as Tate led him onto the deck beside the pool.

"Don't tell me they've never seen a real captain before," Juan said.

"Everybody here has a personal stake in capturing you," Tate said, before raising his hands in victory and yelling to the crowd. "I promised you this day and I delivered! We got him!"

A huge cheer went up from the gathered crew as if they had witnessed the winning goal at the World Cup. The clapping and hooting went on for a full minute.

"That certainly was a warm welcome. But what's the personal stake?"

"You've made all of their lives miserable in one way or another.

You've killed family members, ruined businesses, sunk ships, or caused them to be exiled from their countries."

"So they're all criminals," Juan said. "Like you."

"Only because of your actions. Many of them see themselves as freedom fighters who got caught before they could finish the revolution. Or, like me, they were doing the right thing, and you didn't like the methods. It took me a long time to recruit them, but they've been very motivated to carry out this mission."

"Then they're also deluded. Like you. Why don't you just kill me and get it over with? That's what you all want, isn't it?"

"You're too smart to believe that, old pal," Tate said. "I could have done that already, as you well know."

"Then what *do* you want?"

"To make you suffer the way you made me suffer." Tate raised his arms again to indicate all those around him. "The way you made all these people suffer."

Juan took a breath as he thought about that. "Torture for torture's sake isn't your style. Even for someone as amoral as you."

"You're right. It would be satisfying in the short run, but I want you to live a long life with your failure. You failed to rescue Overholt when you had the chance. Your reputation is in tatters with the CIA and the U.S. government. What else do you have left?"

Tate paused for effect. And Juan realized what he meant.

Juan launched himself at Tate but was restrained by two of the men. "The *Oregon*? What have you done?"

"Nothing . . . yet. Come."

Catcalls and curses rained down on Juan as he was shoved through the exit door behind Tate. They wound through the ship, and Juan knew exactly where they were going since the interior layout was identical to the *Oregon*'s. The sole difference was the lack of artwork adorning the corridors' walls.

"You're so unoriginal, Tate. You had to copy me?"

Tate shrugged. "I think of it more as an homage. Besides, a good idea is a good idea. As you know, I don't mind stealing."

They entered the op center, and the sense of déjà vu was even stronger for Juan. He had the urge to sit in the captain's chair, but Tate settled into it.

"What would be your worst nightmare, Juan?" Tate asked casually. "The death of your crew? The sinking of your ship?"

Juan remained tight-lipped. He didn't think Tate had the means to endanger the *Oregon*, especially with the *Portland* sitting in Buenos Aires.

"I can see that would be difficult for you," Tate continued. "But wouldn't it be worse if I took command of your beloved spy ship?"

Juan scoffed, but he didn't like where this was going. "What are you babbling about now?"

"You didn't think I'd send them to find the real *Kansas City*, did you?"

"Of course not." But they had to risk going to the coordinates Tate gave them in case it was there.

"As I told your dear dead friend Overholt, I needed somewhere much closer than Algodoal for my purposes. I had to lure you with something tangible. And it worked."

Tate nodded to a woman, and a video of the *Oregon* appeared on the main view screen. It was framed by the horizon and bright blue sky. No other ships were visible, and the image seemed to be filmed from far away.

"They'll be ready for whatever you come at them with," Juan said.

A smile curled on Tate's lips. "Is that what you thought in Rio?"

Juan seethed. "I knew you were responsible for that."

"I planned it from the very beginning. CIA officer Ballard here was instrumental in leaking the names of those agents. I knew Overholt would hire you to extract them."

Juan was repulsed by how pleased Tate seemed with himself.

"How did you do it?" Juan demanded.

"I can't give everything away to you. Let's just say it involves a weapon that's been lost for a hundred years. We've tweaked it, naturally, but the principles are virtually unchanged from when it was first developed."

"It may have worked on our sub, but there's no way it'll work on a ship the size of the *Oregon*, whatever it is."

"Oh, it has. Remember the *Kansas City*? Why do you think it went down in the first place?"

Juan was stunned. "You sank a U.S. nuclear sub just to prove you could do it?"

"Among other reasons," Tate said. "But that's not what I want to do to the *Oregon*. Imagine what I could do with another ship like the *Portland*. I think I'll rechristen the *Oregon* as the *Eugene*."

Juan gagged at the thought of Tate ever setting foot on his ship, let alone commanding her.

"They would die before letting you hijack the *Oregon*."

Tate smiled and pointed at Juan. "Exactly. When my helicopter lands on the deck of your ship, there may be a few stragglers who haven't died, but the assault team should be able to take care of that in short order. And guess what?"

Tate nodded at the guards, who pushed Juan down into a chair, the same one Overholt had been sitting in during the video chat.

"You'll get to watch the whole thing," Tate went on. "I've even equipped the assault team with GoPro cameras so we can watch them take over your ship in real time. Won't that be fun?"

Juan sneered at Tate but said nothing. Tate had underestimated his ability to save Overholt, but it looked like Juan had made the same mistake of underestimating his old CIA colleague. Now his crew might pay the price, and Juan would have to see it all happen live. This was Tate's idea of torture.

With a flourish, he pressed a button on his armrest.

"Yes, Commander?" came a voice over the intercom.

"Are you in position?" Tate asked.

"Yes, sir. The disruptor is ready. Helicopter standing by."

"Good." Tate threw a smug glance at Juan. "Commence the hijacking operation."

29

Linda was doing her best to help prep the Gator for the upcoming dive, but she still couldn't hear more than a muffled rumble. Doc Huxley said it might be a few more days before she got some partial hearing back, but Linda was worried that it would never return to normal. In the meantime, she wanted to show she was useful no matter what her condition was. Doing nothing but paperwork for the last few days in her role as the Corporation's VP had bored her to death.

She had Mark Murphy hastily whip up a special speech-to-text app to use in conjunction with his old Google Glass headset. She felt like a geek while wearing it, but now she could understand what someone was saying to her by reading the words projected on the small lens. It wasn't a perfect solution. Background noise was a problem and multiple voices speaking at once could be difficult to decipher. The translation was even worse than when she was dictating a text message to her phone, but it was good enough for her purposes. It allowed her to assist with the checklist of the Gator's cockpit functions before it was launched for the nuclear sub search.

From her seat, Linda had a good view of the technicians in the *Oregon*'s moon pool going over the equipment and MacD doing the final check of the dive gear. Raven was behind Linda in the submersible's main cabin, reading each item off a tablet.

Oil press her? it read on the glasses.

"Oil pressure nominal," Linda replied. She wished she would actually be piloting the sub, but Mark Murphy was going to be coming down from the op center soon to take her position for the dive.

Buttery powder?

"Battery power one hundred percent and delicious."

What?

Linda turned to see Raven's confused expression and smiled. "The speech recognition software on this device is a tad obsolete."

What did hit say I said?

"Buttery powder."

Raven looked down at the tablet and shook her head with a deadpan look.

No, that's write.

Linda laughed and turned back to the instruments.

There was a pause. When it went on for a few more beats, Linda said, "Ready for the next item."

They're here. It's buzzing.

"Now, that one I didn't get," Linda said. "Come again?"

As she waited for the correction, she glanced out the window and was puzzled to see that everyone had stopped moving. She thought perhaps they were listening to a shipwide message that her headset wasn't picking up until she saw MacD abruptly lean down and pick up one of the scuba tanks, raising it high over his head.

"What is he doing?" she asked herself aloud.

MacD's eyes bulged with terror as he looked into the water of the moon pool. His mouth rounded into a scream that Linda couldn't hear, and he reared back as he threw the tank into the moon pool as if he were trying to kill something rising out of the depths, which was impossible because they hadn't opened the keel doors yet.

The rest of the technicians in the cavernous moon pool seemed to go just as crazy, running wildly, fighting each other or hurting themselves.

Linda finally understood what she was seeing. It was happening again. The same thing that had affected the crew of the Gator in Rio.

This time, Linda seemed immune. Maybe being in the sub now was preventing her from being affected.

She turned and saw that wasn't the case.

Raven had dropped the tablet and was prying open the case holding the sub's emergency life raft at the aft end of the cabin. She seemed to be babbling to herself.

We're thinking. There sending us to the bottom.

Linda yelled and leaped out of her seat to stop her, but she had only reached the external hatch ladder when Raven yanked the cord on the inflatable raft.

The pressurized CO_2 canister began blowing it up, and soon neither of them would have room to move. Linda raced up the rungs, and her head poked out of the hatch as the raft began pushing her feet up and out.

She tumbled onto the deck of the Gator and saw complete pandemonium in the moon pool. MacD had run out of scuba gear and was now frantically tossing any random object around him into the water.

Linda remembered how single-minded and insane she'd been in the same condition. Reasoning with any of them was futile. If the rest of the crew was like this, it was just a matter of minutes before people started killing themselves or endangering the ship.

The op center was the only place where she could get the situation under control. As she raced out of the moon pool, Linda realized she might be the sole person on the *Oregon* who was unaffected by whatever was causing this.

But she had been affected before. Why not now?

Julia Huxley dashed by in hysterics, which terrified Linda even more because it was so out of character for the normally calm doctor. She was yelling something that the Google Glass interpreted as *We're going to fly*. It suddenly hit Linda.

She was deaf. Some kind of sound wave had to be the trigger for all of this panic.

Linda had to keep the crew from self-destructing while also getting the *Oregon* away from the source of the sound.

When she passed one of the ship's firefighting stations, she got an idea and snatched a mask with a filter from the cabinet. She put it on as she ran.

When she reached the op center, there were only two people left at their posts. Murph was hunched over his position at the weapons console, tapping furiously on the keyboard and talking to himself. Max sat in the command chair, pointing at the main view screen and shrieking as if he were watching the world's scariest horror movie. Nothing was visible except the horizon.

Her glasses typed out a jumble of messages from both men that didn't make any sense.

I see them!

Won't get us.

Swallow us all!

Nothing left to eat.

Linda didn't bother with either of them. She headed straight for the nearest console and brought up the controls for intruder countermeasures.

Before she could find what she was looking for, she felt a thump reverberate through her chair. She looked up and saw a flash on the view screen, followed by a trail of smoke.

Linda instantly realized what had happened. The thump she'd felt was the launch of a rocket. Murph had fired an Exocet anti-ship missile.

It headed directly south. She glanced at the radar and realized it was racing toward some kind of boat.

Farouk and Li both leaped to their feet when they saw the Exocet shoot into the sky eight miles away.

"You said they were going to kill themselves!" Li shouted at Farouk. "Not us!"

Farouk shook his head in disbelief. "I don't understand." He never imagined that anyone would still have the capacity to take such a complex action as activating a defensive weapons system. "How do they know we should be a target?"

"What do we do?" Li shouted.

With the missile streaking toward the fishing charter at seven hundred miles per hour, there wasn't any time to start the boat and take evasive action.

"Swim!" Farouk yelled.

Both of them dove overboard and swam for their lives.

They had gotten ten yards from the boat when the missile reached them.

And it kept going.

Farouk and Li watched in amazement as it tore past them.

"It missed!" Li said with a whoop. "But how?"

As he was treading water, Farouk thought they'd simply gotten lucky. Maybe the person who fired was as crazed as he'd expected.

He was about to say so when he saw the Exocet change course. It went into a tight arc until it had made a complete one-hundred-eighty-degree turn.

"It looks like I'm going to owe you five hundred dollars," Farouk said.

Li looked at him in confusion. Then it dawned on him. "Our bet?"

Farouk nodded, watching the trail of smoke leading back to the disguised freighter. "The missile didn't miss us. Its target is the *Oregon*."

30

Linda had twenty seconds before the Exocet missile would hit and blow a lethal hole in the *Oregon*. She pushed Murph aside and knocked him to the floor to access the weapons controls and initiate the self-destruct.

She punched the ABORT button, but nothing happened. The missile continued on its course. Murph must have locked it out.

The only remaining option was to shoot it down. Linda brought the port Gatling gun online and set it for autotargeting.

The system required no further input from her. On the outside of the *Oregon*'s hull, the plates slid aside instantly to reveal the six-barreled cannon. Its built-in radar locked on to the incoming Exocet and spun up to firing speed.

She sensed the rapid firing of the gun in vibrations through the hull. On the main screen, at a rate of three thousand rounds per minute, tracers homed in on the missile until the tungsten shells slammed into the warhead, blowing it to pieces, while it was still a mile from the ship.

With the immediate danger passed, Linda raced back to the other workstation and found the controls for the intruder countermeasures.

The *Oregon* was equipped with several mechanisms to deal with enemy boarding parties. The first line of defense was a set of automated .30 caliber machine guns hidden in the barrels strewn across the deck. They would pop out and cut down any gunmen trying to gain access to the interior of the ship.

But if intruders did manage to get inside and take hostages, the venting system could direct a tranquilizing gas to any compartment on the ship. It didn't knock anyone out. Sleeping gases, on the other hand, were too unpredictable and could easily be lethal in large concentrations. But the invisible, odorless tranquilizer did cause the victims to lose any energy or ability to move, as if they'd taken a few Valium.

Linda didn't intend to target any particular part of the *Oregon*. She was going to flood the whole ship with the gas.

As she typed in the commands, she saw Murph edging back to the weapons console. He was going to launch another missile.

Linda ran over and kneed him in the gut. Although she was little, she packed a punch. The wiry computer genius fell back, but she knew he wouldn't be down for long. She snatched a power cord from a nearby laptop and hastily tied his wrists to the base of the anchored helm chair.

She ran back over to the console and switched on the dispenser for the tranquilizing gas. It would take a minute to reach its full concentration, so she kept an eye on Murph, who was tearing at the cord with his teeth to little effect.

Linda thought she was in the clear until she stared in shock at the main view screen as another Exocet missile shot from the *Oregon*'s deck.

She realized her mistake and turned to Max, who was furiously stabbing at the controls on the command chair's arm. Many of the ship's most important functions could be operated from that single seat if needed, including weapons.

It wasn't Murph who had fired the first missile. It was Max.

The Exocet took the same course, racing out before turning to make its final run on the *Oregon*.

Linda ran to the weapons console to reactivate the Gatling gun, but she was tackled from behind. She flipped over to see Max holding her legs and babbling nonsensically, which was projected on the Google Glass she was wearing under the mask.

Nothing left who eat. No thing left to heat.

His words brought back the panic she'd felt on the Gator. He thought something was coming to eat them and he didn't want to leave anything to consume. Linda understood how his thought process seemed crazy to her but logical to him. He was trying to stop her from letting the nonexistent monsters eat everybody aboard.

She glanced at the screen and saw the missile make its final turn and rocket back toward them. If she didn't stop it, the Exocet could penetrate the ship's armor and explode in one of the ammo magazines, tearing the ship in half.

Linda tried to kick Max away, but he was still quite strong despite his age and outweighed her two-to-one. He hauled her toward him and slapped her mask, knocking it askew.

Linda couldn't see, so she flipped the mask off her head, along with the glasses, and held her breath. She got one leg free and jabbed her foot at Max's face. Her heel smashed into his nose, causing a gush of blood to flow, but he wouldn't let go of her other boot. She finally had to take a breath, and she could instantly feel a tingling as the tranquilizing gas hit her system. Her tiny frame would absorb a sedating dose of the drug much faster than Max's would.

The missile was only seconds away from hitting them. Linda angled her foot, and the boot slipped off. Max fell backward, and Linda launched herself at the weapons panel.

She smashed her finger on the GATLING GUN button and it fired on automatic, detonating the Exocet mere yards from the hull. She felt the *Oregon* rock from the impact.

Linda was now getting woozy from the gas. She collapsed to the floor and felt around until her hand clasped the mask. With her last bit of strength, she pulled it over her head.

She sucked in a few deep breaths, and her mind started to clear. When she was back to normal, she saw Max and Murph lying on the floor, conscious but looking like they were blotto from drinking a fifth of vodka.

Linda got to her feet and staggered over to the command chair. Using the armrest controls, she set course due west and brought the engines up to full speed. The *Oregon* leaped forward.

She wondered how far she'd have to take the ship to get out of the danger zone. She guessed fifty miles ought to do it, but she'd be ready to re-release the gas just in case.

Once they were in the clear, Linda knew there would be two main priorities. First, get the whole crew back together, including the Chairman. And, second, figure out some way—any way—to defeat the nasty sonic weapon that nearly caused the destruction of her ship.

31

Juan smiled as he watched the *Oregon* race toward the horizon.

"That probably didn't go the way you were expecting," he said to Tate, who stared at the *Portland*'s op center view screen in disbelief.

"Get Farouk on the line!" Tate yelled. "I want to know what happened."

After a minute of no response, the camera switched from the drone to one on board the small fishing vessel. It showed two drenched men, one Middle Eastern, the other Asian, standing on the deck, puddles of water at their feet.

"They got away," the Middle Eastern man said in what Juan recognized as an Egyptian accent. He had to be Farouk.

"I know they got away, you idiot!" Tate screamed. "How?"

The Asian man shrugged. Farouk shook his head and said, "I don't know. The sonic disruptor was working."

"Where's the helicopter?"

"I told it to turn back," the Asian man said.

"Well, applause for you, Li," Tate said, slowly clapping his hands. "That was brilliant not to have the chopper continue out into the ocean for no reason whatsoever. You two get back here as soon as you can. I want to inspect the sonic disruptor myself."

He slashed across his throat in the universal *Hang up* gesture. Farouk and Li disappeared from the screen, looking terrified.

"Look at the bright side, Tate," Juan said. "The *Oregon* is still around for you to hijack some other time."

Tate stalked over and glowered down at him.

"I'm so glad you're enjoying this because it's the last time you'll enjoy anything."

Juan smirked. "I don't know about that. Do you have another operation you want me to watch you screw up?"

"You're not staying much longer," Tate said, waving over Catherine Ballard to them.

"Where am I going?"

Tate didn't answer. Ballard approached with a handheld scanner.

"Find it and take it out," Tate said.

Ballard nodded and waved the device over Juan, beginning with his head. It remained silent until she reached his left thigh and started beeping.

"Here it is," she said and flipped open a switchblade.

"Careful," Juan said. "This dive suit is my favorite."

"Was he always like this?" she asked Tate as she sliced the suit open.

"It may be hard to believe," Tate replied, "but he's gotten worse. He thinks he can joke himself out of any situation. But not this time, my friend."

Ballard palpated his quad muscle until she found what she was looking for. When she dug the knife into Juan's leg, he didn't give Tate the satisfaction of watching him wince from the pain.

She plucked out a tiny disc and handed it to Tate, who took it from her in a handkerchief. He cleaned the disc and held it aloft to inspect.

"So you thought your crew would find you with this tracker?" Tate asked, his delight returning.

"Seemed prudent to have it, given the psychos I'm dealing with."

"Does that make you feel better? Thinking we're all psychos?"

"Aren't you?"

"Is it psychotic to want justice, to get revenge on the people who've wronged you? Are we psychos for doing mercenary work, which is the exact same thing you do?"

Juan shook his head in disgust. "We don't sink ships for money and kill innocent people in the process."

"You were willing to let hundreds of innocent people die in a terrorist attack in Moscow just because you were squeamish about my interrogation methods."

"You were going to kill that man's whole family. His children."

Tate waved away that point. "They deserved it for supporting a terrorist."

Juan didn't see any reason to keep arguing with him. "You said I'm not staying much longer. Where am I going? Overboard?"

Tate grinned. "After all this, do you think it would be that easy?" He handed the intact tracker to Ballard. "Take this to the international airport and stash it in someone's luggage."

She nodded. "His people will be looking for him on another continent."

"And where will I be?" Juan asked.

"A while ago," Tate said, "it seems you destroyed a joint China–Argentina base in Antarctica, costing them a fortune. Several of the Argentinian officers responsible for the project survived the attack, although they've been demoted or drummed out of the service, pariahs in their own military. They didn't appreciate your role in ruining their careers."

Juan didn't like the sound of this.

"When these officers found out they'd get a second crack at you," Tate continued, "they jumped at the chance and greased the skids for my operation here in Buenos Aires. In return, I promised them you."

Now everybody in the *Portland*'s op center was smiling.

"You don't want to keep me here to torture me?"

Tate shook his head. "This rogue military unit has a secret prison in Las Armas not run by the regular Army. Apparently, it makes the Black Hole of Calcutta look like a Ritz-Carlton. You're going to be spending the rest of your long and very miserable life with a wonderful selection of fellow inmates."

"But then you won't be able to lord it over me when you eventually capture the *Oregon*."

Tate knelt in front of Juan for effect. "I'm not going to attempt another hijacking, my old buddy. That ship has sailed, so to speak. No, I'm going to sink her. It'll be on video, playing on a loop in your cell. I'm going to make you watch your own ship go down and there'll be nothing you can do about it. I imagine that'll be worse than any physical torture I can dream up. The sight of your crew dying over and over will break you. I guarantee it."

Tate stood and took in a deep, refreshing breath. "You know what? I'm feeling better already just at the thought of it all. Let's get him topside."

Juan was unbound and shoved toward the exit. Up on deck, they were met by six soldiers in camo garb. Juan didn't recognize any of them.

"Colonel Sánchez," Tate said to the oldest one, "I present Juan Cabrillo, as we agreed."

Sánchez stepped forward and said to Juan in his native tongue, "You killed my cousin."

"That's funny," Juan replied in Spanish with a fluent Argentinian accent. "I don't recall ever meeting someone as ugly as you. He must have gotten the good genes in the family."

Sánchez sneered at him. "We'll see how many jokes you want to make once we get you to Las Armas tomorrow."

Tate held up a finger. "One more thing, Colonel." He handed the

Argentinian a generic prosthetic leg. "You'll want to replace his fake leg with this one. He tends to keep all kinds of surprises inside his own."

"You've thought of everything," Juan said.

"That's me. Thoughtful. Good-bye, Juan. Maybe I'll deliver the video to you in person so I can see firsthand what a good time you're having."

As the soldiers led Juan away, he called over his shoulder, "Visitors are always welcome!"

Before they left the ship, two of the soldiers held him tightly while another two switched out the prosthetic leg. The new one fit poorly, so Juan had to walk carefully to keep it from slipping off.

Before he got into the waiting truck, Juan pressed three times on his right thigh. That activated the backup tracker Julia Huxley had injected in his leg. Since it hadn't been transmitting, Tate found only the one Juan wanted him to find. Juan's original intent had been to lead the *Oregon* to the *Portland* via his tracker and ambush it, but that operation was obviously off the table.

Now Juan just had to hope the *Oregon* crew could intercept him before he got to the prison. From the sound of it, if he made it all the way to a cell, he might never get out.

32

Eddie Seng opened the top hatch on the Nomad after it surfaced in the *Oregon*'s moon pool. It was six hours after they had rescued Overholt from the diving bell. The smell inside the submersible had gotten noticeably rank from four men in such close quarters, so Eddie was happy to inhale the smell of seawater and oil.

Max and Linda were waiting on the deck next to the pool. Max had a gauze bandage across his nose and a bruise spreading on his face.

"Where's Doc Huxley?" Eddie asked them as he helped Overholt out of the sub.

Overholt shook his head. "Don't bother, I'm fine."

"Still, I think she should give Mr. Overholt a thorough examination. We had to revive him after he inhaled some water."

"The doc is pretty busy right now," Max said with a grim expression.

"Does that have something to do with that bandage on your face?"

"Linda helped me put this on, but yes."

Linc and Eric climbed out and joined them.

"What happened?" Eddie asked.

"We were attacked. It disabled the entire crew except for Linda here. If she weren't deaf, we'd probably all be at the bottom of the Atlantic right now."

"What are the casualties besides your nose?"

"Luckily, nothing too serious," Linda said. "Four broken bones, two concussions, and a good number of stitches required."

Eddie was surprised Linda had responded to him since Max just said she was deaf. When she noticed his puzzled expression, she added, "I can't hear you, but my glasses translate your speech to text."

"How's the ship?"

"Some damage to the port torpedo tubes and the forward operational crane, but it could have been much worse."

"How did all that happen?"

"From a missile fired at us by me," Max said sheepishly, pointing at his nose. "That's how I got this. Linda had to put a boot to my face to keep me from killing us all. I certainly deserved it."

"It's not your fault," Linda said, patting him on the shoulder. "Believe me, I know what it feels like to be out of control from the effects of that sonic weapon."

"We must have escaped the weapon's range since the effects dissipated once Linda evacuated the tranquilizer gas," Max said. "We think it was some kind of underwater device, but we never pinpointed the source."

"Can't wait to hear more about that," Eddie said.

"What about the Chairman?" Eric asked. "Did you get his signal?"

"We're tracking two," Max said. "The original one is currently on a commercial flight headed to New York. We think that's a decoy."

"And the backup?" Eddie asked. "Is that one still on the *Portland*?"

"No. The tracker is currently broadcasting from the Edificio Libertador in Buenos Aires. It's the headquarters for the Army and one of the most heavily guarded buildings in the country. If Juan is in there, we'd need a whopper of a plan to get him out."

"Let me see what I can find out," Overholt said. "Despite my current situation, I still have some friends in the NSA who could tell me if they've intercepted any calls about him."

"Then I'll take Mr. Overholt to Doc Huxley in the infirmary," Linc said.

Max nodded. "Meanwhile, Eddie can fill me in on Buenos Aires, and I'll recap our run-in with the sonic weapon. Let's all reconnect in a couple of hours and come up with a plan to rescue Juan."

Two hours later Max, Linda, Eddie, Murph, and Eric were in the *Oregon*'s executive boardroom. A map of Argentina was projected on the wall monitor behind Max, who sat at the head of the long oaken table. They'd heard that Overholt had acquired relevant information from his NSA contact, so everyone stopped talking and turned their attention to him when Julia escorted him into the room.

"You let me know if you have any subsequent symptoms," she said while she stood at the door.

Overholt eased into a seat. "As I said, I'm feeling much better."

Julia looked at Max. "I could barely get him off the phone long enough to examine him, but he doesn't seem to have any residual effects from his near drowning."

"You have an amazing sick bay facility," Overholt said, throwing a glance at Julia, "and the medical staff seems to be top-notch, if a little overcautious."

Julia ignored his lighthearted complaint. "I'll check him again tomorrow for any signs of pneumonia. In the meantime, I've cleared him to be up and about. I'm going back to the medical bay to tend to my other patients."

She closed the door behind her when she left.

"Glad to see you're doing well, Mr. Overholt," Max said.

"And I appreciate everything you did to rescue me. Has Juan's status changed?"

Max shook his head. "The tracker still has him in the same building in Buenos Aires."

"Then we still have time."

"Why do you say that?"

"Intercepting the right phone calls was a challenge because Cabrillo is a fairly common name in Argentina, but I was able to find out from my NSA contact that Juan is scheduled to be moved tomorrow."

"Did you get any specific intel about the move?" Max asked. He wasn't surprised that Overholt had been able to acquire the necessary intelligence so quickly. The CIA officer had been one of the most well-connected people in Washington for decades and he would still have friends there even if he was under suspicion of treason.

"He's being held by rogue elements of the Argentine Army. They plan to transfer him to a prison near Las Armas tomorrow morning by truck convoy."

Max had Murph plot the most likely routes the convoy would take from Buenos Aires to Las Armas, which was located two hundred miles south of the capital.

"Luckily, there's only one obvious route for the convoy to take," Murph said, tracing a highway through Argentina's coastal lowlands. "Any other option would take them far out of the way."

"Expect the escort to be well armed and ready to fight," Overholt said. "My contact claims that they are under the command of a Colonel Sánchez. For the transfer mission, he's using handpicked mercenaries who are disgraced former soldiers. They plan to throw Juan into a cell under a false name. There would be no way to get him out without a full-scale assault on the prison."

"Then the best option for springing him would be to intercept them en route," Max said.

"That's what I would advise," Overholt said. "Do you have the capability for such a scenario?"

Max thought about it as he inspected the map. Then he pointed to a port just seventy miles south of Las Armas called Mar del Plata.

"We can dock there to unload," Max said.

"Unload what?" Overholt asked.

"The PIG," Eddie said.

Max nodded and said to Overholt, "We've got a truck of our own with a few hidden surprises." He turned back to Eddie. "What would you say about taking Linc and Raven on a road trip?"

33

ARGENTINA

The next morning at the port of Mar del Plata, Eddie stood on the dock as the *Oregon*'s lone functional crane lowered a truck taken out of the ship's cargo hold. The boxy-looking vehicle with the large four-person cab and oversized tires looked as rusted and junky as the vessel it was removed from. Its side bore the faded words VERTEGAS OIL EXPLORATION. The PIG, which stood for "Powered Investigator, Ground," looked completely unremarkable, just as intended.

The customs inspector watched it coming down with a faintly repulsed expression.

"This thing actually is working?" he asked in heavily accented English as he checked his clipboard.

Eddie nodded. "You'd be surprised."

"I *am* surprised. Show me."

When it reached the ground, Raven and Linc detached the cables while Eddie took the inspector on a quick tour of the truck. He opened the rear doors and revealed that the cargo bay was stacked floor to ceiling with six steel drums.

"What are these?" the inspector asked.

"Spare fuel," Eddie replied. "We plan to be exploring some remote regions in the south."

The inspector knocked on one of the barrels and heard the distinctive sound of a full container of liquid echoing back.

"If you want, I can take one out for you to look inside," Eddie offered.

The inspector thought about it, then glanced at his watch.

"You're probably in a hurry," Eddie said, flashing a few hundred American dollars he was holding in his hand. "Maybe we can both get out of here sooner."

The inspector eyed the money and slowly nodded. "I think that is best."

He handed over the clipboard so that Eddie could sign the customs form. He tucked the bills under the paper and gave it back with a smile.

"Thank you, señor."

"*De nada.*"

As the inspector walked off, tucking the money in his pocket, Raven said, "Have you ever had to show an inspector that there really is fuel in those drums?"

Eddie shook his head. "But I always offer, which makes them think that we aren't hiding anything."

Although the six drums were actually full of spare fuel, the ones behind them, that would be exposed by their removal, were simply half shells concealing the real cargo bay.

The PIG was Max's brainchild, and he had designed it from the ground up. The beefed-up Mercedes Unimog chassis was fitted with an armored body strong enough to withstand rifle fire, and the self-sealing tires were driven by an eight-hundred-horsepower turbo-diesel that could be nitrous-boosted for short periods up to one thousand horses.

A .30 caliber machine gun was hidden in the front bumper, and rockets could be fired from racks that swung down from the PIG's sides. A seamless hatch in the roof would slide back to allow the launch of mortar rounds, and a smoke generator could lay down a thick screen of fumes behind the truck.

Eric and Murph had persuaded Max to add a feature to the drive-by-wire system that would let someone operate the PIG remotely with a handheld control. Raven had it in her pocket.

Although the cargo bay could hold up to ten fully kitted soldiers, Eddie, Linc, and Raven would be the only passengers until they were able to rescue Juan.

They got into the cab, which was painted to look filthy. Though the leather seats were torn and stained, they were soft and supportive. Eddie took the passenger seat, while Linc stepped into the back and opened the cargo bay hatch so he could unpack firearms. Raven got behind the wheel and fired up the engine. It burbled like a regular diesel would, but Eddie could feel the immense power coursing through the chassis.

Raven toggled a switch, and the antiquated dashboard retracted and flipped over, revealing a high-tech control panel that gave them access to all of the onboard weaponry. It also had a large LCD screen displaying a map of Argentina. Juan's tracker was flashing in red.

"Looks like they're seventy miles outside of Buenos Aires," Raven said.

Eddie did the math and said, "That makes our intercept point about twenty-five miles north of the prison at Las Armas. It'll be close."

"Don't worry," Raven said. "I'm a leadfoot."

She put the PIG into gear and steered it out of the port. As they left, the *Oregon* was already untied from the dock and putting out to sea.

The convoy from Buenos Aires had been on the road for two hours now, and Juan continued to flex his fingers behind his back to keep the blood flowing to them. The cuffs weren't too tight, but sitting in that position for so long in the back of the SUV was awkward. At least they didn't put a seat belt over the jumpsuit he was wearing. That would have made it more difficult to act if the situation presented itself.

Still, he was impressed with the precautions taken by Colonel Sánchez, who sat in the passenger seat in front of Juan. Tate must have warned him not to take any risks.

Next to Juan was a huge mercenary holding a Heckler & Koch MP5 submachine gun with the barrel aimed at him. He never took his eyes off Juan. Both in front of and behind the SUV were Swiss-made MOWAG Grenadier armored cars that each carried a .50 caliber machine gun mounted on a turret. Juan had also seen the mercenaries loading several Rocket-Propelled Grenade launchers into the vehicles.

If Sánchez had truly taken Tate's advice seriously, he would have ridden with Juan in the armored cars. However, it seemed the colonel preferred the comforts of leather seats and air-conditioning instead and wanted to keep his prisoner close by.

Juan had been nonchalantly watching the road traffic ever since they'd left Army headquarters. If the *Oregon* was tracking him and attempted a rescue, the highway would present the best opportunity. Or he hoped it would.

A few minutes later, a truck with a familiar logo passed them going in the other direction. He saw it for only a moment, but he recognized the false name VERTEGAS on its side.

It was the PIG.

"Colonel, what if I have to go to the bathroom?" Juan asked.

"You'll wait. We're only thirty miles from the prison."

"And if I can't?"

Sánchez turned and snarled at him. "If you mess up my SUV, your stay at the prison will get off to an even worse start than you can imagine."

"I imagine it's not going to be pleasant, although the concrete floor in my cell last night was surprisingly comfortable."

Sánchez looked at the mercenary. "If he doesn't hold it, you have my permission to shoot him in the kneecap."

The mercenary grinned. "*Sí, Colonel.*"

"That's okay," Juan said. "I'll try to hold it."

He knew what was coming and wanted to help out if he could, so Juan shifted his position in apparent discomfort as if he had to go badly. In reality, he was moving his right leg around, loosening the poorly fitted prosthetic limb. After a few moments, he felt it come free, propped up only by the jumpsuit leg.

Now he was ready for the attack.

34

After passing the convoy, going the opposite direction, and turning around in a small town a mile ahead, Raven caught up with them and pulled the PIG up behind the rear armored car as if she were about to pass. There was nothing but fertile farms and grazing land on either side of the four-lane divided highway, and the traffic was light at midday.

Having already passed the convoy, Raven had seen that they were up against some formidable firepower. The Ford SUV was pretty standard, but the two four-wheeled MOWAG Grenadiers looked like genuine war machines, the kind of angular, steel-plated vehicles you'd expect to see patrolling a burned-out town in Syria, not racing down a freeway.

"Can you take out both armored cars?" she asked Eddie.

"Not with Juan in the SUV between them," he answered. "Too risky. We'll have to take out the trailing armored car, then you run the SUV off the road so I have a clear shot at the other one."

"Works for me."

"You ready back there?" Eddie called over his shoulder.

"Armed and dangerous," said Linc, who was standing by the door in the cargo bay. "I'll get the Chairman out of the SUV as soon as we're stopped."

"Okay," Eddie said, peering down at the weapons controls. "Here we go."

He pressed the button, and a rocket leaped from one of the side racks. It shot down the road and blew apart the trailing armored car's left rear wheel. Raven dodged to the right as it veered left into the grassy median and flipped over, throwing sod and metal parts high into the air.

The drivers of both the leading armored car and the SUV stepped on the gas.

"Get closer before that armored car's machine gun can get a bead on us," Eddie said.

"Remember what I mentioned earlier?" Raven asked, flipping the switch on the PIG's nitrous-boost system. "I'm a leadfoot."

The PIG blasted forward.

Vamos! Vamos!" Sánchez shouted at the SUV's driver when he saw the armored car get hit by a rocket and somersault behind them.

The mercenary guarding Juan was distracted because he had turned around to watch the crash and the PIG chasing them, so Juan's moment of opportunity had arrived.

He lifted himself up in the seat and pulled his wrists under him. A two-legged man would have to be a contortionist to pull the hand-cuffed arms past his feet, but Juan was able to get the cuffs past the stump below his right knee. Once that was accomplished, it was easy to get his hands over his left foot.

The whole maneuver took less than two seconds, and by the time the guard turned back around, Juan elbowed him in the head, slamming it against the bulletproof glass.

The guy slumped into unconsciousness.

Juan's cuffed wrists were too close together to use the guard's MP5, so he leaned forward and threw his hands over the driver's neck.

The SUV swerved back and forth as the driver battled with Juan. Sánchez drew his pistol and tried to shoot Juan, so Juan released the driver and grabbed the colonel's hand aiming the gun. They wrestled, as the driver got the SUV back under control, but Sánchez had better leverage.

Juan wrenched Sánchez's hand just as he pulled the trigger.

The bullet went through the driver's head. Blood spattered the ballistic glass, and then he collapsed on the steering wheel.

While Sánchez struggled to get hold of the wheel, Juan recognized that it was a lost cause. He sat back and whipped the seat belt over his torso. The metal buckle clicked at the same time that the speeding SUV swerved through the shoulder and dipped into the ditch next to the road.

The top-heavy SUV tumbled onto its side, and all the air bags went off.

Raven watched in horror as the SUV cartwheeled off the road. It violently flipped twice and came to rest on its tires. She pulled to a stop next to the wrecked vehicle, and Linc and Eddie leaped out of the PIG.

The armored car ahead of them braked, did a U-turn, and crossed the median to the other side of the highway. Raven was about to target it with a rocket, but it shielded itself behind a van that had come to a stop on the opposite side of the highway. The body of the van had IGLESIA DE SANTA MARÍA emblazoned on it. St. Mary's Church.

She couldn't shoot at the armored car without the risk of killing the churchgoers, some of whom had gotten out and were on their cell phones as they looked at the SUV wreckage.

The soldiers in the armored car had no such qualms about

bystanders. Church members dove to the ground as the .50 caliber machine gun in the turret opened fire. The PIG wasn't designed to withstand such a heavy barrage, and the huge rounds started pouring through the cab.

She knew it was time to abandon ship and scrambled out of the PIG through the open passenger door.

Juan shook his head as he regained his senses. The first thing he noticed was Sánchez's face in front of him. Wide eyes stared at him blankly, a broken windshield wiper protruding from his neck. Apparently, the colonel had not been wearing his seat belt.

The next thing that got Juan's attention was knocking on the window. He saw Linc pounding on the glass and looking in. Juan gestured that he was all right, though he did feel some blood trickling down his face.

The door wouldn't open, so he motioned Linc to the driver's side. The guard next to Juan was now lying in the truck bed, which allowed him to lean over and pop the lock.

Eddie yanked the door open while Juan unlatched his seat belt.

"Are you okay, Chairman?"

They were interrupted by the thump of heavy machine gun fire. Shells tore into the PIG as Juan pushed himself out of the SUV.

Eddie and Linc helped him take cover in the ditch behind the PIG. Raven joined them a moment later.

Eddie produced a handcuff key and unlocked Juan's wrist. Then he took out some gauze and pressed it against Juan's forehead.

"You got a nasty cut in the crash," Eddie said.

"Better than the alternative," Juan said. "Life in prison didn't sound fun."

"Thought you might need this," Linc said, handing Juan his spare combat leg.

"And I didn't get a present for you," Juan said, strapping it on quickly. "Now, how do we get out of here with that armored car pouring rounds into our ride?"

"Max assumed this was a one-way mission for the PIG," Raven said, pulling the truck's remote control from her pocket.

Eddie nodded. "We didn't think we'd get it back onto the ship without awkward questions about it suffering serious damage."

"Not to mention the bounty that must be out for me right about now," Juan added.

"That, too . . . Raven, time to lead them away from here so we can make our rendezvous undisturbed."

Raven nodded, and the PIG began to belch dense smoke. After a huge cloud had surrounded them and the truck, she revved the engine. The PIG barreled down the highway toward Las Armas.

Moments later, the armored car crossed back across the median and gave chase, continuing to fire at the fleeing truck.

"We'll wait for them to get a few miles down the road," Eddie said.

Juan didn't have to ask what they were waiting for. He heard it. The throbbing rotor blades of a helicopter.

The smoke dissipated completely with the arrival of the *Oregon*'s MD 520N, a chopper without a tail rotor that steered itself using the turbine's exhaust gasses. Gomez, who was wearing mirrored shades and a Houston Astros baseball cap, smoothly settled the aircraft on a field of grass next to the highway and gave a jaunty wave when he was down.

Eddie handed out black balaclavas in case any curious onlookers in traffic were filming the action, and they all pulled them over their heads before rushing over to the helicopter and climbing on.

Juan got into the seat next to Gomez, who pointed at the bloody gauze sticking out of the balaclava.

When Juan had his headset on, Gomez said, "You okay?"

"I'll be fine," Juan replied. "Thanks for coming to get me."

Gomez gave him a movie star wattage smile. "My pleasure, Chairman. Just glad to have you back. The *Oregon*'s waiting for us twenty miles off the coast. For some reason, Max didn't want me to rise out of the cargo hold in the middle of Mar del Plata Harbor."

When the doors were closed, Gomez pulled back on the collective, and the helicopter rose into the air. As they flew east across the highway toward the *Oregon* and gained altitude, Juan looked south, where he could see the PIG racing down the road with the armored car in hot pursuit.

"Anytime it's clear," Eddie said to Raven over the intercom.

She waited until there weren't any other cars within three hundred yards.

"Activating self-destruct," she said. "That'll do, PIG."

The mortar rounds inside the PIG detonated. In combination with the fuel drums in back, it created an enormous fireball that engulfed the entire highway. The armored car careened off the road to avoid the explosion.

With a blast that huge, there would be little left of the truck, and certainly nothing to trace back to the *Oregon*. Still, it was a big price to pay for Juan's freedom, and he couldn't help but think of everything that Zachariah Tate had cost them already. He was sick of being on the defensive.

It was time to fight back.

35

Once he got back to his cabin aboard the *Oregon*, Juan took a long—very long—hot shower, a luxury he had even more appreciation for now after his night in the filthy cell. As he put on his leg and clothes in his bedroom, he heard a knock at the outer door. That would be Maurice with a late lunch specially prepared by Chef.

"Come in!" Juan called out.

He didn't hear the door open, but the sound of dishes and glasses clinking on the table in his office/living room soon followed.

When he was dressed, he went out to see Maurice completing an immaculate setting for two.

"It's a pleasure to have you back on the *Oregon*, Captain," Maurice said. "I trust that you are on the mend."

Juan touched the spot on his temple where Julia had put in four stitches.

"Just a little bump on the noggin," he said. "Thanks for the meal. The jail I was in last night isn't exactly Michelin-rated."

"No, I suppose not. Chef has prepared filet mignon with béarnaise sauce, garlic scalloped potatoes, and Brussels sprouts in a blood orange balsamic reduction. I have taken the liberty of pairing it with a Château Montrose Bordeaux." Maurice poured the decanted rich red wine into large crystal goblets.

Juan's mouth began to water at the savory aroma wafting from the feast. "I trust your judgment implicitly, Maurice."

"The feeling is mutual, Captain."

That was about as gushing a compliment as Juan could ever expect from the unflappable steward.

There was another knock on the door, and Juan opened it to see Langston Overholt waiting outside.

"Lang, welcome to the *Oregon*," Juan said, shaking his old mentor's hand. "Please come in and join me for dinner to celebrate your first visit to the ship. Not the way I would have liked it to happen, of course."

"Thank you," Overholt said as he entered. "It smells delicious." He glanced at the bottle in Maurice's hand. "Château Montrose. Excellent choice. Is it the 2007?"

"It is the 2006, Mr. Overholt," Maurice replied.

"It sounds like you two have met."

"Not yet, actually," Overholt said.

"I'm not surprised Maurice knows your name," Juan said. "Not only is he the best steward on the Seven Seas, he's also the most well-informed person on the ship."

As the two older men shook hands, Maurice had an odd look on his face.

"Forgive me, sir, but haven't we met?"

Overholt wore a similar expression of recognition. "You look familiar to me as well. For some reason, Admiral Beale of the Royal Navy comes to mind."

Maurice nodded. "I served under Admiral Beale when he was captain of the HMS *Invincible*."

"Yes, I remember now," Overholt said. He turned to Juan and said, "This was long ago, back in my days as a field officer at the Agency.

We brought a defecting KGB officer back to Maurice's aircraft carrier, and the Royal Navy generously hosted us for a few days until we could get him back to America. I imagine Maurice and I were both at the start of our careers during that mission." He turned back to Maurice. "I'd love to reminisce with you a little later over drinks. Not many people in our cohort left to remember the olden days."

"I would be honored." He looked at Juan. "Captain, please ring when you'd like me to remove your dishes."

"Thanks, Maurice."

The courtly steward picked up the silver tray and left as quietly as he had entered.

Juan and Overholt sat down and ate heartily, each of them recounting the events of the past two days.

When they were done with the recap, Juan brought up the theory about the sonic weapon that Julia had told him while she was suturing his wound.

"She thinks that the metal hull of the *Oregon* vibrated in a resonant frequency when this sonic device hit it, transmitting the signal throughout the ship and affecting the entire crew."

"I'd say her theory's correct given the immunity that Linda Ross seemed to have," Overholt said.

"The question is, how do we fight a weapon like that? I can't very well make my entire crew deaf."

"What about earmuffs or -plugs?"

"It's worth a shot, but Julia doesn't think it would work. The harmonic tones could be infrasound, and the low frequencies aren't as well blocked by hearing protection. The resonance might be carried by bone conduction, like our molar mics."

"I know the U.S. military has done experiments along these lines, but no one has produced results anywhere near what your crew has experienced."

Juan shook his head in frustration. "They tell me that they would have jumped overboard or destroyed the ship to escape their hallucinations. We got very lucky that Linda was unaffected. I don't want to count on luck again, but if we don't have an effective countermeasure, we'll be at Tate's mercy if we battle the *Portland*. There's got to be some way to neutralize it."

Overholt sat back and got a faraway look in his eye.

"Tate did let something slip while I was on board the *Portland*. He said they sank the *Kansas City* partially because someone aboard had critical knowledge he seemed to consider dangerous. I recall the exact quote because it seemed important. 'That SEAL was too curious about his cousins' deaths.'"

"So there was a Navy SEAL on the *KC* who Tate was so concerned about that he sank a nuclear sub to conceal it?"

"That seems to be the case. Could they still be alive?"

Juan considered that before saying, "Although it's been more than ten days, it's possible. If the hull wasn't breached, there could be enough air for the crew to survive that long. I know bottoming tests on Los Angeles–class subs have shown crews can last up to two weeks with battery power and by burning emergency O_2 candles."

"But where are they?" Overholt asked. "It doesn't seem the Navy has found it yet. If Tate led them to the wrong location with that SEPIRB, the search could be going on hundreds of miles away from the *KC*'s actual wreckage site."

Juan snapped his fingers. "Tate revealed something else to me as well. He said the sub was somewhere off the coast of Algodoal."

Juan tapped on his tablet and put a map of Brazil on his HD wall screen. He pointed to a small town near the mouth of the Amazon River.

"There. The *Kansas City* has to be somewhere off the coast of that region."

"That's a lot of ocean to cover," Overholt said.

"Three thousand square miles, depending on how far out the *KC* was when she sank. The search could still take weeks. And if she bottomed out deeper than two thousand feet, the hull would definitely be crushed."

"No," Overholt said, "Tate mentioned that the depth he told you was accurate. The *Oregon* was just looking two thousand miles from the right place."

"So the *KC* really is lying in two hundred fifty feet of water?"

Overholt nodded. "Is that significant?"

Juan didn't answer. Instead, he put up the Atlantic Ocean depth chart on the screen and then zoomed in on the Brazilian coast. He stood and went over to the monitor.

"Here's the edge of the continental shelf," he said, tracing a line vaguely mirroring the coastline. "The seafloor averages about a hundred feet in depth until it gets to this ledge. Then it drops rapidly to the abyssal plain. The edge of the shelf is the only place where the ocean is two hundred fifty feet deep."

"Do you think the *Kansas City* came to rest on a ledge?" Overholt asked.

"That's what Tate is implying. All the Navy would have to do is follow this line and they'd find the *KC* in a day."

"We have to call the U.S. Navy and tell them they need to alter their search grid."

"Do you think they'd believe you?"

"I doubt it," Overholt said. "I've used up most of my governmental favors."

"To rescue me?" Juan asked ruefully.

"It was worth it, my boy."

"Thanks."

"I'll see what I can do with the Navy."

Juan looked at the map and did some calculations in his head. "In case they don't believe you, we have the capability to dive on the sub at that depth." He picked up the phone and dialed the op center. "Hali, have Eric set course for Algodoal, Brazil, maximum speed."

"Algodoal, Brazil," Hali replied. "Aye, Chairman."

Juan hung up and looked at Overholt. "We'll be there in a little more than two days."

Not only did they have to hope that someone among the *Kansas City*'s crew was still alive, they also needed an answer for why Zachariah Tate wanted so badly to sink it.

36

The soundproof chamber inside the *Portland* was one of the few features that she didn't share with the *Oregon*. The room was designed to test the effects of the sonic disruptor without harming the rest of the crew. Now thirty-six hours after the unsuccessful attack on the *Oregon*, it was activated again, with two men in it this time. Today, it was being used for punishment. Each man was in a straitjacket.

From the observation room, Tate watched the men, who were tied to chairs, struggle to get loose from the bindings. The cameras provided a panoramic view of the room and a close-up of Abdel Farouk's and Li Quon's faces. Both of them were terrified by the gruesome visions that the disruptor was creating in their minds.

Tate turned to the operator and said, "How long until they succumb to a psychotic break?"

"Hard to say," the man replied. "Could be in as little as ten more minutes. They've been in there for twenty already."

The inability to combat visions had to be excruciating. A man could take only so much before breaking.

"Shut it down," Tate said.

The operator pushed the ABORT button, and the disruptor was turned off. Farouk and Li, who were sweating profusely, immediately slumped in the seats, exhausted by the ordeal.

Tate activated the intercom. "I hope we've learned a lesson here. Failure is not tolerated on this crew. You were responsible for the *Oregon* and you allowed her to get away. I assume you won't botch an operation again in the future."

Both men vigorously shook their heads.

"Good to hear. You two are valuable to the team, but penalties are an unfortunate necessity when you let the team down." He looked at the operator. "Go in and untie them."

The operator left the room and went into the chamber to unstrap the men. Tate cut the camera feed.

He could have killed them both—wanted to, in fact—but they had skills that couldn't easily be found again. And whittling down the number of his crew was inefficient. They got the message, and so did the rest of the men. The camera feed of the punishment had been broadcast throughout the ship to reinforce for everyone that they should be diligent.

As he left the observation room, he was met by Catherine Ballard, who had a worried look on her face as they walked back to their shared cabin.

"You didn't like the show?"

Ballard shook her head. "No, I did, it was very effective."

"Then what is it?"

"We just received a notification from our contact in the Argentinian military. Juan Cabrillo got away."

Tate abruptly stopped. "What?"

"The convoy they were transporting him in was attacked."

"And we're just finding out about this now?"

"It made the news, but was reported as a terrorist event. Three vehicles were destroyed, including the one that initiated the assault. At first, they thought Cabrillo was killed when the attacking vehicle exploded, but they realized later that it was empty. The investigators found no bodies."

"I told Sánchez to be set for something like that," Tate fumed as he continued walking. "I could kill him."

"Too late," Ballard said. "He was found in the wreckage of his SUV impaled by a windshield wiper."

"He was punished for his failure. If Juan wasn't in the vehicle, how did he get away?"

"Some of the witnesses reported a helicopter taking off. They assumed it was a medical rescue flight."

Tate burst into the cabin and sank into the sofa to think. Ballard followed him in and closed the door behind her.

"What do we do now?" she asked. "We still haven't had any success tracking down the *Oregon*'s current position."

"If we had known they were rescuing Juan, we could have intercepted them two days ago," Tate said, pounding his fist into a cushion. "Maybe I should have left Farouk and Li in that chamber until their brains turned to jelly."

Ballard looked at him like she wanted to say something but hesitated.

"What?" Tate demanded.

"You mentioned Algodoal to Cabrillo. He'll know the general area to search for the *Kansas City*."

Tate sat up when he realized what that meant. "Do you think he's going after the sub?"

"Possibly. If he finds Jiménez still alive . . ." she said, her voice trailing off as she contemplated the implications.

"They can't be alive down there in that tin can."

"Do we want to take that risk?"

"If he's really going there, the *Oregon* has a nearly two-day head start on us. We'd never catch up in time."

"Maybe we don't have to. What if we reveal the location of the sub before they get there?"

"Then the U.S. Navy will rescue the sailors if they're still alive."

"But Cabrillo won't have any access to them. They might as well be on Mars, as far as he is concerned."

Tate nodded and smiled. "You see? That's why I fell in love with you. Always thinking ahead."

"Should we call the Navy?"

"No, I have a better plan. You and I will fly up there and take a helicopter out to drop the activated SEPIRB in the water right where the *KC* is. That'll bring every warship in the area running. The *Oregon* won't be able to get close."

"We're going personally?" Ballard asked.

"I'd send Farouk and Li alone, but no doubt they'd need some supervision. Besides, we have another task to complete in that region. The real key is keeping Juan from finding the *Bremen*. Since Jiménez knew where it was, someone else might locate it, too. You and I are going to find it first and wipe it out once and for all."

They had some clues about the German U-boat's location, but Tate had thought killing the Brazilian cousins who originally stumbled upon it would take care of the problem. Now he realized he needed to erase its existence.

Ballard grinned back at him. "Going back to wipe out the source of the sonic disruptor? I like it."

"Once that's done, we can spend all of our time locating Juan and destroying his ship."

The germ of a plan for ambushing the *Oregon* was forming in Tate's mind. But this time, he wanted the odds overwhelmingly in his favor. During the flight to northern Brazil, he'd call his friend in the Chinese Navy. The contact badly wanted to get his hands on the plans for the sonic disruptor after seeing what Tate had done to the *Kansas City*. Instead of money, Tate would ask for help in sinking the *Oregon*.

37

OFF THE COAST OF THE STATE OF PARÁ, BRAZIL

As Juan had feared, the U.S. Navy ignored Overholt's plea to change their search grid, so the *Oregon* had rounded the eastern tip of Brazil and raced up the edge of the continental shelf. The trip took just fifty-four hours, from the time they left the coast of Argentina until they stopped just short of the Amazon River Delta. They started the sonar search for the *Kansas City* at a spot southeast of the small coastal town of Algodoal.

The *Oregon*'s sensors swept the shelf's underwater cliff, focusing on a depth of two hundred fifty feet. For the first four hours, they found nothing, and Juan, who was seated in his command chair in the op center, was beginning to wonder whether this had all been an elaborate ruse planted by Tate.

When they were at nearly the same latitude as Algodoal, Linda called out from her spot at the radar station. Her Google glasses didn't seem to be hindering her too much, especially because everyone in the op center was wearing a lavalier microphone to help Linda distinguish who was speaking.

"Chairman, I'm picking up a stationary vessel twenty miles dead ahead."

Stationary? Juan frowned. Could it be the *Portland* lying in ambush?

"Tate couldn't possibly have gotten here ahead of us, could he?" Max asked from his engineering post, echoing Juan's concern.

"Slow to five knots," Juan said.

"Five knots, aye," Eric replied from the helm.

"What type of vessel is it?" Juan looked at Linda.

"It's not broadcasting an AIS signal. Too small for a cargo vessel. Bigger than a fishing trawler. Might be a warship."

Commercial vessels over three hundred tons were required to send out an Automatic Identification System signal to help prevent collisions. Although naval vessels also carried them, they tended to use them intermittently or only in poor conditions to prevent enemy ships from tracking them.

"Hail them," Juan said to Hali.

"Unknown vessel to the north," Hali said into his headset mic, "this is the cargo vessel *Anacapa*. Please respond."

"Put it on speaker so I can talk to them," Juan said.

After a moment, an accented voice replied, "*Anacapa*, this is the Brazilian Navy corvette *Barosso*. We need no assistance."

"We picked up an odd signal from this area," Juan said, even though they hadn't. "It seemed to be centered on your current location. That's why we were worried when we saw you stopped."

"We need no assistance," the voice repeated. "Do not approach us. Stay at least two miles away."

"Understood, *Barosso*. Over and out."

"Communication ended," Hali said.

"Yeah," Max said. "They found the *Kansas City*."

"Murph," Juan said, "do you think they have any rescue capability on the *Barosso*?"

Murph, who was an expert on foreign navies' weaponry, shook his head. "Not unless they brought the equipment specifically for that purpose. The Inhaúma-class corvettes are designed for anti-submarine warfare."

"How long until the U.S. Navy can arrive with a DSRV?"

A Deep-Submergence Rescue Vehicle was a mini-sub built to connect to a nuclear submarine stranded underwater and transfer its crew to safety.

"If the Navy already shipped it down here and attached it to another sub, maybe twelve to eighteen hours, depending on where they are right now. Twice as long if the DSRV is still in the U.S."

With a disabled sub, every minute counted. If any of the crew was still alive, that could easily change if they had to wait another twelve hours.

"What if we go down and check on it ourselves?" Juan asked Max. "Nomad's air lock can double as a decompression chamber. If there are survivors, we could get some of them out."

Max shrugged. "It's worth a shot. But I don't think that corvette would take too kindly to us just hanging around in the vicinity when they're protecting a sunken U.S. sub."

"We'll pass by slowly enough to launch the Nomad when we're two miles out. You take the *Oregon* out past their radar range and turn around with a new name on the stern. Pick us up on your way back."

"Oh, no," Max said. "I'm going with you this time. Eric can handle the *Oregon*."

Even though Eric was the best ship driver on the *Oregon* other than Juan, his first inclination was to have Max in command in case things got dicey.

When Juan began to object, Max added, "Don't make me mutiny."

Juan laughed. He obviously had no choice. "Fine. You can pilot Nomad. But we'll go light in case we need room for passengers. Just you, me, and MacD."

"Because of the heliox?"

Juan nodded. At a depth of two hundred fifty feet, they'd need drysuits and a combination of helium and oxygen in the tanks instead of just oxygen. But breathing that mixture could be tricky without proper training, and MacD was the only other crew member rated for heliox diving besides Juan.

Since they had readied the Nomad for launch in case they found the *Kansas City*, it would only take twenty minutes to go through the checklist and put it in the water. The *Oregon* could get to the *Barosso*'s two-mile limit in that time from twenty miles out, but seeing a cargo freighter move at such a high velocity would be highly suspicious to the captain of the Brazilian warship.

"Stoney," Juan said, "adjust your speed to put us within two miles of the *Barosso* in forty-five minutes. You have the conn."

"Aye, Chairman," Eric replied.

"Hali, call MacD and tell him to meet us at the moon pool."

"Aye, Chairman."

As Juan and Max left the op center, Juan said, "Remember, this is an anti-submarine corvette. If they detect an unknown submersible around the *Kansas City*, they'll probably be very upset."

"No problem," Max said. "I'll take us in below the thermocline and put Nomad's motors into quiet mode. The corvette will never hear us coming."

38

Once the Nomad was released from the underside of the *Oregon*, it took the submersible a half hour to reach the location where the *Barosso* was station-keeping. Max brought them up from a depth of eight hundred feet, following the contours of the steep slope of the continental shelf.

As they rose, the Nomad's lights illuminating the way, Juan, Max, and MacD crowded into the polycarbonate nose cockpit, straining for a glimpse of their target. While Max was in shirtsleeves, Juan and MacD were already in drysuits. All they'd need to don before getting in the air lock would be the masks.

The depth gauge read three hundred feet when MacD said, "There she is. Man, she's a big sucker."

The *Kansas City*'s bow was protruding over the lip of a ledge. Juan could make out the port torpedo tube doors.

"At least she went down upright," Max said. "I don't see any damage yet."

"Let's check her out from stem to stern," Juan said.

Max put the Nomad in front of the bow and kept rising until they were at the same depth as the *KC*'s sail—what submariners in old days called the conning tower. He pushed the Nomad forward, and it didn't take long to see what sank the *Kansas City*.

A gash thirty feet long had been carved into the starboard side near the bow. From the scrapes on the hull, it looked like the sub had collided with the cliff's edge.

"Ah'm no expert," MacD said, "but that is not a good sign that we'll find survivors."

"We made it this far," Juan said, despite his shared pessimism, "we might as well do our due diligence. There doesn't seem to have been an explosion on this end. Let's keep going."

Max piloted the Nomad toward the stern. As they maneuvered around the sail, they could see that it was intact. When they got past it, a large cylinder the size of the Nomad was visible resting on the deck just aft of the sail.

"What in the name of Fat Tuesday is that thing?" MacD asked.

"That's right," Juan said. "I keep forgetting you aren't a Navy man. That's called a dry deck shelter." Even though MacD had spent the last few years on the *Oregon* becoming an expert diver, his military experience was as an Army Ranger.

"The tube holds three compartments," Max said. "A decompression chamber on the bow end, an air lock in the middle that's connected to the forward escape trunk, and a hangar for a SEAL Delivery Vehicle in the aft end."

"Ah get it," MacD said. "They use it for infiltration missions the way we use the moon pool on the *Oregon*."

"Exactly."

"Then we won't have easy access to that escape trunk," Juan said. "Besides, since the only damage we've seen so far is in the bow, the stern is the most likely place to find survivors."

Max pressed on, and they spotted no other hull breaches. What they did see was an avalanche of rocks that had slid from the cliff above and landed on the portion of the hull where the stern escape trunk hatch was located. What had to be a ton was covering it.

"No wonder nobody got out," Max said.

"We need to find out if anyone is conscious inside," Juan said. "Apply the contact transceiver."

They could have used the robotic arm to tap out Morse code on the *KC*'s hull, but the banging would have been loud enough for the *Barosso* to hear, alerting the corvette to the Nomad's presence. Instead, they'd fitted a special device that they could press against the nuclear sub's hull to communicate with anyone inside by voice, just like pressing an ear to the wall.

Max lowered the transceiver until it touched the *Kansas City*.

"Go ahead," Max said.

Juan spoke into the microphone. "Attention, USS *Kansas City* crew members. Is there anyone in there?"

Nothing but static played through the Nomad's speakers. Juan repeated the hail.

"You think we'll be able to hear their voices?" Juan asked Max.

"Never really tried this before, so they may not even be hearing us. The hull does have sound insulation."

Juan picked up the mic again. "*KC* crew members, if you can hear this, tap on the outer hatch."

They waited. Still nothing. Juan tried again. This time, he heard a tap of metal on metal.

It was Morse code. Since MacD wasn't a Navy vet, Juan interpreted the letters as they came in.

We . . . hear . . . you . . .

"'We'?" Max repeated, sounding elated that they'd found anyone at all. "How many are in there?"

Juan relayed the question.

Twenty-six in engine room. Rest of sub flooded.

Out of a normal crew complement of a hundred twenty-nine—maybe more, since there were Navy SEALs on board—only twenty-six were still alive. Tate had killed over a hundred U.S. sailors to cover his crimes.

"What's your situation?" Juan asked them.

Have immersion suits. But hatch jammed.

Immersion suits were emergency survival gear stored on the sub. To escape a downed sub, the sailors would put them on and enter the escape trunk's air lock. When the hatch opened, the buoyant suits, which were equipped with short-term breathing apparatuses, would float to the surface and double as life rafts until help arrived. The problem was, the sailors couldn't get the hatch open to escape.

"There's about a ton of rocks covering the hatch. How much air do you have left?"

CO_2 building. Estimate three hours O_2 left.

"I don't think the U.S. Navy will get here before then," Max said.

"Then we have to get those rocks off so they can get out," Juan said.

"I agree. But if we start moving them around with the robotic arm, the *Barosso* might hear us."

"Let's do it," MacD said. "We gotta get those boys out."

Juan nodded. They'd have to risk it.

"We're going to clear the hatch so you can get out," Juan told the desperate men below them.

Thank you.

Max detached the transceiver and moved the Nomad to the hatch. With careful precision, he controlled the submersible while Juan operated the robotic arm. He began lifting rocks and carrying them away one by one. It was a tedious task, but there were no shortcuts. It would be worse to cause a second avalanche that covered the hatch all over again.

Fifteen minutes in, MacD said, "Do you hear that?"

Juan was so intent on picking up rocks that he hadn't heard anything.

"What was it?" he asked MacD.

"Ah thought Ah heard a faint tapping."

Juan told Max to pause for a moment. Perhaps the sub crew was trying to tell them something.

Then he did hear it. Taps on metal. But it had a higher pitch than the ones they'd heard before.

The tapping continued.

"It's another Morse code message," Juan said.

SOS. In DDS.

Max looked at Juan in surprise when he understood the message.

"What are they saying?" MacD asked. "Is there a problem in the engine room?"

"It's not coming from the engine room," Juan said. "Someone is still alive in the dry deck shelter."

39

When Michael Bradley first heard the faint voices emanating through the hull, he thought he'd become delusional after spending days in the dry deck shelter's decompression chamber, hoping to be rescued. Then he recognized a few words and realized with great relief that he was no longer alone.

Situation . . . Air . . . left . . . Hatch . . . Get . . . out . . .

There was a rescue team outside, and it sounded like they were talking to someone, which implied there were survivors in the stern section of the *Kansas City*.

He had to let them know he was alive as well. That's when he picked up a wrench with his good arm and began slamming it against the wall.

He did that for fifteen minutes before he had to drop the wrench due to exhaustion.

When he first entered the chamber twelve days ago, he thought he had a few hours to live at most before his air ran out. He even wrote a good-bye message to his family and recorded the events leading up to the sinking in his little notebook.

But then something strange happened. The lights, heat, and air never went off. The *KC* was still feeding power to the DDS, so he actually had a chance to make it out if the Navy found him before the batteries died. He'd set his broken arm and secured it with duct tape to keep it in place before ransacking the decompression chamber for supplies. He discovered a small tool kit, as well as several Soldier Fuel energy bars and some bottles of water, in an emergency pack. Even with rationing, he had eaten the last bar four days before, and drank the last of the water six hours earlier that day, so he thought it really was the end until he heard the odd voices.

After a minute's rest, he picked up the wrench again and beat it against the metal, tapping out the same message.

SOS. In DDS.

He didn't get any response. The voices had disappeared.

But he wouldn't give up. Not until his last breath was gone. That's one thing the Basic Underwater Demolition/SEAL training course had taught him. BUD/S was all about carrying on through pain, fatigue, hunger, thirst, and cold. Anyone who wasn't up to the challenge could Drop on Request, DOR, which meant ringing a brass ship's bell three times. The people who washed out were the ones lacking the will to go on in the face of agony and desperation.

If Bradley could make it through the Hell Week of BUD/S, he was not going to ring the bell now.

He continued banging until his muscles were on fire. He screamed to get through the pain.

Then he heard something and stopped, dropping the wrench to the floor. There was a mechanical sound, as if a hatch were opening.

He looked through the tiny window into the air lock and saw nothing but darkness. He used a flashlight and shined it on the hatch down to the *Kansas City*'s escape trunk, but it remained motionless.

Then he heard another sound and was amazed to see a light bouncing around in the SEAL Delivery Vehicle hangar. The wheel on the hangar hatch turned.

When it opened, a man in a black drysuit and yellow dive helmet entered. He was carrying a large dive bag with him. He saw Bradley's flashlight and came over to the decompression chamber hatch. Bradley could see that his equipment included a rebreather for the heliox tank on his back.

The diver motioned to the air lock controls on his side. Bradley gave him the *OK* signal.

A few minutes later, the lock had drained and filled with air. The diver removed his helmet and twisted the hatch wheel until it opened. The man had a blond crew cut and blue eyes that glittered with intelligence.

"Hi, there," he said in a high pitch that lowered as the helium left his lungs. "I'm Juan Cabrillo. Time to get you out of here."

"Michael Bradley," the man said, still stunned that he was free of the decompression chamber. "What ship are you from?"

"That's a little complicated. I'm not in the Navy."

"You're not? Who are you, then?"

"Just a Good Samaritan. We don't have much time before your crewmates start coming out and getting the attention of the Brazilian warship above us."

"My crewmates? How many are still alive?"

"Twenty-six."

Bradley was both elated that some of his fellow sailors had made it and heartbroken that it was so few.

"Only twenty-six," Bradley repeated softly.

"I hate to break it to you, but it has become a bit ripe in there," Cabrillo said, pointing inside the chamber. "Let's close it up so we can leave."

The only thing Bradley wanted to retain from his ordeal was the notebook. He pocketed it and stepped into the air lock while Cabrillo unpacked what he'd been carrying. It was another drysuit and helmet.

"How did you know it would only be me in here?" Bradley asked.

"I didn't. Figured I might have to make multiple trips. Have you ever used heliox?"

"Once."

"I hope the suit fits, because we don't have any other options. MacD looks about your size."

Bradley started putting on the suit. "MacD?"

"The guy who was wearing this suit until a few minutes ago. He's back on Nomad, helping clear off the rear escape trunk. Besides, we only have room for two at a time in our air lock."

None of this was making any sense to Bradley, but he didn't have much choice but to go with Cabrillo.

He'd finished gingerly pulling his suit over his broken arm when they heard a loud ping.

"Was that from your sub?" Bradley asked as Cabrillo handed him the helmet.

Juan shook his head. "That's from the *Barosso*. We need to get out of here."

The corvette on the surface had just scanned them with their active sonar.

Captain Tomás Vega, the *Barosso*'s commanding officer, doubted that his sonar officer really had heard a scraping noise coming from the *Kansas City*, but he couldn't take the chance that something else was down there. He was responsible for the nuclear sub until the U.S. Navy arrived and he wasn't going to give his country a black eye by letting something happen to it before the Americans could attempt a rescue.

"Anything on the scope?" Vega asked the sonar man.

"Contact bearing two-seven-five!"

"Identify."

"Small submersible. Unknown origin. It has moved away from the *Kansas City*."

Vega turned to the communications officer. "Radio the U.S. Navy. Find out if they have any ships or subs operating in the area."

After a minute, the comms officer said, "Negative. The U.S. says they don't have anything close to us."

"Then we have to consider an unknown sub hostile," Vega said. "Put some distance between us and the *Kansas City*." He looked at the weapons officer. "Prepare to fire an anti-submarine torpedo."

40

Juan's mind was racing as he tried to put himself in the *Barosso*'s captain's shoes. They would likely consider a strange sub hovering near the *Kansas City* a threat. That meant the Nomad was in danger, and it was defenseless.

When Juan had squeezed past the SEAL Delivery Vehicle to get access to the air lock, he had noticed that it was equipped with two mini-torpedoes.

The dry deck shelter air lock was nearly full of water when Juan said to Bradley, "Does that SDV work?" Their helmets used acoustic transducers for underwater communication.

"The batteries should still be charged," Bradley said in a chipmunk-pitched voice now that his lungs were full of the heliox.

"Have you operated one before?"

"Only in base exercises as the weapons officer. I was supposed to take it out on my first operational training mission before we went down."

"Then consider this your replacement mission. If the Brazilians fire a torpedo, my submersible is too slow to evade it."

"They don't know you're here?"

"We had to make this a covert rescue operation. I can't explain why right now."

"What can we do?" Bradley asked.

"Do those mini-torpedoes on the SDV have active warheads?"

"Yes, but we can't fire on a friendly warship."

"That's not what I'm thinking. Let's get it out of the garage. I'm driving."

Juan opened the hatch to the hangar and found the controls for extending the cradle holding the SDV. The external cap was already pivoted to the side from when Juan entered, so the cradle motored back until it reached its limit.

The SDV was intended to be a method for SEAL teams to approach shore without being seen. It had the cigar shape of most other submarines, with a large propeller powered by rechargeable silver-zinc batteries. Unlike other subs, however, the SDV's six seats were open to the sea, which allowed for easy ingress and egress by SEALs in their scuba gear. All electronics were sealed, but the controls were exposed to the water.

This SDV was armed with two Compact Rapid Attack Weapons, or CRAWs, which were miniature torpedoes meant for attacking small surface vessels or subs. They were mounted one to a side on fuselage clasps. With a warhead weighing just forty-five pounds, the CRAW wouldn't inflict much damage upon a two-thousand-ton corvette even if Juan wanted to target it. But the CRAW could provide them with some defense against an anti-sub torpedo launched from the *Barosso*.

He and Bradley swam out of the hangar. It was too dark to see the rear escape trunk hatch, but Juan spotted the Nomad's lights a hundred yards off the *KC*'s port stern. While they unmoored the SDV from the cradle, he called Max.

"Did you get the rocks cleared?"

"It was going to take hours to pick them up one at a time because they were so small, so I bulldozed the rest of them off. I told the sailors inside, and the first two crewmen are getting in the escape trunk now to evacuate. But we have a new problem."

"The ping?" Juan asked. "I heard it."

"We're pretty exposed out here," Max said. "Did you find anyone? Are you ready to go?"

"Got a sailor with me. He was the only one."

"We'll come pick you up, then."

"No, take shelter by the cliff edge. We'll come to you in the SEAL Delivery Vehicle. I'm worried that we may need it."

When the SDV was completely detached from the cradle, Juan got into the driver's seat while Bradley sat in the passenger seat next to him. Juan went over the joystick and trim controls. It looked like a standard mini-sub layout. He switched on the power, and the control panels on both sides lit up.

"No time to go through a checklist," Juan said. "Are you ready?"

"Aye, sir," Bradley replied.

Juan put it into reverse and backed away slowly from the dry deck shelter. When they were clear, he lifted from the deck and motored toward the Nomad.

He was about to tell Max that they'd escort him to a spot farther along the cliff's edge and out of view of the *Barosso* when he heard a splash.

"Fish in the water!" Bradley squeaked. The effect would have been comical if they weren't being shot at.

"Bearing?" Juan asked.

"One-seven-five."

Right behind them. Juan swung the SDV around to put them head-on with the approaching torpedo.

"It went out and now is turning around as it descends," Bradley said. "One thousand yards and closing fast."

"Fire CRAW One," Juan ordered.

"Torpedo away!"

The mini-torpedo unlatched from the side of the SDV and shot forward, playing out a hair-thin wire behind it.

"Impact in twenty seconds. They're both doing more than fifty knots, so this is going to be like hitting a bullet with a bullet."

Juan peered over at Bradley's sonar screen and saw the two dots racing toward each other.

Juan counted down the last ten seconds in his head. When the dots fused as one, he steeled himself for the explosion. But nothing happened.

The dots raced away from each other.

"It missed!" Bradley yelled, pounding the bulkhead in frustration.

"Fire Two!" Juan called out.

"Two away! Ten seconds to impact."

"Does the torpedo have a self-destruct?" Juan asked.

"Yes."

"We can't afford to miss again. On my mark, activate self-destruct."

"Understood." Bradley placed his finger over a red button. "Ready."

Juan was hoping to overload the enemy torpedo's sonar array or disrupt the guidance system with a nearby blast.

He looked at the screen and counted down in his head again. Three . . . two . . .

"Now!"

Bradley jammed his finger on the button.

The CRAW detonated, the flash visible in the distance. It was immediately followed by a far bigger explosion.

A second later, the SDV was buffeted by a huge shock wave. It tossed the submersible sideways, and Juan struggled to stay in his seat as it slewed around.

When the shock wave had passed, he looked at Bradley and said, "Are you all right?"

Bradley gave him the OK.

"Juan, come in," Max's worried voice said over the comm system. "Are you still with us?"

"The Lollipop Guild is alive and well," Juan said through his helium-soaked voice box. "Heading back to the Emerald City now."

He could see the Nomad hovering below an outcropping. As soon as the SDV was alongside, Juan and Bradley would abandon it and enter the Nomad's air lock for the decompression cycle while Max took them back to safety below the thermocline.

As they passed the stern of the *Kansas City*, the hatch of the rear escape trunk opened, and two men in yellow immersion suits swam out. One began the ascent to the surface. The second man pushed the hatch closed behind him before joining his crewmate.

At the same time, a second ping emanated from the *Barosso*. They were trying to confirm that they'd destroyed their target.

Using a pair of binoculars, Captain Vega watched the geyser of water finish erupting and waited for his sonar operator to give the all clear.

He lowered them and turned to the seaman. "Did we get it?"

"No, sir. The torpedo exploded prematurely. It was hit by the second defensive torpedo. I'm reading a small sub leaving the stern of the *Kansas City*."

He still had an unidentified hostile down there, one that had fired two mini-torpedoes.

"Prepare to fire torpedo number two," he ordered.

"Aye, captain. Torpedo Two ready to fire in all respects."

Before he could give the command to launch it, he heard a sailor yell, "Men in the water!"

It was an officer on the bridge wing. He was pointing in the direction of the *Kansas City*'s location.

Vega raised the binoculars and saw two men in yellow bobbing in the water. He recognized the immersion suits worn by submariners in an emergency. Could they be from the *Kansas City*? Was the phantom sub actually helping them?

"Stand down the torpedo!" Vega shouted. "Get a rescue boat in the water."

Before the boat got out to them, another two men appeared on the surface. Over the next two hours, twenty-six sailors miraculously came up.

The mystery sub eventually surfaced. Empty. It was identified as the *Kansas City*'s SEAL Delivery Vehicle. Vega theorized that a crewman somehow made it out of the dry deck shelter and saved his fellow sailors before succumbing to nitrogen narcosis at that depth and exiting the SDV in a stupor. They'd keep searching for his body until the Americans arrived.

Vega was so busy with the extensive search and recovery effort that he paid little attention to the cargo ship that sailed slowly by two miles away.

41

Having completed the decompression in the Nomad's air lock, Juan gave Lieutenant Bradley some clean overalls, a bottle of water, and one of the sandwiches they'd brought along. After wolfing down the sandwich and draining the bottle, Bradley dozed during the long ride back to the *Oregon*.

When they surfaced in the moon pool, Julia Huxley was there to meet them and take Bradley to the infirmary. Once she had treated his injuries, she brought him to the boardroom, where Juan and Max were waiting with a spread of food laid out by Maurice. Bradley came in with a fiberglass cast on his arm.

"You sure have been keeping me busy," Julia said as she escorted him into the room. "I've delivered so many patched-up patients to you over the last week or so that I feel like I'm in *Groundhog Day*."

"How's our new friend doing?" Juan asked as Bradley cautiously took a seat.

"Hairline of the radius and ulna. But they've been healing nicely, thanks to the excellent temporary duct tape cast that Lieutenant Bradley made for himself."

"What is this ship?" Bradley asked. "Your medical bay is way better than any I've seen in base hospitals."

"By the way, he's been asking a lot of questions," Julia said. "I told him to wait, but he kept pestering me. Now you and Max can answer them."

She closed the door, leaving Bradley looking at Juan and Max with a skeptical expression.

"I imagine this is all pretty disorienting for you," Juan said.

"You think?" Bradley shot back. "When can I get back to my unit?"

"I'm not sure. I think you'd better hear what we have to say first."

"I have no idea what's going on. You rescue twenty-six of the KC's crew, plus me, but you're being shot at by the Brazilians? And you're not with the Navy?"

"We're a private organization," Max said. "But we do most of our work for the U.S. government."

"Then why a covert mission to save us?"

"We're not exactly in the U.S.'s good graces right now," Juan said. "They think we've been sinking ships."

"Have you? Did you sink the KC?"

"No. A former CIA agent named Zachariah Tate did. Before you went down, did your crew experience any strange behavior?"

Bradley shifted uncomfortably in his chair. "How did you know that?"

"He has developed something called a sonic disruptor. We believe it uses sound waves to affect people's minds. It makes them have terrifying hallucinations and drives them to harm themselves and others."

Bradley nodded slowly. "That's what happened to everyone else on the KC."

Juan frowned. "It didn't happen to you?"

Bradley shook his head. "I seemed to be the only one who didn't go crazy."

Juan and Max glanced at each other, then Max asked, "Did you have some kind of hearing problem that day?"

"I had an ear infection. Couldn't make out anything that people were saying. It finally cleared up a few days ago."

"That's why you were immune," Juan said. "The same thing happened to our ship, but our crew managed to get away from it . . . You're sitting in the *Oregon*, by the way."

"Can you tell us if you had any cousins that died recently?" Max asked.

Bradley narrowed his eyes. "Why do you want to know?"

"Because we think a SEAL aboard your sub was the reason Tate sank her. He had some knowledge that Tate was afraid of."

Bradley sat back in his chair and crossed his arms. "Why should I trust you? You could be working for Tate. You could *be* Tate, for all I know."

"I thought you might be skeptical," Juan said. "Maybe this will help." He pressed a button on the tablet in front of him. "Come in, Linc."

A few seconds later, Franklin Lincoln opened the door and breezed in. He took a seat next to Bradley, whose eyes lit with recognition.

"It's you," Bradley said with awe. "I mean, Lieutenant Commander Lincoln."

Linc grinned at him. "I'm a civilian now, but it's good to know my rep in the SEALs is as good as ever."

"You hold most of the records at the InterService Rifle Championships. The six-hundred-yard mark you set is unbelievable. You're a legend. They still have your photo up at Coronado." Coronado, California, on San Diego Bay, was where BUD/S training took place.

"I'm impressed with what you've survived. Living in that decompression chamber for almost two weeks? That took some guts."

"Thanks. Man, wait 'til my buddies hear I . . ." Bradley's voice trailed off, waning from excitement to sadness.

"I'm sorry about your friends," Juan said. "But we're on your side. We want to find out why they died so it won't be in vain."

"Are you going to stop this guy Tate?"

"That's the plan."

Bradley took a breath. "I didn't have any cousins die recently. But I know someone on the *KC* who did. Carlos Jiménez. He was my best friend."

"Could he be one of the men who was in the engine room that survived?" Max asked.

Bradley shook his head. There was a catch in his voice as he spoke. "He went nuts, like everyone else, and attacked me. That's how I ended up in the DDS. He was in the forward escape trunk when it flooded."

"I'm sorry," Juan said again. "But it's very important that you tell us anything you can if we're going to stop Tate from doing something like this to another ship."

"Carlos had been pretty upset when we put to sea," Bradley said. "His mother, who passed away a few years ago, came from Brazil, and he had some cousins from a small town in the eastern Amazon jungle. Carlos had been emailing them and planned to go visit. But they were killed before he could go."

"Do you know how they died?"

"They were gunned down. The police said it was drug dealers, but Carlos didn't believe them. He thought it was related to something they'd found."

"Which was what?" Max asked.

"It's going to sound crazy, but they said it was a German U-boat called the *Bremen*. When they started asking around about it, no one took them seriously until some American guy showed up and pressured them to reveal the location. Carlos's cousins wouldn't give up the info. They were scared of him and emailed Carlos about the man's strong-arm tactics. After our mission, he was going to go down there to look into it with them. But then, just before we set sail, he got word they'd been murdered."

Max looked at Juan and said, "That sounds like Tate's handiwork. But what does he want with a U-boat?"

"It must be related to the sonic weapon somehow," Juan said, before turning to Bradley. "Do you know what town these cousins were from?"

"Somewhere near a tributary of the Amazon River, but I don't remember the name offhand."

Juan sighed with disappointment. They were so close to finding out what Tate was protecting, and now it seemed just out of reach.

"But it doesn't matter," Bradley continued. "I can show you exactly where they claimed the U-boat was."

Juan leaned forward with renewed hope. "How?"

Bradley smiled for the first time. "I have a map."

42

From the open door of a chartered Agusta six-passenger helicopter, Zachariah Tate watched the jungle pass below, a nearly unbroken expanse of thick green carpet that was slashed only occasionally by one of the muddy brown tributaries of the Amazon. On his headset, he listened to Catherine Ballard recount the latest news about the discovery of the *Kansas City*. She was sitting across from him next to Farouk, who had his face buried in a laptop.

"Reports say that it was found by a Brazilian Navy corvette," she said as she read from her sat-link phone, "and that twenty-six survivors have been transferred to an American Navy destroyer that arrived twenty-four hours later. A massive effort is currently under way by the Navy and the National Underwater and Marine Agency to raise the sub and bring it back to the U.S. NUMA is concerned that the nuclear reactor could contaminate the Brazilian coast if it leaks."

"Did they report the names of any of the survivors?" Tate asked.

Ballard shook her head. "It's only been a day and a half. They're still notifying relatives."

"Then it's good we came here. If Jiménez is still alive, it's only a matter of time before someone comes looking for the *Bremen*." He turned to Farouk. "Any sign of it yet?"

Farouk shrugged without looking up. "It's a big jungle. If we could ask the people who originally found the U-boat where it was, this would be a lot easier."

Tate glared at him. "You think that it was a mistake for me to kill them?"

Farouk looked up from the computer with alarm. "N-no. I just meant it's difficult to find it with limited data. You were right to stop them from revealing the U-boat to the world. It could endanger everything we've worked for."

Tate laughed. "Relax, Farouk. I'm just messing with you. We both thought the *Kansas City* was a total loss. How could we know some of the sailors would get out two weeks later? Anyway, Jiménez may have died in the wreckage. This search is just for insurance."

Farouk smiled weakly. "No problem." He went back to studying his screen.

Strapped to the underside of the helicopter was another piece of technology put together by Farouk. It was a LiDAR—a Light Detection and Ranging—imaging system. As the Agusta flew over the jungle, laser beams were being fired downward thousands of times every second. Most of the beams were blocked by the trees, but a good percentage got through to the ground, enough to form a picture of the terrain below by subtracting the tall jungle foliage from the image. It was the same tech archeologists used to map Mayan ruins hidden in Central American rain forests. Farouk's computer was analyzing the data in real time and creating a map on his laptop. If the distinctive shape of a World War I–era U-boat was within their search grid, it should be easy to spot.

They had started by scanning all of the tributary banks in the area, but Tate thought the *Bremen* was unlikely to be found there. It would have been discovered long ago by fishermen cruising along the rivers.

So now they were searching the jungle's interior. The U-boat had been abandoned in 1922, and the smaller rivers had shifted course many times in the nearly one hundred years since then. It was very possible that the U-boat had gotten stranded in a cut-off tributary and swiftly overwhelmed by the foliage that raced to cover any bare ground.

"This is taking forever," Tate said.

"We must be methodical," Farouk said. "Any deviation from the search pattern and we could miss it."

"And you're sure that Horváth didn't reveal the location of the U-boat in his rants?"

"I wish he had. This is tedious."

Istvan Horváth, the Hungarian scientist who invented the sonic disruptor toward the end of World War I, had emerged from the Amazon jungle in 1922 with wild tales of a German U-boat stuck in the middle of the rain forest. He claimed the *Bremen*, a sub built to be a blockade-runner, had escaped the war unscathed and used a remote Amazon River outpost as its base to raid ships for four years after hostilities had ended.

No one had believed him, even though the *Bremen* had indeed disappeared before the war was over and was never seen again. The problem was that Horváth was certifiably insane, driven mad by sickness and his long trek through the bug-infested jungle. He told his rescuers that a disease struck everyone on the sub and killed them before they could put to sea. He was the only survivor and managed to hike his way down the river to the coast, but his wild-eyed stories were considered too fanciful to be anything other than the ravings of a madman.

Horváth was sent to an asylum in Budapest, where he spent the rest of his life scribbling on the walls of his cell. It was only decades later when Farouk was conducting his own research in sound weapons that he came across an old photo of Horváth in his cell that was printed in a psychiatry journal. Farouk recognized the equations the scientist had written on the walls as the formulas for developing the sonic disruptor. He and Tate snuck into the still-standing asylum and found that the cell had been repainted long ago, but they recovered a trove of archived photographs from Horváth's time there. To Tate's delight, Farouk was able to re-create the Hungarian's work, and even perfect it.

Then Brazilian locals stumbled across the U-boat, and Tate knew he needed to protect his investment. Horváth's plans for the sonic disruptor could still be on board, rendering Tate's monopoly of the weapon useless. He had to keep anyone else from getting their hands on it.

"We're running low on fuel, Commander," the pilot said. "We need to return to gas up."

Tate grimaced and looked at the sun in the western sky. "How long will that take?"

"Including travel time to the heliport and back? An hour."

Tate turned to Farouk. "Do we have time for another run?"

"Just barely."

"Okay," Tate said to the pilot. "Take us back."

"Li will be waiting for us," Ballard said. "I just heard from him on the radio."

"Did he get the supplies?"

She nodded, which meant Li had acquired two hundred pounds of C-4 plastic explosives. Once they located the *Bremen*, Tate would make sure no one else found any remnant of the original sonic disruptor or its plans by blowing the entire U-boat to smithereens.

43

The *Oregon* navigated the tangle of forks in the vast Amazon Delta until she reached as far inland as she could without going aground. She dropped anchor in the muddy silt, far from any of the major river ports. When the boat garage door slid up, Juan could smell a mixture of flowers, fungus, and mold, which were all critical to the life cycle of the jungle. He didn't have any worries that they'd be spotted by curious onlookers. Even this close to the coast, towns and settlements were sparse, and the nearest farms were fifty miles away.

Since the RHIB was a casualty of Overholt's rescue in Buenos Aires, they'd have to use two Zodiacs to make it the rest of the way up river. In addition to Eddie, Linc, Raven, MacD, and Murph, Michael Bradley had insisted on coming along. Although the Navy SEAL still had the cast on his arm, Doc Huxley had molded the fiberglass in such a way that it allowed him to grasp objects, so he felt that he was up to partaking in the mission.

Juan initially denied his request to join them, preferring instead to return the lieutenant home to his unit, but Bradley had refused to leave until he helped them find the *Bremen* and guarantee that his crewmates hadn't died for nothing. In exchange for bringing him with them on the jungle expedition, Bradley agreed to share his map, which turned out to be a photo of a drawing Carlos Jiménez's cousins had sent him. Bradley's phone had gone down with the *KC*, but he had backed it up to the Cloud before leaving port, so he could retrieve the picture simply by connecting to the internet.

When Murph and Eric got hold of the map, they cross-referenced it with a detailed satellite chart of the region. Within minutes, they had the supposed location of the U-boat pinpointed to a region south of the Amazon River in the Mapuá Extractive Reserve, a vast, protected rain forest that was crisscrossed by streams and supported a tiny population of native peoples. Jiménez's cousins had lived in one of the reserve's small riverside communities.

Juan was with Linc, Bradley, and Murph in one Zodiac, while Eddie, MacD, and Raven took the other one. All of them were armed with MP5 submachine guns except for Bradley. Despite his request for a weapon, that was one point on which Juan wouldn't budge.

"We've got about four hours of daylight left to conduct our search of the jungle today," Juan said. "Depending on how accurate that map is and how thick the jungle is, it might take several days to cover the whole area."

"I'll be keeping track of our search pattern," Murph said, holding up a GPS locator. "Should keep us from getting lost and backtracking on grids we've already covered."

Juan looked at Bradley. "You understand the terms of this deal, right?"

"I'm a Navy SEAL, not a baby," Bradley grumbled.

"But when you're with us, you're under my protection and command. Deal?"

Bradley nodded and glanced at Linc. "I have to stay by his side at all times."

"Well, don't make it sound like torture," Linc said, wiping his sweaty brow. "I don't think I smell that bad yet."

"In this humidity, it won't be long," Murph said, spraying himself with a generous dusting of DEET to ward off the rain forest's wealth of bugs. "I wish I had something that repelled snakes."

Linc tapped the machete on his hip. "That's why I have this. For close encounters."

Murph smiled at Bradley. "I'd stay by his side."

They traveled two miles upriver to the point closest to the search area. The rest of the journey would have to be on foot.

They hauled the Zodiacs out of the river and walked into the dense forest. Trees soared high above, blocking most of the light trying to make it to the ground. In the few places where there was a gap in the canopy, the thick undergrowth was virtually impassable. Birds, frogs, and insects chirped constantly, and the sound of moving water and branches waving in the wind surrounded them. Dead leaves crunched underfoot, the remains of the dry season.

The term "dry season" was relative in this rain forest. They still had to wade through a multitude of sodden bogs and knee-deep creeks as they tramped through the jungle, guided by Murph and his GPS, which needed to be reset continually when its signal was obstructed by the foliage. Within fifteen minutes, Juan's pants were soaked through, and his boots were caked with mud.

For two hours, it was a monotonous trudge through the forest, without any sign of a single man-made object.

Juan then heard a sound that was definitely made by man. The throb of a helicopter rotor was approaching. He held up his hand, and they all stopped.

The chopper passed to the south of them, the noise faded into the distance.

"Must have been a surveyor," Eddie said.

"Or a transport," Raven suggested.

"Out here?" MacD asked.

"Let's keep going," Juan said, although the close proximity of the helicopter bothered him.

They continued on for another fifteen minutes. Juan, who was right behind Murph, looked at his watch and saw that they had just another forty-five minutes before they had to give up the search for the day and return to the Zodiacs.

That's when he heard Murph's foot clank as he stepped up onto what looked like a decaying brown log.

Everyone halted. Juan put his foot against the object and tapped it with his toe. It rang out with a hollow sound. He bent down and wiped dirt away until he saw gray paint and rusted steel.

A stand of bushes was blocking the view to the right, so Juan walked straight ahead for another forty feet and turned to face the rest of the group, who were all gawking at the discovery. It was only now that he could make out the conning tower sticking out of the ground like the stump of an immense tree. He had just walked across the stern of a World War I U-boat sitting in the middle of the Amazon rain forest.

The entire surreal shape was unmistakable, even though it was partially camouflaged by vines and other vegetation. The only part that had been uncovered completely, the muck and grime having been wiped away by the previous visitors, was the German Iron Cross and the name stenciled on the conning tower.

BREMEN.

44

It took five minutes of pounding with the sledgehammers they'd brought to knock away the rust and loosen the gears enough to turn the wheel on the top hatch of the conning tower. A musty smell drifted from the interior, over ninety years of air closed off from the world. Juan put on his headlamp and descended the ladder.

When he stepped onto the deck of the control room, his light settled on a mummified corpse, sitting up and leaning against the periscope. Two more bodies were sitting at the dive controls, mouths agape.

As more of the team came down after him, their lamps gave a fuller view of the tiny room crammed with pipes, dials, levers, and switches, all of them labeled in German. There were dozens of valve wheels on virtually every surface for operating the ballast and compressed-air tanks. Although everything was filthy from its operational days, being closed to the humid air outside all these years had kept corrosion to a minimum. The *Bremen* still looked as if she were ready to put to sea.

"Fan out and look for anything about the sonic disruptor," Juan said.

Raven and MacD went forward, while Murph and Eddie took the stern.

Bradley was the second to last to enter, and he easily came down despite his broken arm. Linc followed close behind.

"And I thought the *Kansas City* was cramped," Bradley said, taking in the room that now looked even smaller with Linc's huge frame taking up so much space.

"This was actually a huge submarine for the era," Juan said, having studied up on the *Bremen* during the trip on the Amazon. "Over two thousand tons, with an extended range of twenty thousand miles."

"How many crew members?"

"Eight officers and sixty enlisted."

Linc whistled. "I hope they were all good friends."

"If they weren't at the start of the cruise," Juan said, "they would be by the end."

"As long as they didn't kill each other first," Bradley joked, before clearing his throat, embarrassed, when he realized his statement echoed what happened to the *KC*. "Why is it so big?"

"She was designed as a blockade-runner," Juan answered. "The Brits were trying to keep any materials from reaching German ports, so the *Bremen* and other U-boats like her were meant to sneak under the blockade. She could carry up to seven hundred tons of cargo."

"The question is, how and why did it end up in the middle of the Amazon jungle?" Linc said.

"The how is probably a little easier to answer," Juan said. "I'm guessing that we're currently standing on what used to be an old riverbed. This whole area is one big floodplain. Every time they get a major storm, it's possible for the higher river waters to carve out new pathways. That would have left the *Bremen* stranded here. Assuming it's been here since the First World War, that's plenty of time for the overgrowth to swallow it."

"And the why?" Bradley asked.

Juan shrugged. "If we find the captain's log, it might tell us."

As they began a search of the control room, Bradley said, "I don't speak German. What will it look like?"

"It might say *Kriegstagebücher* on the cover," Juan said. "That literally means 'War Diaries.'"

"Long German word," Linc said sarcastically. "Gotcha."

They rifled through the maps and code books, but they found nothing that looked like a logbook.

Then Juan glanced down at the body propped up against the periscope and saw the corner of a book protruding from under the corpse's leg. He bent down and tugged at the cover until it came free.

The letters KTB were etched on the cover. He gingerly opened it. Although the pages were yellowed, the neat German handwriting was easily legible. The date on the first page read "Der 7.9.16."

September 7, 1916.

"Found it," Juan said as he flipped through the book.

Bradley and Linc came to him and looked over his shoulder.

"What does it say?" Bradley asked.

Juan shook his head. "I don't know German, either. Murph can help us translate it. But what's strange is that the last date in the book is June 18, 1922."

"That's four years after the war ended," Linc said.

"I'm guessing they went into business for themselves," Juan said.

"Why do you think so?" Bradley asked.

"Because as I was scanning through the pages, I saw the names of some American vessels, including the *Carroll A. Deering.*"

"That sounds familiar," Linc said.

Juan nodded. "It's a pretty famous maritime mystery. She grounded herself near Cape Hatteras after a storm. The ship was completely intact, but the entire crew had vanished and was never seen again."

"We still don't know why Tate went to so much trouble to kill

Jiménez and sink the *KC*," Bradley said. "Why would he care if we found this ancient U-boat?"

Juan was about to give his theory for Tate's motives when he heard a call from the bow.

"Chairman, I think we'd better leave as soon as we can!" Raven yelled.

Juan gave the log to Linc and hurried forward until he reached the torpedo room. He found Raven and MacD standing with their backs to the bulkheads, as far away as they could get from the two torpedoes strapped to cradles at the center of the room.

They were fully intact, but one of the winch chains used to move the torpedoes into the tubes had fallen onto the torpedoes. It was hanging from the contact fuse at the front of one of the weapons.

"Was it like this when you entered?" Juan asked.

"Yes," Raven said calmly. "It's exactly as we found it."

"Ah wouldn't go anywhere near those things," MacD spluttered.

"All right," Juan said. "Don't touch them. We don't know if the warheads are still active or if the chemicals inside have broken down and become more volatile."

"What about the fuel?" Raven asked.

"I don't see a leak, but the kerosene might also be sensitive to vibration."

"Not to mention a spark," MacD added.

Juan nodded. "We don't want to give it a static shock. Let's back out of here slowly."

As they eased away from the torpedoes, Juan said, "Did you find anything?"

Raven shook her head. "Seven more bodies. No papers, except for a few personal letters and some novels."

"Then let's hope Murph and Eddie have had more luck. In any case, we're leaving in five minutes no matter what."

As they walked back toward the control room, Juan noticed for the first time the bodies that Raven mentioned. All of them were lying in bunks that he had raced by.

Juan went toward the stern, past the captain's minuscule cabin, and found Eddie and Murph going through the crew's lockers.

"Anything?" he asked.

"A lot of clothes and personal effects," Eddie said, "but nothing related to the sonic disruptor."

"There's got to be an operator's manual or plans, or something," Murph said, frustrated at coming up empty.

"They wouldn't have kept something that valuable in the open where anyone in the crew could get to it," Juan said.

"And they'd want it to be watertight."

"Somewhere only the captain, and maybe one other person, would have access to it," Eddie said.

Juan went with them back to the captain's cabin, and they ran their fingers along every joint and seam.

Finally, Murph yelled, "Eureka!"

He pulled a panel open to reveal a hidden compartment. Inside was a stack of notebooks.

Murph opened the top one and said, "I've never seen this language."

He showed it to Juan, who spoke Spanish, Russian, and Arabic, but he didn't recognize the finely printed words, either.

Murph pointed his phone at the page and snapped a photo. "Just using my translation app."

After a few seconds, he said, "Hungarian. According to a rough translation, the first sentence reads 'Notes for the producing of sound systems to advance mind revision and conduct by Istvan Horváth.'"

"There's German words there," Eddie said, pointing at two scrawled at the bottom of the page.

Irre Waffe.

Murph translated again. "Crazy weapon."

"This is what Tate was trying to keep secret," Juan said. "Pack it all up, and we'll decipher it back at the *Oregon*."

He went back to the control room and smiled at Bradley. "We found what we came for. It was hidden in the captain's room."

Bradley sighed in relief. "I'm sorry Jiménez couldn't be here to see this. You're going to find Tate and bring him down, aren't you?"

"That's the plan. But I don't think you can be part of it."

Bradley nodded. "It's time for me to go home."

"We'll drop you off at the nearest city with an airport and put you on a plane."

"What should I tell the Navy?"

"The truth. But they might not believe you."

"When I bring them back here, they will. I never thought—"

Juan put up his hand to interrupt him. It was the vibration in his feet that he noticed first. Then a rhythmic beat against the steel hull became audible. If they had been underwater, he would have thought it was the sound of a destroyer's screws as it approached to depth-charge the U-boat.

But to Juan's mind, the reality sounded just as ominous.

Linc looked upward, as if he were peering at the sky through the ceiling of the U-boat, and said, "The helicopter is back."

45

The Agusta had been flying the pattern set by Farouk, who was now in the front seat next to the pilot, and Tate had grown bored. They'd been at this all day, and he was getting sick of staring down at the featureless green expanse of trees. Ballard was dozing opposite him, and Li was checking the crate of C-4 plastique he'd loaded onto the helicopter, twelve bundles in all. They'd been fitted with time detonators, and he was adjusting the settings. Half a minute would give them time to get free of the explosion.

He sighed in irritation, but he sat up when Farouk spoke.

"Go back," he said to the pilot.

"Did you see something?" Tate asked.

"A long cigar shape. It could be a log, but it seems particularly large."

The helicopter swung around and retraced their path.

A few seconds later, Farouk raised his fists in triumph.

"That's it!" He held up the laptop. Sure enough, Tate could make out the distinct outline of a U-boat.

Farouk guided the pilot until they were hovering.

"We're right over it."

Tate leaned out the open door, but he could see nothing unusual. The canopy of trees completely shielded the ground from view.

"Where can we land?" he asked the pilot.

"I haven't seen a clearing for miles," the pilot replied, "at least none big enough for the chopper."

"We'll have to get a boat and come back upriver," Ballard said. "We can hike in and plant the explosives."

"No," Tate said. "That'll take too long. Li, can we drop those bricks without them blowing on impact?"

Li nodded. "The C-4 is very stable. And I've installed the detonators so that they won't be dislodged when they hit the ground."

"You've got enough bricks to completely destroy the U-boat?"

"More than enough. Half that number should be plenty."

"Then we'll drop them from here," Tate said. "After the explosions, we'll make another pass, and Farouk can take a look at the aftermath. If anything is left, we'll do it again."

Li rubbed his hands together in anticipation. "Sounds good to me. I've been waiting all day for this."

With Farouk's help, Li set the timers on the bricks and dropped them into the trees. When the sixth one was away, the pilot wheeled the helicopter around and raced away at top speed.

Tate looked back out the door while Li counted down.

"Five . . . four . . . three . . . two . . . one . . ."

There was a series of bright flashes visible through the canopy, and the surroundings swayed from the blasts.

But that wasn't all. A moment later, a huge fireball erupted in the same spot, throwing whole trees into the air. The immense shock wave pummeled the helicopter, and Tate had to hold on to keep from falling out the door.

"What was that?" he yelled at Li.

Li, wide-eyed at the result of his handiwork, shrugged helplessly. "It shouldn't have been nearly that big of an explosion."

"I bet I know," Ballard said. "It's a U-boat, right? Maybe they had some torpedoes left."

Tate nodded as he thought about it. "That must be what happened."

"It made the job easier for us," Farouk said. "There won't be much left of it now."

Tate breathed easier when he realized Farouk was probably right.

"Still, we should go back and make sure."

"Yes, Commander," the pilot said. He turned and headed back to the site of the explosion.

When they arrived, the foliage was still aflame. Smoke drifted into the sky, marking the location for anyone who might see it.

Tate wasn't worried about that. As long as the U-boat was destroyed, all that curious locals would find was charred wreckage.

They hovered out of the smoke, and Farouk inspected the screen.

"Is there anything left?" Tate finally asked.

"Not much that I can see," Farouk answered. "There's a huge crater where the bow used to be. Most of the rest is just twisted metal."

Since some of the trees had fallen over or had been blasted in half, Tate could now see some of the debris. It was now unrecognizable as a submarine. Large pieces of the hull were ripped to shreds, and anything flammable in the interior was burning.

"Good work, people," Tate said with a big grin. "I'm buying dinner tonight."

The pilot banked to the side and began the flight back to the heliport.

"Commander?" Farouk said in a hesitant voice. "There's something wrong with the recording."

"Like what?" Tate asked with a chuckle. "Did we get the wrong U-boat? There can't be that many stuck out here in the Amazon jungle."

"It's not the U-boat."

"Then what is it?" Tate demanded. Farouk was really starting to ruin his good mood.

"I was looking more closely at the images from when we first found the U-boat, to compare them to what we're seeing now."

"You're testing my patience, Farouk."

"I zoomed in on the video," the Egyptian engineer said, turning in his seat, an expression of dread on his face. "It's pretty faint, but I think there were people coming out of the sub."

46

Juan opened his eyes and wiped mud from his face as he coughed and gasped for breath. His chest reverberated from the explosion that had thrown him into a bog. He and the others had taken cover a hundred yards from the *Bremen*, and it had barely been enough distance between them and the now smoldering wreckage of the U-boat. Just how close Juan had come to dying was represented by the jagged piece of steel that was embedded in the tree next to his head.

He pushed himself to his feet and called out, "Everyone all right?"

He'd been the last one out of the U-boat when they'd heard the helicopter passing overhead. He'd made the mistake of thinking they were safe crouching behind trees surrounding the *Bremen*. It wasn't until he saw the bricks of C-4 falling from the sky that he ordered the team to run for it.

One by one, each person said they were okay, just scrapes and bruises, and Juan breathed easier.

"Will you get off me!" Bradley yelled, and Juan saw Linc rising to his feet. Since the lieutenant was his responsibility, Linc had thrown himself on Bradley to protect him from the blast.

"Just doing my job," Linc said, pulling Bradley up.

"I'd rather take my chances getting pummeled by an explosion."

"You're the one who wanted to come along. My boss is right here, and it would look very bad on my next evaluation if you got killed on my watch."

"I hate to break up your sparkling repartee," Juan said, "but that helicopter is coming back."

It had to be Tate tying up loose ends.

"They want to blow up the U-boat again?" Murph asked. "It's already a slag heap."

"Did they see us?" Raven asked.

"With all those trees up there?" MacD said. "Doesn't seem likely. Ah could barely see it when it was right above us."

"Then how did they find the *Bremen*?" Eddie wondered. "They could have flown over a hundred times without seeing it. We literally had to trip over it, and we had a map."

Juan realized that Eddie was right. Apparently, Tate had sensors in the chopper that could see into the jungle. Infrared wouldn't work in this heat, so he guessed it was a LiDAR system like the one they had on the *Oregon*.

"We may have been spotted!" Juan shouted. "Double-time back to the Zodiacs!"

Murph led the way using his GPS locator. Because they hadn't followed a trail, there was no other way to retrace their steps.

The helicopter came to a standstill and hovered over the spot where they'd been standing just moments before. As they ran, Juan looked back over his shoulder and saw another brick of C-4 fall from the sky.

"Get down!"

They all hit the dirt just as the explosive went off. Dirt rained down on them, but they were too far from the blast for anyone to be injured.

"Move!"

They jumped to their feet and made their way through the lush undergrowth as fast as they could. Juan was bringing up the rear, and Eddie was right in front of him.

"I don't think they can see us in real time," Eddie said over his shoulder as he ran. "They keep hitting at us where we were."

"I thought the same thing," Juan called back. "The software may need some processing. That's why we need to keep going."

The helicopter came toward them again. Juan considered just having his team run until the copter's fuel ran out, but it was beginning to get dark. If the chopper had infrared sensors, they'd be sitting ducks. They had to get back to the safety of the *Oregon*.

This time, the helicopter flew ahead of them and dropped another brick in their path, anticipating that they were heading to the closest tributary. They all dove to the ground again, and the C-4 took out a swath of trees. Juan fired his submachine gun at the helicopter, and the others joined in, but the tree cover was nearly impenetrable, and he couldn't tell if any bullets were hitting the mark.

"Cease fire!" Juan yelled. "How far out are we, Murph?"

"Two hundred yards."

"Let's go. We'll have a better shot at the chopper from the river."

"We'll also be more exposed," Eddie added.

"It's worth the risk," Linc said.

They avoided one more blast on the way there. As Juan shook the dirt from his hair, he could imagine Tate's delight in tormenting them.

When they reached the Zodiacs, they hustled the boats into the water and started the motors. Since Bradley didn't have a weapon, Juan gave the controls to him while he, Linc, and Eddie aimed at the sky. MacD and Raven were doing the same thing in their boat while Murph drove.

The river here wasn't very broad, only a few dozen yards across. The *Oregon* was anchored at a fork two miles away. At max speed, it would take less than four minutes to reach it.

"Stay close to the bank," Juan said to Bradley. Then he called Max on his comm link. "Max, we're taking fire out here."

"Gunfire in the jungle?"

"No, a chopper. Tate is dropping bombs on us. No casualties, but they're getting closer. Can you get a lock on it?"

"It's not on our radar. It must be hugging the trees."

"We're bringing it to you."

"We'll be ready," Max said.

Juan heard the chopper coming from the direction of the U-boat. The helicopter, the Agusta, flashed from one side to the other and disappeared again. For a split second, Juan saw Tate's smug face smiling down at them from the open door.

"They'll be coming around now that they know where we are!" Juan shouted. "Get to the other side of the river!"

Both Zodiacs veered across the water until they were next to the opposite bank. At the same time, the Agusta appeared out of the trees. Tate tossed a C-4 packet down where they would have been seconds before and it exploded almost the moment it touched the water. The resulting geyser drenched the boats but wasn't close enough to damage them.

Juan had them slow down to mess up Tate's timing again, and when the chopper came around for the next pass, Juan and the rest of them fired their weapons as it crossed the river. The submachine guns were designed for short range in tight quarters. It was unlikely the rounds hit anyone, but it would give Tate something to think about before the next bombing run.

By now, Juan recognized where they were. If they could get around the next bend, the *Oregon* would have a clear shot at the helicopter.

"Max, we're about to lure Tate into the open. Prepare to fire."

"Aster ready," Max replied. The anti-aircraft missile was radar guided, so as soon as the Agusta was in the *Oregon*'s sights, it would transfer the target lock to the weapon.

The next time the helicopter flew over, Tate dumped the C-4 right behind Juan's Zodiac. The explosion tossed the boat into the air, which luckily landed upright instead of capsizing. Juan's teeth rattled from the impact, but he was able to stay in the Zodiac, as were Eddie and Bradley. Linc, however, was thrown overboard into the water.

"Keep going!" Juan ordered the other boat while Bradley circled around. Linc grabbed the side of the Zodiac, and Juan and Eddie hauled him in.

"Go! Go!"

Raven, MacD, and Murph were now two hundred yards ahead and past the bend in the river and in full view of the *Oregon*. Bradley raced toward it, and the helicopter emerged from the trees and hovered over the water behind them.

Tate stared at them. The Agusta didn't move.

The Zodiac reached the bend, and Juan saw the *Oregon*, its missile battery ready to launch.

The helicopter stayed where it was.

Juan told Bradley to slow down, then turned back to Tate. Juan waved his arm, trying to goad his nemesis into following them.

Tate cocked his head, which was followed by a huge grin. He wagged his finger at Juan and spoke into his headset. The Agusta turned and flew away along the path of the river.

"He knew the *Oregon* was waiting," Eddie said.

Juan thought about that wagging, scolding finger. He should have known taking Tate down wouldn't be all that easy.

"Don't worry," he said as he watched the Agusta vanish behind the trees. "We'll get another chance."

47

A sailor opened the hatch in the deck of the Chinese *Wuzong*, and, for the first time in two weeks, Admiral Yu Jiang smelled that salty tang of the ocean. He climbed the ladder until he was standing on the observation platform and took a deep breath, happy to be free of the body odor and diesel fumes that permeated the sub despite its air filters. He raised his binoculars and scanned the horizon. The only vessel visible in any direction was a Panamanian-flagged fuel tanker called the *Diamond Wave* that was idling five hundred yards dead ahead.

The seas were calm, and it took Yu's eyes a few moments to adjust to the dawn's sun. He would have preferred to surface at night, but it would have made this operation much more difficult.

Yu didn't think there was much risk of being spotted. He'd selected this point specifically because it was so isolated. They were far from any shipping lanes, and U.S. satellites wouldn't be looking in this region of the ocean a thousand miles from the nearest land.

The executive officer joined him on the deck, and Yu said, "What does the traffic look like?"

"According to the marine tracking system, the closest vessel is the containership *Lookout Bay* one hundred twenty miles north of us. It won't pass within fifty miles of this place."

"Good," Yu replied, pleased with his choice of location. "Maneuver us alongside the tanker."

The *Wuzong* eased up to the oiler on the last of its battery charge. The sub was a Type 039A Yuan-class diesel-electric boat with air-independent propulsion, meaning it could operate for long periods underwater without snorkeling to provide air to the engines. Its design made it much quieter than a nuclear sub. Its batteries were virtually silent, while a nuclear power plant's coolant pumps had to always be running to prevent meltdowns.

The disadvantage was its range. A nuclear sub could circumnavigate the earth multiple times before the reactor fuel had to be replaced, but diesel fuel eventually ran out.

The *Wuzong* had been running on fumes for two days before the tanks finally emptied the morning of the day before, and the batteries were draining at a rapid rate. It was a huge risk, crossing the entire Pacific in a sub intended for guarding the Chinese coastline, but it was one Yu had been willing to take for this mission.

This operation was well outside the People's Liberation Army Navy chain of command. It was a covert mission, and he'd handpicked the crew himself, all volunteers. They knew what they were signing up for, that if they were discovered or captured, they'd all be sent to re-education camps as mutineers and traitors. Yu was protecting his superiors, and his own beloved service record, giving them all plausible deniability if things went badly.

He didn't have the authority to redirect a nuclear attack sub for this operation, but he did have enough clout to take command of a diesel-electric boat. He'd been a sub commander for decades before transferring to headquarters in Beijing, but he'd arranged this mission after he was contacted by Zachariah Tate and given evidence that could finally let him exact revenge for his brother's death.

Years ago, Yu Tien was the commander of the destroyer *Chengdo*, which was sunk under mysterious circumstances. Jiang and Tien had been close, enlisting in the Navy together and competing to see who could rise fastest through the ranks, Tien in surface warfare, Jiang in the submarine force.

Tien had been a brilliant commander, so Jiang was shocked and devastated to learn that the *Chengdo* had gone down. It had been last reported overtaking a cargo ship to launch a boarding party for inspection, and then it simply disappeared. It took six months to find the remains of the ship, which was riddled with holes from missiles, torpedoes, and gunfire.

It was long rumored that the cargo ship had inflicted the damage, which seemed absurd to Yu, but he investigated it all the same and came up with nothing. The tramp steamer had seemingly vanished into myth.

Then Tate had come along and shown him documentation that a spy ship called the *Oregon* was responsible. It was under the command of a former CIA officer named Juan Cabrillo, Tate's ex-partner.

Yu confirmed that a man and ship of the same description had departed Hong Kong just before the *Chengdo* was sunk in the South China Sea. He believed Tate's allegation. His subsequent proposal was too tempting for Yu to pass up. He would finally get revenge for his brother and at the same time acquire a new sonic weapon for the Chinese military.

All he had to do was help Tate sink the *Oregon*.

The *Wuzong* stopped next to the tanker, which loomed like a skyscraper over the low-slung sub. Its crew members swung a fuel line over on a boom, and the sub's sailors quickly attached it to begin pumping diesel into its empty tanks.

"Admiral," the XO, the executive officer, said with a smile as he lowered a radio, "the captain of the tanker says they have fresh fruit and fish to transfer over."

"Excellent," Yu said. "Give my thanks to the captain." He thought that would definitely help morale after two weeks of rice and canned vegetables.

A small crane lowered crates onto the deck, where they were greedily unpacked and passed down the hatch by his happy crew.

Everything seemed to be going smoothly until his XO turned to him with alarm.

"Admiral, the tanker has spotted a sailboat two miles out. Apparently, it's so small that their radar didn't pick it up until a minute ago."

Yu cursed his luck. If the sailboat reported seeing a Chinese sub this far south in the Pacific, it would surely draw notice from the U.S. Navy, which would alert its allies in South America.

"What direction is it heading?" Yu asked.

"North. It passed Cape Horn on a round-the-world trip, and it's now heading for Easter Island. At its current speed, we'll see it in less than ten minutes."

The huge tanker was currently shielding them from view, but the sailboat's course would allow its crew to spot the *Wuzong* as soon as it went by the tanker's stern.

Yu had a decision to make. If he had to sink the sailboat, it would be missed, but it wouldn't guarantee that the captain hadn't called in a report on the sub.

Better not to take any chances, not when he'd traveled eight thousand miles for his vengeance.

"How much fuel have we loaded?"

"We're three-quarters full," the XO answered.

"That's enough," Yu said. "Inform the tanker captain to wait to refuel us for the return trip. If we aren't here in one week, we won't be coming back."

The XO shot him a grave look and then nodded. "Understood, Admiral."

"Detach the fuel lines. Make ready to dive the boat."

The sailors scrambled to finish their work and get inside the sub. When Yu saw that he was the last on deck, he climbed down the ladder to the control room.

"Emergency dive!" he ordered.

The Klaxon sounded, and the ballast tanks filled with water. He watched through the periscope as the *Wuzong* slipped beneath the surface. The tip of the sailboat came into view just before the scope was swallowed by the waves. They'd made it without being seen.

The next stop was the rendezvous with Tate and the long-deserved destruction of the *Oregon*.

"Set course for Tierra del Fuego," Yu said. "Maximum speed."

48

It took a day to get the *Oregon* off the Amazon and back into the Atlantic. The only stop the ship made was to drop Michael Bradley in Macapá, where he could contact the American military attaché and arrange a flight back to the U.S. Juan didn't want to risk a bystander's life any longer, no matter how brave or qualified he might be. He imagined that the Navy would have a lot of questions for Bradley when he returned, and Juan left it to the SEAL to reveal whatever he deemed necessary.

Once they were safely away from the Brazilian coast, Juan went to Mark Murphy's door and knocked. Normally, he'd expect to hear heavy metal blasting from the cabin combined with explosions and gunfire from a first-person shooter video game. Instead, it sounded like dialogue from a movie he vaguely recognized.

Murph yelled, "Door's open!"

Juan went in and saw Murph, Eric, and Hali watching a film on the room's wide-screen TV. Trays piled with dishes of half-eaten food and empty cans of Red Bull were scattered around the black leather sofa, and Murph and Eric were sitting on the floor with backs leaning against the couch. Each had a laptop on his knees and another on the carpet next to him. Hali was sitting on the couch, munching a club sandwich.

"Am I interrupting movie night?" Juan asked as he watched the screen. Then he realized that the movie playing was *The Princess Bride*. But in this case, all of the major male characters' faces had been replaced with the face of Shrek. Although it was strange to hear the green ogre say, "Hello, my name is Inigo Montoya," the effect was seamless.

"Hey, Chairman," Murph said. "Hali stopped by to help us with the deepfake technology that Tate has been using to mask his identity on voice chat."

"At least you're not using my face this time," Juan said.

"We wanted to see if we could substitute anything we wanted," Hali said.

"What's the purpose?"

Eric sat up and brushed crumbs from his button-down shirt and khakis. "I read a story in the news that malware can be used to trick radiologists into thinking someone has cancer. They use the deepfake-type software to infect computer-scanned MRI or CT images and make it look like there is a tumor on the screen."

"Or to remove one entirely so that the radiologist thinks the patient doesn't have cancer," Hali added.

Juan shook his head. "Scary, but where does that get us?"

"Murph and I think we can insert malware into the video chat data stream," Eric said. "The intent is to disable his deepfake technology. Hali is here to help us figure out how to use the chat's feedback loop to launch the software without Tate knowing."

"Would he realize that the deepfake had been disabled?"

Hali shrugged. "I guess we could make it so that it still looks like it's working on his end even though disabled on ours."

"Good work, gentlemen," Juan said, his mind churning through the possibilities that the malware raised. "I have an idea how we might use that. Let me know when you've got it up and running. Now, to the work you were supposed to be doing?"

Murph held up his hands in a gesture that said *My bad*. "The translation of Horváth's notebooks wasn't as straightforward as I thought it would be. The Hungarian is a bit difficult for the scanner to decipher because of his handwriting, but the real issue is that he used some sort of code. I wrote an algorithm to decrypt it, and it's running now. Should be done in a half hour. I can't promise how complete it will be. Some of the pages were severely mildewed."

"And the captain's log?"

Eric handed him a stack of paper. "Here it is. I also emailed it to you. Some interesting stuff in there."

"Murph, when you're done decrypting the scientist's notes, get together with Doc Huxley and see if you two can come up with a way to neutralize the effects of the sonic disruptor. We can't go up against Tate again without some kind of protection."

"Do you want us to keep working on the malware?" Hali asked, pointing first to himself and then to Eric.

"Yes. Tell me as soon as you know it works. Then we'll give Tate a call."

Juan left and went back to his cabin, where he spent an hour reading the captain's log. It was slow progress as he kept cross-referencing items on the internet.

He was almost finished when there was a knock on the door. "Come in." Overholt entered with two mugs of coffee. Juan offered him a seat, and Overholt put one of the mugs in front of Juan.

"Maurice said you'd want this," Overholt said.

"It's very welcomed," Juan said, taking a drink of the rich Brazilian brew. "I think he has a sixth sense for anticipating the crew's needs."

"He's an interesting fellow. We spent the last two hours trading tales, me from the CIA, him from the Royal Navy." Overholt winked. "Heavily redacted, of course."

"I'm just sorry I wasn't there to hear them. Been too busy with this."

He passed the pages to Overholt, who thumbed through them. He stopped when he was about halfway.

"I recognize this name," Overholt said. "The *Carroll A. Deering*. Why is that familiar?"

"It's a maritime mystery that's never been solved. Until now, that is."

Overholt slowly nodded. "Didn't she show up on the East Coast without her crew?"

"On the shoals of Cape Hatteras in North Carolina. There were lots of theories for why the crew abandoned ship. Battered by a storm? Hijacked? Mutiny? None of them were very convincing. Now we know the answer."

"Which is?"

Juan sat back and looked at the view of the ocean on his 4K video screen. "According to this log, in the early 1920s the *Bremen* was running up and down the Eastern Seaboard hijacking valuable ship cargo and she never had to fire a shot. All they did was unleash the sonic disruptor on an unwary vessel, and the crew jumped overboard or killed themselves. Because the *Bremen* was a blockade-runner, she had more than enough space to transfer cargo."

"It sounds like the *Deering* wasn't the only victim."

"Not even close," Juan replied. "There were seven other unexplained ship sinkings or disappearances during that time that correspond to hijackings in the *Bremen*'s log. And that was only along the American coast. The *Bremen* ranged throughout the Caribbean and South America, changing their hunting grounds often to avoid raising suspicion. They even ventured to the West African coast once, before the raids stopped in 1922."

"What happened?" Overholt asked.

"Disease. They were using the Amazon as a base, sailing upriver after nightfall, and off-loading cargo onto standard freighters to be shipped to ports around the world. But in the summer of '22, one of the ships they were trading with brought a disease that sounds like Ebola or some other hemorrhagic fever. The whole crew was wiped out within days. The Hungarian scientist who created the sonic disruptor fled into the jungle with as much food as he could carry."

"And the Amazon tributary changed course after everyone died, miring the sub in the jungle," Overholt said, marveling at the sequence of events.

"Once Murph completes his translation of the Hungarian's notebook, we'll have proof that the sonic disruptor exists. That should be enough for you to take back to the CIA and clear your name." As with Bradley, Juan didn't like putting his old friend in danger aboard the *Oregon* any longer than he had to. The *Portland* was out there somewhere, and Tate was eager to hunt Juan down and sink his ship.

Overholt shook his head. "You don't get to my lofty position at the Agency without making some enemies. The story Ballard planted was good, and she's been nurturing it for years. Tate embezzled billions from black accounts and pinned the crime on me. There are plenty of people back in Langley who are willing to believe that I'm a traitor if it helps them get ahead. And the people who do believe me won't want to put the Agency through another public scandal, especially if they have to put their reputations on the line to weather the storm."

"Then what can we do?"

"We need to stop Tate. Or get solid evidence that he was responsible for sinking the *Kansas City*."

"The sonic disruptor plans—"

"—are not enough. Sure, the surviving crew will tell the investigators about the symptoms, and Michael Bradley will tell them that you saved him and the others, but they'll believe it was all a setup. We need something more concrete."

Juan sat back and thought about the deepfake malware Eric and Hali were perfecting.

"I might have a solution to our problem," he said. "I'll have to make a backchannel connection with NUMA. It's time to call in a favor from Dirk Pitt."

49

Tate hoped that he had destroyed the *Bremen* before Juan could get anything useful from it. But he couldn't be sure. Now, he couldn't count on the sonic disruptor to disable the *Oregon* again. Juan's presence did, however, confirm that Jiménez had provided information about how to find the U-boat. Tate was sick of making mistakes, like not searching for the *Bremen* earlier to blow it up. He wasn't going to underestimate his opponent again.

Unlikely as it was that Juan and his crew could quickly develop a countermeasure for the weapon, even a small chance was still a chance. It was also possible that Juan could build his own version, but that would take weeks or months. Not that it mattered. The *Portland* was shielded from sonic effects.

Since he couldn't depend on his superweapon anymore, he had a backup plan for sinking the *Oregon*. He'd flown straight back to Montevideo with the others and ordered the *Portland* to set sail immediately. They had a rendezvous to keep.

"They're right on time," Tate said as he watched the one-hundred-ninety-foot missile boat on the main view screen of the *Portland*'s op center.

"A fine craft," Pavel Durchenko said. The gruff Russian executive officer nodded appreciatively at the screen. "It has been too long since I had a ship of my own."

"Just like I promised you," Tate said, before turning to Farouk. "Prepare to engage the sonic disruptor."

"Aye, Commander," Farouk said. "Ready in all respects."

The Israeli-made Reshef-class warship was on a transatlantic crossing to its new owner, the Chilean Navy. The boat, renamed the *Abtao* after a famous sea battle, had originally been made for the South Africans and served in their Navy for over forty years. Chile had bought the heavily modified vessel to join the three others like it in its fleet.

For such a small ship, the *Abtao* carried an imposing array of armaments. She could fire up to four Harpoon anti-ship missiles, which were supplemented by two 76mm guns and twin 20mm Oerlikon cannons. For the delivery, though, she was unarmed. The ammunition was to be loaded once she arrived in Valparaiso.

Normally, the ship required a crew of forty-five, but the South Africans had installed automated controls that would let her be run by just twelve people for short periods of time.

Perfect for Tate's purposes.

When she passed within a mile of the *Portland*, Tate said, "Fire the disruptor. Full power."

"Firing," Farouk responded.

For a number of seconds, nothing seemed to happen. Then the *Abtao*'s engines abruptly shut down, and her bow plowed into the water. A minute later, the first of the crew emerged on deck. They ran around, confused and shrieking. One by one, twelve men tossed themselves into the ocean until no one was left on board.

"Is that all of them?" Tate asked.

Durchenko nodded. "Twelve were on the manifest."

"Good. Nice to see that they even stopped the ship for us. Take your crew over and bring her alongside the *Portland*."

"Aye, Commander," Durchenko said and left the op center.

While he waited for Durchenko to get over there, Tate walked over to Ballard and put his arm around her. "What did Admiral Yu say? Good news, I hope."

She smiled weakly at him before reading from her tablet. "He expects to be in Tierra del Fuego in four days."

"A day after the next step in our operation. Not bad."

Ballard lowered her voice. "You don't seem concerned about our setbacks."

"This was never going to go exactly the way I wanted," Tate said. "Although you worked closely with Langston Overholt, Juan's mentor, you never had much contact with Juan himself. He's a formidable guy."

"I never thought he'd be able to find the *Kansas City*, let alone the *Bremen*. Does he have a sixth sense?"

"He's not a superhero. He's a man, just like me. But he does have a major weakness, as you've seen. He can't stand to see a friend or an innocent person suffer. That's why we're undertaking this operation. I had a feeling I'd need a fallback, and I was right yet again. Don't worry. This will all work out."

Ballard's smile brightened. "I told Admiral Yu to surface for a radio message when he reaches the islands around Tierra del Fuego. He sounded eager to see the ship that killed his brother."

"If I decide to be a nice guy, I may let him make the kill shot." When she looked at him dubiously, he added, "Just kidding. I want that pleasure all to myself. Admiral Yu will be there to herd him into my waiting arms."

Several minutes later, Durchenko called from the *Abtao*.

"Commander, except for some minor cosmetic damage from the crew before they left, the ship is in complete working condition."

"See?" he said to Ballard with a grin. "Just like we planned."

He ordered Durchenko to bring the *Abtao* next to the *Portland* so they could begin the resupply operation. Although she didn't have any weaponry on board, that was about to change. The containers that they were supposed to transfer to the *Manticora* before Tate sank her held all the munitions they needed to bring the missile boat to operational status. They even had a full load of fuel to transfer.

Despite the setbacks Ballard brought up, Tate was pleased with his growing fleet. He now had a mighty armada at his command. The three ships together—the *Portland*, the *Wuzong*, and the *Abtao*—had more than enough firepower to sink the *Oregon*, with or without the advantage of the sonic disruptor.

Once they had the *Abtao* fueled and armed, they would head to the southern tip of South America and the vast archipelago that snaked up the Chilean coastline. He'd never be able to ambush the *Oregon* in the open ocean, Juan was too smart for that. Tate needed a place to hem the *Oregon* in, and the maze of channels and islands near Tierra del Fuego suited his plan nicely.

Now he just had to get the right bait. Tate had considered a cruise ship, but corralling a thousand or more passengers and crew was too unwieldy. Instead, he'd found something smaller, a vessel with just enough crew aboard to be useful as hostages. And it was an American ship, the likeliest to bring Juan running to the rescue.

"Is the *Deepwater* still in port?" he asked Ballard.

She tapped on her keyboard, checking the tracker they'd secretly planted on the *Deepwater* more than a week before just in case, and nodded. "According to the port's computer system, she'll be docked in Punta Arenas for the next two days. Then she leaves for the Alacalufes National Reserve, and is scheduled to return in twelve days."

Tate looked at his map and put a finger on Punta Arenas, the most populous city in southern Chile. It was a two-day sail from their current position. By the time they caught up with the *Deepwater*, she would be a hundred miles from the nearest Coast Guard station.

And they would catch her. It wasn't as if the research vessel could outrun them.

NUMA hadn't built the *Deepwater* for speed.

50

The last place Juan saw Tate and the *Portland* was in Buenos Aires Harbor, so he had ordered the *Oregon* to head back in that direction at top speed in hopes of intercepting the *Portland*. He knew full well that she could be thousands of miles away from there by now, but with no other information to go on, it was better than idling in the middle of the ocean waiting for another taunting message from Tate.

He entered the infirmary to find Murph and Julia Huxley with sheets of paper strewn across one of the examination tables. Neither of them looked like they'd slept more than a couple of hours.

"I hope you didn't stay up all night for nothing," Juan said. "Tell me you found some useful information in that Hungarian's notebooks."

"We wouldn't have made you come all the way down here if we didn't," Julia said.

Murph tilted his head back and forth, like he didn't exactly agree with her. "More like so-so news." To Julia he said, "Don't get his hopes up."

"You're not going to let Eric and Hali outdo you, are you?" Juan asked.

"Yeah, yeah, I know," Murph said sheepishly. "I heard they had a breakthrough on the deepfake malware."

"They said it's all ready to go for Tate's next video chat."

"How is that going to help us?" Julia asked.

It was Juan's turn not to get their hopes up, so he kept it vague. "I've set something up that might clear our names if Tate cooperates with us."

"That sounds cryptic and noncommittal," Julia said.

"I can't wait for that surprise," Murph said. "But we do have something that might help us with the sonic disruptor."

"A way to neutralize it?" Juan asked.

"Partially. Horváth's notes were even harder to decipher than I thought they'd be. Plus the mildew obliterated some of the writing, so it's not complete. I couldn't reconstruct a duplicate of Tate's weapon with what I have, but the notes sketch out the principle behind how it works. I'll let the doc explain it."

Julia picked up one of the sheets that had a series of formulas and waveforms on it. To Juan, it looked like a random series of numbers and letters with some squiggly lines thrown in.

"This shows the combination of resonant infrasound frequencies that are generated by the sonic disruptor. Although the sound is emitted at a powerful amplitude, it's much too low in frequency to be audible. When the sound waves hit the inner ear, they cause vibrations that have a profound psychological effect. Neurotransmitters are released that put the brain into a fight-or-flight mode. Essentially, the response is an extreme panic psychosis."

"It makes you go crazy," Murph summed up. "But only while the signal is hitting your ear. That's why the effect goes away so quickly when the sound stops."

"How can it affect everyone on the ship?" Juan asked.

"Because the infrasound is so intense that it causes the ship's hull itself to act as a resonator, possibly even an amplifier, as would be the case with a submarine, whose entire hull could be hit by the disruptor when it's underwater."

"Do you have a countermeasure?"

Murph did the head tilt again. "Maybe. If we can cause our own hull to vibrate at the same frequencies, it could cancel out the waveforms."

"But it would have to be something loud," Julia said.

"And the only thing on the ship that can create a sound that loud is our sonar dome," Murph said. "We'd have to modify it to focus it directly on the hull."

"Which means we couldn't use it as a sonar anymore," Juan said, getting why Murph had not been as gung ho about the solution.

Murph shook his head. "It's a trade-off. But it's probably better than all of us going crazy. The good news is, we don't have to go into port. I can make the modifications while we're under way."

"Can we use it as a weapon ourselves?"

"It might disrupt other sonars in the vicinity," Murph said.

"But I don't think it would cause the kind of effects that we've experienced," Julia added.

Juan thought about his options. "And if Tate uses his weapon on us while we have this countermeasure in place, what happens to us?"

"I'm hoping the effects on us are mild. Maybe some unease or agitation, but no full-blown psychotic breaks. That's the theory. But there's no way to know until we actually experience it."

Juan noted how many *ifs*, *hopes*, and *maybes* there were in the assessments, but he trusted their abilities. Besides, there was no other choice.

"You have my permission to make the modifications to the sonar."

"I'll get started pronto," Murph said. He packed up the papers and equipment that he needed and left the infirmary.

"Do you really think this will work?" Juan asked Julia.

"I don't know. If I could inoculate the whole crew against the effects, I would. Since the sound is conducted through the bones in our skulls, earmuffs or -plugs won't work. Short of making everyone deaf, I don't know what else I can do. This is our best shot."

Juan's phone buzzed, and he saw a text from Max.

Come to the op center. I have something to show you.

"Get some rest," Juan said. "You look beat."

Julia smiled wanly. "First, I've got to resupply the medical bay from the cargo stores. Then I'll take a nap."

"I'm sorry we've been keeping you so busy."

"A beach vacation would make it up for me," she said with a mischievous grin.

"Sounds like a great idea for all of us."

She was going through her inventory as he left.

When Juan got to the op center, he found Max at the engineering station.

"You rang?" Juan asked.

Max looked up, startled. When he was deep into his work, he often didn't notice anything around him.

"When did I text you?" he asked.

"A few minutes ago."

Max raised his eyebrows. "I could have sworn it was a half hour ago."

"That must mean you have something interesting."

"I do indeed. The *Portland*."

"What about it?" Juan asked.

"You said it's identical to the *Oregon*, right?"

"From what I saw of it, it looks like an exact copy. Of course, Tate doesn't have our taste in décor, but functionally I'd guess it's the same. Same op center, same moon pool, same armory, same weapons. Except for the Metal Storm gun, that is. Remember, we added that later."

"Which means the engines are probably identical, too," Max said.

Juan shrugged. "I can't see Tate improving on what you designed.

He doesn't have that kind of engineering know-how or creativity. What are you getting at?"

"The engines on the *Oregon* are unique. Or they used to be. Now, there's one other ship in the world that has the same magnetohydrodynamic engines that we do. Listen to this."

Max played a file that sounded like a laser battle from a science fiction movie, with zaps at different pitches pinging back and forth in rapid succession.

"Is that from the trailer of the latest *Star Wars* movie?" Juan asked.

Max shook his head. "What you heard was recorded from sensors orbiting earth inside the Van Allen belt. Lightning bolts generate electromagnetic pulses in the atmosphere that travel from the North Pole to the South Pole and back. The sound is what you get when you convert the light signals to auditory signals. They're called whistler waves. They're also found in the electromagnetic containment chambers of nuclear reactors."

He played another recording. This one sounded similar to the first one, but the sounds were less rapid and lower in pitch.

"More whistler waves," Juan said. "So?"

"Those came from our own engines. The supercooled electromagnetic coils that are strong enough to propel water through the ship's venturi tubes are also generating those waves as a by-product, and they interact with the atmosphere."

Juan finally understood where Max was going with this.

"You're saying that the *Portland* creates these waves as well? Can we detect them?"

Max smiled. "Yes. In fact, we're the only ship in the world that can detect them."

"Why?"

"The waves are far too faint to observe at long distances without very sensitive specialized equipment that requires far more stability than you could get on a ship. But since our engines are the same as the

Portland's, they resonate with each other due to the atmospheric effect of the whistler waves. It's very faint, but I tuned the engine instrumentation to approximate the distance to the *Portland*. It won't show us the direction, but it'll tell us if we're getting hotter or colder."

"I can work with that," Juan said with a grin. "Wait, you said you 'tuned' the engine, past tense. You mean you've done it?"

"I figured you would be okay with it. Besides, I wanted to see if it would work before I called you in. And guess what. It does."

Juan clapped him on the shoulder and laughed.

"You like surprising me, don't you?"

"I do get a certain pleasure out of it. It doesn't happen very often."

"So, where is Tate?" Juan asked.

Max pulled up a map of the South Atlantic. "I've been tracking him for several hours now. From what I can tell, he's heading west at twenty-five knots."

"So he's not in a big hurry." Like the *Oregon*, the *Portland* could easily double that velocity. Juan traced the path. "That puts him on course for either the Falkland Islands or Cape Horn." He did the math in his head. "At our current speed, we won't catch up to him until we get to Tierra del Fuego."

"If he doesn't change course," Max said. "This tracking method is not very precise, so it might take time for me to see if he turned."

"It's far better than anything we've had up until now. We finally have an advantage over Tate." Juan had a sudden thought. "If we can track him, then he can track us, can't he?"

Max shook his head slowly and cocked it at Juan. "That's very unlikely. Because you're forgetting one thing, my good man."

"What's that?"

"I'm not on the *Portland*."

51

Even though it was summer, Rashonda Jefferson wore a ski cap over her tight ebony curls and a peacoat to ward off the brisk wind that swept across the Strait of Magellan, the narrow channel of water between mainland South America and the island of Tierra del Fuego that served as the main shipping route between the Atlantic and Pacific Oceans. Although she was originally from Atlanta, Jefferson had spent most of her adult life at sea, first with the Navy and now with NUMA. She preferred missions in tropical waters, not at the frigid ends of the earth. Not that she'd ever let her crew know that. As the master of her ship, the *Deepwater*, she had to be willing to endure any conditions they did without complaint.

Still, she was eager to get back inside after spending the entire day overseeing the loading of supplies for the upcoming mission. At three hundred twenty feet long, the aqua blue NUMA ship was small enough to maneuver close to shore while big enough to provide amenities to her crew of fifty-three that made life on board comfortable. Jefferson impatiently leaned on the deck railing and drummed her fingers, looking out over the busy port that served the city of over one hundred thousand, and wondered where her navigation pilot was.

The scientific equipment needed for their mission had arrived a day early, so they were ahead of schedule. But because the waters in the area were so unpredictable and the quarters so tight, Chile required all ships traversing the strait to carry a local pilot knowledgeable about the region.

This time of year, there was high demand for pilots, so she supposed she was lucky she got one at all. She counted a cruise liner, two icebreakers, and four Antarctic supply vessels among the ships in the harbor. And that didn't account for the ships in transit through the strait. Of course, freighters and cruise ships could go around Cape Horn without a pilot, but the sea was so treacherous outside the protection of the islands that most of them took the calmer path through the strait.

A Land Rover drove up and screeched to a stop beside the ship. A young woman hopped out and pulled a duffel bag from the backseat. She hustled up the gangway, a long, dark ponytail swinging behind her. Even from this distance, Jefferson could see that she was fit and pretty, which was sure to be noticed by the mostly male crew.

Jefferson met her at the top of the gangway and stuck out her hand. "Rashonda Jefferson. Welcome to the *Deepwater*."

The woman took her hand in a strong grip. "Amelia Vargas. Nice to meet you, Captain. Sorry I'm late." Her Spanish accent was noticeable, but her English seemed fluent.

"I'm just glad you made it," Jefferson said. "I'm hoping to get out of port today. We'll go to the bridge first to brief you on the route I'd like to take, and then I'll have my executive officer show you to your quarters."

"I would be happy to do that." They began walking to the superstructure perched near the bow of the ship, right behind the helicopter pad that extended over the prow. The arrangement left plenty of room at the stern of the ship for cranes, sensor equipment, and the tender used for shore excursions in the remote locations they'd be accessing.

"You have a fine ship," Vargas said.

The pilot looked even younger close up, like she was barely out of her teens.

"Thanks," Jefferson replied. "I didn't get much information about you when you were assigned to us. How long have you been a pilot?"

Vargas smiled. "I know, I look very young. But I've been a pilot for four years now, and that was after three years with the Coast Guard."

"So you know the area well?"

"Very. I was born and raised in Punta Arenas. My father owned a fishing boat and took me with him all summer long since I was little. I think I've seen every inlet from here to Valparaiso. You are in good hands."

"I hope so," Jefferson said, impressed by the woman's confidence. "We're going to be traveling into some very tricky waters."

"I like a challenge," Vargas said.

They entered the bridge, and Jefferson introduced Vargas to the crew. She pulled up the map of the vast archipelago that stretched hundreds of miles to the north and west along the Chilean coast.

"Do you know anything about this research mission?" Jefferson asked.

"You're tracking whale migration patterns in the Alacalufes National Reserve, I believe."

"Right. Primarily humpback and blue whales. We'll be placing passive sonobuoys along many of the channels between the islands to trace their movements. We're also going to be installing webcams at penguin rookeries at seven locations." The spots were lit up in red. "Each will have a satellite linkup and will be solar-powered. The camera will be uploading video in real time, and we'll be recording it to count the penguin population in those areas. We'll have to anchor at each location and send our boat to shore."

"I hope you have a long anchor chain," Vargas said. "The water can be over three hundred meters deep in places." She leaned down and ran her finger from point to point, then shook her head.

"What's the matter?" Jefferson asked. "Can't you get us through those straits?"

"I can. It's just that the weather over the next week or so is going to be unpredictable there."

"Storms?"

"No, but the conditions will be perfect for low cloud cover and thick fog. The mountainous . . . What's the word?" Vargas paused as she searched for it. "Ah, yes. Topography. The mountainous topography makes it hard to tell when the fog is rolling in. It could happen very suddenly, and then we would have to move very slowly to avoid obstacles. There are many glaciers in the area, so we could run into calving bergs."

"Then the sooner we start, the better," Jefferson said. "After you stow your belongings, I'd like you back here in fifteen minutes so we can get going." She ordered her XO to ready the ship for departure.

As Vargas hefted her duffel and walked toward the bridge door with the crewman who was to show her to her quarters, she turned to Jefferson and said, "There's one advantage that will make it easier to navigate your route."

"What's that?" Jefferson asked.

"We'll be in a very remote and isolated area," Vargas said. "I doubt we'll see another ship."

52

Two days after hijacking the missile boat, the *Portland* passed the tiny Isla Hornos, marking the transition from the Atlantic to the Pacific. The *Abtao* was following behind, crashing repeatedly through thirty-foot waves, while the *Portland*'s powerful engines and larger size made for little more than a mild bobbing. Tate could imagine Durchenko clutching the bridge console of his smaller vessel with every breaching crest. The Russian was actually lucky. It could have been far worse. The Drake Passage had a well-earned reputation for wicked gales and rogue waves that made it a ships' graveyard.

Their target, the *Deepwater*, had left Punta Arenas a day earlier than expected, but it didn't change the schedule by much. They would simply seize her crew farther north in the National Reserve, where the research ship had been planting webcams. Tate had even watched the webcast from a few of them and once caught a glimpse of the *Deepwater* in the background. In fact, that location would be even better. Less chance of running across a random fisherman or tourist boat. The tracker they'd installed made the future interception a done deal. The crosshairs indicating the *Deepwater*'s position pulsated on the main view screen.

Ballard, who looked a little seasick from the rocking motion in the op center, said, "Zach, we've got a call coming in on Overholt's phone. It's Juan Cabrillo."

Tate frowned. Not because he was worried that the phone was being tracked. Its signal was being routed through a series of internet connections through a satellite feed that made it impossible to trace.

He was frowning because he was planning to call Juan later that day for another round of taunting and to lure him into the planned ambush.

"Do you want me to ignore it?" Ballard asked when she saw Tate's expression.

"No," Tate said after a moment's hesitation. "Might as well get the call over with now. Make sure to patch it through the deepfake software. I like Juan looking at himself when he's talking to me."

"Done," she said, and his old friend's face appeared on-screen.

"Juan," Tate said. "How did you know I was thinking about you?"

"Rough seas, Tate?" Cabrillo speculated. "That must be Catherine Ballard behind you. She looks like she's sitting on a seesaw. I bet if I could see her face, it would be a pale shade of green."

"And I'd bet you'd like to know where we are."

"Why don't you tell me?"

"You know what? I will. We're near Tierra del Fuego. Where are you?"

Cabrillo shrugged. "You don't expect me to make it that easy for you, do you?" He was throwing Tate's expression back in his face.

Tate laughed. "Touché. But it doesn't matter. You'll come find me anyway."

"And fall into another trap? How dumb do you think I am?"

"Please, Juan. I would never underestimate you. Why else do you think I didn't follow you down the river? I knew you had the *Oregon* waiting to blow my helicopter out of the sky. By the way, did you find what you were looking for? I mean, before I destroyed the *Bremen*?"

"The secret behind the sonic disruptor? Of course. We found everything."

Tate narrowed his eyes at Cabrillo, then smiled and wagged a finger at him. "Very good, Juan. I can't tell if you're bluffing or not. Again, it doesn't really matter."

"We did find Jiménez," Cabrillo said. "That's who you were trying to kill when you sank the *Kansas City*, wasn't it?"

Tate sneered at Cabrillo's smug expression of satisfaction. "Apparently, I didn't do the job well enough if he survived."

"You shouldn't have used the sonic disruptor to do it. You should have used a torpedo from the *Portland*."

"But I'm saving them all for you."

"Right," Cabrillo said. "You didn't even have to use them to sink the *Manticora* and the *Avignon*."

"Why waste a perfectly good torpedo on them when guns and missiles could do the job just as well? That is, when the *Oregon* sank them. I mean, who would believe there was an identical ship to yours out there?"

"Langston Overholt knew we didn't sink those ships."

"But Overholt is now dead."

That got a rise out of Cabrillo, whose face flushed red at the mention of his old mentor's demise.

"You didn't have to kill him."

"Come on, Juan. We did the U.S. government a favor. He embezzled hundreds of millions destined for black projects."

"Evidence that Ballard planted."

Tate was about to agree, then stopped himself. He understood exactly what Cabrillo was doing and applauded his misguided effort.

"Please, Juan. You're humiliating yourself. If you're trying to get me to admit to crimes against the U.S. government, it's a fool's errand. You're just implicating yourself if you try to show this video to anyone."

Juan smiled. "It was worth a shot."

"Not really, but whatever . . . In any case, let's get down to the reason I was going to call you."

"To gloat some more?"

"That's always fun, but no. It's time we got together again. Therefore, I'm going to hijack the crew of a ship and hold them hostage. All you have to do is come and get them."

Cabrillo slowly rose, his jaw clenching in anger.

"What ship?"

"And have you warn them? I don't think so. You'll find out the name soon enough. I'll send you a video of the crew. We'll keep them well fed and happy until you arrive. I just wanted you to know where to head. Tierra del Fuego, if you didn't get that before. It might take you a few days if you're still in the Amazon."

"Tate, you don't have to do this," Cabrillo said, his face contorting in rage. "There's no need to involve more innocent people in your games."

"I think there is. You've always had a soft spot for the innocent. I like that. It makes you predictable. Oh, and if I don't see you two days after I hijack their ship, I'll send you videos of you killing them one by one. I'll also send them to the CIA, just for posterity."

Finally, Cabrillo couldn't take it anymore and began to scream, stabbing his finger at the camera as he lunged toward it. "You're a dead man, Tate! We're coming for you! I'm coming for you!"

"Good," Tate said calmly. "We'll be ready."

Then he gave a mocking wave good-bye and hung up as Cabrillo continued to rage at the screen.

53

CRUISING ALONG THE ARGENTINE COAST

Tate's irritating face disappeared from the screen. Tate's face, not Juan's superimposed over Tate's.

Juan took a breath to settle himself, turned to Max, and coolly said, "How was my acting job?"

"You're definitely in the running for a Golden Globe nomination."

"Not Oscar-worthy?"

Max wagged his hand side to side and smiled. "But, then, I know you better than Tate does."

"I thought you were quite convincing," Overholt said as he walked from the side of the room where he couldn't have been seen on camera. "I'm sure Tate thinks your rant is still going on."

"As long as he didn't realize that the deepfake software was overridden."

Eric and Hali, who were sitting at the communications console, high-fived each other.

"The deactivation was invisible," Eric said.

"I agree," Juan said. "There's no way he would have continued the conversation if he had known. Let's bring back our friends on-screen, Hali."

"Aye, Chairman," Hali said. "They should have been able to see everything from both sides."

Juan wished he could have revealed that Tate gave himself away and rubbed in his face the fact that his plan to frame Juan had been utterly wrecked, but Juan had resisted the urge, knowing that tipping Tate off would just make him go into hiding. Juan was playing the long game, and clearing their names and finding the *Portland* was more important than the momentary satisfaction of seeing his old partner enraged about being bamboozled. Tate, on the other hand, would have had no such impulse control.

All the time they had been talking, there was another video chat going on in the background, and now the participants in it appeared on the view screen. Two people sat at a conference table while a third lounged behind them, leaning casually against the wall.

The first person was Patricia Kubo, Director of the CIA. The former senator from Hawaii rubbed her forehead like she was massaging away a headache.

"What a mess," she said in a strained alto. "If I hadn't seen you talking to Zachariah Tate and Catherine Ballard in real time, I wouldn't have believed they were teaming up together. We were so sure he was dead, and now he basically admitted to sinking a U.S. nuclear attack submarine and a covert CIA cargo ship."

The other seated person had flaming red hair, a Vandyke beard, and was dressed in a bespoke gray suit. Vice President James Sandecker, the original founder of NUMA, chewed on his unlit cigar and nodded slowly.

"True, it's a mess," he said. "But it's a mess we created for ourselves. And don't forget the civilian freighter *Avignon*. There doesn't seem to be much that Tate won't do for revenge."

The room's tall and lean third occupant had a shock of black hair, tanned and rugged features from many hours in the sun and salt of the ocean, and opaline green eyes that glittered with sly intelligence just as Juan remembered from their first encounter. Dirk Pitt, the current Director of NUMA, seemed to be the only one in the conference room who was amused.

"That was quite a performance, Juan," Pitt said. "I thought you were going to blow a gasket."

"I had to make Tate believe that he won," Juan said. "He's a sore loser."

"You've done a good job keeping him on the losing end recently."

"I've got a better team than he has."

Sandecker shook his head. "I have to say, Mr. Cabrillo, that I was reluctant to indulge your request when Dirk brought it to me. But as you've experienced in the past, he can be quite convincing himself."

Pitt was on board the *Oregon* long ago when the Corporation was helping NUMA out with a secret mission in Hong Kong. It was during that operation that the *Oregon* had the encounter with the Chinese destroyer that cost Juan his leg. If it hadn't been for Pitt's quick thinking, Juan probably would have lost the whole ship and everyone on it.

"I know," Juan replied. "That's why I called Dirk to bring you on this call. I figured that the VP and the CIA Director wouldn't believe fugitives like us without someone to vouch for us."

"I was willing to give you the benefit of the doubt since you saved my life several years ago," Sandecker said. He was referring to the time when the *Oregon* destroyed enemy drones that were trying to down Air Force Two.

"I believe you now," Kubo said. "Seeing Tate and Ballard in a replica of your op center was very convincing. Langston, I'm sorry for ever doubting you."

"I understand, Patricia," Overholt said. "Catherine Ballard has been concocting this plan for years. She duped me completely."

"I assure you that the CIA will do everything in its power to bring her to justice."

"Quietly," Sandecker said. "I've spoken with the President, and he wants to keep the political blowback from this situation to a minimum."

"That's up to Zachariah Tate, Mr. Vice President," Juan said.

Sandecker waved his hand dismissively. "Tate wants you dead and your reputation ruined. He knows the best way to do that is to make you a pariah to the U.S. government, not the public."

"Plus he wants to keep the *Portland* off the radar of the other countries," Pitt added. "At least until he wants to sell his services to them after he's sunk the *Oregon*."

"We can't have that happen, either," Kubo said. "The President has declared the *Portland* a threat to national security. That gives us latitude for how to deal with him."

"But we can't undertake any operations that will jeopardize international relations with other countries," Sandecker said. "Therefore, the U.S. Navy will not be going after him in foreign waters."

"Like the seas around Tierra del Fuego," Pitt said.

"Exactly. This has to be dealt with covertly." Sandecker looked directly at Juan. "And from what I hear, you have a way to find the *Portland*."

"We do, thanks to Max back there." Juan pointed him out, and Max gave a breezy salute.

Sandecker continued. "Then I authorize you to track down the *Portland* and take whatever measures you deem necessary to subdue the ship, up to and including sinking her."

"And Tate?"

"Use your best judgment," Kubo said. "I'll tell you, though. We sure don't want him back."

"Understood. We're moving at maximum speed right now to intercept him. Tate thinks we're still somewhere near the Amazon, so I'm hoping to get to him before he attacks that unnamed ship."

"We have a ship in the area called the *Deepwater*," Pitt said. "I'll have the captain keep an eye out for the *Portland* or any ship that looks like her."

"That's probably a good idea," Juan said.

"Sounds like it'll be a battle for the ages. Two identical state-of-the-art spy ships going at each other." Pitt smiled. "Wish I could join you, but I've got a few fires of my own to put out around here."

Juan chuckled at that. "From what I remember about you, Dirk, I'm not surprised by that at all. You always seem to have . . . let's say 'interesting' adventures. I'd love to swap war stories with you someday."

Pitt nodded in agreement. "Likewise. Next time you're in Washington, we'll get some steak and cabernet at a grill I know. Happy hunting."

"Thanks."

"I think our feelings about Tate are all the same here, Mr. Cabrillo," Sandecker said as he and Kubo stood to leave. "He and his people need to be brought to justice for what they've done, one way or the other. Go get him."

54

As she watched the crew anchoring the seventh sonobuoy from the *Deepwater*'s bridge, Rashonda Jefferson was proud of her crew's efficiency. The ship had placed three of the penguin rookery webcams, all of which were getting hits on the NUMA website, and the sonobuoys had been just as successful. Three of the sensitive hydrophones had picked up pods of humpback whales traversing the tight confines between the myriad islands in the expansive nature reserves.

Their current location, a junction of five waterways where they expected to capture the sound of migrating whales, was surrounded by snowcapped mountains on all sides, and the spaces between the islands were so narrow that the *Deepwater* had to proceed at a crawl to navigate them.

Luckily, Amelia Vargas had been as good as advertised, confidently guiding the ship through the most dangerous and unpredictable waters with ease. The navigational pilot had been right about both the water depth—over a thousand feet in places—and the hazards caused by the multitude of glaciers. They'd seen several huge icebergs calve into the sea.

Vargas had her finger on the route map while frowning at the latest weather report.

"What's the matter?" Jefferson asked.

"I think we're going to have to change direction. We could get socked in very quickly by fog."

Vargas pointed toward clouds sweeping over the islands to the south, clinging to the islands like a blanket. As usual, Jefferson agreed with the pilot's instincts.

"You're right. I don't want to be stuck in here with zero visibility. We'll head north as soon as we're done anchoring this sonobuoy. Even turning around in here will be tricky."

The intersection was not much wider than a quarter mile. The *Deepwater* was maneuverable, but executing a U-turn here would take skill, concentration, and nerves of steel.

By the time Jefferson got word from her crew that the sonobuoy was installed and secure, she could see the fog creeping toward them from the south, snaking its way ominously through the channels between the islands.

"Not a moment too soon," Vargas said.

"Captain," the XO said, "we've identified a radar contact heading toward us from the north."

Jefferson grimaced. That would make backing out even more of a challenge. She raised a pair of binoculars, but the ship had disappeared behind a small island in the middle of the northern channel.

"Fishing boat?"

The XO shook his head. "Far too big for that. I estimate her length at nearly two hundred feet."

That got a raised eyebrow from Vargas.

"Any idea what she could be?" Jefferson asked her.

Vargas shook her head. "No cargo ship would come this way. And we're far from any ferry lanes."

"Hail them," Jefferson ordered.

"Aye, Captain." The XO spoke into the radio. "Unidentified ship to the north, this is the NUMA vessel *Deepwater*. Please respond."

After a moment, a voice came over the loudspeakers in accented English. But the accent sounded Russian, not Spanish. "This is the Chilean Navy ship *Abtao*. Shut down your engines and prepare to be boarded for inspection."

Jefferson gaped at Vargas, astonished by the command. She took the mic from the XO.

"*Abtao*, this is Captain Rashonda Jefferson of the *Deepwater*. We have authorization from the Chilean government to conduct a research mission here. For what purpose do you want to board us?"

The *Abtao* emerged from behind the island, and Jefferson could see a 76mm gun on her foredeck. It was aimed directly at them. Men were manning two 20mm Oerlikon cannons that were also pointed in the direction of the *Deepwater*.

"*Deepwater*, we have reports of smugglers operating in this area. As you must be aware, the Chilean Navy has the absolute right to inspect any vessel operating in Chilean waters."

The *Abtao* came to a stop in front of the mid-channel island next to a glacier that ended at the water's edge. It was at point-blank range, bristling with menace.

Jefferson turned to Vargas. "What is going on here?"

"I have no idea. The Coast Guard should be in charge of stopping ships for inspection, not the Navy."

Jefferson handed her the microphone. "You were in the Coast Guard. Explain that to them."

Vargas spoke in rapid Spanish.

The response came back in English and ignored whatever Vargas said. "I repeat, prepare to be boarded."

Vargas shook her head. "I told them who I was and asked them to check with the Coast Guard about our mission. It's very strange that they didn't respond in Spanish." Her brow furrowed and her eyes widened. "Wait a minute. The *Abtao* isn't scheduled to go into service for six weeks. I know because her home port is supposed to be Punta Arenas. Something is wrong."

"New contact, Captain," the XO said. "Another ship to the north behind the *Abtao*."

"A second Navy ship?"

"I don't know. But it's much bigger. I'd say five hundred feet long."

She raised the binoculars again and caught a glimpse of a dilapidated steamer before it, too, disappeared behind the island.

The name on the bow read PORTLAND.

Now she was even more confused. A ship that size in these channels was nearly suicidal. And why was it following the Navy ship?

"This is absolutely absurd," Jefferson said, snatching the mic back and speaking into it. "*Abtao*, I'm calling NUMA, and they will contact your government to confirm who we are. We all need to get out of here before that fog covers us."

She turned to the XO. "Get NUMA headquarters on the line."

As the XO picked up the satellite phone, Jefferson saw fire spit from one of the Oerlikon cannons.

She shoved Vargas to the deck and yelled, "Everyone get down!" just as the 20mm shells blasted the *Deepwater*'s superstructure.

55

Because the *Portland* was still behind the island, with no clear view of the *Deepwater*, Tate was watching the feed from the *Abtao*'s camera. The Oerlikon's gunfire ripped into the satellite dish and antennae mounted on top of the bridge, blowing them to bits. Now there was no way for the ship to call for help.

"Good shooting, Durchenko," Tate said into the radio.

"Thank you, Commander," Durchenko replied.

He switched the comm channel to the boat garage.

"Is the assault team ready?" he asked Catherine Ballard, who was in charge of the boarding party.

"Li has the RHIB ready to go," Ballard answered. "Shouldn't take us long to get over there. I'm not expecting any resistance, but we're set if they're foolish enough to try."

"Excellent," Tate said with a grin. The ambush had gone exactly as planned. "As soon as Durchenko has disabled their ship, head on over."

"Can't wait."

He switched back to the *Abtao*. "Durchenko, take out the engine room. We don't want them trying to escape into that fog. But remember, we want hostages, so don't use your 76mm gun and sink her by accident."

"Aye, Commander."

The *Portland* was now rounding the edge of the island, so Tate had the main view screen in the op center switch to a view of both the *Abtao* and the *Deepwater*. The man on the Oerlikon swung its aim over to the *Deepwater*'s stern and began to pour shells into the hull.

Tate was capturing it all on video, a rogue Chilean Navy ship destroying an American research vessel. He wanted to see the CIA make sense of that.

The NUMA ship was turning, so the engine obviously hadn't been disabled yet. However, it would only take a few more seconds of concentrated fire to tear the engine room completely apart.

The *Abtao* didn't get the chance. An Exocet missile shrieked out of the fog and smashed into the bow of the Chilean boat. The resulting explosion was so powerful that it ripped the 76mm gun off its mount and shredded the men on the Oerlikons. The bridge's windows shattered, and the hull was set aflame.

Tate leaped out of his chair. "What just happened?"

The missile boat began to take on water through the gaping hole in its front. It would go down quickly. Durchenko must have realized the boat was lost. He fired all four of his Harpoon anti-ship missiles at the same time that a second Exocet lanced out of the mist. It struck the *Abtao* amidships, breaking it in two. The bow end capsized while the stern settled into the water. They'd both be gone within a minute.

None of the four Harpoons targeted the *Deepwater*. Instead, they disappeared into the fog where the Exocets had come from.

The *Deepwater*'s screws were churning water behind it. It was about to escape into that same fog.

Tate screamed at Farouk, who was gawking at the screen. "Engage the sonic disruptor! We're going to stop them one way or the other."

The Egyptian engineer nodded. "Engaging the weapon."

As he said it, a familiar shape loomed out of the mist like a nightmare. Tate recognized the distinctive bow of the *Oregon*.

The front of the ship was on fire, and there was a hole in the deck where the Exocets were launched from. The forward crane was dangling over the side. Still, with all that damage, she steamed forward like a juggernaut.

She passed the *Deepwater* and turned smartly to shield the NUMA ship, protecting it from the effects of the sonic disruptor. Obviously, the weapon was not having the desired effect on the *Oregon*.

"Fire our Exocets!" Tate yelled at the weapons officer.

"At which ship?"

"Both ships, you idiot!"

"Firing."

Four Exocets leaped from launchers in rapid succession. Two streaked toward the *Oregon*, the others toward the *Deepwater*, which was now moving away from the *Portland* at top speed.

The *Oregon*'s Gatling guns emerged from hidden positions, and the six-barreled weapons began unleashing three thousand rounds per minute. The heavy tungsten tracer shells homed in on the missiles. Two of the Exocets were shot down halfway to their targets. One slammed into the bridge of the *Oregon* and erupted in a huge fireball.

Tate cursed because he knew there was nothing of value on the bridge. It was merely an observation post and decoy used for fooling visitors. Juan and his command crew were nestled deep within the ship in the op center, protected by the ship's armor cladding just like he was.

The fourth missile shot past the *Oregon* and looked like it might take out the *Deepwater* before it could get away, but the Gatling gun on the opposite side of the *Oregon* blew it apart moments from impact.

The *Deepwater* was swallowed by the fog. At the same time, the *Abtao*'s two sections went down in a swirl of white water and foam. There was no sign of survivors.

Tate was furious. Unlike Juan, whose own anti-ship missile launcher looked too damaged to function, Tate could fire another spread of missiles. That was a futile tactic. They'd probably be shot down just like the last ones.

"Prepare to launch torpedoes at the *Oregon*!" Tate shouted. "I want that ship sunk!"

56

In the *Oregon*'s op center, Juan couldn't get comfortable in his command chair. The sonic disruptor was setting his teeth on edge and making his skin crawl, like he'd had sixteen cups of coffee, and everyone around him looked just as uneasy. But they weren't going crazy. Murph and Julia's hull vibration solution to partially neutralize the acoustic weapon seemed to be working.

For the last two days, they'd been traveling at maximum speed to intercept the *Portland* before she reached her target, yet it wasn't fast enough. Juan had been planning to surprise the *Portland* as she came through the islands. He was just going to wait until he saw her bow pass by as he hid in a cove, slamming four torpedoes into her before Tate knew the *Oregon* was anywhere near him. The planned sneak attack wasn't sporting, which was exactly the point. Juan would have been very happy to send the *Portland* to the bottom without her firing a shot.

The radio traffic they overheard between the *Deepwater* and the *Abtao* changed everything. Juan recognized Durchenko's voice from when he'd been held captive on the *Portland*. He couldn't let the NUMA ship be taken by Tate. It would have changed everything. Juan ordered the *Oregon* into the fog using the ship's LiDAR system to guide them through the narrow straits. As soon as they had a lock on the missile boat, he fired.

Unfortunately, so did Durchenko. Three of the Harpoons missed, but one of them made a direct hit on the *Oregon*'s missile launcher. It would take days to fix it even if it were in dry dock.

The rest of the damage report wasn't much better. The same blast that took out the launcher also destroyed the controls for the torpedo countermeasures. And although the bridge in the superstructure was cosmetic only, the explosion from the Exocet also wiped out the radar atop it so any range-finding would have to be done manually. Luckily, the LiDAR was still operational, so they could disappear back into the fog after they'd given cover for the *Deepwater* to escape.

"Murph," Juan said, "launch two torpedoes at the *Portland*."

"Aye, Chairman," Murph replied. "Torpedoes away."

On-screen, Juan could see the torpedoes ejected from the launchers and splash into the water.

"Two minutes to target," Murph said.

"Hali, what is the *Deepwater*'s status?"

"Her engines are severely damaged," Hali replied. "Captain Jefferson says they're limping along. No way they can make it all the way back to Punta Arenas without effecting repairs."

"Tell her to take shelter where she can, and we'll try to keep the *Portland* away from her."

"Aye, Chairman."

Hali was in secure radio contact with Jefferson. Although she couldn't call out for help on the satellite link, she still had an operational short-range radio on board. The disabled satellite dish didn't matter anyway. By the time any Chilean Navy ships could arrive, this would all be over, one way or the other.

Once the *Deepwater* was past the island, she could turn in any one of multiple directions, making it difficult for the *Portland* to find her.

But they had to give her time.

"Chairman," Hali said, his tone urgent. "I just got a call from the *Deepwater* that the sonobuoy they installed in this channel is detecting two unknown high-pitched signals heading our way. At the speed they're going, they'll hit us in one minute."

"Torpedoes," Juan said. It was the drawback Murph had warned him about when he modified the sonar to counteract the sonic disruptor. They were blind to anything coming at them from under the water.

"Thirty more seconds for ours," Murph said. "The *Portland* is backing behind that small island and has released countermeasures."

Juan pounded his armrest in frustration. Those were exactly the tactics he would take himself, except he didn't have the cover of an island to hide behind and he couldn't deploy his audio decoys to lure the torpedoes away from the *Oregon* because they had been destroyed by the *Abtao*'s Harpoon missile.

Tate's gambit worked. The *Oregon*'s torpedoes impacted harmlessly against the island, blasting chunks of rocks off the cliff that tumbled into the water in a minor avalanche.

There was one advantage to the *Portland* withdrawing behind the island. Juan could no longer feel the sonic disruptor's effect ricocheting through his brain.

Murph's jury-rigged version of the same weapon tied to the *Oregon*'s sonar, however, was ready to deploy.

"Murph," Juan said. "See if you can disrupt the passive sonars on those torpedoes."

"Activating it now."

The sonar dome was now blasting out a signal that should cause the torpedoes' sensors to malfunction. Theoretically.

"Stoney, move us out of the direct path the torpedoes would have been taking."

Eric took a deep breath and said, "Not much room to maneuver in here, but I'll see what I can do."

He eased the *Oregon* over toward the closest island as near to it as he dared. The *Portland*'s torpedoes ran too deep to spot them visually, so the only way to know they'd missed would be by seeing them explode. Hopefully, far away.

A geyser erupted by the shore opposite to them. Murph's disruptor had worked, causing the weapon to swerve off course.

But it didn't work the same way on the second torpedo. It must have swung in the other direction because it exploded off the *Oregon*'s port bow, rocking the ship from water hammer effect. Juan had to grip his chair to keep from falling out.

Alarms went off, indicating a hull breach.

"Closing watertight doors in sections three, five, and seven," Max called out as calmly as he could. "I've lost engine power in the port venturi tube, and maneuvering thrusters have been damaged. Flooding starboard ballast tanks to compensate for the portside flooding."

With the *Oregon* severely wounded, they couldn't wait any longer to give the *Deepwater* more of a head start. Juan had to get the *Oregon* out of there before the *Portland* could take another shot at them. But if they simply made a dash into the fog, the *Portland* would run them down before the *Oregon* could lose her.

What Juan wouldn't give for some kind of roadblock . . .

His eyes snapped to the mid-channel island separating them from the *Portland*. It was only a matter of time before she came back around the island, and she had to take the port side because the starboard side was far too cramped for her to squeeze through.

But it was the remnants of the avalanche that caught Juan's attention. He looked at the glacier flowing into the narrowest part of the channel. The ice came right down to the water's edge.

"Murph," he said. "I want you to fire two more torpedoes. But the target isn't the *Portland*. I want you to hit that glacier dead center. Run them as shallow as possible."

Murph followed Juan's gaze and nodded when he understood what Juan was going for.

He tapped new coordinates into the computer and said, "Torpedoes away."

As the *Portland* began to emerge from behind the island, the torpedoes sped toward the glacier, the propellers leaving bubbles churning behind in their wake just below the surface.

Fifteen seconds later, they blew up right beneath the part of the glacier that overhung the channel, causing massive chunks of ice to collapse into the water. The explosions set off a chain reaction that cleaved huge bergs off the glacier, blocking the path that the *Portland* would have to take. Even with her armored hull, ramming them could tear sizable holes in the ship.

Juan had to hope Tate wouldn't take that chance. He would back out of the channel and go around the island to try to cut Juan off. By that time, Juan was betting he could disappear into the vast labyrinth of channels and fjords within the National Reserve.

"Stoney, get us out of here."

Eric rotated the *Oregon* and steered her back in the direction she had come. Before the *Portland* could fully reappear from behind the island, the *Oregon* limped away into the fogbank.

57

Tate knew he had badly damaged the *Oregon*, and now he just needed to finish her off. But with the icebergs that Cabrillo threw in his path, he had to dash around the island by a different route to catch him. The longer course, coupled with the dense fog, meant that when he arrived at the other end of the channel, the *Oregon* and the *Deepwater* were gone.

He was now poring over a map of the area in the op center with Ballard, trying to plan their next move.

"Maybe we should wait for the *Oregon* or the *Deepwater* to come out of the Reserve," Ballard suggested. "If they're as damaged as you think they are, we could easily destroy them in the open ocean."

"I don't think, I know. You saw how the *Oregon* was listing right before it vanished in the fog. At least one of the torpedoes hit."

"Then let's wait—"

Tate slammed his palm against the screen. "No! We don't know how long it will take for Juan to make repairs or if he's called someone to come help him. We have to find him now."

Ballard shook her head at the map. The intricate web of channels, fjords, and coves provided too many places for the *Oregon* to hide.

"But the *Abtao* is gone. Even with the *Wuzong* coming, our advantage is cut by a third. We can retreat and try this again another time."

Tate rounded on her, enraged. "Are you insane or just stupid? We hit the *Oregon* three separate times with torpedoes and missiles. And we have a Chinese diesel-electric sub on our side. We'll never get another chance like this. You haven't shown a lack of nerve before. Don't start now."

Ballard looked around the op center to see Farouk and Li giving her embarrassed sideways glances, then she turned back to Tate and glared at him. Tate didn't care. She needed to grow a pair.

Finally, Ballard put up her hands in surrender.

"Fine. What's your plan?"

"Good. Nice to see you're back on the team." Tate calmed himself and turned back to the map. "Now, even though we're looking at a maze of channels in here, as far as I can see there are only two ways out. One here in the north, the other here in the south. We'll direct the *Wuzong* to enter from the north, we'll come in from the south. If we conduct our searches methodically, we'll run across the *Oregon* or the *Deepwater* eventually. When either is found, it's game over."

Ballard nodded. Tate could tell she liked his plan.

"We either sink the *Oregon* and then find the *Deepwater* at our leisure and dispose of the witnesses," she said, "or we take the *Deepwater* crew captive, like we originally wanted to, and force the *Oregon* to come to their rescue."

"Right. And with the *Oregon* damaged, we'll have the upper hand in any fight. If Juan wants to battle toe to toe, we'll be able to outlast him. In fact, I'd welcome—"

Farouk interrupted him.

"Commander, we're getting another call from Juan Cabrillo."

Tate smiled at Ballard. "Maybe he's calling to surrender."

"From what I've seen of this guy," Ballard said, "I highly doubt that."

"Come on," Tate said as he took his command chair. "You don't have to harsh my buzz."

He looked at Farouk. "Put Juan on-screen, deepfake us as usual."

After a moment, Cabrillo appeared, and he was more composed than the last time they spoke.

"Hello, Juan. You're looking good. I don't see any broken blood vessels in your face, like I thought I would, after your blowup during our previous talk. You do seem a bit stressed, though."

"I've had a lot on my mind the last few hours, Tate."

"I bet. But I'm glad to see you're still afloat. I wouldn't want you to sink before I found you and take all the fun out of it."

"You won't find us," Cabrillo said. "Look at your map of the region."

"I have. Yes, it's a complicated mess of islands and straits, but I think we'll run into each other sooner or later."

"Maybe you should get out of here while you have the chance."

Tate laughed. "I saw what happened to the *Oregon*, Juan. Even though things look hunky-dory in your op center, I'd guess you have damage control crews working double time all over the ship."

"A few minor dings," Cabrillo said. "Nothing that won't buff out."

"You are such a good liar. No wonder you had such an illustrious career in the CIA."

"The CIA is the reason I called. They know."

"Know what?"

"They know that you're alive. They know that Catherine Ballard abducted Langston Overholt and joined you to frame me and my crew for crimes we didn't commit. They know that you've built an exact replica of the *Oregon*."

Tate grinned at Juan and gave him his favorite finger wag. "Liar, liar, pants on fire. That might have been what you claimed, but it sounds so outrageous. Why would they ever believe you?"

"Because I've got you on recording," Cabrillo said evenly.

"You've got *you* on a recording, you mean."

Cabrillo turned to someone and said, "Play it back."

Suddenly, Tate was watching himself at their last conversation, and his stomach dropped. He was looking at his own face. In the background was Ballard, with that sickly look she got as they were battered by the waves. There was no way Cabrillo could have re-created that expression without having seen her at the time.

Tate slowly rose out of his seat. He walked over to Farouk and slapped him hard.

"You let this happen!" he screamed, before turning back to the screen.

"Now who's going to blow a blood vessel?" Cabrillo asked, the corners of his mouth turning up in a slight smile. He was enjoying this reveal.

"It doesn't matter," Tate said, waving his hands.

"I think it does. Vice President Sandecker and CIA Director Kubo were watching in real time. They saw everything."

"They're going to believe you? Maybe I'll just say we're working together."

"I don't think that'll work, either," Cabrillo said. He looked to his side and nodded.

To Tate's shock, into the frame stepped a very much alive Langston Overholt.

"Hello, Mr. Tate. I'm happy to still be on two feet, but I'm sorry to see you again."

Tate sneered at the two of them. "You think you're so smart."

"Not that smart," Cabrillo said, "but smarter than you. If you were really smart, you'd leave Chile right now and find some hole in the world to climb into. Because the U.S. government is going to come looking for you."

Tate could feel himself losing control. He took a seat in his command chair and held the armrests in a vise grip.

"You're the dumb one, Juan, if you think I'm going to leave now. Not when I've got you on the ropes. I'm coming to find you, and there's no place for you to hide."

He slashed across his throat, and the feed cut out.

Everyone in the op center was staring at him, but no one dared speak.

"Contact the *Wuzong*," Tate barked at Ballard. "Tell Admiral Yu that we're going to war."

58

With Vargas's expert help, Jefferson steered the damaged *Deepwater* through a passage so shallow and narrow that the much larger *Portland* could never follow. However, the winding waterway ended a mile later in a circular cove. They were safe for now, but trapped. At least they hadn't had any casualties more serious than wounds requiring a few stitches.

"How long will it take to effect engine repairs?" Jefferson asked her XO.

"A day at best," he replied. "We barely made it here before we had to shut the engines down to keep them from seizing up completely. Even if we get them running again, we'll only be able to run at ten knots max."

"I don't care. I want us moving as soon as possible. Make it so."

"Aye, Captain." The XO left for the engine room.

"We'll never outrun the *Portland*," Vargas said.

"We wouldn't have anyway," Jefferson said. "Dirk Pitt himself told me that she could cruise faster than forty knots. I thought he was pulling my leg until I saw that old freighter firing missiles."

"Then, what do we do? We won't even have the fog to conceal us."

It had been five hours since the devastating sea battle, and the fog was beginning to lift.

They hunched over the map of the area. Jefferson traced several routes through the islands, but they all led back to two exits into the Pacific, one to the north and the other to the south. It would take them hours to get out, and the *Portland* could be waiting between them at either choke point.

"Why don't we wait here until the Chilean authorities arrive?" Vargas suggested.

"You saw the *Portland*'s armament," Jefferson said. "A Coast Guard vessel would be cut to shreds by the *Portland*, and it might take two days for Chile's Navy ship to get here. It doesn't matter anyway. Our radios and satellite transmitter are toast."

"I thought your chief scientist said they're still getting data from the sonobuoys and the webcams."

"We are. That's why I could warn the *Oregon* about the torpedoes. The data is coming in, but we can't send anything out to the *Oregon* except by short-range radio."

"From what their captain told us about *Oregon*'s own damage," Vargas said, "I don't think they'll be much help, either."

"Then we need to sit tight here until we can make headway."

The mission's chief scientist, Mary Harper, burst onto the bridge. The slender woman, in her fifties, was breathless from running.

"Mary, what's going on?" Jefferson asked.

Harper planted a laptop on the console. She clicked, and it brought up a waveform from one of the sonobuoys. Jefferson recognized it as the signature of the song of the humpback whale.

"We just heard this from Sonobuoy Two," Harper said.

She played the audio clip. It was the familiar hoots, rumbles, and whistles of a humpback whale communicating with its pod.

"What's so unusual about that?" Vargas asked, confused as to

Harper's sense of urgency. "We hear whale songs all the time in the waters around here."

Harper shook her head. "No, *this* is what you hear."

She played a second audio clip. To Jefferson, it sounded similar to the first one.

"Isn't that the same thing?" Vargas asked, even more puzzled now.

"Not at all," Harper said. "The second one you heard is the song of the southern ocean humpback whale. The first one you heard—the one detected by our hydrophone—is the song of the northern Pacific humpback whale."

Now Jefferson was just as bewildered as Vargas. "What are you saying?"

"Humpbacks learn songs from each other," Harper said. "The songs are very distinctive to each community of whales. The whales from the northern Pacific never interact with the ones in the Southern Hemisphere. They each have their own language, so to speak."

"So we shouldn't be hearing this song in Chile?" Vargas asked.

"It would be unprecedented for a northern Pacific humpback to travel this far south. They usually only leave the Arctic to breed in Hawaii or Mexico and never come below those latitudes."

Jefferson was getting exasperated with the discussion.

"Dr. Harper, I applaud your scientific enthusiasm, but, if you didn't notice, we're a little busy with trying to stay alive right now."

"I know, I'm sorry," Harper said. "But there is a point to this. When I heard the song repeat, I compared it to the previous version. It was exactly the same. And I do mean exactly. That just doesn't happen."

Vargas raised a quizzical eyebrow at Jefferson. "She said she has a point, but I don't get it. Is this a critical whale thing that I don't understand?"

"Dr. Harper has a Ph.D. in marine biology," Jefferson said. "I'm sure she wouldn't be wasting our time if this weren't important."

"Thank you, Captain Jefferson," Harper said, annoyed but plowing ahead. "I wasn't finished. When I heard the repetition, I turned up the sensitivity of the hydrophone and canceled out the waveform of the whale song. When I did that, I heard this coming from the same direction as the humpback signal."

She played another audio clip. This one was fainter, and it took a moment for Jefferson to recognize it for a man-made sound. When she did, she looked at Harper with surprise.

"Am I crazy," Jefferson said, "or is that the sound of a ship's propeller?"

59

The extreme depth of the fjord they were navigating allowed the Chinese sub *Wuzong* to glide through the channel at one hundred feet below the surface, making it undetectable by any aircraft flying overhead. So far, they'd detected no ships.

Admiral Yu Jiang calmly watched the depth gauge and asked for constant updates from his sonar officer.

His executive officer, on the other hand, had been agitated ever since they had left the vast empty spaces of the open ocean.

"These underwater canyons are getting narrower the closer we get to the mainland," the nervous XO said. "Perhaps we should have stayed at the entrance to the northern pass as Tate wanted us to."

Yu sneered at him. "And simply wait for the *Oregon* to come to us?"

"Tate said that he would herd the ship in our direction. You would get the glory of sinking her."

"Of course that's what he would say. But he wants revenge just as much as I do. I could sense it in his voice. He will attack the *Oregon* the moment he sees her. He's just using us to keep her from escaping."

"The *Wuzong* was not meant to operate this close to shore."

"Don't you trust our country's scientists?" Yu asked him.

"I do," the XO said. "But we have never tested the new sonar system in real-world conditions."

"Then consider this the test. Not only will we get our revenge, we will prove the viability of our experimental sonar and acquire a valuable new weapon when Tate hands over his designs for the sonic disruptor."

Underwater, a submarine was virtually blind, relying on inertial navigation and existing maps for plotting its course. In the open ocean, where undersea obstacles were few and well documented, this type of navigation was sufficient. Passive sonar provided positional information on moving objects like ships and other subs.

But to see subsurface obstacles closer to shore required the use of active sonar, which sent out a powerful ping that reflected off of stationary objects. The echolocation provided a detailed image of the surrounding topography, but it also revealed the sub's position and its proximity to any ships in the vicinity.

For that reason, military subs rarely ventured into shallow waters unless they were in friendly ports and had the benefit of seeing traditional navigational markers like buoys and lighthouses, while either on the surface or below, using the periscope.

But Chinese researchers had come up with a compromise that allowed their nation's subs to venture into foreign waters without being detected. They had installed an active sonar on the *Wuzong* that simulated the call of the humpback whale.

The sonar signal was emitted at the same intensity as the song produced by an actual whale. This meant that its reflected signal was less powerful than that produced by a traditional sonar, so the sub had to move much more slowly than normal, like a car creeping through pitch-black night with weak headlights.

Any ships hearing the signal would simply think a whale pod was passing by, never suspecting that the song had been recorded from a whale in Hawaii. And since humpbacks ranged over the entire world, the sonar could be used anywhere without raising suspicions.

"Any ships in the area?" Yu asked the sonarman.

"No, sir," the executive officer replied. "The only man-made object on my scope is that buoy we just passed."

Yu knew that the *Deepwater* was conducting oceanographic research in the area. He suspected it was something boring, like the analysis of water temperature or tidal movements. His sub wouldn't trip any of those types of sensors.

"Clearance?"

"One hundred meters from the bottom," the sonarman said. "Three hundred meters on either side."

Yu smiled at his XO. "You see? Plenty of room."

The XO pointed at the map. "It will get narrower soon."

"Then we will go even more slowly. We're going to check every channel that the *Oregon* could fit into."

"Certainly not this one, though." The executive officer was pointing to a waterway that bent around on itself and dead-ended in a cul-de-sac. It was more than two miles long, and entering it would require a tight U-turn. One mile in, then another mile back to the end after the turn.

Yu nodded firmly. "Yes, that one, too. The end widens enough for us to make the turn to exit."

"I highly advise against us entering that fjord. We don't want to get stuck in there."

"I'm not going to pass it and risk missing the *Oregon* because we lost our courage."

"It's not courage, sir. It's just that—"

Yu put up a hand to interrupt him. "Your objection is noted. Is there anything else?"

The XO backed down and shook his head.

"How long until we reach that offshoot?" Admiral Yu asked.

"Thirty minutes."

"Fine. When we reach that point, I will guide us in personally."

"Should I raise the antenna and inform the *Portland* of our status?"

Yu bored through his executive officer with an icy glare. "We will contact Zachariah Tate when we have something to report."

"Understood, Admiral."

The XO didn't say another word, and Yu leaned down to continue poring over other potential hiding places for the *Oregon*.

60

T hank you for the heads-up, Captain Jefferson," Juan said after hearing the audio clip that the NUMA commander had played for them over the encrypted radio channel. Everyone in the op center had gone quiet to listen to the underwater propeller.

"What do you make of it?" Jefferson asked.

"I'm not sure."

"Is it the *Portland*?"

"No, I can say for sure that it isn't." The jets of water produced by the magnetohydrodynamic engines would never be mistaken for a ship's propeller. "Can you play it again?"

After several repetitions, Linda Ross, whose hearing was still diminished but now functional again thanks to two weeks of recovery time, said, "Chairman, I ran the sound of the screw through our military database. The sound fidelity isn't very good through the radio connection, but the computer says it most closely matches the audio profile of the screw on a Type 039A Chinese diesel-electric submarine."

A murmur went through the op center. Juan certainly hadn't expected that result.

"Although I never considered the possibility it was Chinese, I thought it might be a sub," Jefferson said. "My chief scientist, Mary Harper, thought the screw was too far below the surface to be a ship."

"And you said it's heading toward us?" Juan asked Jefferson.

"Yes. Dr. Harper estimates that at the rate it is traveling, the sub will be able to see you in less than thirty minutes. That is, if her captain is crazy enough to enter the channel where you're anchored."

The *Oregon* had taken refuge in a long fjord that was the shape of a U-bend pipe used in plumbing. The *Deepwater* had come this way two days ago because one of the biggest penguin rookeries they were studying was located on one of the fjord's pebble beaches. Jefferson said she briefly saw the *Oregon* on the operational webcam before the ship went out of frame.

On the map, it seemed that the fjord had only one way in or out. However, what used to be a peninsula that separated the two long arms of the fjord was now an island. Until recently, a glacier flowed down to the sea near the entrance to the fjord, but the ice had melted after the latest maps had been created just a few years before.

That left a gap barely wider than the *Oregon*. Only the most desperate circumstances would spur an effort to squeeze through it. One wrong move or rogue current and the jagged rocks would rip a mortal gash in the hull. While the sub would never come through the cut through the peninsula, it might attempt going down the length of the fjord.

"I wouldn't discount anything at this point," Juan said, "including Tate attacking your ship."

"But we went through a channel that even I was reluctant to enter. There's no way the *Portland* could get to us in here."

Juan looked at the map. The *Deepwater* was ten miles to the south in a broad cove surrounded by mountains. Jefferson was right that the *Portland* couldn't get in there, but that wouldn't stop Tate.

"If he finds you, Captain Jefferson, Tate could come at you with small boats or a helicopter. You've seen too much for him to just let you go. He'll either take you hostage or wipe out your whole crew and scuttle the *Deepwater*. Do you have any defensive armaments to repel boarders?"

"Does a flare gun count?" she asked sarcastically.

"Won't hold a candle to the kind of firepower he'll be bringing. I'm going to send you some help."

"That would be much appreciated," Jefferson said. "But how will they get here?"

"We've got a helicopter, too." He told her the tail number so she wouldn't be afraid to see it approach.

"Our landing pad is clear."

"They'll be in the air in ten minutes." Juan knew it was risky. The helicopter might be seen by the *Portland*, but he felt that it was better than leaving the *Deepwater* defenseless.

"Thanks for sending them."

"It's the least I could do for warning us about the sub. I look forward to meeting you when this is done."

"Same here," Jefferson said and then signed off.

Juan turned to Linda. "Get Gomez to fire up the helicopter. Take MacD and Raven with you. Bring some extra weapons along to share. And tell Gomez to stay as low as possible. I don't want the *Portland* to spot you and shoot you out of the sky."

"Neither do I," Linda said and hurried out of the op center.

Juan would use drones to keep a watch out for the *Portland*, but they'd used them all up during the battle in Rio and hadn't had time to replenish them.

He went over to Max and asked, "What's the latest casualty report?"

"Three injuries. Doc Huxley is treating them and said none of them requires surgery."

"That's good to hear. And the damage report?"

"Not much better than the last one," Max said with a shake of his head. "Both port venturi tubes are out of commission."

"Any way to fix them?"

"Not without a dry dock. Which means we're down to half speed at best. Plus we have major damage to our maneuvering thrusters. I know you were thinking we might be able to head through the eye of that needle where the glacier used to be, but there's almost no chance we'd get through unscathed. The radar is gone, and the sonar is non-functional because we're using it for protection against Tate's sonic disruptor."

Juan mulled over all that information, then said, "Weapons?"

"Port torpedoes are empty. Starboard torpedo launchers are off-line because of the flooding. Exocet missiles are down. We're lucky they didn't cook off after that Harpoon hit. We might be able to get missiles to operational status with a day of repair work."

"Which leaves us with what?"

Max sighed. "The 120mm cannon and the Gatling guns are still functional."

"Neither of which are powerful enough to sink the *Portland* without a sustained barrage. Any good news?"

"The flooding is under control. We're not in imminent danger of sinking."

"I suppose it could always be worse," Juan said.

"Sorry I don't have a more optimistic report."

"We don't have time to slip out of here before the sub arrives. Looks like we're going to have to fight them. No way a Chinese sub is in these waters unless it's working with Tate."

"How can we fight them?" Max asked. "Our torpedoes are out, and we have no sonar. We won't even know if the sub is in the fjord."

"We still have some sonobuoys, right?"

Max shrugged. "They're not nearly as powerful as the ones the

Deepwater installed. We'll never hear the sound of a diesel-electric sub running on batteries."

"We don't need to," Juan said. "We only have to hear the whale's song."

Max nodded. "That might be enough. I'll send out Hali and Murph in a Zodiac to drop it in the water near the U-turn of the fjord. But how are we going to fight it with no torpedoes of our own?"

"We have to get it to the surface. The sonar alterations that Murph made might work."

Max looked skeptical, but there was no other choice. "If the sub sees us before we spot them, she'll plant a couple of torpedoes in us, and then it's game over."

Juan knew he was right. This entire strategy was a long shot, and the situation looked dire for the *Oregon*. Even if they survived an encounter with the Chinese sub, they still had to get past the *Portland*, which was looking more improbable by the minute.

"I have an idea how to bring the sub to the surface," Juan said. "I'll let Hali and Murph know what they need to do. You find Maurice and tell him to come see me."

"Maurice?" Max asked, puzzled why Juan would want to see the chief steward at a time like this.

Juan gave Max a solemn look. "I have an important task for him. And I don't think he's going to like it."

61

The hydraulic platform in the aft hold of the *Oregon* rose out of the deck while Gomez Adams untied the skids of the MD 520N five-passenger helicopter. Unlike most choppers, this one had no tail rotor. Instead, rotation of the aircraft was controlled by exhaust from the turbine that was vented through slots in the tail boom.

He climbed in and rapidly went through the checklist to get the chopper airborne as quickly as possible. While Gomez was busy starting it up, Linda, MacD, and Raven loaded a complement of assault rifles into the helicopter, enough to outfit a squad of soldiers. All three were dressed in combat gear and body armor.

"Do you think they'll have anyone on the *Deepwater* who can fire those things?" Gomez asked Linda.

"NUMA always has a few Navy vets on board," she said. "And, we know how to handle our weapons."

"Ah just hope we get there in time," MacD said.

"As far as we know, they haven't been spotted," Raven said, handing up the last of the ammunition. Now there was barely room inside the cabin for the three of them. Linda got into the front seat beside

Gomez while Raven and MacD squeezed into the rear. All of them put headsets on.

"Everyone buckled in?" Gomez asked.

They all said yes, and he started the engine and engaged the five-bladed rotor. Within seconds, it was up to full speed, and he deftly lifted off from the *Oregon*. He wheeled around and sped down the fjord, waving to Hali and Murph as he flew over, each in his own Zodiac.

Gomez could have chosen a direct flight path from the *Oregon* to the *Deepwater*, but instead he flew overland as much as he could to minimize the chance that he'd accidentally pass over the *Portland*. If her anti-aircraft missile system was the same as the one on the *Oregon*, Tate could easily blow him out of the sky.

He passed over one last mountain and saw the *Deepwater* anchored in the isolated cove. The sole waterway into it was so tiny that he gave the captain credit for squeezing through successfully. If the *Portland* tried the same thing, it would be wedged in place.

He circled the *Deepwater* once so they could see he was from the *Oregon*. Then he dived down and hovered over the bow landing pad, settling onto it so gently that it was hard to tell they'd even made contact.

Two women approached the helicopter as Linda, MacD, and Raven got out. He couldn't hear what was said among them because he didn't stop the rotor, but each of the women expertly checked the magazine on the assault rifle given to her and slung the weapon over her shoulder. Raven and MacD carried the rest away toward the bridge.

Linda came back over and spoke into the headset.

"We don't want Tate to know we got here," she said. "If they see the chopper on the pad, they'll be wary about approaching. We want to catch them by surprise. Better go back to the *Oregon*."

"Roger that," Gomez replied.

Linda closed the door and backed away. As soon as she was clear, Gomez took off.

When he neared the top of the mountain, he noticed movement out of the corner of his eye.

It was a drone. The quadcopter was just cresting the ridge to the south. The only reason he saw its gray body was because it stuck out against the white snow on the mountaintop. It had to be from the *Portland*.

He radioed the *Deepwater* about the drone, but he didn't hear a response. He was too distracted by the flare of a missile's exhaust racing toward him over the mountain from behind the drone.

He shoved the joystick forward in an attempt to duck under the missile's path. It wasn't fast enough.

Even though the warhead didn't make a direct impact, the missile's proximity sensor detonated, showering the chopper with shrapnel.

The windscreen was peppered with metal shards, and two of them hit Gomez, one in the head and one in the leg. Blood gushed down his face, obscuring his vision, but he didn't feel any pain. Not yet.

The explosion also hit the engine, and smoke poured out. Alarms blared, and the control panel warning lights flashed like it was Times Square.

He could feel the lift decreasing, and the helicopter swung crazily from side to side. It wasn't going to stay in the air much longer.

"Mayday! Mayday! Mayday!" Gomez shouted into the headset as he wrestled with the controls. "I'm going down. Repeat, I'm going down."

He didn't get an answer, so he didn't know if his radio had been hit as well.

The mountain was rugged and steep, but there was a small glacier on one side of the island. He aimed the MD 520N for the flattest portion.

As he approached, the engine suddenly cut out, and he had to glide in as best he could using autorotation. His depth perception was gone, so gauging his speed as he headed for the white expanse was nearly impossible.

He used his thousands of flight hours to guess when to flare out. Too early and he'd drop like a stone. Too late and he'd slam into the ground at high speed.

He was too early, but only a little. He was hovering just feet over the glacier when the last of the lift gave out. The helicopter lurched downward, but the soft snow cushioned its fall, and then it remained upright as the skids sank into the powder. The rotor blades slowly came to a stop and the cabin went eerily silent.

Gomez keyed the radio, but all he heard was static.

Then the pain finally hit. His leg throbbed and his head ached. He reached in the first-aid kit and grabbed and ripped open some gauze, pressing it against his temple to stanch the blood flow. His thigh was bleeding, too, but it didn't look serious.

If the drone saw him, it certainly saw the NUMA ship, and it meant the *Portland* was somewhere nearby. Getting off this glacier was going to be a problem. He leaned back and closed his eyes. That was nothing compared to the trouble coming for the *Deepwater*.

62

That helicopter had to have spotted the drone," Tate said from his command chair in the *Portland*'s op center. The smoking MD 520N that was now resting on the glacier was similar to the *Portland*'s own chopper. "It must be from the *Oregon*."

"What was it doing there?" Ballard asked.

"I don't know. Maybe Juan is in communication with the *Deepwater* and sent someone to evacuate them." The NUMA ship was motionless in the cove where it was hiding.

"That won't happen now," Farouk said. "The chopper is a wreck."

"Now it is. But the pilot might have been able to warn *Deepwater* that we're nearby."

"We can't get in there," Li Quon said. "The *Portland* is too big to fit."

"What about firing a missile to sink her?" Tate asked.

Li shook his head. "We can't get a lock from here."

"Don't we want hostages?" Ballard asked.

Tate nodded. "I was just considering my options. What do you suggest?"

"The *Portland* may not be able to get in," Ballard said, "but I can take our chopper over there." No sense in sending it out on a search for the *Oregon* when it could be shot down without ever seeing the ship.

"I can go with her," Li said. "I should be able to steer the *Deepwater* back out of the cove."

"If she's seaworthy," Tate said. "Durchenko's men put a lot of holes in her engine room before the *Abtao* went down."

"If the ship isn't able to make headway, we can hold them hostage on board," Ballard said. "Or we can start ferrying them back here."

Tate grimaced. There were supposed to be more than fifty crew on board. Bringing them all back two or three at a time would take too long.

"Ten people at most," he said. "Officers only. Execute the rest."

"I'll take some charges along, just in case," Li said. "That way, I can plant explosives to scuttle the ship."

"How long will it take you to get over there?" Tate asked.

Ballard shrugged. "Ten minutes."

Tate thought about that. The range on the chopper was three hundred miles, so there was no need for the *Portland* to hang around and wait for them. If Ballard saw the *Deepwater* try to make a run for it, Tate could always turn around and come back to intercept the ship. If not, he could take the *Portland* and continue searching for the *Oregon*.

"Okay," he said. "You and Li assemble an assault team. Land on the *Deepwater* and take control of the ship and crew. They're a bunch of scientists, so I don't think you'll encounter much resistance, but don't hesitate to eliminate anyone who fights back. We don't need all of them."

"Understood," Ballard said. "We'll land, and then I'll have the helicopter take off again and cover us while we commandeer the bridge."

On the main view screen, Tate saw the helicopter pad rising from the aft hold. Its pilot was checking the weapons. Unlike the *Oregon*'s civilian chopper, Tate had sprung for the military version. It was equipped with twin 7.62mm mini-guns and two seven-shot rocket pods. The weaponry wasn't enough to sink a ship of the *Deepwater*'s size, but the machine guns and rockets could take out anyone on deck who caused trouble.

Li left the op center, and Ballard was about to follow when Tate grabbed her arm and planted a kiss on her.

"What was that for?" she asked with a smile.

"Because I can," Tate said. "Plus I love it when you say 'comman-deer.'"

As she pulled away, her hand trailed down his arm. She was still grinning as she went out the door.

Tate turned and caught Farouk smirking at him. The rest of the op center crew members were studiously averting their gazes.

"What are you looking at?" Tate sneered at Farouk as he returned to his chair.

"Nothing at all," Farouk said, but he chuckled under his breath.

Tate made a mental note. Once he sank the *Oregon* and sold off the plans for the sonic disruptor for a hefty price, he'd have no more use for the Egyptian engineer.

When Ballard got back from her mission, she and Tate would have a lot of fun planning how to kill him.

63

Juan's blood ran cold regarding Tate when word came back from the *Deepwater* that Gomez's helicopter was shot down after he dropped off the team. He wished he could go in search of his friend and crewmate, but right now his responsibility was to the *Oregon*. The sonobuoy Hali had anchored near the other end of the fjord was picking up the humpback whale's song, which meant the Chinese sub was approaching.

Even though clouds still passed over the tops of the mountains surrounding them at regular intervals, the water and air at the surface of the fjord were relatively calm. The tranquil conditions made Juan's plan possible.

A magnified view of the fjord's opposite end showed nothing.

"I'm picking up the signal rounding the U-bend," Hali said. "If I'm reading this right, they'll be completing the turn in a minute. Then they'll have a straight shot at us."

"Start up our sonic disruptor," Juan ordered Murph.

"Starting her up," Murph said, activating the crude version of the weapon that he had improvised.

"Let's see what that does to their sensors," Eric Stone said from his position at the helm.

"If it doesn't work," Murph said, "we'll know soon enough."

Too true, Juan thought. The sound of an explosion hitting the ship might be the first indication the submarine hadn't been affected. The sub would fire torpedoes the second its commander saw the *Oregon*. The disruptor had diverted the *Portland*'s torpedoes, but that was no guarantee it would deflect the Chinese's. In any case, the *Oregon* might not be able to survive even a near miss in her current state.

"Hali, trigger the fog generator."

Juan had ordered Hali and Murph to leave one of the Zodiacs out there to hold a large remote-controlled smoke machine.

A white cloud began to belch from the Zodiac. Soon, it would cover a large section of the fjord. The generator would produce a good approximation of the fog they'd seen before, but it wouldn't last long. If Juan had worked this out correctly, all they would need was a minute or two of the dense coverage.

"Murph," he said, "prepare to fire."

"Opening hull doors," Murph replied. The steel plates would now be retracting to expose the ship's 120mm cannon.

Murph looked down at the targeting reticle on his weapons monitor, which was also displayed on the main view screen. The reticle was aimed at the center of the expanding cloud.

"This may be tricky without the radar," he said.

"I trust your aim," Juan said.

All they could do now was wait for the sub to show itself.

Admiral Yu was not pleased when he heard from the sonarman. They were in a critical maneuver rounding the bend in the fjord, and the crewman was telling him that the *Wuzong* was effectively blind.

"Is the sonar malfunctioning?" Yu demanded.

The sonarman looked perplexed. "I don't know, Admiral. There might be some kind of interference, but I can't tell where it could be coming from. Our signal still seems to be emitting, yet I can't see the fjord walls on my monitor anymore. We could drift right into the cliffs or any underwater obstacle."

Yu cursed his luck. "Reverse engines! All stop!"

As the *Wuzong* came to a halt, Yu waited for the sound of the hull scraping the rocks, but all was silent. They'd stopped in time.

"It looks like we'll have to use visual navigation," Yu said. "Bring us to periscope depth."

He raised the periscope and peered through it. When the scope cleared the surface, he still could see nothing. This time, however, it was because of fog. He did a complete three-hundred-sixty-degree turn, but the cover was so dense that he couldn't even see the nearby cliffs.

It might only be low-level, Yu thought. The periscope was just a meter or so above the surface. They had to get above the mist.

"Surface the boat," he ordered.

"But we will be visible, sir," the executive officer objected.

"Not in this soup, we won't," Yu said. "We can't just sit here. Do it."

The XO looked dubious, nonetheless saying, "Yes, sir."

The ballast tanks were emptied, and the *Wuzong* breached the surface.

Yu once again looked through the periscope. The fog was less dense at this level, and it looked like it was starting to clear. He turned, seeing just how close they'd come to running straight into the side of the canyon. The rock face was less than fifty meters from the starboard bow of the boat.

He kept rotating and suddenly stopped when, out of the parting gloom, he saw a ship a mile away at the dead end of the fjord. It was either the *Oregon* or the *Portland*, he couldn't tell which.

"Radio the *Portland*. Now! Tell them our position and ask for theirs."

The radio officer made the call, but Admiral Yu didn't need to wait for a reply to realize he'd made a grave mistake. There was a muzzle flash from the bow of the ship.

"Crash-dive!" he yelled. "Fire torpedo tubes one and two!"

A second later, a huge splash from an explosion erupted off the port bow, and the sub shook from the impact.

The crew scrambled to follow his orders, but Yu realized it wouldn't matter.

A second muzzle flash told him he was too late.

Juan watched as the second shell struck the bow of the submarine. The armor-piercing round must have plunged all the way through to the torpedo room because the entire front of the submarine blew apart in a spectacular blast.

The remainder of the sub settled in the water until its tail fins tilted up skyward, then plunged beneath the surface like a diving whale.

The op center was quiet for a minute as they waited for the possibility of a torpedo hitting the *Oregon*. But when nothing happened, everyone breathed a sigh of relief.

"Sorry about the first shell missing," Murph said to the room. "I'll have to adjust the aim on that targeting system."

"Yeah, you stink at this," Eric teased. "It took you two whole shots to sink an enemy sub."

"If you keep shooting that badly," Max said, "we just might give you a Christmas bonus this year."

Juan didn't want to dampen the mood. He knew it was only a temporary victory.

"Hali, did you intercept any signals coming from the sub?"

Hali shook his head. "No, but that doesn't mean anything. They could have sent out an encrypted radio message."

"Then I don't think we can celebrate just yet," Juan said in a somber tone. "It's very possible Tate now knows exactly where we are."

64

The *Portland*'s helicopter circled the *Deepwater* twice, but Ballard, who was sitting next to the pilot, couldn't see anyone at all.

"They must be cowering inside," she said to Tate over the radio.

"I wish I could be there with you," he said.

"And I wish I could trade places with you. How long until you reach the *Oregon*?"

"An hour. I have to take the long way around the island to get to the fjord. But there's no way Juan could get past me even if he leaves right now. I've got him."

"How are you going to do it?"

"Guns, torpedoes, missiles—the whole works. I want to see the *Oregon* reduced to a hulk before she goes under." She heard him talking to someone else, and then he came back on the line. "Farouk would like to sink her from here with a couple of Exocets, but it's the same problem as with the *Deepwater*. We can't get a lock on them until we're in the fjord."

"You said you've lost contact with the *Wuzong*?" Ballard asked.

"They got cut off right after the call saying that they saw a ship that could either be us or them. I even heard screaming before they went off-line. I'm guessing Admiral Yu underestimated Juan, and he paid the price."

"Don't make the same mistake."

"I won't. I can poke our bow in just far enough to get a lock with our radar and sonar. Then the *Oregon* will be history." Tate sounded absolutely giddy.

"Record it for me. I want to watch later."

"Absolutely. We'll put it on the big screen."

"I'll bring the popcorn," Ballard said. "We're about to land. I'll call when we have the hostages under control."

"Hurry back." Tate signed off.

Ballard pointed the pilot toward the pad on the bow of the *Deepwater*. "Take us down. As soon as we're out, take off and cover us."

The pilot nodded and dove toward the stationary ship. He touched down, and Ballard, Li, and two other men in her assault team, all armed with Heckler & Koch G36 automatic rifles and wearing Kevlar vests, leaped out of the helicopter. They dropped to their knees as the rotor spooled up again.

The bridge directly aft of them was empty. No movement anywhere as far as she could tell. They were going to have to search the ship room by room.

She waited as the chopper took off, her rifle at the ready.

Raven and MacD were waiting on either side of the bridge, lying below the windows until they heard the helicopter lifting off the pad. Raven nodded at MacD, and she shoved open the door on the portside bridge wing while MacD opened the door on the starboard side.

She took aim at the ascending chopper. Raven's target was the engine while MacD was shooting for the pilot. She unloaded her magazine on full auto. She must have hit something vital because the turbine started coughing black smoke. Either MacD hit his target or the pilot just wasn't as good as Gomez because the helicopter spun, out of control, toward the jagged slope nearest to the *Deepwater*. It slammed into the island sideways, and a rocket pod exploded, ripping the copter to shreds. Pieces tumbled down to the water below.

Raven dove to the deck, bullets pinging against the bulkhead above her. She didn't engage the four people in combat gear on the helicopter pad, who were now firing weapons in the direction of the bridge. They were Linda Ross's responsibility.

Linda was surprised to find that the only people on board the *Deepwater* who'd ever fired an assault rifle before were Captain Jefferson, a Navy vet, and Amelia Vargas, who used to be in the Chilean Coast Guard. She gave each of them a weapon and sketched out a plan, with the help of Raven and MacD, to repel boarders.

They'd kept a lookout until they saw the MD 520N approaching with rockets and machine guns. That necessitated a quick revision to the plan, with Raven and MacD taking out the helicopter after it took off.

Linda, Jefferson, and Vargas, meanwhile, readied themselves to pop up from the emergency stairs at the bow since the focus of anyone on the pad would be Raven and MacD, shooting from the shelter of the solid bridge wing railings.

Linda had no intent on fighting fairly, not when it was clear that Tate would likely murder all of them.

When she heard the gunfire, Linda waved her hand forward, and the women went up the stairs until they saw four people in combat gear on the pad.

Catherine Ballard was the leader, so Linda took her down first with a single round. Jefferson and Vargas each shot one of the other men. Linda hit the last man, center mass, in the back, and he flopped to the deck. The entire assault took less than two seconds.

"Stay here and cover me," she said to Jefferson and Vargas, both of whom looked wired but in control.

They nodded, and Linda crept forward, her rifle at the ready.

She got to the four attackers and saw that two of the men were dead from headshots. Both Jefferson and Vargas had good aim.

Catherine Ballard was lying on her back and bleeding from a severe neck wound.

Linda shook her head in disgust. "You're going to die a traitor to your country."

Ballard smiled up at Linda with scarlet teeth.

"And your captain is a dead man. Your ship is . . ." Her voice trailed off.

Linda leaned down and grabbed her vest. "What about my ship? Tell me!"

Ballard didn't answer. She sputtered blood from her lips before wheezing her last.

The final man was lying facedown. Linda flipped him over with her foot, her finger on the trigger.

He was an Asian man, grimacing in pain.

"Move and you die," she said with the barrel of her rifle in his face.

She nodded for Jefferson and Vargas to join her.

"Cover him."

While they did, Linda kicked away his rifle, removed his sidearm, and searched him. He didn't have any other weapons. Her shot in his back had been stopped by body armor.

"Who are you?" she demanded.

He coughed and said, "Li Quon."

"Are you going to tell me anything useful, Mr. Li, or should I shoot you now?"

She wouldn't shoot an unarmed man, but he didn't know that. By the horrified looks on their faces, neither did Jefferson nor Vargas.

"Don't shoot!" Li cried. "I'll tell you whatever you want to know."

"Where is the *Portland*?"

"It's heading to the *Oregon* right now. Tate knows where it is."

"We know that," Linda said, shoving the rifle even closer to his nose. "How far away is it?"

"It'll be there in less than an hour," Li yammered, terrified. "Tate said there's no way for the *Oregon* to escape."

65

Juan stood on the ruined bridge of the *Oregon* and looked down at the battle scars riddling her deck. Charred and twisted metal bore witness to the damage she had survived. Despite the toppled crane, the blasted gaps in the hull, and the wreckage where he was standing, his ship still had life in her. To someone else, the blackened paint and misshapen steel might have looked ugly, but to Juan the blemishes were a testament to the reasons why he loved his home on the sea.

Footsteps stomped up the metal stairs to the bridge wing outside, and Juan smiled. He didn't have to turn to know who it was.

"She's a tough old gal," Max said. "Any other ship would have been at the bottom of Davy Jones's locker by now."

"The *Oregon* can take a lot of punishment, in large part thanks to you," Juan said. "You designed a fine ship."

Max sighed. "Which means I also designed the *Portland*. I never thought we'd be fighting against ourselves."

"And now we're fighting with both hands tied behind our backs. Tate's ship is undamaged, and we're about to face him with half an engine and minimal weapons. At least you got the maneuvering thrusters back online."

The outlook hadn't gotten any rosier when they'd received a brief call from Linda telling them that her team had defeated the assault on the *Deepwater* and that the *Portland* was on the way.

"We can still deliver a punch," Max said. "The sub sitting on the bottom of this fjord is proof of that."

Juan shook his head. "It's not enough. Tate has torpedoes and missiles."

"We've got the Gatling guns for defense, and Murph's pseudo sonic disruptor has worked so far to deflect torpedoes."

"Tate saw what happened the last time he used torpedoes. He's too smart to make the same mistake twice. He'll use umbilical wires to guide them in. We'll be an easy target. And we can't outrun him. I've looked at the map. He'll easily catch us if we try to make a break for it."

Max leaned against the railing next to him. "You sound pretty glum. I've never known you to give up. You're not thinking of surrendering to Tate, are you?"

"If I thought surrendering would save the crew, I'd do it. But you've seen Tate's MO. He won't stop at killing me and sinking the ship. He'll murder every single survivor of the battle, and then he'll go back and finish off the *Deepwater* for good measure."

"Then we go down fighting," Max said resolutely. "Not a bad way to die."

"I don't want to die. I don't want anyone on the *Oregon* to die. That's why there's only one option."

"Maurice didn't like what you told him. And I bet I'm not going to like what I'm about to hear."

Juan pointed at the narrow gap in the peninsula separating them from the fjord's entrance. Before he could say more, his phone buzzed. Even out this far in the middle of nowhere, he could get a signal from the shipwide network. He answered and put it on speaker.

"What's going on, Hali?" he asked.

"I've got Linda on the line again."

"Patch her through."

The connection clicked. "Linda, I've got Max here with me. What's the latest?"

"Li Quon has been spilling his guts, and he told us something that I thought might be useful."

"That the *Portland* has some critical weakness we can target?" Max asked. "Like an exhaust port two meters across that will let us blow up his whole ship with one shot?"

"I wish," she said. "But Li did mention that Tate has been monitoring the webcams that the *Deepwater* set up to watch the penguin rookeries. He even saw the *Deepwater* in the background of one of the videos."

"One of those webcams is in this fjord, isn't it?" Juan asked, turning toward the long canyon. "I can see penguins on the beach about a half mile away." The recent explosions hadn't seemed to bother them at all. They were probably accustomed to the sound of cracking ice and calving glaciers.

"Not sure how that can help us," Max said, "but it certainly doesn't hurt us. I checked, and the camera is facing the opposite direction. He can't see us right now."

"I was just thinking about that deepfake technology," Linda said. "Captain Jefferson said the webcams are designed to be updated remotely. If I gave the access code to Eric and Hali, do you think they could install some software to make it look like the *Oregon* is in the frame? It might buy you a few critical seconds if Tate thinks you're somewhere that you're not."

Max looked at Juan and made a face like it could work. "I do have some footage of the *Oregon* that we could use."

"It would have to be subtle. If it's too obvious, Tate will know it's a fake."

"I'll get Eric and Hali to work on it right away," Max said. He took out his own phone and began texting.

"Okay," Linda said. "I'll give Hali the access codes."

"Before you go," Juan said, "did Li tell you anything about the state of the *Portland*?"

"He claims everything was in working condition when he left. But he did say that Tate would be broken up about the death of Catherine Ballard. He thought they were in love."

"Thanks, Linda, that helps. I'm passing you back to Hali."

Max put away his phone and said, "Eric thinks he can do it in the next hour before Tate gets here." He looked skeptical about its effectiveness, though. "I'm not sure how much of a difference it will make. We're still at a huge disadvantage."

Juan looked again at the tight walls of the gap that the carved out glacier had left behind. Linda's idea made his mad plan seem a bit less crazy.

"Even a little edge might help," he said. "It might be the difference between life and death."

66

The *Portland* was half an hour away from intercepting the *Oregon*, barreling around an island to make a run toward the fjord, but Tate was more concerned that he hadn't heard back from Ballard. She was supposed to check in after she took the *Deepwater*, but he'd heard nothing.

"Try her radio again," he told Farouk.

Farouk made the call, shaking his head after a few moments. "No response."

Tate stewed about what that might mean. "Could her radio be out?"

"Maybe," Farouk said, "but I can't reach the helicopter, either."

Tate didn't like it, yet he couldn't let himself be distracted. He had to prepare for his attack on the *Oregon*. "You've made the changes to the torpedo guidance systems?"

Farouk nodded. "Wire-guided only."

"I want to use the sonic disruptor again on the *Oregon* crew."

"It didn't seem to affect the ship the last time we saw them. They must have developed a countermeasure."

"I know that!" Tate spat. "I'll use it on any lifeboat that makes an escape once we sink her. I want them to suffer."

"That's a good idea. I doubt their countermeasure will be installed on small boats." Farouk suddenly held up the finger of one hand and pressed the other hand to his headset. "I'm getting a call from Ballard's radio."

Tate jumped out of his seat and felt a flush of relief. "Put her on."

"You're connected."

A woman's voice came over the speakers. It wasn't Ballard.

"Zachariah Tate?" she asked.

"Who is this?" Tate demanded, his heart racing. "Where is Catherine?"

"I'll let someone else explain."

There was a pause, and then a familiar voice spoke.

"It's your fault that I had to contact you this way, Tate," Juan Cabrillo said, much to Tate's shock. "You weren't answering my calls."

For a moment, Tate was speechless.

"I bet you're surprised to hear from me," Cabrillo went on.

Finally, Tate found his voice. "You can't be on the *Deepwater*."

"I'm not, although it would have been amusing to let you think so. No, I had Linda patch me through using Catherine Ballard's radio since your girlfriend wasn't using it. Linda tells me you've been pestering her nonstop with attempts to get in touch with Ballard."

"Where is she?" Tate growled.

"Ballard? She is currently dead. Not what I would have wanted, but she tried to kill my people, so it was justified."

"I don't believe you."

"Well, that's just wishful thinking on your part. Could I be talking to you through her radio if she were still alive?"

Even though Tate couldn't see Cabrillo's self-righteous expression, he could imagine it. The image in his head was enraging.

"I will kill you!"

"You keep saying that, but it hasn't happened yet. And I don't think it will. I'm sure you'll go on trying, though."

"I'm on my way to the *Oregon* right now," Tate said. "The *Wuzong* radioed your position to me."

"Is that the name of the Chinese sub that's now lying in four hundred feet of water with her entire front half blown away?"

"You can keep up your smug little game," Tate said, "but I'm coming for you, and nothing can stop me from sinking the *Oregon*."

"You started this 'little game,' as you call it. I'm going to end it. Come and get me, Tate."

The signal abruptly cut out.

Tate let out a primal scream and kicked his chair until his foot ached.

Farouk cleared his throat. "Commander, you should look at this. It's a live shot from the fjord where the *Oregon* is hiding." He nodded at the main view screen.

It was the webcam video from the penguin rookery. Behind the birds, waddling around amid lounging sea lions, the *Oregon* drifted into view. She was listing badly and was maneuvering to get her bow gun facing the end of the fjord where the *Portland* would be appearing. Smoke wafted up from her superstructure until disappearing into the low cloud cover above.

Tate focused his anger on the on-screen image and said to Farouk, "We won't even have to show ourselves. Can you use this image to guide the torpedoes?"

Farouk nodded. "It shouldn't be a problem. But I don't want to try steering them around any tight corners."

"Keep an eye on the webcam to make sure they don't move." Tate checked the map. "Once we get to the far end of the fjord, we'll launch our torpedoes from behind the cliffs. At that point, Cabrillo won't even know they're coming."

Tate thought about his promise to Ballard. She wouldn't be able to watch the *Oregon*'s final moments. But he would. And then he would chase down the *Deepwater* to avenge her.

67

Juan stood on the deck of the *Oregon* next to the HOB, short for Hoverbike. It looked akin to one of Gomez's small drones, only bulked up on steroids. This one was more than twelve feet across, with six propellers, two bicycle-style seats with handlebars for both passengers, plus seat belts and stirrups. Each of the props was encircled by a protective casing to keep riders' hands from being sliced by the blades.

Linc walked toward him, a .50 caliber Barrett sniper rifle slung over his shoulder. He had nothing more than some extra ammunition with him to keep the load light, which was a relative term given the former SEAL's bulk.

"For the record, I'm not loving the idea of being a passive passenger on this thing," Linc said.

The HOB had no pilot controls on it, another weight-saving measure. Instead, the drone was controlled remotely, using the tiny cameras and sensors on board to guide it.

"It's very stable," Murph said from behind him. "Gomez taught me everything I know about how to fly this thing."

"Did he teach you everything he knows?" Juan asked, specifically using the present tense even though he didn't know Gomez's fate yet.

"Probably not. I'm sure I can work out the rest." He winked at Juan without Linc seeing him.

"You better be kidding," Linc said as he pointedly checked the magazines holding the huge bullets for his rifle. "This ammo has a two-mile range, you know."

Murph put up his hands in surrender. "I will do my best."

Eddie was the last to join them. All he was carrying was a pair of high-powered binoculars. He would be Linc's spotter. Both of them were wearing white-camouflaged cold-weather gear and had goggles around their necks.

"It's going to be chilly up there," Eddie said, pointing to the top of the glacier where they were headed. "Wish I could bring a thermos of coffee."

"Don't worry," Murph said. "I'll bring you back down as soon as you give me the word."

Linc and Eddie were going to give Juan advanced warning of the *Portland*'s arrival. The top of the glacier had an expansive view of the fjord below, but it would have taken the two of them too long to climb to the top over the icy terrain. The HOB was the only way to get them up there in time.

"Linc needs to ride in front to balance the load," Murph said.

Linc held out his hand to Juan, an unusually serious look on his face.

"Chairman, it's an honor to serve with you."

Juan shook his hand and said, "The honor is mine."

Linc climbed on, and Eddie shook Juan's hand as well.

"I can't believe we're doing this," Eddie said. "I hate it, but I understand it. We'll give you our best, Juan."

"I know you will, Eddie," Juan said. "I'll do the same."

Eddie got on the Hoverbike, and Juan backed away until he was next to Murph, who was sniffling.

"I think I'm getting a cold," Murph mumbled, but Juan could hear him choking up.

Both Linc and Eddie gave them the thumbs-up, put on the goggles, and gripped the handlebars.

Murph tapped on the control tablet, and the propellers whirred to life, sounding like a sextet of giant bumblebees.

The HOB gently lifted off the deck and banked toward the glacier. It rose until it was even with the crest of the ridge, almost a thousand feet high, and Murph found a flat spot to land. The trip that would have taken hours on foot had been completed in less than a minute.

Linc and Eddie waved as they dismounted, and Juan checked the comm system.

"How do you read?"

"Loud and clear," Eddie replied. "Shouldn't take us more than five minutes to get to our vantage point."

"Good. Let me know when you're in place."

"Roger that."

Juan turned to Murph, who pocketed the tablet.

"Let's get you down to the moon pool," Juan said.

He had taken a walk around the ship, a naval tradition for captains before major battles, but he was glad to take one more tour.

As they entered the nearest door and headed down the stairs, Murph said, "The ship controls should have all been transferred to the command chair. You'll have everything you need at your fingertips."

"Thanks, Mark," Juan said. "You do exceptional work. I hope you know that."

Murph nodded quietly. For once in his life, he seemed tongue-tied.

When they reached the moon pool, they found a hive of activity, with the crew swarming around the two submersibles. The Gator was in the water, while the Nomad was being moved into position above it by the gantry crane.

Eric and Hali came over to stand next to Murph. Juan was impressed by how composed his three young officers were.

"The Gator is ready to launch, Chairman," said Eric, who would be driving it.

"Thanks, Stoney," Juan said. "You stay hidden until the coast is clear. Literally."

"I will. Smooth sailing to you."

Juan put a hand on Eric's shoulder. "I know you'll do what you need to. You always have." Juan gave him a bittersweet smile, before turning to Hali. "Keep in touch with the *Deepwater*. Let them know what happens here."

"Aye-aye, Chairman. Godspeed to you."

"You as well."

The three young men went over to the Gator and climbed in. Murph was the last one, and he gave Juan a final look before closing the hatch behind him. A few moments later, the Gator sank into the water and disappeared.

Juan looked up and saw Max on the catwalk above, guiding the cradle holding the Nomad. He climbed the stairs, and by the time he was standing beside Max, the Nomad was settling into the water.

"I saw your good-bye down there," Max said. "Those guys really look up to you."

"I couldn't ask for a better crew. Speaking of which, did you get everyone else into the lifeboats?"

Max nodded without looking away from his task. "The first one has been launched, and the second will be in the water in a few minutes."

Not everyone could fit into the subs, so the lifeboats were necessary even though they would be more vulnerable to the *Portland*. However, if Juan's mission worked as planned, they'd be safe. He wished he could shake hands with every one of them, but there wasn't time.

"Where's Maurice?" Juan asked.

"Finishing the job you gave him," Max grumbled.

"You know this is the right call."

Max looked too focused on his work to answer. When the Nomad was floating in the water, the technicians below detached the gantry crane, and Max raised the lifting cradle out of the way. He set the controls down and finally looked at Juan.

"The only wrong call you've made is not letting me stay behind with you," Max said.

"Tate is my problem. I've inflicted enough of him on the crew already, including you."

Max held his gaze steady. "You always look out for everyone but yourself."

Juan forced a grin. "It's my fatal flaw."

"And it's your biggest strength. That's why Tate is going to lose."

"Fingers crossed. Give my best to Julia. We've both been too busy in the last few hours to see each other."

"I will." Max unexpectedly wrapped Juan in a bear hug.

"I'll be seeing you, old friend," Juan said.

"In this life or the next, brother," Max replied.

Max pushed him back and took one last look before he turned away to finish prepping the submersible.

Juan left the moon pool and headed toward the stern, pausing only to retrieve a small box from his cabin. He didn't run into a single person as he navigated the bare corridors. With everyone leaving, the ship felt decidedly hollow.

He climbed the stairs and emerged on the afterdeck. He was confronted with the empty helicopter pad, where Gomez's chopper should have been, and hoped the pilot had made it somehow.

Juan walked to the very end of the fantail and saw the second of the lifeboats motoring away from the ship. He saluted the faces look-ing up at him and received melancholy waves in return.

The jackstaff was currently displaying the national flag of Iran. To keep a low profile, the *Oregon* often flew the banner of a rogue coun-try like Iran, Syria, or Myanmar, or sometimes one signifying more of a mainstream registration, such as Panama or Liberia. It was done to better keep the ship's true registry hidden.

But there was one flag that had never before been raised on the *Oregon*.

Juan lowered the Iranian flag and tossed it in the sea. He opened the box he was carrying to reveal another, folded flag, its blue field with white stars crisp and clean.

He carefully unfolded it, making sure that it didn't touch the deck, and lashed it to the line. With sure hands, he ran it up the pole until the stars and stripes of the U.S. flag fluttered in the light breeze.

Juan heard a distant cheer erupt from the previously gloomy crew on the lifeboats, and he pumped a fist in the air as a response.

If he was going to go down with his ship, Juan wanted to do it in service of his country.

Even though she was gravely wounded, the *Oregon* still had some fight left in her, but there was no reason for anyone else to pay for Tate's homicidal revenge plot. Thanks to Murph, Juan could operate the ship by himself for this one last task.

He was going to ram the *Portland* with the *Oregon*.

68

Tate was still seething over his call with Cabrillo, but he had the *Oregon* right where he wanted her. She was still in the same place near the beach with the penguins. She hadn't moved in the last half hour.

In his mind's eye, Tate had a vision of the *Oregon*'s demise. From the safety of the bend in the fjord, he would plant two torpedoes in her port side, where she had the most damage. Big, beautiful geysers of water would shoot into the sky, and the *Oregon* would be rocked by the explosions. She would start listing immediately as water gushed into the gaping holes.

Then Tate would have the *Portland* come around the bend so he could see the ship's misery with high-definition cameras. He would launch every Exocet he had and watch the *Oregon* try to shoot them down. At the same time, he'd order his 120mm cannon and the Gatling guns to unleash their fury on the ship. Anyone caught on deck trying to escape would be cut to ribbons.

Finally, the *Oregon*, by this point an utter ruin, would turn turtle and break in half. She would suffer the disgrace of sinking keel up. Then after mopping up any survivors, Tate would head back to the *Deepwater* and destroy her as well.

356 | CLIVE CUSSLER

His only regret was that he wouldn't be able to force Cabrillo to watch with him. Tate would try to call him, perhaps make him beg for mercy, but he doubted his old friend would answer. It didn't really matter. Cabrillo would know that he'd been beaten. Tate had to be satisfied with that.

"We've reached the fjord's entrance," Farouk said. "Should I send up a drone to verify their position?"

"And risk them spotting it?" Tate asked. "Do you think we should let Juan know we've arrived just to strike a little terror in him?"

Farouk looked horrified. "I didn't think of that."

"You may be a brilliant engineer, Farouk," Tate said. "But you're a moron when it comes to tactics. Of course we're not going to announce that we're here. He'll know the moment our torpedoes have dealt a killing blow to his beloved ship."

He took one more look at the stationary *Oregon* on-screen and said to the helmsman, "It's time to party. Make the turn."

They entered the fjord.

Linc and Eddie found a stable perch at the top of the ridge and had an expansive view of the fjord's entrance. From a prone position, they could see the opening of the gap leading to the other arm of the fjord, but from this angle they wouldn't be able to see the *Oregon* until she emerged from the narrow canyon.

"Chairman, the *Portland* is coming into the fjord," Eddie said into his molar mic as he watched the ship make a sharp turn in their direction.

"Acknowledged," Juan said. "I'm in position. Let me know when to begin my run."

"Roger that."

"What do you think are the chances that this will work?" Linc asked Eddie, the scope of the sniper rifle against his eye.

"I don't know," Eddie said. "Even with half an engine, the *Oregon* can build up some good speed. That'll be a lot of force. As long as Tate can't evade the hit, it might be enough to sink the *Portland*."

"And if it isn't?"

Eddie lowered his binoculars and looked at Linc. "Then the *Portland* will kill all of our friends, and all we'll be able to do is watch."

"You're a fresh breath of optimism," Linc said.

"You asked."

"Next time, lie to me."

Eddie turned back with his binoculars. The *Portland* was fully in the fjord now and approaching the opening. He calculated the ship's speed and the distance to the point where it would be directly opposite the gap. To hit the *Portland*, Juan would have to start his charge before he could see his target. He had to lead it, just like a duck hunter, except in this case both the shot and the prey were eleven-thousand-ton ships.

"Chairman," Eddie said. "The *Portland* is now in the center of the fjord, two hundred fifty yards from our side. At her current speed, she will be directly in front of you in forty-five seconds."

"Roger that," Juan said. "Beginning my run."

Eddie put down the binoculars, but kept an eye on the *Portland* in case she changed course.

Quietly, he said, "Happy hunting, Juan."

Murph and Hali had crowded into the Gator's cupola with Eric, who had partially surfaced the submersible so they could see the *Oregon* one last time. They watched water shoot from behind the ship as she accelerated toward the gap.

"That still looks awfully narrow," Hali said as the *Oregon* approached the glacier-carved canyon. "And it looks tighter the closer the ship gets."

"The Chairman is the best ship driver I've ever seen," said Eric, who was no slouch himself. "If anyone can get a ship that size through there, it's him."

"Isn't it harder to keep the ship straight with only the right venturi tubes functional?" Murph asked.

"Max said he got the maneuvering thrusters working," Eric said. "If the Chairman puts them at full power toward starboard, it should be enough to keep the *Oregon* on a direct path."

As he said that, the bow of the *Oregon* shot into the gap.

"Come on, Chairman," Eric said under his breath. "You've got this."

Within seconds, the *Oregon* was swallowed by the fjord.

Juan tried not to blink as he watched the cameras on the op center's main view screen and made tiny adjustments to the *Oregon*'s course using the joystick on the command chair armrest. Murph had altered the LiDAR system so that it beeped at Juan every time he got too close to one of the canyon's walls, like the backup sensor in a new car that was backing into a parking space between two concrete pillars. The warnings sounded almost constantly.

For the first time that he could recall, Juan had his command chair seat belt snugged tight around his waist. It felt wrong to have the op center to himself, but it gave him peace of mind knowing that he was the only one in imminent danger. His eyes flicked back and forth from the port to the starboard cameras, and he had to remind himself to breathe. The jagged rocks filled the camera's view on either side, like serrated teeth ready to chew into his ship.

When he was three-quarters of the way through, Juan felt the current suddenly pull the *Oregon* off course, and he heard a mournful screech as metal was torn from the ship's hull. He rapidly corrected his path. There was no point in slowing down now. Through the canyon's exit ahead, he could now see the bow of the *Portland* nosing into view.

This was it. He was committed. Juan ratcheted the throttle to full power, and the *Oregon* blasted forward, her armored prow aiming right for the midsection of the *Portland*.

Contact directly left!" shouted the *Portland*'s radar operator.

"On-screen," Tate said.

The port camera view appeared, and Tate's blood ran cold when he saw the *Oregon* racing toward them.

"No! No! That was supposed to be a solid wall of ice." On the map, there was no gap indicated there, yet here was the nightmare image of the *Oregon*'s bow growing larger on-screen at a fantastic rate.

"Flank speed!" he screamed.

"Flank speed, aye!" the helmsman answered.

"Go! Go!" Tate shrieked, but the crewman's reaction time was too slow. There was no way to avoid the impact now.

As he scrambled to latch his belt, Tate realized that he had done exactly what he warned others against doing. He had underestimated Cabrillo.

It had simply never occurred to Tate that Juan would sacrifice his own ship.

Eddie's heart raced as he could do nothing more than watch the terrible sight of the *Oregon* plowing into the center of her doppelgänger.

With a mixture of pride and sadness, Linc said, "You got him, Chairman."

The *Oregon*'s bow plunged into the *Portland* like a dagger into an

360 | CLIVE CUSSLER

enemy's heart. The *Portland*'s thick, steel-plated hull ripped apart as easily as a sheet of tissue paper. The *Oregon* didn't stop until she was buried halfway into the other ship. If the ships were truly identical, Eddie guessed that the *Portland*'s op center had taken the full brunt of the blow.

The two freighters were now joined as one. The *Oregon* was a barbed spear embedded in her quarry, and there would be no pulling her loose. The force of the collision pushed the *Portland* all the way to the opposite cliff, where the linked vessels finally came to a halt. Dense black smoke rose from the point of impact.

Eddie clicked his molar mic. "Chairman, do you read me? Juan?"

There was no answer.

69

Tate shook his head to clear it, but that only worsened the whiplash in his neck. He opened his eyes to see that the op center was now a complete wreck. He was the only one who had a seat belt on, so he had stayed in place even though his command chair was now pushed up at a thirty-degree angle. No one else was moving. Bodies were sprawled on the floor or had been crushed beyond recognition by the *Oregon*'s rusted hull, which now filled the space where the view screen had been.

Sparks flew from exposed electrical conduits, Klaxons blared, and the emergency lighting had flickered on. Tate checked the ship status on the pad on his armrest, and it winked on and off with a long series of warnings.

Engines down. Weapons off-line. Fire suppression systems disabled. Flooding in multiple compartments. The list went on.

With a hole as massive as the one the *Oregon* had punched in the *Portland*, it was just a matter of time now before the ship went down. He had to get out.

He unlatched his belt, but a new alarm sounded that caught his attention. It was the fire signal.

He looked at the pad and zoomed in on the 3-D image of the ship's layout. There was a fire raging in the section right next to the ammunition magazine. If it ignited one of the shells or missiles stored there, the resulting explosion would slash the ship in two.

He heard a cry from his right and saw Farouk pinned against the bulkhead by his console, which had been torn from the floor. He was holding out his arm in a pathetic plea for help.

"Please, Commander!" he bawled. "I can't move."

Tate shook his head. "Serves you right for failing me. You're on your own."

He ran out of the room, Farouk's miserable wail receding behind him.

Tate headed for the nearest stairs, but they were blocked. He doubled back and tried a different path. That corridor was a tangle of girders, leaking pipes, and dangling wires. He'd electrocute himself trying to climb through.

The third route he tried took him past the ship's shooting range and armory. He was confronted by the sight of the *Oregon*'s hull, which had been peeled open so cleanly that the chasm was big enough for him to fit through. It seemed to be his only way out.

It was also highly dangerous. For all he knew, the *Oregon*'s crew was waiting to kill him if he tried to escape through their ship. He had to arm himself.

He sprinted back into the shooting range, opened its inner security door, and dashed into the armory. After he snatched a G36 assault rifle from the wall, along with two spare magazines and a flashlight, he raced back the way he'd come.

When he reached the union of the *Oregon* and the *Portland*, Tate pointed the G36 into the darkened opening. He clicked on the flashlight and saw an empty corridor.

The way was clear. He climbed into the *Oregon*.

Juan unbuckled his belt and took stock of himself. Surprisingly, he was unscathed from the massive collision. Too bad he couldn't say the same about his ship.

He was proud of the punishment the *Oregon* had been able to take, but the impact must have damaged the engines beyond repair. He tried to reverse out of the *Portland*'s death grip. No response. The *Oregon* wasn't going anywhere.

Juan had to abandon ship. Water was pouring in through holes in the side and bow of the ship. Some of the emergency bulkheads had closed, but not enough of them. The clock was ticking for the *Oregon*, and it wouldn't be long before it hit zero.

He tried contacting Eddie. He got no response. Communications were off-line. Soon the *Oregon* would be covered by a thousand feet of water, and he didn't want to be inside her when that happened.

He went to the door and spun around to take one last look at the op center. It was his favorite spot on the ship, the place where he felt most comfortable, and he treasured the camaraderie he'd experienced with the rest of his officers during the most harrowing of missions. But now it was empty. The room—and the ship—had done their jobs.

It was time to go.

Juan turned and ran for his life.

70

Both Eddie and Linc frantically searched in vain for any movement on the *Oregon*'s deck, scanning the ship from stem to stern with the sniper scope and binoculars.

"If he's still alive," Linc said, "shouldn't we have seen him by now?"

"He might be trying to save the ship," Eddie replied.

"I don't see how. Look at that big gash in the starboard side."

Movement on the *Portland* caught Eddie's attention. Several people were stumbling toward the only lifeboat that remained undamaged.

"What was that?" Linc asked.

"Where?" Eddie switched his view back to the *Oregon*. "Do you see him?"

"No, I meant on the *Portland*. I thought I saw a flash of light near the midsection."

Eddie refocused the binoculars on the other ship. "I don't see any—"

A massive fireball erupted from the center of the *Portland*, engulfing the few people on deck and tossing huge sections of the vessel high into the air. A few seconds later, the blast wave reached Eddie and Linc, battering their eardrums.

"Whoa!" Linc said.

"That's an understatement."

"I bet something set off the ammo magazine."

"I bet you're right."

The explosion finished what the *Oregon* had started and split the *Portland* in two. Each half rolled away from the cliff and listed over until both abruptly capsized. Soon, the sections would be lying at the bottom of the fjord.

The *Oregon* would quickly follow them. Nothing could stop that now. Her entire bow had been sheared off by the immense explosion, which also pushed her toward the center of the fjord, where she had drifted to a stop.

"Come on, Chairman," Linc said. "Get out of there."

Juan's eyes blinked open, and he found himself lying on the landing of the stairwell with a painful welt on his head. He'd been thrown down the steps by some kind of blast. Since he wasn't dead, it had to have come from the *Portland*.

He picked himself up, regained his senses, and continued up the stairs until he emerged onto the deck and into the bracing cold. He had come out on the starboard side just forward of the superstructure.

He looked toward the *Oregon*'s bow and saw that it wasn't there anymore. All that remained was a ragged tear in the deck, which was now beginning to tilt downward. Farther over toward the side of the fjord were the two halves of the now overturned *Portland*. The bow end gurgled as it was claimed by the sea. The stern went vertical and then plunged straight down like a rocket aimed at the ocean's floor.

No matter how much Juan hated the thought, the *Oregon* was going to suffer the same fate. He went to the nearest life raft canister. He grabbed the nylon rope and yanked on the quick-release chain. The cylindrical canister rolled overboard and landed in the water. He pulled on the cord until it activated the CO_2 cartridge. Its clamshell case popped open, the raft inflated.

He was about to jump over the railing when gunfire peppered the raft with holes. Juan threw himself on the deck as bullets ricocheted around him. He felt one of the rounds tear into his left arm. A chillingly familiar voice called out to taunt him.

"Hey, Juan!" Tate shouted with undisguised glee. "Don't you know the captain is supposed to go down with his ship?"

71

Did you see where that came from?" Linc asked.

Eddie, searching the deck for the source of the bullets that shredded the life raft, couldn't see who was responsible.

"No, but Juan is still alive," Eddie said.

"He was. Is there any blood on the deck?"

"Not that I can see, though it's hard to tell from this far away." Then Eddie saw Juan push himself up to his hands and knees. "Wait, he's moving. He's sitting up, against a bollard."

"We need to find whoever is hunting him."

"Hold it, I just saw the guy's leg. He's retreating behind the super-structure. You see it?"

"Got him," Linc said. "But I don't have a shot. How did he get on board?"

"I have no idea. Juan was the first person I saw set foot on the *Oregon*'s deck."

"Can you get him from here?" Eddie asked.

"If he comes into view and then stays put for a few seconds. The difference in wind speeds between up here and down there will be tricky to compensate for . . . Still nothing on the comms?"

"No." It was frustrating to see Juan yet not be able to talk to him.

"I was hoping you could get the Chairman to lure this guy out into the open," Linc said.

"That would be helpful. Maybe he'll remember we're up here."

Juan used the ceramic knife from his combat leg to cut a length of the lifeboat rope and made a tourniquet for his bleeding arm, using his good hand and his teeth to secure it. He couldn't bend the elbow without excruciating pain, but it didn't seem like the round had fractured his bone.

He'd worn the prosthetic leg with the hidden compartment just in case. Now he was glad he had. He took out the .45 caliber ACP Colt Defender, which held seven rounds in the magazine and one in the chamber. Clearly it was no match for the firepower he was up against. He recognized the sound of a G36 assault rifle.

Juan looked up at the top of the ridge where he knew Linc and Eddie could see him. The distance and their camouflage made them invisible. He hadn't heard the boom of the deafening Barrett sniper rifle, which meant Linc couldn't see Tate. The advantage Juan had was, Tate had no idea they were up there.

Juan had to lure him into the open. The fog was closing in on the ridge, so he didn't have much time.

"I noticed you didn't go down with your ship, Tate!" Juan shouted.

"Do you think I believe in that stupid cliché?" Tate yelled back. "That's only for Boy Scouts like you. Besides, I wanted to come see you one last time."

"I'm right here. Come and get me."

"Nice try. I've heard about that trick leg of yours. You've probably got a handy little gun in there. You probably don't have an assault rifle like I do."

"You got me there, Tate." Juan leaned around the bollard and shot off three quick rounds, trying to flush Tate out.

"Still here, Juan! You could try to hide, but remember that I know the *Oregon* as well as you do. Why don't you save me some trouble and jump overboard right now? In water this cold, you'll be dead in a couple of minutes from hypothermic shock."

Tate seemed happy to wait Juan out and have them both go down with the *Oregon*, which was steadily sinking at the bow. Juan looked toward the nearest door going into the interior of the ship. Too far. Tate would cut him down before he got halfway there.

It was time to take more drastic measures and trust that Eddie and Linc were ready to help him.

He stood up and emptied his magazine in Tate's direction until the click of the trigger was audible. He then tossed the gun on the deck and remained standing.

Tate peeked from behind the superstructure. "Well, that was pretty stupid of you. Or you're just suicidal because I beat you."

Juan shook his head and held his arms up in the air. "Neither. Just practical."

Tate emerged with a pompous grin and the G36 held lazily at his side. He ambled toward Juan.

"I've waited a long time for this," he said.

Juan nodded. "So have I."

"Good-bye, Juan."

"Just shoot already," Juan said.

"With pleasure." Tate stopped and took aim.

"I didn't mean you."

Through the tendrils of fog that were beginning to envelope them, Eddie saw that Tate was in the perfect position, in plain view, standing still. Tate said something and raised his rifle.

"Take him down," Eddie said.

Linc pulled the trigger.

72

The *Oregon* shuddered, just a minor slip downward, as some interior spaces filled with water. It was enough to save Tate's life.

Something sliced along his cheek, and he flinched as if he'd been slapped. Then he heard the crack of a rifle from somewhere high above and realized that Juan had placed a sniper on the mountain overlooking the fjord. Cabrillo had deliberately coaxed him from his hiding spot just to blow his brains out. It almost worked.

Tate emptied his magazine in Juan's direction. He ducked back into his hiding spot just in time to avoid two more rounds that dug craters in the deck right where he'd been standing. When he was protected by the safety of the superstructure, he ejected the mag from his rifle and slapped a new one in. Blood dribbled down his chin and onto his shirt, but Tate felt no pain. He was jacked from the adrenaline surging through his veins.

"That was smart!" he called out. "You nearly got me. But your own ship let you down."

No answer.

"You still out there, Juan? I didn't hear a splash."

"Time to make this a fair fight, Tate!" Cabrillo shouted back.

Tate heard the sound of a bulkhead door slamming closed.

Fair fight? To make it a fair fight, Cabrillo would need an assault rifle of his own.

He headed to the armory, just two decks below. Instead of Tate worrying about Juan getting a weapon to take him on in a gun battle, he was elated by the gift.

He risked a peek around the superstructure and saw fog blanketing the mountain. The sniper was now blind.

Tate ran for the door, one of the hidden ones that led into the secret areas of the ship. In his haste to get to the armory, Cabrillo had left it ajar.

Tate threw it open and followed Cabrillo into the bowels of the sinking *Oregon*.

Juan didn't dwell on his bad luck as he ran down the stairs. Linc's shot was right on the mark. It was the ship that moved Tate out of the bullet's path.

It didn't take long for Juan to settle on a new strategy. The fog that rolled in and took Linc out of the equation forced him to consider a Plan C. Or maybe he was up to Plan F, at this point. It didn't help that the ship was rapidly sinking. Juan knew that he had only a few minutes left before she went under.

He'd told Max that he didn't want to die, and that still held true. But Tate wasn't going to let him off the *Oregon* alive. And Juan didn't have another gun in his combat leg.

It was something that Tate had said up on deck that made him think of this new tactic. Tate said he knew the *Oregon* as well as Juan did.

But Tate didn't. Only a member of the Corporation knew the ship as intimately as Juan. There were things on board that he had modified since the *Oregon* was first designed and built. Changes that wouldn't have been in the original plans Tate had stolen to construct the *Portland*. Minor alterations that made the *Oregon* absolutely unique despite her doppelgänger.

The armory had one of those modifications.

He just hoped that Tate took the bait and followed him.

73

Tate took the stairs down two at a time. He was racing to reach the armory before Cabrillo could come out with a weapon. If Tate caught him while he was still in the armory, he could lock Juan inside. Then the captain really would go down with his ship.

Two levels down, Tate sprinted along the hallway until he reached the door of the shooting range. Drops of fresh blood on the elegant carpeting ended there.

Tate knelt and pulled the door of the range open slowly in case Juan was plotting an ambush. Tate swept the interior of the firing range with his rifle, but it was clear. The blood drips continued to the armory.

Cabrillo was still in there.

Tate smiled. He lifted the G36 and fired a burst of rounds at the security pad next to its door. On the *Portland*, the portal was designed to go into lockdown mode if the pad was tampered with. This one had just been tampered with big-time.

To be sure, Tate tested the handle. The door wouldn't budge.

He didn't know if Juan would be able to hear him through the soundproofing, so Tate pounded with the butt of his rifle.

"You hear that, Juan?" he shouted. "Sorry I had to do it this way. The *Oregon* will make a nice tomb for you!"

He heard nothing in response. Cabrillo would probably try to use an RPG to open the door, killing himself in the process, so it was time for Tate to make his exit, find a life raft, and figure out a way back to civilization.

Of course, he might be captured by the crew of the *Oregon*, if they were still around, but he'd gotten out of prisons tougher than anyplace they could take him. He still had millions hidden in offshore accounts, plenty to start rebuilding his life with. The important thing was, he'd finally gotten his revenge.

Tate turned the handle and pushed.

It wouldn't open.

For Juan, going down to the armory was never about getting a weapon to fight Tate.

A few years back, Juan got tired of having to go through the noisy shooting range just to get to the armory, so he had a second door installed on the opposite side of the large room for easier access. He guessed Tate hadn't gone to that trouble.

So when he heard Tate enter the range and fire his rifle, Juan had sprinted back behind him and keyed in his code for locking all fire doors on the ship, which included those to the shooting range and the armory.

Juan heard muted pounding, followed by rifle fire and bullets hammering the door. He activated the intercom to the range.

"You said you know this ship as well as I do, Tate. You're obviously wrong. I thought you'd realize that this door is fireproof, waterproof, and bulletproof."

"You coward!" Tate screamed. "That's a cheap move, locking me in here!"

"Isn't that what you were trying to do to me?"

"Come in here and fight me face-to-face. No weapons, just skill against skill. See who the better man really is."

"I don't have to fight you to know the answer to that."

Juan desperately wanted to punch Tate in the face for what he had been made to do, for sinking his ship, but this was his best chance to survive. The *Oregon* was saving Juan's life one last time.

Freezing water rushed up the sloping corridor and rapidly covered his feet. The irony was not lost on Juan that Tate was going to go down in the very ship he had promised to sink.

"Time to leave now," Juan said. "It's been fun seeing you again, Tate."

He clicked the intercom off before Tate could respond. No reason to let him have the last word.

Juan sloshed through the water toward the stairs as the *Oregon* tilted ever higher.

74

Juan had to stay dry as long as possible. His toes were going numb from their brief dip in the water that was quickly devouring the *Oregon*.

Every second, the floor's incline was increasing, making it difficult for him to make his way up the stairs. At the same time, the ship was sinking faster and faster, and it felt like the flood was chasing him with each step.

He hauled himself up the stairway by clasping the railing with his good arm and wedging his boots against the wall, as if he were scaling a steep cliff.

By the time he reached topside, behind the superstructure, the *Oregon* was sloped at an acute angle, and half of the ship had been engulfed by the water. He climbed over to the railing and used the chains on it to pull himself toward the stern.

When Juan was within a hundred feet of the fantail, the unnatural torque at the base of the aftmost crane caused it to collapse. The steel girders smashed into the superstructure, and the boom crashed into the gunwales just behind him, sweeping down the deck until it plum-meted into the sea.

There wasn't much time left. No life jacket was within reach. Juan looked around, didn't see any lifeboats nearby. Not that that surprised him. He had ordered them to stay in the safety of the fjord's other arm in case it took longer than expected for the *Portland* to sink. He didn't want to sacrifice the *Oregon* just to see Tate wipe out Juan's crew anyway.

His best chance was to swim for the shore and wait for someone to pick him up. The closest flat land where he could pull himself out of the water looked to be three hundred yards away, behind the ship's stern. Normally, Juan could swim that distance without breathing hard, thanks to regular laps in the *Oregon*'s ballast tank that doubled as a pool.

But in these bone-chilling waters, and with one arm useless, his strength would be sapped rapidly as his system stopped blood flow to his extremities to conserve heat and energy for the vital organs in his torso.

With the angle of the ship increasing steadily, it was now virtually impossible to pull himself all the way up to the fantail one-handed. Even assuming he was able to get there, he'd have to jump past the venturi tube openings. If he got sucked into one of them as the ship went down, he'd have no chance.

There was only one choice. Without a second thought, Juan leaped over the railing and steeled himself for the cold as he plunged into the water.

He was not prepared for how shockingly icy the water was, as it enveloped him. He nearly inhaled a lungful. He swam for the surface, his fingers losing feeling. His head broke into the air. The piercing cold felt even worse because of the breeze blowing across his wet face.

He started swimming, with good force for the first fifty yards, through the water churned up by the sinking ship. But he could feel his muscles losing strength like batteries losing their power.

Juan kept at it, refusing to give up, but when he looked up again, the shore seemed no closer than it had a minute before. His strength was nearly gone, and extreme fatigue was setting in. He could keep himself afloat for a little while longer, nothing more. He wasn't going to make it.

Over his shoulder, he heard several loud bangs. He turned and saw the *Oregon*'s stern sliding toward the water's surface, white froth bubbling around it. The superstructure was already submerged. Juan must have heard bulkheads popping as the pressure got too great to hold back.

He watched with a heavy heart as the ship's elegant fantail, shaped like a champagne glass cut in half, approached the water, which rushed into the gaping maws of the venturi tubes that had reliably powered the *Oregon* through countless critical missions over the years.

Water swept up the flaked and rusted hull, washing away letter by letter the name OREGON that was written in iron filings magnetized to the stern. The last part of the ship to descend into the water was the jackstaff holding the American flag waving in the wind. The Stars and Stripes came to rest flat on the water, as if it didn't want to go, and then it was pulled down into the abyss.

Only swirling water marked the ship's passing. The seemingly indestructible *Oregon* was gone.

Juan, his energy flagging, turned slowly in a circle and saw no one. Not even Linc and Eddie could see him because of the thick fog cover. He was utterly alone.

He felt a remarkable sense of peace. His crew was safe. He'd done what he had to do. This isolated spot, with natural beauty all around him, would become his final resting place.

Juan stopped paddling. He closed his eyes, and his head slipped beneath the waves.

T ate pounded on the door to the armory, desperate to get inside and find a weapon to break himself out of this prison. His G36 rifle lay on the floor, its ammo magazines long since emptied. Bullet holes peppered both the doors.

He was nearly standing on the forward wall by now. He couldn't tell how much of the ship was underwater, but nothing had seeped past the watertight portal yet.

Tate was hyperventilating. The Chechen prison had been torture, but this was worse. He didn't want to die like this.

His throat was raw from screaming, yet he continued just the same.

"Juan! I know you can hear me! I'll make you pay for this!"

He heard something like a knock from the outer door. He went over to it and had to reach up to press his palm against it. The metal felt cold to the touch. Freezing.

Then Tate felt the door push against his hand.

Hope surged through him. The Boy Scout Juan was showing mercy.

"I knew you'd come back!" Tate yelled with joy.

But it was short-lived. A tiny laser jet of water lanced through a seam in the door.

Then another. And another. One caught Tate in the arm, and the pressure was so high that it sliced his skin as neatly as a scalpel.

Then Tate realized with horror that no one was outside the door. The ship was diving to the bottom of the fjord. The intense water pressure was bowing the door inward.

Tate backed away. With nowhere to go.

Finally, the door could hold back the water no longer. It burst from its hinges and was hurled to the back of the firing range, a tsunami gushing in.

Tate open his mouth to scream again. The sea instantly filled his lungs, and the last thing he felt was the agonizing pressure of a thousand feet of water crushing the life out of him.

75

As Juan sank into the fjord, he opened his eyes and saw that he was far enough from the surface that darkness had closed in around him. With all of his extremities numb from the cold, Juan couldn't tell if he was moving his limbs or if they were just drifting lazily with the currents. He was too tired to care. His mind must have been numbed as well. He felt oddly relaxed, as if he were in a sensory deprivation chamber.

Still, he resisted the urge to inhale as long as he could. He could sense the slowing of his heartbeat and realized he might be able to set a new personal record before he had to breathe. When he did, it would be his last. I'll go out on a high note, he thought.

Then something changed. At first, his mind was so fuzzy that he couldn't tell what it was. Finally, he blinked and understood.

It was getting lighter. He was moving toward the surface.

He couldn't be swimming. He had neither the strength nor the will to move his arms or legs. He looked down to see if he was doing it involuntarily and noticed something metal on his arms. Bracelets? Handcuffs? It didn't make sense until he got closer to the light.

The shiny metal objects were holding on to him, propelling him upward. They were jointed. Like hands, yet different.

Not hands. Claws. A robot's claws.

The surface was close now, but Juan couldn't fight the compulsion to not breathe any longer. He convulsed as he sucked water into his lungs.

At the same time that his head broke into the air, everything went black.

When Juan came to, he was no longer in the water. He was lying on his back with heat packs and a thermal blanket covering him. While his chest and throat ached, he was breathing air again.

Julia Huxley hovered over him with a concerned expression.

"Welcome back to the company of the living," she said. "It was touch and go for a while there."

Juan coughed and sat up with Julia's help. He saw a submersible cockpit in front of him and realized he was inside the Nomad.

"How long have I been out?" It felt like his voice box was being dragged across a cheese grater.

"About an hour. You heaved up a lot of water after I performed CPR on you, then you immediately passed out again once you'd been revived. I thought I was going to lose you."

"At least I set a record," he said.

"What?"

Juan shook his head. "Not important. How did I get here?"

"It's thanks to those two." She pointed to his right, and he turned to see Max, leaning against the sub's inner wall. Kevin Nixon was seated next to him, wrapped in a towel. His hair was damp.

"I know you told us to stay away," Max said, "but sometimes I'm not so good at following orders. I trailed after you. Figured you might need some backup. So when I saw you go under, I raced over and snagged you with the robotic arms. It was Kevin who did the hard work."

Kevin shrugged. "Once Max grabbed you with the robot, I saw that you weren't conscious. All I did was dive into the water and pull you over to the side so we could get you on board. When I hit that cold water, it knocked the wind out of me. I was in it for just a few seconds, with a life jacket on. I don't know how you lasted as long as you did with that bum arm and no flotation device."

Juan had forgotten about his arm. He looked down and saw that it was neatly bandaged.

"I guess I need some stitches," he said. Now that he'd warmed up, the feeling was back, and the entry and exit wounds in his biceps were throbbing.

"Actually, you don't," Julia said. "The bullet missed the bone. So all we'll do is wash and dress the wounds regularly. Stitches would just keep foreign contaminants from draining. You should be good as new in a couple of months."

Julia handed Juan a cup of water. He was parched from inhaling so much seawater and gulped it down.

"How's the crew?" he asked Max.

"Everyone's safe and accounted for. We even found Gomez."

Juan dreaded asking the next question. "Alive?"

"Oh, yeah," Max said. "Sorry I didn't mention that part. He sent up a flare, and the *Deepwater* homed in on it with a short-range drone. Seems he crash-landed as pretty as a picture on a glacier. Eddie and Linc were able to fly down from the ridge above us through a break in the fog, and they're on the way there now in the Gator with the Hover-bike so they can retrieve him."

"Any survivors from the *Portland*?"

Max shook his head. "Seems like the only person on that side who got out of this alive was Li Quon. Linda has him under lock and key on the *Deepwater*. Apparently, the authorities in Singapore will be very happy to get their hands on him."

"And the valuables? Did Maurice get them out?"

"I did indeed, Captain," said a soothing British voice behind Juan.

Juan edged around to look at the rest of the Nomad's cabin and saw Maurice and Overholt sitting beside a large pile of boxes and a dozen rolled-up paintings.

"Good to see you back from the brink, Juan," Overholt said.

"Glad to be here. Thanks for your help, Maurice. I knew I could count on you."

"Although I didn't relish the implications of the task you gave me," Maurice said, "it was the proper thing to do. We couldn't let the *Oregon* go down without rescuing our dearest possessions. Mr. Overholt and I were able to collect the Corporation's valuables from your safe, as well as the most important mementos from the crew's cabins. We also salvaged all of the artwork on board."

Maurice knew more about the ship and the people on it than anyone else, so he had been the perfect person for the job.

"Good work," Juan said. "I'm sure the crew will be appreciative."

"Speaking of which, there they are," Max said, pointing out the cockpit window. The two *Oregon* lifeboats bobbed twenty yards away. "Captain Jefferson thinks the *Deepwater*'s engines can be fixed by tomorrow morning. Once they're up and running, they'll swing by, pick up the rest of us, and tow all the vessels back to Punta Arenas."

Juan nodded with admiration for the pluck and resourcefulness of his crew. Although the *Oregon* had been sunk, they'd saved what really mattered. Each other.

'm sorry you lost your home," Overholt said.

Juan almost replied, "There's never been a ship like her," but thought about her doppelgänger and stopped himself.

"The *Oregon* was a good ship," he said with a bittersweet smile and a hollow pit in his stomach. "I sure will miss the old gal."

EPILOGUE

Across Guanabara Bay from Rio's bright lights, Juan rode on a small ferry with a dozen workers heading to the tiny Ilha do Viana for the night shift. It was long past sunset, and cargo ships crowded around the island, shuttling goods in and out of the brand-new transshipment warehouse located there. It stood next to an abandoned fish-processing plant that dated back fifty years. When they pulled up to the dock, Juan could see the giant letters painted on the side of the new building.

FERREIRA INDÚSTRIAS GLOBAIS. Ferreira Global Industries.

Juan shuffled off the ferry with the others, yawning like he was still waking up from a night's sleep. An armed guard stopped the group coming in and checked ID.

Juan handed his over. It read "Lucas Calvo." The prosthetic appliances glued to Juan's face by Kevin were a perfect match for the real Lucas Calvo, who was currently being detained in his apartment by Hali. During their observations of the warehouse laborers, they discovered that Calvo wasn't the chatty type, which was the reason they'd chosen him for impersonation. Juan hadn't had to talk to any of the other workers during the ferry ride.

The guard gave the ID back after a thorough review and said, *"Vá para dentro." Go inside.*

Juan, who'd been studying Portuguese for the last six weeks in preparation for this mission, replied, *"Obrigado."* He entered the warehouse and followed the men to the opposite side of the cavernous space holding goods and materials from Ricardo Ferreira's factories all over Brazil.

They took a freight elevator two levels down. The doors opened to a broad tunnel that extended two hundred yards ahead of them. Juan trudged along, flexing his left arm. Just as Julia had said, other than a slight pull in his skin from the two puckered scars, it felt no different than before he'd been shot.

When they reached the end of the tunnel, they entered another elevator that was located under the seemingly abandoned cannery. Two stories up, the doors opened to reveal a vast, well-lit manufacturing plant.

The only product on the assembly line were dozens of Slipstream submarine drones. Juan had only seen a prototype on Ferreira's yacht. Orders from drug dealers and smugglers had been so good that it had gone into full-scale production. The first finished copies were about to roll off the line.

Juan saw a palatial office overlooking the factory floor, and a man inside wearing a tailored suit was excitedly talking on his phone. The man turned, and Juan recognized him instantly as Ricardo Ferreira. He was alone.

Thanks to Calvo, Juan knew exactly where the stairs up to the office were. He peeled away from the other workers and headed down the hallway toward the stairs where a single guard was on duty. As soon as he was in the corridor, he took out a handkerchief and held it to his face like he had a bloody nose.

"Eu preciso do banheiro," he said. *I need the bathroom.*

"The bathroom is on the other side of the building, *idiota*," the guard replied in English and Portuguese mixed, pointing as he did so.

When his hand was up and away from his weapon, Juan elbowed him in the ribs and slammed the guard's head against his knee. The man crumpled to the floor. He wouldn't be out long, but it would be long enough.

Juan pocketed the guard's semiautomatic pistol and looked at his watch. He went to the nearby fire exit, which was chained shut and alarmed. Juan swiftly picked the padlock and deactivated the alarm.

When he opened the door, four people clad in black combat gear and ski masks swarmed in. Each was armed with a suppressed AR-15 assault rifle. One of them also had a carbon fiber crossbow.

"Right on time," Eddie said.

"Have any trouble?" Juan asked as they crept toward the stairs.

"A couple of guards are going to have headaches in the morning," Linc said.

"And need ice packs for their groins," Raven added, handing Juan a pair of handcuffs.

MacD held out his assault rifle to Juan, who said, "I'd prefer the crossbow this time."

"Really?" MacD asked. "Ah can't blame you. She's a beauty."

"I promise you I'll give her back once we're in the Gator." Linda was currently idling at one of the vacant docks.

Once they were outside the foreman's office, Juan said, "Give me sixty seconds. Then we're out of here."

He left them behind and bounded up the stairs. Ferreira must have felt secure in this building. There was no guard outside his office.

Juan burst in, and a surprised Ferreira stared at him in utter shock. Juan pointed the crossbow at his head.

"*Quem é você?*" Ferreira demanded indignantly.

"Who am I?" Juan answered in English. "Don't you recognize me?"

"No."

"I made a promise to Luis Machado. You knew him as Roberto Espinoza."

Ferreira was confused for a moment. "That traitor? How did—"

While keeping his aim with the crossbow, Juan pulled the prosthetic appliances off his face. "He found out where this factory was. I told him I'd use the information to get you. So here I am."

It finally dawned on Ferreira who Juan was. "Jorge González! You were there the day my yacht was attacked."

"The same day you murdered Machado. And my name isn't González. It's Juan Cabrillo."

"Whoever you are, you won't get out of here alive."

"I think I might."

The fire alarm sounded.

"*Evacuar del edifício*," came Eddie's voice over the loudspeakers. Juan had taught him how to say "Evacuate the building."

Down on the factory floor, workers scrambled for the elevator, which was the only usable exit. As soon as they were gone, Eddie, Linc, Raven, and MacD fanned out to plant explosives.

"You can't do this," Ferreira growled.

"Watch me."

"I own the police. They will take you down."

"I'm shaking in my boots."

Juan lowered the crossbow to get the cuffs out of his pocket, and Ferreira saw his moment. He reached for the pistol that Juan had noticed in his shoulder holster. Before he could get it halfway out, Juan snapped the crossbow up and shot him in the heart.

Ferreira gaped down at his chest in surprise, then keeled over, his now unseeing eyes staring at Juan.

"Promise made, promise kept," Juan said.

He ran back downstairs and met the four others by the exit. The disarmed guard had fled.

"Let's go," Juan said. "They'll figure out what happened any minute."

They ran across the empty storage lot to the crumbling dock. The Gator was waiting there, and they quickly climbed inside. As Juan stood in the hatch, a series of explosions tore apart the abandoned fish factory. The Slipstream drones were destroyed.

Juan handed MacD his crossbow and closed the hatch. Linda submerged the boat.

From the cockpit she said, "I'll have us back home in fifteen minutes."

"Home" for the Gator right now was a rented boat shed on the other side of the bay.

"By the way," she added, "Max called. He sounded pretty excited."

Juan got out his phone and called him.

"How'd it go?" Max asked as soon as he picked up.

"Mission accomplished," Juan said. "It took a lot longer to plan and execute from our temporary quarters, though."

"I might have a solution for that. Here, I'm switching to video."

A second later, he was watching Max walking through a port. Juan couldn't see any distinguishing features, so he didn't know where it was. All he could tell was that Max was somewhere on the other side of the world. The bright sunlight gave it away.

For the past month, Max had been on an epic quest to find a new ship for the Corporation, one that could be modified the way the Oregon had been transformed from a lumber freighter to a high-tech spy vessel. Langston Overholt and Vice President Sandecker made it clear the money would be there, some from CIA funds recovered after tracking down Tate's hidden offshore accounts and some as a reward for turning over the plans that would allow the development of countermeasures against a future sonic disruptor.

Max had been scouring ports, scrapyards, and shipbuilders from Italy to Malaysia to South Korea searching for the perfect replacement. He had been morose since losing the *Oregon*, but, for the first time in months, Juan saw joy and anticipation on his face.

"You are not going to believe what I found," Max said. "You know those designs we've been working on? This ship is exactly what we were hoping to find. I can't wait to tell you about it."

Max's enthusiasm was infectious. Juan felt a jolt of the same thrill he got when he originally created the Corporation and began recruiting a crew. He knew his friend had discovered something special.

"Don't just tell me about it, Max," Juan said. "Show me."